Praise for the novels of *New York Times* bestselling author Beth Kery, recipient of the *All About Romance* Reader Poll for Best Erotica

"One of the sexiest, most erotic love stories that I have read in a long time."
—*Affair de Coeur*

"A sleek, sexy thrill ride."
—Jo Davis

"One of the best erotic romances I've ever read."
—*All About Romance*

"Nearly singed my eyebrows."
—*Dear Author*

"Fabulous, sizzling hot . . . You'll be addicted."
—Julie James, *New York Times* bestselling author

"Action and sex and plenty of spins and twists."
—*Genre Go Round Reviews*

"Intoxicating and exhilarating."
—*Fresh Fiction*

"The heat between Kery's main characters is molten."
—*RT Book Reviews*

"Some of the sexiest love scenes I have read this year."
—*Romance Junkies*

"Scorching hot! I was held spellbound."
—*Wild on Books*

"Nuclear-grade hot."
—*USA Today*

Because You Are Mine series

BECAUSE YOU ARE MINE (ALSO AVAILABLE IN SERIAL FORMAT)
WHEN I'M WITH YOU (ALSO AVAILABLE IN SERIAL FORMAT)

Titles by Beth Kery

WICKED BURN
DARING TIME
SWEET RESTRAINT
PARADISE RULES
RELEASE
EXPLOSIVE

One Night of Passion series

ADDICTED TO YOU (WRITING AS BETHANY KANE)
EXPOSED TO YOU

One Night of Passion Specials

BOUND TO YOU
CAPTURED BY YOU

When I'm
With You

Beth Kery

BERKLEY BOOKS, NEW YORK

THE BERKLEY PUBLISHING GROUP
Published by the Penguin Group
Penguin Group (USA)
375 Hudson Street, New York, New York 10014, USA

USA I Canada I UK I Ireland I Australia I New Zealand I India I South Africa I China

Penguin Books Ltd., Registered Offices: 80 Strand, London WC2R 0RL, England
For more information about the Penguin Group, visit penguin.com.

Berkley trade paperback / Target edition ISBN: 978-0-425-27256-5

The Library of Congress has catalogued the Berkley trade paperback edition of this book as follows:

Kery, Beth.
When I'm with you / Beth Kery. — Berkley trade paperback edition.
pages cm
ISBN 978-0-425-26935-0
1. Rich people—Fiction.   2. Chicago (Illinois)—Fiction.   I. Title.   II. Title: When I am with you.
PS3611.E79W44 2013
813'.6—dc23
2013008937

PUBLISHING HISTORY
Berkley trade paperback edition / September 2013

PRINTED IN THE UNITED STATES OF AMERICA

10 9 8 7 6 5 4 3 2 1

Cover photograph of "String of pearls wrapped around fork"
copyright © John Manno / Getty Images.
Cover design by Sarah Oberrender.

When I'm With You

Part I

When We Touch

Chapter One

I t was past midnight when Lucien opened the rear entrance to his restaurant and immediately went on high alert, hushing his movements. In the distance he heard the sound of a low male voice. An intruder had breached his restaurant's security. Although Fusion was frequently bustling with the chic late-night dinner and nightclub crowd, it was closed on Sunday and Monday. There definitely shouldn't be anyone inside. Quietly, he closed the rear door, his fist tightening around the polo mallet he carried. He'd been planning on replacing this cracked one with an intact one from his storage closet at Fusion. He had different plans for it now.

For the most part, Lucien maintained the vaguely amused, cynical stance of an experienced, world-weary libertine, a man who claimed no family, no country, no creed, and few of the worldly possessions to which he was entitled by law, which were many. But what he *did* claim, he fought for. Always. He just hadn't realized that the restaurant he'd recently bought had gotten so deeply into his bones until this very moment, when he was ready to do battle for it.

He eased down the dim hallway, following the glow of a light shining around a partially closed door that led to the large bar area of the restaurant. He turned his head, his hearing pitched to pick up the slightest sound. A tingle went down his spine at the sound of female laughter. A man's low chuckle twined with it—rough and intimate. He heard the unmistakable sound of glassware clinking, as if in a toast.

Lucien approached the door and leaned his head into the crack.

"Why do you play games with me?" he heard a man ask.

"Play games?"

Lucien's escalated heartbeat seemed to hesitate for a moment at the woman's voice. Strange. She was from the country of his birth. The female's tone was amused, melodious and light, her French accent laced with a British tinge. Perhaps he recognized the accent because it was very similar to his own.

"You *are* taunting me," the man said roughly. "You have been all night. Not just me. There wasn't a man in that restaurant tonight who wasn't bewitched by you."

"I'm actually being very cautious. We are going to work together, after all," the woman replied, her tone suddenly brisker, cooler. Lucien got the impression she was sending up red flags.

"I want more than just to work with you. I want to help you. I want you in my house . . . my bed," the man said, ignoring the female's warning. Lucien went from high alert to irritated in a second flat when he recognized the man speaking. He hadn't interrupted a burglary on his premises.

He'd walked in on a seduction.

Disgusted, he pushed open the door and strode into the dimly lit, sleek restaurant. The couple stood next to the shining mahogany bar facing each other, their hands curled around crystal brandy snifters. He noticed the woman backing away slightly from the man, as if repelled by his hovering. Distantly, he registered that she wore a blue and silver evening gown that clung to full, firm breasts and taut curves. The dress plunged in the back, revealing a glimpse of white, flawless skin that shone luminous in the soft lighting. The vision of

Mario Vincente's hand splayed across that expanse of bare skin inexplicably ratcheted up Lucien's irritation to anger. The extremely talented chef Lucien had hired from a top-rated restaurant in Las Vegas was a bit of a diva. Mario didn't notice Lucien until he was just feet away. When he did, his brown eyes went wide.

"Lucien!" The brandy-filled glass sagged in Mario's hand. Lucien's gaze flicked rapidly to the singular bottle sitting on the counter—Cognac Dudognon Héritage, an item from the private stock in his office. Lucien tossed the polo mallet he'd been carrying on the mahogany bar, the sound of it ringing in the air like a remonstrance.

"I hadn't realized I'd provided you with Fusion's security code. Or permission to access my office and private bar. Explain yourself, Mario," Lucien said, his tone crisp but neutral now that he understood the nature of the intrusion on his property. True, he was irritated at Mario's infraction, and he would make sure his employee knew it. He just hadn't yet decided if he'd terminate the idiot. He'd never had a soft spot for Mario, but chefs as talented as him were hard to come by, after all.

"I . . . I didn't expect to see you," Mario fumbled.

"Clearly."

Lucien noticed the woman's bare, lithesome arm dip, the liquor in her glass sloshing in the curved bowl. For the first time, he gave the other occupant of the room's face a cursory glance. He did a double take.

"Merde."

"Lucien."

"What are you doing here, Elise?"

Surely he was seeing things—a face from his past . . . a beautiful face, but one he'd most definitely rather not appear at this juncture of his life. What the hell was Elise Martin doing in his restaurant in Chicago, thousands of miles from their country of origin, leagues from the gilded cage of their common past? Was this some sort of cosmic joke?

"I might ask the same of you," Elise replied rapidly, dark blue eyes flashing. Understanding made her features flatten. "Lucien . . . *you're* Lucien *Lenault. You* own this place?"

"*What?* You two know one another?" Mario asked.

Lucien threw Elise a repressive glance. Her lush lips snapped closed, and she gave him a defiant glare. She'd caught his warning for silence regarding their association all right, but that didn't guarantee anything. Knowing Elise, she hadn't decided yet whether she'd keep quiet or not. A flicker of anxiety went through him. He had to get her out of Fusion at all costs . . . out of his life here in Chicago. Elise Martin would cause havoc anywhere she set a perfectly pedicured, elegant toe. More specifically, she could ruin everything he'd gained on his mission with regard to billionaire entrepreneur Ian Noble.

"I . . . I'm sorry. Surely one glass wouldn't hurt," Mario was sputtering. Lucien dragged his gaze off Elise's face. "I know it's your personal stock, but—"

"You're fired," Lucien interrupted succinctly.

Mario blinked. Lucien started to walk away.

"Lucien, you can't do that!" Elise exclaimed.

He whipped around at the sound of her voice. For a second he just stared at her.

"How long has it been?" he asked her, his quiet question for her, and her alone. He saw a strange mixture of emotions cross her beautiful face—discomfort, confusion . . . anger.

"It's been close to two years since that night at Renygat," she said, referring to his successful nightclub and restaurant in Paris. He had to hand it to her. Despite the riot of emotion that'd flickered across her face, she was all cool aristocrat by the time she spoke. Damn her. Any man who tried to decode the enigma of Elise was doomed to a lifetime obsession. Who *was* she? Uncontrollable bad-girl heiress or luminous, golden, elusive ray of sunshine that beckoned and taunted?

"Lucien, don't be so hasty," Elise said softly, a witch's smile shaping lips that could probably tempt a man to do murder. "It would be silly to fire Mario because of how you feel about me."

"I'm not firing him because of how I feel about you," he said levelly. The vision of Mario's hand on her white skin flashed into his mind's eye. *Liar*. He willfully ignored the taunting voice in his head. "I'm firing him because he underhandedly procured the restaurant's security code, broke into my private property, and stole from my personal stash."

She'd cut her long, glorious mane of blond hair since he'd last seen her two years ago. She wore it short now, the gleaming waves combed behind her ears. He'd have thought the shearing of those curls and tresses might have symbolized the taming of Elise's infamous wild spirit, but he'd have thought wrong. Elise's rebellion came from her eyes. Anger stiffened her features. She must have forgotten that her typical charms didn't work on Lucien.

"You can't fire Mario," she stated, all traces of seductive allurement replaced by annoyed stubbornness. Lucien had to force himself not to smile at the abrupt alteration.

"I can do whatever I please. This is my place."

He saw a familiar defiant expression tighten her features, the same one she'd worn when she was fourteen and he'd told her that a stallion in his father's stables was too strong and dangerous for her to control—an expression he was very fond of, despite it all.

"But—"

"There's no but about it," Lucien said, forcing his tone into its usual calm cadence and volume. He would *not* let the presence of Elise set him off balance. She had a habit of doing just that—of whipping the usually staid upper crust of European society into a scandalized whirlwind with her outrageous stunts . . . of sending a man spinning with her unparalleled beauty and the temptation of taming her. He remembered all too well how he'd nearly succumbed to her siren song during their last meeting at Renygat. He recalled

Elise looking up at him as she unfastened his pants, her fingertips
brushing against a cock that teemed with hot, raw lust, her lips red
and puffy from his earlier angry possession of her mouth, her eyes
shining like fire-infused sapphires, her taste lingering on his tongue,
addictive and sweet.

*"You want to forget your past, Lucien? I'm going to make you feel so
good, you're going to forget everything that happened with your father.
That's a promise."*

His body tightened at the memory. He'd believed her. If anyone
could make him forget for one glorious, nirvanic moment, it was
Elise. It had cost him to send her away that night, but he'd done it.
She manipulated as easily as she breathed. She knew precisely how
to slip the most formidable foe in her hip pocket and make him beg
like a hungry dog.

And to add to that risk, Elise knew too much, after that night at
Renygat.

She still did, damn it.

There's only one way he would ever invite Elise into his life, and
she would never agree to play by those rules. Not Elise Martin.

Would she? a small voice in his head taunted.

"I want both of you to get out of here. You're lucky I don't call
the police," Lucien stated, starting to turn again. He paused when
he noticed Mario move jerkily toward him from the corner of his
eye. Apparently, the chef had regained some of his typical hauteur
in the intervening seconds.

"Don't be a fool. You have to open Fusion tomorrow. You need
me. What will you do for a chef?"

"I'll manage. I've been in this business long enough to know how
to deal with stealing employees."

"Are you calling me a thief? An *employee*?" Clearly, Mario
couldn't decide which label was more insulting: criminal or paid
worker. His color faded beneath his olive-toned skin.

Lucien paused, gauging, taking in the glassiness of Mario's eyes.

Apparently, Mario had imbibed his fair share before he'd brought Elise here to ply her with Lucien's brandy. Did he plan to make love to her on the leather couch in Lucien's private office as well? The thought sent his anger to a low boil. He supposed Mario might be attractive enough to some women, but he was in his forties, and far too old to be seducing Elise. No matter that Elise had probably taken four times as many lovers as him, Mario was still a rutting cradle robber, as far as Lucien was concerned.

"I hadn't yet called you a thief, but that's precisely what you are. Among other things."

"You *cannot* fire him!" Elise blurted out. Lucien glanced sideways at her, startled by the panic in her voice but unwilling to look away from Mario when the other man's hands were balled into fists. Why was she so desperate over Mario? He'd definitely gotten the impression she was cool about the chef's seduction.

"Stay out of this. It's none of your business," Lucien muttered.

"It *is* my business. If you fire Mario, what am I supposed to do?" Elise exclaimed, setting her snifter on the bar.

"What are you talking about?" Lucien bit out, but Mario wasn't interested in their tense, private exchange.

"You've always been a smug French bastard, thinking you could lord it over me," Mario bellowed. He grabbed Elise's upper arm roughly. "Well, you can't fire me because I quit! Come, Elise. Let's get out of this devil's lair."

Elise kept her feet planted and jerked when Mario yanked on her. "Nobody tells me what to do," she exclaimed. Lucien clamped his fist around the other man's forearm and squeezed. Tight. Mario yelped in pain.

"Let go of her," Lucien warned. He saw the flash of aggression in Mario's expression and resisted rolling his eyes in exasperation. He really wasn't up for this tonight. "Are you *sure* you want to start something?" he asked mildly. "Do you think it's wise?"

"*Don't*, Mario," Elise warned.

For a brief second, Mario hesitated, but then the alcohol he'd consumed must have roared in his veins—not to mention an Elise-inspired testosterone surge—mounting his blustering vanity. He released Elise and lunged, fist cocked. Lucien blocked Mario's punch and sunk his fist beneath his ribs.

One, two, done. Almost too easy, Lucien thought grimly as air whooshed out of Mario's lungs followed by a guttural groan of pain.

Lucien shot a "this is all your fault" glare at Elise and then put his hands on the shoulders of the now hunched over Mario. He grabbed Mario's jacket off the bar stool and urged the gasping, moaning man toward the front door of the restaurant with a hold on his shirt collar.

When he returned a few minutes later alone, Elise still stood next to the bar, her chin up, her carriage held every bit as proud and erect as her aristocratic ancestors, her gaze on him wary. He walked toward her, unsure if he wanted to shove her into the back of a cab like he just had Mario, shake her for her foolishness, or turn her over his knee and punish her ass for the infraction of peering into his private world.

"What did you do with him?" she asked shakily when Lucien stalked toward her, his fierce, gray-eyed gaze causing her to quail inwardly, even though she didn't show it. She understood what a potential threat Lucien Sauvage was. He could handle a drunk like Mario in his sleep. Elise knew of his athleticism, not to mention his years of experience in maintaining peace and the law in his popular, luxurious restaurants and hotels across the world. Many times organized-crime elements had tried to get a foothold in his establishments and failed, thanks to a combination of Lucien's acute intelligence and raw power.

"I put him in a cab. Now—what to do with you?" he asked, his gaze dropping over her.

Her nipples tightened beneath a stare that was fire and ice at once. Her spine stiffened; her throat froze. The truth was still ricocheting around her skull: *Lucien Sauvage owned Fusion*. She'd unknowingly put her future in the hands of a man who had rejected her.

And nobody rejected her.

Well, *hardly* anybody, at least when she wanted otherwise. She'd definitely wanted *otherwise* with Lucien. *Just my luck.* Of all the restaurants and gin joints in all the towns in all the world, she'd had to walk into his, she thought with a panicked sense of amusement.

"You're going to do the only thing you can do with me," she replied, her voice cool enough for someone who was playing the poker game of a lifetime with a crap hand. It was a mark of their shared past—their onetime friendship—that they spoke English to each other. Both of their mothers were English, their fathers French. It was a commonality they shared, a small intimacy that used to seem significant to a fourteen-year-old girl who craved the feeling of closeness to a beautiful young man who seemed forever unattainable to her. "You're going to have to let me fill in as Fusion's chef now that you've made such a mess of things with Mario."

He blinked and his expression went flat. "What are you rambling about? Are you drunk?"

Anger bubbled up in her chest. "I had one glass of wine all night," she said honestly. She noticed his sarcastic glance at her brandy snifter on the bar. "Mario handed it to me; I took it. Lucien, what are you doing here?" she asked again, her curiosity about him trumping her worry about her future. "You disappeared from Paris over a year ago. None of your employees in Paris will say where you are. My mother spoke to yours recently. Even Sophia doesn't know where you are. She's miserable with worry."

"Right," he said sardonically. "My mother is sick to death at the idea of me not touching all that money she wants for herself ever since my father has been locked up in prison."

Elise blinked. He had a point. She *had* heard he was being strangely stubborn and elusive about accepting his ancestral fortune.

"If you tell a soul you saw me here, I'll make you pay, Elise."

Quiet. Succinct. Completely believable.

Her heart leapt into overdrive. He'd paused a few feet away from her. She had to stretch her neck back slightly to see his face, and hoped he didn't notice her pulse throbbing at her throat. He struck her as even larger than she remembered—tall, lean, hard, and supremely formidable. He'd cut his dark hair since she'd last seen him; now he wore it in a short, very sexy shakeout style that emphasized his masculine, chiseled features and an effortless sense of masculine grace. She'd always had a desire to run her fingers through that soft-looking, thick hair . . . wantonly fill her palms with it. He'd grown a very trim goatee since then, too. He wore jeans and a buttoned ivory cotton shirt, the color along with his silvery-gray eyes creating a striking contrast to smooth, caramel-hued skin. Mario wasn't the first to refer to Lucien as a devil. Men said it with bitter envy. Women said it with covetous lust.

His size and undeniable aura of physical strength had always thrilled her, but Lucien intimidated her as well. His quiet, calm voice; contained, confident manner; and brilliant, charming smiles belied a coiled power inside him. There was a darkness to him that didn't exactly match the white, flashing smile and easygoing manner with which he charmed the upper strata of the social world and his affluent hotel and restaurant guests.

She had no doubt that Lucien could be dangerous when he chose. She also knew he'd never really harm her—not the young man who had once showed her kindness and taken her under his wing.

But that didn't make his threat any less intimidating.

"Now," he said calmly, stepping closer still and placing a hand on the rail of the bar. She suddenly felt cornered. "When are you leaving Chicago?"

"I'm not leaving. I plan to live here."

"What?"

"That's right. Chicago is my new home," she said with supreme confidence, even though she didn't feel it. Elise was nothing if not an actress, and spirited aplomb was her finest role.

Unfortunately, her father had been contemptuous of her plans to become a chef and relocate to Chicago, refusing to fund her new career. She couldn't access her trust fund until she was twenty-five. Six months had never felt so far in the future to Elise. The nest egg she'd squirreled away after almost a year of waitressing in Paris had never seemed so pitifully small.

"Why would you come to Chicago? It hardly suits you," he said, his downward glance at her evening gown infuriating her.

"You really don't know, do you?"

"Know what?"

"My culinary school in Paris has matched me up with Mario Vincente for my training. I'm staging with him, Lucien," she said, referring to the process whereby a new chef trained for a period of time under an established chef. She studied his stoic expression anxiously. "I have a contract," she added defensively when he seemed unmoved by her confession. "You can't send me away."

"You're mad," he said dismissively, picking up the brandy snifters on the counter and starting to walk away. The panic amplified in her chest. She despised the sight of Lucien's back.

"I've completed my training at La Cuisine in Paris. The only thing remaining is for me to stage with a master chef—the master chef you just fired!"

He turned around and she saw he was smiling. Her heart swelled and seemed to press against her breastbone. *Merde.* Lucien's smiles— the white teeth, the twin dimples, the firm, shapely lips. If the devil did exist, he'd definitely take on Lucien's form in order to sow as much sin in the world as possible. She'd never seen a more handsome man in her life, and unfortunately, she'd seen more than her fair share of men.

"You're serious, aren't you?"

"Yes," she said, her spine stiffening. She took offense at his condescending tone.

He chuckled. Her stomach felt hollow, seeing him laugh at her aspirations. *She* felt hollow.

"So you're going to be a chef this week."

"I'm going to be a chef for the rest of my life."

He shook his head, his smile fading. "This is the latest item on your crazy to-do stunt list. You've already tried race-car driver, sommelier, and photographer."

"I've grown up. I've turned my life around. I want my life to have . . . *substance*. I'm trying to create a career for myself."

"Why does an heiress need a career?" he asked. He had a decadently sexy voice. Rumor had it that women were regularly seduced by it alone, forget the rest of the package. Not that anyone would ever forget the smallest detail of Lucien. Elise knew she never had. She watched him as he moved behind the bar.

"Why does an heir?" she countered. "You've always worked, first at your father's hotels and then in your own hotels and restaurants. You of all people shouldn't be questioning me."

He glanced up, all traces of amusement gone. Her lungs couldn't expand as he held her stare. Pain welled up in her—shame about her past wild behavior and cynical attitude toward life, lancing fear that her plans for a future were hollow, that she truly didn't have what it took to be a functional adult who could give and take and make the world a bit of a better place. She hadn't possessed any role models for such a thing. She was afraid that greatly diminished her chances of success.

It was Lucien's stare that made her feel her shortcomings so completely. He saw a lot with those X-ray eyes. He always had.

He'd immediately seen her foolishness when they'd first met at his parents' estate in Nice. Elise had been a headstrong, wild thing, desperate for her preoccupied parents' attention, for the staff's, other houseguests' . . . *anyone's*. Lucien had been a coolly elusive twenty-one to her fourteen years that summer. From the beginning, he'd seen her ragged neediness, although she hadn't realized it at the time. He'd befriended her, much to her delight. She'd been like a pitiful, neglected puppy, in awe of every scrap of attention he threw her way. It had been the best summer of her youth, those golden months on the shore of the Mediterranean.

Of her life.

She hadn't realized until years later that their fathers had implored Lucien to take her under his wing. More than likely he'd been paid well for spending time with her, riding, swimming, and boating during that unforgettable summer. The knowledge shamed and infuriated her to this day.

"You must realize this is an unexpected—not to mention ridiculous—situation, Elise," he said, his tone softer than it'd been before. She tensed when she suspected it was from pity. "You can't work at Fusion."

"I told you. I have a contract."

"You have a contract with Mario, not with Fusion or me. I understand that master chefs take on stages. I allow them to arrange that on their own, respecting a talent I don't possess. You aren't one of Fusion's paid employees, however, and as you just witnessed," he said, wiping off the snifter he'd just washed, "Mario no longer works here."

She stood there, panic gripping her, her thoughts coming a mile a minute. Had she failed so quickly in her plans? Were they so brittle? Was she? Would she be forced to return to the sterile emptiness of her existence in Paris, once again the vanquished fool?

No. It would *not* happen.

"Why did you change your name?" The random question just popped out of her throat, she was so frantic.

For a moment, he didn't speak, just finished wiping off the snifter and hanging it with the other glassware, leaving her with her thoughts. Taking his time, he strolled around the bar. He approached her and stood close. Closer than she'd expected. The spicy scent of his cologne filtered into her nose.

"I'd actually already changed my name during our last meeting in Paris. Apparently, you'd been partying too much. You likely are a bit cloudy about a *few* things that occurred that night."

She stilled, suddenly growing wary. Something about his reference to their encounter at Renygat and the subtle suggestion that she might be *mistaken* in her memories of it triggered a warning signal in her brain.

She'd left her companions and sought out a private meeting with Lucien that Saturday night two years ago, nervous but eager to reconnect with her childhood infatuation now that she was a woman. True, she'd known he was in Paris for a while, but her parents' pushy desires about Lucien had made her standoffish about approaching him. She'd been embarrassed, lest he think she was just enacting her parents' wishes like some kind of robot socialite, bent on marriage to one of the most eligible males in the country.

She'd tapped lightly on the only door in the hallway, taking a moment to realize when she got no response that the door only led to a shorter hallway—an entryway of sorts. It led to the true door to Lucien's office. The outer door had been shut, but as she went through it, she'd seen that the inner one was cracked open an inch. Standing in the entryway, she'd accidentally overheard that puzzling conversation between Lucien and a German-accented stranger.

"I'll need top-notch insider information on Noble—his background, his family, his financials."

"That won't be easy. Ian Noble is known for being a control freak about security."

"That's why I hired you," Lucien had replied, sounding preoccupied. *"You're supposed to be the best."*

There had been a grunt of acknowledgment followed by a pause.

"What's that expression on your face?" the German man had asked, sounding vaguely amused. *"You're not feeling guilty, are you? About what you plan to do with Noble?"*

"Subterfuge isn't pretty, no matter how you dress it up. Sins of the father haunting me, I suppose," Lucien had said in a subdued, sardonic voice. *"We carry those ghosts with us, no matter what."*

The man had given a harsh laugh. *"Forget all that, and focus on your prize. Trust me. What you're planning with Noble doesn't compare to the crimes committed by your father."*

"I'm not cloudy about that night, Lucien. I remember it all," Elise said, hesitant to bring up the volatile topic in this delicate situation. His expression remained impassive, but something flashed in his eyes. She swallowed through a tight throat. "I don't recall you saying anything about changing your name, though."

"I think you know why I changed my name and left France." His quiet voice rolled over her like a sensual wave.

"You shouldn't let your father's crimes taint you. You're your own man," she whispered, referring to the fact that his adoptive father, Adrien Sauvage—wealthy industrialist, hotel chain owner, and head of a media empire—had been sent to prison two and a half years ago for corporate espionage. She knew Lucien had been questioned by the police about the possibility of his colluding with his father in the stealing of high-level corporate secrets. Elise had never believed he was guilty for a second. She had firsthand experience of Lucien's quiet, restrained disdain when it came to Adrien Sauvage. In the end, Lucien had never been charged with anything, but it seemed the taint still clung.

"I don't let his crimes affect me. I'm very aware that I'm not him."

His voice had gone quiet and husky as his gaze ran over her face. She stilled, the back of her neck prickled in anticipation. He reached up and touched her hair. She shivered at the sensation of his fingers sliding over it and gently tucking a lock behind her ear. Her entire body quickened, tingling with excitement. It felt strange, being so acutely aware of a man. She hadn't let herself get close to many men romantically—let alone a man as attractive as Lucien—since she'd thrown herself into her cooking career and begun to support herself. She hadn't *ever* let men get too close to her, truth be told. She'd had a major crush on Lucien as a girl, of course, even though he hadn't known she'd existed in a romantic sense. But this was different. She was a grown woman now, one who was much clearer on what she wanted out of life.

"I would have thought I wouldn't like your hair short," he murmured distractedly, his warm breath striking her temple. "But it suits you perfectly. Elegant sass."

"Lucien—" she began breathlessly when she saw the heat in his eyes as he caressed her again. He interrupted her by stepping back.

"I'll help you to arrange moving back to your parents' home in Paris, if you like. Are you set for money? Do you need any?"

"No. I'm perfectly fine," she muttered, jarred by his abrupt change of topic and the absence of his touch.

"You can't stay in Chicago," he said so resolutely that she blinked in surprise.

"Who are you to say I can't live here? Did you buy the city or something?" she fired, forcing herself to ignore the flicker of delicious sensation between her thighs, a direct effect of his touch . . . his nearness. Her anxiety mounted at his droll, unmoved expression. "You need a chef! Let me fill in for you at least until you find someone else."

"No. That's out of the question. I'm sorry."

Anger rose in her, stiffening her spine and making her stand tall.

How could he sound so resolute? Was she that disgusting to him? "I won't have you ruin everything I've planned," she declared.

"I won't have you doing the same to me."

"What?" she asked, set off-balance by his rapid-fire response. "How could *I* possibly ruin anything for you?"

He leaned against the bar, displaying lean, honed muscles to optimal effect. "That night at Renygat? In my office?" he prompted significantly.

She flushed with heat. After they were alone, she'd confronted him about what she'd overheard. He'd been furious about her eavesdropping, and their angry exchange had turned heated. The tension had segued to the sexual variety. She'd broken his rigid restraint that night . . . momentarily. He'd kissed her angrily and completely, fully acknowledging the fact that the girl he'd known was now a full-blooded woman. She knew she'd pushed him too hard with her flirtatious taunts. She just hadn't realized how fearsome Lucien could be when his control broke. . . .

How thrilling.

She noticed Lucien's narrowed gaze on her.

"Of course I remember," she said. She suddenly found it difficult to meet his stare. "I don't see how that relates to me ruining anything for you."

"I have enough distractions in my life at the moment. I don't need you adding to the mix." Her heartbeat escalated. Was he suggesting he was attracted to her? Or was he referring to that overheard conversation she could make no sense of whatsoever? Elise couldn't decide if she should be flattered or offended by his declaration.

"I'm not going to distract you. I came to Chicago for one reason and one reason alone—to get the training I need to be an excellent chef. I'm very good at what I do."

"I have no doubt of it. But you're forgetting one thing—there's no longer a chef here to train you, *ma fifille*."

"I don't care. I'll find another chef in this city. I came to this place to start a new life, a fresh start, and I won't let anyone—not even you, Lucien—set me off track. And I'm not a little girl," she added fiercely, referring to the French endearment he'd given her as a child.

His nostrils flared slightly as he shoved himself off the bar with a graceful, sinuous movement. Her heart started to throb in her ears as he reached for the silk wrap she'd draped over a stool earlier. He was going to send her away. *Again.* She remained frozen in place when he held up the garment, a challenge in his gray eyes.

"You are a child. A beautiful, stubborn one, but a child nonetheless," he said. "It's time for you to go, Elise."

Fury ripped through her like lightning. "You bastard," she hissed. She grabbed the wrap out of his hands. "I should have known you'd never help me. You're as selfish and narcissistic as your father . . . as *any* of our darling, beloved parents."

He caught her arm in an iron grip as she stormed past him toward the doors. "I'm not like my father," he grated out. Elise balked at the evidence of his sudden, potent anger, but she rallied. She jerked at her arm, but her reaction was just for show. Lucien's restraint triggered a completely different response than Mario's had.

"Let go of me," she said shakily, not sounding convinced it was what she wanted, even to her own ears.

"You should be glad I do let go and worry about the day I don't."

Her chin went up, pride and anger and hurt battling for room in her consciousness. "I'm not afraid of you."

He pulled on her, drawing her closer, so that her body brushed against his hard length and the fullness behind his fly. He scorched her with that almost otherworldly stare. She waited on a sharp ledge of anticipation, her breath burning in her lungs, when he lowered his head until their mouths were just inches apart.

"You've always tested me. You'll always be that girl I remember, foolishly poking at a sleeping snake. You'd better get out of here.

You've been begging without words to be disciplined since you were a girl, and you have no idea how much I'd love to give you what you so richly deserve . . . what you *need*."

He noticed her wide-eyed, shocked expression and smiled grimly. "Not so sure of yourself now, are you?" he asked, his voice a low, purring threat. "What do you say? Do you want to stay with me and get what you need, *ma chère*?"

Something in his low, rough voice made her flesh prickle with excitement and adrenaline to run in her blood, but mostly she was confused. Hating to show vulnerability in front of a man like Lucien, she fell back on the brittle armor of pride.

"I said to let go of me," she repeated.

When he released his grip, she staggered several steps in her heels, not because he'd pushed her, by any means—he'd actually been quite gentle—but because her mind was reeling. Something had happened to her at Lucien's touch. His words. It was like a sealed door inside her had been thrown wide open, and what she saw in the depths of her being had excited and bewildered her in equal measures.

Discipline. Need.

Her heart raced faster yet as she recalled the words uttered in Lucien's low, silky tones. She headed toward the doors. Out of pure habit, she threw a rebellious glance over her shoulder.

She took flight at what she saw—an angry, aroused, primal male animal. She hoped Lucien didn't notice how fast she moved as she scurried out the door, feeling as if the devil truly was on her heels.

Chapter Two

Lucien looked up when Sharon Aiken, his manager, tapped lightly on his office door late the next morning.

"Sharon. You are the picture of loveliness, as always, but I hope your beauty is accompanied by good news this morning. I could use it."

The middle-aged woman laughed. "Do they teach French men to charm just like they teach you to say please and thank you?"

"Haven't you heard, it's part of our genetic makeup." He raised a brow expectantly while Sharon laughed. She noticed and silenced her mirth.

"Don't worry, the interim chef you hired has indeed arrived. We are saved," she said.

"Bless you," Lucien said feelingly. He took a final swig of the café au lait he held in his hand and stood, ready for business. Even though he was relatively new to Chicago, he'd managed to create a network of professional contacts in the restaurant industry. A friend had informed him that a qualified chef had recently been let go from Chez Pierre. Having once sampled Baptiste's cooking, Lucien had leapt at the chance, despite the warning accompanying the referral. "John Baptiste is an exceptional chef, but he's very temper-amental," his friend had said.

"Is there a chef that exists that isn't?" Lucien had asked wryly.

He'd risen early and set about the task of contacting Baptiste, who had proved to be elusive, both in the physical sense and the practical. Baptiste had been insulted by Lucien's offer of a provisional contract, with its renewal based upon how well he fit at Fusion. But Fusion was known for its blend of French Moroccan fare, after all, and not all chefs felt comfortable with the subtleties of the combination. The Spanish-born chef had been infuriatingly vague about showing up this morning, thus Lucien's immense relief at Sharon's news. He'd figured Baptiste was a fifty-fifty gamble.

"Can you please send him back to my office so that we can take care of his contract?" he asked Sharon.

"Him?"

Lucien looked up in the process of gathering the contract from his desk. His skin prickled with wariness when he saw Sharon's dumbfounded expression.

"It's a *she*?" he asked slowly, filling in the blanks reluctantly.

"Well . . . yes. I was surprised at how young she is, but she's got Evan and Javier hopping to her every command," Sharon said, referring to two of their culinary assistants. "She certainly has a way about her." Sharon studied him anxiously when he dropped the papers in his hand and stalked around the desk. "Lucien? Were you expecting someone other than Ms. Martin?"

"Yes. More fool me," he muttered with barely restrained anger. That little demon's imp had more *couilles* than a tanked-up bull rider. How dare she challenge him? Sharon backed up against the wall, looking slightly alarmed, as Lucien swept past her.

His blood boiling, he peered through the kitchen door window, assessing the situation and attempting to gather himself before he entered. Elise stood behind a metal table with a saucepan in her hand and was talking animatedly, grinning as she did so. For a few seconds, he remained still and watched her, enthralled despite himself. She was like a quick, flickering flame.

She'd come back, even with his warning. He was going to have to deal with this godforsaken attraction he had for her. It wouldn't be vanquished. He could only hope to control it. He'd been a coward by sending her away before. Yes, she was a handful, but some things were inevitable. Elise had made it so by defiantly walking back into his life again.

"Mincing isn't so bad," he heard her saying through a crack in the door. "I had a little game I used to play whenever Monsieur Eratat—he was my meanest, foulest instructor at La Cuisine—set me to it. I'd pretend I was his barber, and I'd imagine mincing up his stupid little mustache to within a hairsbreadth of his fat nose. Of course I had to do tiny, perfect little slices to prolong Monsieur Eratat's torture." Elise's silvery laughter twined with masculine chuckles. "Even Monsieur Eratat had to admit to the class that no one had a finer mince than me," Elise added, a smile in her voice.

"I would never imagine that about you, Ms. Martin. Everything about you is too perfect to ever . . . er . . . mince," Evan, one of his culinary assistants, stuttered awkwardly. Lucien flung open the door when he registered Evan's worshipful tone.

Yet another mouse in her trap.

Evan and Javier immediately ceased their furor of chopping. They stared at him wide-eyed, Javier standing before mounds of porcini mushrooms and Evan before cloves of garlic. Only Elise continued in her task, glancing up at him with infuriating calm as she continued to dribble a sauce over dozens of duck fillets.

"What the hell do you think you're doing?" Lucien asked glacially, ignoring Javier and Evan.

"Roast duck with cèpes and green beans. It's on your lunch menu."

"I know it's on our lunch menu," he grated out. Elise looked calm enough when she glanced at Javier and Evan, but he noticed the pallor of her already fair skin.

"We're going to be pushing it for the lunch crowd, you two. Better get going," she urged in a friendly, competent manner. Much to Lucien's deepening fury, his two employees went back to chopping with enthusiasm.

He raised his eyebrows in a challenge. "May I see you in my office, Ms. Martin." It was worded like a question, but it was a command. He saw her bite at her pink lower lip as if to still its quaking. He felt a surge of satisfaction at her subtle show of nerves. She looked much younger than her twenty-four years at that moment. Her figure seemed especially slight in her white chef's jacket and loose black pants, her face appearing dewy and freshly scrubbed. For some reason, the vision of her youthful, glowing beauty combined with her competent manner sent him into a higher pitch of rage and helplessness.

He was going to have to handle her, once and for all. Unfortunately, she couldn't be dealt with like just any beautiful woman. No, she'd been right about her cutting ability. Elise sliced to the bone.

"It's not really a good time—"

"Get into my office this second before I drag you there, Elise."

All the chopping sounds ceased again, although Evan and Javier kept their heads lowered. The remaining color in Elise's cheeks faded.

"Lucien."

His heart jumped. He glanced around at the sound of the crisp, unexpected voice. Ian Noble stood with his hand holding the kitchen door open.

"Ian, what can I do for you?" he said smoothly. It wasn't unusual for Ian to stop by and see him—Ian owned the tower where Fusion was housed after all. It was just that his presence there today was highly inconvenient. From the corner of his eye, he noticed Elise set down the saucepan. He sensed her focused attention, ratcheting up his anxiety.

"I wanted to stop by to tell you that I won't be able to meet you for our fencing appointment tomorrow afternoon."

Lucien nodded. "Going out of town?"

"No, there's something very important I'm considering buying for Francesca," Ian said, referring to his very lovely artist girlfriend, Francesca Arno. "It takes a bit more research and thought than the common gift." Lucien rapidly took note of his friend's distracted air.

"You're not going to rely on Lin's shopping expertise?" he teased. Lin was Ian's exceptionally talented executive assistant.

"I'm a busy man, but I'm not a fool," he returned. Lucien laughed. He'd gathered from a few things Ian had said in the past that he'd gotten into trouble a time or two with Francesca for allowing his assistant to plan a little bit too much of the gift-giving and romantic outings. Francesca definitely preferred Ian's personal touch, and it was a sign of Ian's devotion to her that he freely gave her his most prized asset: his time. A man like Ian Noble had precious little of that commodity.

Ian's gaze flickered over to Elise. Lucien stiffened when the sharp blue eyes stuck. It wasn't just that Elise was lovely. She was like a luminous flame that radiated sexuality.

"Where's Mario?" Ian asked quietly under his breath, referring to the disgraced chef.

Damn Elise and her intrusions.

"I fired him last night," Lucien replied.

Ian's brows rose in subdued curiosity. "And this is your new chef?"

"I'm Elise Martin," Elise said, wiping off her hands with a towel and coming around the table.

"Ian Noble," Ian said.

Lucien stood there, steaming in a vat of helplessness as he watched Ian and Elise shake hands. He couldn't think of a way to deny that Elise worked with him without highlighting their past association and possibly causing her to reveal something he wanted kept secret at all costs.

"*Ian* Noble. Noble Tower?" she murmured under her breath. He saw when it clicked into place for her. She cast an amazed, curious glance at Lucien that made him stiffen. "I knew Fusion was in the Noble Tower building, but I didn't realize the *Noble* referred to you. This is your headquarters?"

"That's right. I look forward to sampling your creations. Francesca and I are regulars here at Fusion," Ian said.

Lucien frowned when he noticed Elise's upturned face as she studied Ian. Ian couldn't help it that he was very attractive to the opposite sex. Ian's greeting and gaze were politely interested, nothing more, but Elise's inspection of him didn't have to be so openly curious, did it? Her sapphire-blue gaze transferred to Lucien and her smile widened. Lucien ground his teeth in impotent fury, unsure what the little minx would do next and wondering how quickly she could ruin in seconds what had taken years to create.

"I've heard so much about you," Elise told Ian, although she was goading Lucien, of course.

"You're French?" Ian asked.

"Yes. I understand from some of the articles I've read about you that you are as well."

Ian nodded. "I was born in France, raised in England, schooled in the States. Where did Lucien find you?"

Lucien flashed her a warning glance, which she ignored.

"In a pot of trouble, I'm afraid," Elise said, her grin gamine, not to mention sexy as hell. Lucien's body responded to that smile against his will. An uncomfortable blend of fury and lust simmered in his blood, sending an alarm blaring in his brain. She opened her lips to explain further, but Lucien cut off the potential catastrophe of Elise's mouth.

"Elise and I just met. She's a friend of Mario's," Lucien said. It seemed imperative at that moment of crisis that the lie he told was simple and easy for Elise to understand. They needed to be on the same page for this unexpected—undesirable—encounter.

"You're very kind to step in and help Lucien in a pinch," Ian said.

Elise's gaze flew to Lucien, gauging his reaction to what Ian had said. Unwilling to say much else that might cause further inquiry on Ian's part, not to mention unsolicited revelations on Elise's, Lucien remained silent. He scowled when he saw her face grow radiant with triumph. She'd gotten just what she wanted, and she knew he knew it.

I'm going to punish you for this.

He wondered if she'd read his mind, because her triumphant expression faded.

"I was wondering if I could talk to you about something in private?" Ian asked Lucien, giving him just the excuse he needed to get Ian away from Elise.

"Of course. In my office?" Lucien suggested, extending his hand toward the door.

"It was a pleasure to meet you, Ms. Martin," Ian said before turning.

"The pleasure was mine."

Lucien waited until Ian had cleared the kitchen before he spoke in a low, confidential tone to Elise. "You have given me no other choice. Consider your challenge accepted, *ma fifille.*"

Before he turned to follow Ian, he had the thin satisfaction of seeing her eyes widen in panic.

Lucien waved at the bar in his office. "May I get you a drink?"

Ian shook his head and sank into one of the deep leather chairs in front of Lucien's desk with a swift, graceful movement for a man so large. He glanced distractedly at the polo mallet Lucien had never gotten around to replacing last night.

"Been practicing at your club?"

"A bit. The field is still soaked from all this rain. It's probably better to just get it off your chest," Lucien added mildly as he settled into the chair behind his large mahogany desk. He knew perfectly well that Ian had no interest in horses or polo. He'd much rather discuss his love of motorcycles.

Ian gave him a quick glance. "It's that obvious, is it?"

Lucien smiled. *Yes, it was that obvious.* He'd first met Ian several years ago in his restaurant in Paris, and they'd become quick friends. Lucien had moved to Chicago a little over a year ago, upon Ian's request, in order to open and oversee the restaurant in Ian's brand-new tower headquarters. When Lucien had decided his position was more secure in Chicago, he'd given in to his entrepreneurial nature and bought the restaurant from Ian last Christmas. Their friendship had entered a new level of closeness. Ian Noble was never an easy man to read, but Lucien suspected he'd learned his mannerisms and moods as well as most anyone on the planet, save a few.

"Let's put it this way: damn you for canceling our fencing match today. I'd bury you, as distracted as you are," Lucien said.

Ian gave a mirthless smile. "You're undoubtedly correct."

"What is it? Is it business?"

"No," Ian said almost before Lucien had finished asking.

Lucien leaned back in his chair. "Ah. Francesca, then," he said with finality. Of course. Only his lover could have the power to make Ian this distracted. The passionate flash in Ian's eyes confirmed his guess. Lucien waited patiently, knowing that Ian would eventually get to the point if given the opportunity. Ian had become one of the most powerful, wealthy men in the world because of his singular focus. If he'd come here to speak to Lucien about something, he'd get to it. Eventually.

Lucien began to wonder about that, however, when Ian continued to sit in morose silence.

"I've been considering asking Francesca to marry me. In fact, I'm more than considering it. I plan to choose her ring tomorrow," Ian said abruptly, his crisp, British-accented voice somehow not matching his almost tangible tension.

Lucien blinked. "That's wonderful."

"You're surprised, aren't you," Ian stated, studying him from beneath a brooding brow.

"No. I know how much you two love each other. It's a wonderful thing to witness, seeing you and Francesca together." He didn't flinch under Ian's laser-like stare.

"You're telling the truth, but still . . . you doubt that I could make a commitment like that. Deep down, you thought you and I were alike in that way."

Lucien grinned. "I have no idea what you're talking about."

Ian gave him a droll glance and stood, pacing in front of the desk and reminding Lucien very much of a trapped tiger. "We both like women, but neither of us has ever been the settling type. What about that woman—Zoe Charon? You were serious about her last year. But when her manager offered her a promotion in Minneapolis, you let her go without a second glance."

"That's not true. I glanced."

Ian gave him a skeptical look, but Lucien didn't blanch. He *had* hesitated about letting Zoe Charon walk away last winter. He'd liked her a lot. But in the end, there was always an unavoidable rift between him and intimacy. Now more than ever.

"What has my past experience with women got to do with the fact that you're considering asking Francesca to marry you?" Lucien wondered.

"Nothing, of course," Ian said. He unbuttoned his suit jacket, fell again into one of the chairs, and crossed his long legs. "It's just that . . . I have never once in my life considered myself to be the marrying type. I'd assumed the same thing about you. Perhaps I was wrong?"

"No, you weren't," Lucien replied. "But again, I hardly see how my preferences—or shortcomings as a man—apply to you."

"Because I have *more* shortcomings."

"You worry that you can't be faithful to Francesca?"

"No," Ian responded grimly. "It's not that at all. She's everything I want. Another woman would never do now that I've touched Francesca."

Lucien experienced a flicker of envy.

"I don't understand your hesitance, then. If you know you can be faithful to Francesca, what's the problem?"

Ian grimaced and glanced away. Lucien sensed his hesitation . . . his bitterness. "I feel that I might poison her somehow after a lifetime of association with me. I thought you might understand. I know how ashamed you are of what your father did, of his crimes. I, too, have a sort of . . . taint on me that I feel I can't make disappear. It's in my blood," he added irritably, glancing at Lucien. "I know. I realize how melodramatic I sound. But Francesca is so . . ."

"Fresh. Genuine. Lovely," Lucien supplied when Ian faded off.

"She is light itself. And I'm not."

For a second, neither of them spoke as Lucien absorbed Ian's words. A powerful kinship with the other man rose in him, an amplification of a connection that neither of them spoke of but seemed to mutually sense from their first meeting. They shared dark souls, stained from the moment they first drew breath in this world.

"I just feel that if Francesca and I marry, no matter how happy we are, a dark cloud hovers on the horizon. My decision to bind her to me could change things, open up"—Ian paused as if trying to find the words—"*un sac de nœuds.*"

Lucien smiled sadly at the French phrase—a sack of knots. He thought of Elise out there in the kitchen. He sighed resignedly. Well, sometimes there was nothing for it. Knots must be untied, one by one, no matter how intimidating the task. He would not back down from his personal *sac de nœuds* now that it'd been shoved in his face so provocatively by gorgeously packaged trouble.

"Who isn't afraid of the future when making such an important decision?" Lucien asked quietly. "You must believe in yourself and your ability to make your own fate. Everything else is bowing down to fear."

A strange look came over Ian's fierce expression, a distant light dawning in shadow. "You think it's just a matter of cold feet then?"

"I do. You must trust in yourself. You must trust in Francesca."

Ian's glance was like a blue-skied storm. "In Francesca, I have complete trust."

In myself, I have precious little.

Lucien remained seated as his friend gave his thanks and left the room, the unsaid words ringing like a familiar echo in his head, the voice his own—not Ian's.

The lunch rush had died out by the time the elegantly dressed woman who had introduced herself as Sharon Aiken entered the kitchen.

"Lucien has asked to see you in his office, Ms. Martin."

Elise paused in the process of arranging vegetables on a plate of grilled shrimp and pearl couscous.

"Can't it wait?" she asked warily. She'd been expecting the summons from his royal highness, but that didn't make hearing it now any easier.

"Lucien says Evan can finish up for you. There's only one table left to serve. He says for you to report to him immediately. He has a polo match later this afternoon, and he wants to speak with you before you become involved in the dinner prep."

"Of course," Elise said, taking pains to keep her voice cool and professional when she noticed the pointed curiosity in Sharon's expression. Obviously Lucien had warned the manager that Elise might try to wriggle out of a meeting with him.

"You have given me no other choice. Consider your challenge accepted, ma fifille."

The memory of Lucien's low, ominous threat played back in her head for the hundredth time. Well, the moment had come. What was he going to say? What was he going to *do* about her bold decision to show up here today, pretending to be his new chef? Part of her still couldn't believe she'd done it. Another part—the part that had stared hopelessly at the rundown décor in the Cedar Home Extended Stay Hotel last night—told her that she'd *had* to do something, no matter how crazy or brash, to try to keep her dream for a future from dying. She would not concede failure this time. Lucien was a fearsome presence, but he was a familiar face in a country full of strangers. He was furious at her, but he would help her when no one else would.

Wouldn't he? He sent you away once before.

Yes, but he'd said something about the dinner prep to Sharon, as if he expected Elise to be completing her day there. That was a good sign, wasn't it? Her brain had been spinning in overdrive ever since Ian Noble had walked into the kitchen earlier. She'd sensed Lucien's edginess, even though he'd outwardly appeared calm. The voice of the strange man she'd heard in Paris echoed yet again in her brain.

"You're not feeling guilty, are you? About what you plan to do with Noble?"

Had Lucien relocated his entire life to Chicago because of *Ian Noble*? If so, why? What did Noble have that Lucien wanted? It made no sense to her, given everything she knew of Lucien. Lucien was an extremely wealthy man in his own right, so she couldn't imagine that his motives were financial. Although extreme wealth never vanquished greed. If anything, it did the opposite, she thought, reminded of Lucien's father.

One thing was certain: Lucien hadn't denied it when Ian assumed that Lucien had hired her as an interim chef. Clearly, Lucien hadn't wanted the compelling billionaire to know about their past connection . . . or about what she'd overheard in Paris.

But what did Lucien's father's crimes have to do with Ian Noble?

She washed her hands, her anxiety mounting by the second. Irritation spiked through her when she turned to wipe off her hands and saw that Sharon waited for her. Did she plan to escort her like a jailer to Lucien's office?

"Thank you, I know the way," she said, even though it was a lie. Mario had disappeared alone last night when he'd apparently gone to raid Lucien's private store of premium cognac. She lifted her chin and breezed past the manager, noticing from the corner of her eye that Sharon followed her out of the kitchen. In the main dining room, she paused next to a busboy.

"Which way to Lucien's office?" she muttered without moving her lips.

"All the way at the end of the rear hallway, last door on the left," the busboy said so loudly that she grimaced and rolled her eyes.

She started down the long, empty hall, the sounds of the restaurant becoming muted until she could hear only the throb of her escalated heartbeat in the thick silence. By the time she knocked on the massive carved door of Lucien's office, she felt as if she were willingly walking to her own execution.

She started when the door whipped open suddenly. He looked dark and intimidating standing there, wearing a pair of black trousers that hung elegantly on his tall, athletic form, a dark gray shirt, a black and silver silk tie . . . and an unreadable expression. He nodded once and she entered the room, glancing around nervously at the masculine, luxurious office. The heavy door closed behind them with a loud click. She heard another snick of metal and spun around, alarmed.

"Did you just lock that door?" she asked, her already rapid heartbeat redoubling its tempo.

His nostrils flared slightly as he stared at her. "If you decide to stay, I think you'll prefer that the door was locked."

"What's that supposed to mean?"

"Come. Sit down," he said, waving his hand at the chairs before his desk. She sat slowly, watching him warily as he leaned against the edge of his desk directly in front of her. He had beautiful thighs—long and powerful. She had a sudden urge to see them naked, to run her hands over the sleek, hard muscles, to absorb his strength. . . .

She blinked, shocked by the thought in this tense situation, and looked away. Feeling vulnerable, she thought the best defense might be a strong offense.

"Lucien, did you come to Chicago because of Ian Noble?"

"Of course I did," he said. "He asked me to open the restaurant in his new tower. I did it as a personal favor to a friend."

"How long have you two known each other?"

"I didn't ask you back here to discuss Ian."

"But why didn't you deny to him that I was the interim chef?" she asked suspiciously.

"Why do you think?"

She glanced at his face skittishly.

"Because you didn't want me to mention anything about our past association, your past identity . . . about your father?" It wasn't precisely what she'd meant to say. She meant that conversation she'd overheard. On that night in Paris several years ago, she'd hidden in the rear entrance area of Renygat when she'd realized the mysterious German man was taking his leave, glimpsing only the back of the man as he left Lucien's office. Then she'd approached Lucien, who was now alone in his office, and confronted him about what she'd overheard. He'd been furious at her when he realized she'd been eavesdropping on his conversation.

She didn't want to specifically mention it presently for fear he'd send her away again.

His expression was bland. He crossed his arms below his chest and shifted his hips, bringing her attention downward to his crotch area. Her cheeks heated. Had he suggested she sit in the chair as he towered over her, his blatant masculinity right at eye level as a subtle power play? She wouldn't put it past Lucien.

"Why should it matter to you what Ian Noble thinks?" she pushed.

"I own a business in his tower. It matters."

"But I don't think your father's crimes say anything about—"

"What you think isn't of consequence here. I had to make a decision quickly out there, given what you pulled, and I think it'd be the best—the cleanest—solution for no one here in Chicago to know about our past connection for now."

She leaned back in the chair, considering. "No wonder you wanted me to disappear so fast last night," she mused. What was Lucien up to? It made her uncomfortable. She didn't like to think of Lucien getting himself into any trouble. And yet—this was powerful information that had fallen so unexpectedly into her lap. . . .

He narrowed his gaze, studying her. "Don't even think about it, Elise."

"Don't even think about what?"

His gray eyes flashed. "Blackmail. Don't give me that innocent look. You were thinking you have something to hold over my head now, something to use to control me. You were thinking that you would promise to keep quiet if I didn't interrupt this fantasy of the week of yours about becoming a chef."

"I was thinking no such thing," she lied hotly.

He laughed softly. "Do you think I'm a fool? I know how you operate. You learned manipulation from the cradle."

"I'm just trying to make a life for myself, Lucien. A good life . . . an honest one. I'm willing to work hard. Have you truly grown so callous that you would turn your back on a friend?"

"Friend? You never had *friends*. You had sycophants that thronged around society's aristocratic darling; you had the bucks lining up, panting to be the next one or two or three you chose for your bed—"

"How dare you!"

"You probably had the most elite drug dealers in the Corsican mafia at your beck and call—"

"I never used illegal drugs—or legal ones, for that matter."

"My point is, you *never* had friends, Elise."

She flung herself out of her chair.

"Well, maybe I need one now."

For a few seconds, they faced off in silence, her breathing slightly escalated. She listened to her heartbeat throb in her ears. He pinned her with his stare.

"I didn't ask you into my office just now because I want to be your *friend*."

She found herself staring at his hard, gorgeous mouth, wondering if she'd imagined what he'd said . . . his tone. She thought about what he'd proposed last night, when he'd dared her to stay there with him. Her gaze skittered to the door he'd locked and back to his face. Her heartbeat grew impossibly louder, until it felt like the thundering drum of it became her whole world. Was he saying what she *thought* he was saying?

"You . . . you want to be more than friends?" she asked weakly.

His gaze looked hungry as it flickered over her face. "You must know I find you attractive. If you recall, at one time, our parents even wanted us to marry."

She couldn't believe she was hearing him say this. *Of course* she recalled it. "My mother told me you completely dismissed the idea."

"Naturally, I dismissed it. I was twenty-six when they first mentioned it. You were nineteen. I hadn't seen you in five years. Do you really think I'd do anything but shoot down the idea before they got too far in spinning their web?"

Elise thought of the four people who were Lucien's and her parents and his reference to them as calculating spiders.

"No. Of course not," she said, perfectly seeing his point. If she recalled correctly, she'd been equally as dismissive when her mother oh-so-casually mentioned the topic. Her blood had quickened at the idea of seeing Lucien again—of something happening between them—but as in all things, she would never consider letting her mother notice that something mattered to her. She routinely downplayed romantic interests to Madeline, knowing the firsthand consequence of putting her heart on her sleeve when it came to her mother. It'd happened once, when she was very young, that she'd confessed her childish hopes to her mother about a beautiful teenage boy named Aaron. The day she'd accidentally witnessed Aaron's body twined around her mother's voluptuous curves like an adolescent boa constrictor had silenced Elise forever in that regard.

Besides, the scions of old, wealthy families were always contemptuous of their parents' territory building through arranged marriage. Defiance was the only defense they possessed. She'd said something flippant and hard every time her mother brought up the topic of Lucien.

"Why are you bringing up our parents' ancient wishes now?" she asked slowly.

"Not because I'm proposing marriage," he said, a slow, sardonic smile shaping his mouth. *Damn those dimples.*

She blinked. "No, of course not. I realize that," she assured quickly, embarrassed.

"I just bring it up because the concept of us having a relationship isn't all that far-fetched, although what I'm proposing is hardly something our parents would have condoned. No. This is just about you and me and our needs."

You and me and our needs.

For a moment the silence seemed to press down on her until she felt as if she couldn't breathe. She'd wanted Lucien for so long, but he'd remained an impossible, elusive fantasy. Was all that about to change?

"Did you know what you were doing when you walked in here today, pretending to be my chef?" he asked quietly.

Her mouth fell open in surprise at his question. "I was fighting for something I want. Very much. I was hoping to convince you."

"I don't think that's what you were doing. Not entirely anyway."

She laughed at his absolute confidence. "Please, enlighten me then."

"I think you came here because of what I said last night. You've always run like an out-of-control wildfire, Elise. You knew I would give you a limit to your world, a measure of control that you sorely need. You threw down the gauntlet when you walked in here today and pretended to be my new chef. Well, I accept your dare. If you play by my rules."

His quietly spoken words roared in her ears.

"I'm not sure what you mean." She meant it, but something about the hard edge to his voice and the dangerous glint in his light eyes caused her skin to prickle with heightened awareness. Was it fear that mingled with her confusion, or was it excitement?

His gaze flickered over her face thoughtfully. "The wild child of the European social circuit, partying with the royals, flitting from one career to another . . . from one man to another. You've been the very embodiment of self-indulgence," he mused.

"That part of my life is over," she stated with much more confidence than she felt. It was her greatest fear that she wasn't strong enough, that her lofty goals and aspirations were a façade draped over a hollow center. Ever since her friend Michael had been found dead, she'd vowed to change. But what did she really know about taking control of her life, of making it worthwhile? Precious little.

"It's very hard to turn over a new leaf. If you are to be successful in this venture, a degree of self-control will be required."

"I'm perfectly capable of looking out for myself," she said with regal dismissiveness.

"I look forward to witnessing it."

"Well, you will," she retorted hotly, realizing too late how defensive she'd sounded in response to his calm manner. She bristled, self-doubt and uncertainty rising in her when he merely studied her. "But what about . . . the other?"

"The other?" he asked, eyebrows going up. Helplessness twined with excitement in her chest. She had never been so confused by a man in her life.

"You were insinuating you wanted us to . . ." She trailed off as she lamely pointed at him, herself, and him again in a joining gesture. Join *how*, precisely? He wasn't saying. Her desperation grew when he didn't rush to assist her. "Do you *want* me, Lucien?"

"Of course I want you. You're the most tempting creature I've ever laid eyes on."

Her mouth fell open in shock at that. He was usually so stoic, so understated. Nothing could have taken her more off guard than his bald admission.

"You sent me away. In Paris, that night." She listened to her heart pounding in the silence that followed.

"I didn't send you away because I didn't want you, Elise. I sent you away because you're dangerous."

"To your person?" she laughed.

"To my peace of mind. You're like a thorn in a man's flesh," he muttered. "But none of that matters now. You walked in here today, and as I said, I think you were telling me something significant by doing that. Don't you?"

She found it hard to meet his steady stare. "Maybe," she conceded breathlessly.

"I'm not asking you to leave. If you go, it'll be by your choice."

Something about his honesty helped her find her courage. "You must know I'm attracted to you as well. I have been for as long as I can remember," she admitted shakily.

His body jerked slightly. He caught himself and remained unmoving. For a split second, she thought he was going to straighten and . . . do *something*. Hold her?

"I will be the one to set the rules, Elise," he said instead.

"Why?" she asked, back to being bewildered.

"Because it's in my nature to be the dominant during sex."

She just stared at him. A frisson of excitement went through her belly and flickered between her thighs.

"Surely you know about such proclivities?" he prompted.

She swallowed thickly. Yes, she knew. Not by direct experience. Typically, Elise liked to be the one to call the shots. Not in a dominatrix manner. It's just that she typically got her own way, and that included sexual interaction. What Lucien said had struck her as both alien and exciting at once.

"Of course I do," she blustered, trying to hide her confusion. She didn't want him to think she was naïve, but well . . . she *was*, in many ways. Most of the people who considered her the irrepressible, wild *coquine* would be shocked to know just how inexperienced she was.

"It's very simple. You're very beautiful. I want you. It would give me great pleasure to see you submit, for once in your life. You require discipline," he said firmly, his mouth curving into a god-awful sexy smile. "Besides, if you are determined to stay in Chicago, I want you close."

"So you can keep tabs on me? Keep me in line?" she asked, insulted.

"Yes, to be honest."

Their eyes met and he sobered. "And if we are to see each other, I will be the one to call the shots. Do you agree to this? Can you give up control to me?"

She bit her lip uncertainly. "Will this be an exclusive arrangement?"

"Yes. I won't be sexually involved with another woman for the time period we are together. I expect sexual fidelity from you as well. In fact, I demand it," he said in a harder tone with a pointed glance.

Her heart seemed to have swelled past its typical confines and was pressing into her throat. "And just how do you plan on keeping me in line?" she managed sarcastically, still insulted by his insinuation that he wanted to engage in this relationship to control her while she was in Chicago.

"At the moment? I will spank you by hand."

She noticed him studying her reaction closely and strained for a neutral expression. Her heart gave up pretending, however, and started running a race in her chest cavity.

"As I said, even though you may not have been entirely aware of it, I believe that's why you came here. I want you to know that I won't put up with your manipulation. I will punish you every time you defy me in the future. I will punish you every time I see you engaging in impulsive or unsafe behaviors. I will discipline you every time you lie to me."

Nothing could have prepared her for what he'd said. The word *punishment* took on layers of new meaning when uttered in Lucien's low, sexy voice . . . dark, forbidden, exciting complexities. Part of her was shocked, and yet another part wasn't surprised at all.

She laughed incredulously, even though panic started to rise in her as she observed his calm, unruffled manner.

"You're flipping mad," she breathed out, hiding her bewilderment.

He regarded her through a hooded gaze.

"Those are my terms. I have told you that I want you. But I won't have you running amok in my life if you plan to live in Chicago. One, I don't need the drama. Two, I couldn't abide witnessing it." Her breath caught when she heard the emotion ringing in his compelling voice. "If your spoiled, oversexed mother was too weak to teach you to control yourself, and your father was too self-involved to bother, then someone has to do it. When you strutted into this restaurant today like you owned the place, you made that *someone* me.

"Now unfasten your pants and lower them, then lean against my desk," he continued, his matter-of-fact manner only amplifying the surreal sensation fogging her brain. *He couldn't be serious.* He wanted to spank her? Lucien Sauvage? "You can go if you choose," he said, not unkindly, when he noticed that she didn't move and continued to stare at him in disbelief. "We won't do this thing unless you are in full agreement."

"*That's* blackmail," she whispered.

"No. You are not my employee, Elise. I have never offered you a job. I have never offered you anything but this relationship, which will be carried out by my rules, and mine alone. You pushed yourself in here. This isn't about blackmail or harassment. This is about what you need, what I think you were asking for by marching in here uninvited today. If you plan to live here in Chicago, if you are to be in my life, I will not allow you to manipulate and defy me. You will receive the discipline you require—and if I sense that you submit, there will be pleasure as well. If you can't agree to that, then there's the door."

She didn't move. She couldn't.

He nodded once, seeing that she'd made her decision. Elise realized dazedly that she had, indeed, decided. He turned and walked over to a large antique cabinet. He opened one of the doors and she glimpsed an expensive stereo. Suddenly, the sounds of Beethoven's rich, penetrating Fifth Symphony filled the air. She stared at Lucien stupidly as he returned to her.

"Do as I told you," he said, not unkindly.

She glanced once at the door and back at him. His face was hard, but she saw something in his eyes—not gentleness, necessarily, but compassion . . . understanding that this was not an easy thing he was asking of her, but that he asked it anyway.

"I hate you, Lucien Sauvage," she said as she began to unfasten her pants, the hissing sound of her voice barely rising above the swell of the music.

He nodded once matter-of-factly. "But you will still do as I say."

She jerked down her pants as a defiant reply.

"Lean over the desk," he said.

Her held breath burned in her lungs and blistered her throat as she did what he said. She'd never been punished before. She'd never voluntarily given up control to a man. This was an entirely new experience. She couldn't believe she was allowing it to happen. What did it mean that she was? Anger, bewilderment, and excitement twined in her and tightened around her lungs. Her breath hitched when Lucien stepped closer.

Something hot and forbidden surged through her pussy. She felt his hand at her hip. His long fingers slipped beneath the waistband of her underwear. A tendril of excitement flickered through her clit.

"Do you have to?" she asked shakily as she felt him lower her panties.

"Always," was his reply. He released the skimpy underwear, and it bunched next to her pants at her knees. She squeezed her eyes tight when she felt him lift her chef's smock, fully baring her to his gaze. Mortification swept through her. Lucien would never believe it if she told him—so she didn't say a word—but she wasn't used to such intense intimacy.

She trembled with excitement when Lucien's hand brushed against the sensitive skin of her right buttock. He cupped the flesh and squeezed. Liquid heat rushed through her pussy, the strength of her response confusing her. It was as if her body had a mind of its own. Her brain certainly hadn't given her permission to find his possessive touch on her ass so arousing.

"You're lovely. I will find it exciting to punish you. Very," he murmured. "You may find it arousing as well, but it will also sting. That's the consequence of your behavior. Even though I will enjoy this, today it will only be a punishment. As I mentioned, we will take things at my pace."

She turned her chin. He saw her bewildered expression.

"We won't be having sex after I finish," he explained patiently. "That will come another time."

She listened to all of this in anxious amazement.

"Elise?" he prompted. "Am I making myself clear?"

"Yes," she croaked.

"I will spank you with my hand twenty times. It will burn, but you need never fear that I will cause you any lasting harm. It isn't my intention, now or ever, to harm you. Do you understand?"

No, she didn't understand. She couldn't comprehend anything that was happening. Why was she letting him do this to her?

Discipline. Need.

She recalled him saying those words last night and bit her lip, her anticipation more acute than she'd ever experienced in her life. Was it true? Was that the reason she'd come on her flagrantly rebellious mission today? Hadn't he hinted what would happen if she stayed with him last night?

And she'd returned, determined to provoke him . . . into this?

"Elise?" he prompted.

"Yes, I understand," she said in a choked voice.

He lifted his hand from her ass.

Smack.

She whimpered at the burst of sensation. He spanked her again, a brisk slap of skin against skin, and her eyes sprang wide.

Oh. It stung, but it was also exciting to feel Lucien's hand come into contact with her bottom, that quick flash of sensation. It was intimate, too; something about the secretiveness of what he was doing here in the midst of a business—the fact that she was *letting* him do something so personal to her, so illicit—was also thrilling.

She stared sightlessly at the blotter. His hand landed again, and she suppressed a gasp, not of pain, but of an incendiary emotion she couldn't name or control. It was as if his spanks were causing some friction in her, forcing something to the surface with his blows that she'd rather keep buried. He paused with his hand on her, his light caress almost as volatile as his punishment.

"Are you all right?"

"Yes," she grated out, hoping he heard the anger in her voice and not the other bewildering feelings brewing in her chest.

He spanked her again. She bit her lip to stop herself from moaning. He knew what he was doing. His slaps were quick and brisk, meant to sting, not bruise or harm. He smacked her on the lower curve of her right buttock twice. A cry flew out of her throat. She shifted her hips instinctively, trying to avoid another swat on her prickling flesh. He bracketed her hips with his hands and kept her steady.

"Hold still, or you'll earn more," she heard him say, his voice thicker than before. Was he getting turned on? Arousal pinched at her clit for some reason. She crunched her eyelids closed in rising bewilderment. He rubbed the patch of flesh on her bottom as if in apology for making her nerves sizzle. Her ass felt hot beneath his big hand.

He smacked her again. She gasped. Distantly, she realized he'd turned on the stereo to muffle the sound of her spankings. His office was already remotely situated in the restaurant, the door was thick, and the luxurious furnishings and paintings likely muffled interior sounds.

Did he punish women in his office often?

The disconcerting thought fractured when he landed another spank. She was horrified when a tear burst from her clenched eyelids.

"Mario was right. You are a devil, Lucien Sauvage," she accused, shifting her bottom. He popped the moving target with increased force.

"If you don't keep your ass still, you will discover what a devil I can be."

She bit her lower lip as she forced herself to still. He smacked her again. Her ass was on fire, and her pussy was growing wet. The nerves on her behind stung, but it was nothing compared to the pleasurable tingling of her clit. At the same time, she was truly humiliated by the fact that she was allowing Lucien to spank her bare-assed.

Yet . . . she wanted it. Needed it.

"Just get it over with, please. I can't take much more," she said brokenly when he paused to soothe her burning flesh with caressing fingertips.

"You will take what I give you." He raised his hand again. The music swelled in her ears.

Smack, smack.

It was as if he were pushing something out of her with his punishment, building friction, trying to create a fire of feeling in her flesh. It was too much. Emotion exploded out of her. She shuddered uncontrollably.

Suddenly he was lifting her by the shoulders and she was in his arms. She pressed her hot, wet cheek against his silk tie and shook with feeling.

"I hate you. I hate you," she muttered, not even sure what she was saying in her tumult.

"No you don't," he said quietly, his fingers moving gently in her hair, soothing her. "We are alike, you and I. Both alone. Both misfits. I struggled to escape the golden cage, too, *ma chère.* I'm trying to help you, if you'll only listen."

"Lucien," she whispered, so much feeling infused into that one word, so much longing. She rubbed her cheek against his tie, drying unwanted tears. His clean, spicy, citrusy scent permeated her misery. So did the sensation of his hard body.

He was clearly, awesomely aroused.

She stilled at the realization, her misery fading. The inexplicable ache at her core amplified.

What would happen now?

His long fingers skimmed against her skin and he lifted her chin. She stared up at him, defiant even in her utter confusion. "I'm going to give you what you need."

"I don't understand you," she whispered.

"Such a beautiful, wild thing, such a pure, strong flame," he murmured, his gaze traveling over her face as he caressed the line of her jaw. "But you will burn yourself to ashes if left unchecked. You've been grasping for an outer limit to your world for years now, something to contain you. Now you've run into it. And I'm not turning away this time," he said simply, skimming her cheek with his fingertips.

She stared up at him mutely. He leaned down and kissed her lips, his mouth so tender and so cherishing that she felt as if she were dreaming.

"Now bend back over the desk so that we can finish."

She arched against him. She'd rather just skip the spanking, hot as it was making her, and possess what she'd desired for half her life. Who knew that she'd respond so strongly to a bit of kink? She wasn't the only one responding. What she felt of Lucien—his size and hardness—made her fevered. She'd love to stroke and suck the awesome cock she felt pressing against his trousers.

"Do as I say," he said, avoiding the come-hither gyration of her hips, his gray eyes flashing, his tone hard. "Don't try and grab control of this, Elise. Don't test me. You'll lose."

She gasped at the realization that he understood precisely what she'd been doing with her seduction. She let him turn her in his arms, despite her sharp disappointment. He pressed gently at her lower back, prompting her to bend over. His hand moved up her spine, massaging, molding, working the muscles.

"So much tension in your muscles . . . so much pain," he said quietly. He didn't seem to be expecting a response, which was fine with her. She was too overwhelmed by his touch to speak. His hand brushed against her prickling, hot ass. Her clit pinched in arousal, the sharpness of her response shocking her. The anticipation was killing her.

"But why? *Why* are you doing this?" burst out of her throat, her voice going high in panic.

"Because I care," he said. Her eyes sprang wide when he pressed his hand to her buttocks. Then it was gone, and she knew he was drawing his hand back in preparation to strike. Her sex clenched tight in anxious excitement. "I wouldn't be doing this if I didn't, Elise. And you wouldn't be letting me if you didn't know that."

Part II

When You Defy Me

Chapter Three

His hand struck the lower curve of her ass cheeks, causing a burst of sensation.

"*Ouch.*"

"*Je suis désolé,*" she heard Lucien apologize huskily behind her. He touched her buttocks, his palm warmed from her spankings. Her breath hitched. "It will take me a time or two to learn what you can tolerate . . . what you need."

Her clenched eyelids sprang open. "What I need is for you to stop torturing me this way."

His hand disappeared. *Smack.*

"Wrong. You need a consequence for your actions."

The nerves on the surface of her bottom stung and burned. There was an inexplicable link between those nerves and her sizzling clit. She bit her lip, experiencing an almost overwhelming desire to touch herself . . . to staunch the ache growing between her thighs.

"Brace yourself," Lucien warned, his voice a low, sexual purr that washed over her exposed, flaming ass and tickled at her damp pussy. She firmed her hold, following his order instinctively, and clenched her teeth. His hand landed again and again, the brisk cracking sound of skin against skin creating a strangely erotic contrast to the rich yet highly controlled notes of the symphonic music filling her ears.

The tail of her smock flipped down over a buttock. She inhaled shakily when he paused and took a moment to carefully replace the edge of her smock at her waist, once again revealing her ass. She could just imagine how pink it must look to him. The breath burned in her lungs when he spread his hand over the crack between her buttocks, his fingers spread, his fingertips below his palm.

"So beautiful," he murmured.

She whimpered softly at the hint of awe in his tone. He was so large that he encompassed her. He rubbed, and her vagina clenched tight. She moaned feverishly, wanting . . . needing his touch on her sex. He was only inches away from her pussy. She gyrated her hips slightly, rubbing him back in an open invitation.

Smack. She gasped at the unexpected, sharp pain of his hand cracking against her ass.

"Damn it," she seethed.

"You're doing it again," he said, a thread of amusement in his hard voice.

"What?"

"Trying to grab for the reins."

"Ouch . . . ooh . . . *merde*," she mumbled incoherently when he spanked her.

"Every time you attempt to seduce me, I'll spank you an extra time. Submit, *ma chère*. Let go. I'm taking control for the time being."

A tear leaked down her cheek, but she remained determinedly still. For a few seconds, she and Lucien were as one. She feared the flex of Lucien's muscle, the swing of his arm, but she also anticipated it, sensed it perfectly . . . wanted and needed it. There, for a few seconds, she understood precisely what Lucien had meant.

Discipline. Need.

"Two more," she heard him growl.

She twisted her chin and saw his arm stretched back. He looked awesome in that moment, his long legs spread slightly, nostrils flared, eyes blazing, muscles coiled and tense. He paused with his hand back and met her stare. It happened so quickly that later she wondered if she'd imagined it. He cupped her hip with his free hand and pressed her burning ass to his crotch, grinding her against rock-hard thighs and cock.

Her eyes sprang wide when she fully absorbed his dimensions . . . his heat. Liquid surged at her core, an answer to his primal call. Abruptly, he was gone.

"Damn those eyes," he muttered thickly. "Look at that desk or I swear you won't sit comfortably for a week."

She turned, staring sightlessly at the leather blotter on his desk, panting shallowly as he cracked off the last two strokes.

Through the swelling sounds of the symphony and her own pounding heart, she heard the rough, soughing sound of Lucien's breath behind her. She didn't move.

What would he do now? Her pussy was hot and wet between her thighs. She felt his arousal behind her like a distant but powerful fire, his heat seeming to emanate against her naked ass, teasing her sex. Surely he wouldn't walk away? Perhaps he'd take her from behind? The thought panicked and excited her. She hadn't prepared for this. She started to raise herself in order to touch him . . . in order to pleasure him . . . to satisfy him . . .

. . . in order to take control of this volatile situation.

That she could handle. He'd said they wouldn't have sex, but that was before they'd generated all this heat. She stood and turned, gratified to see the fixed, rigid expression on his face as he stared at her ass. He grabbed her wrist lightning quick when she reached for his pants. Suddenly, she was spinning and her back was pressed tightly to his front, her bottom pressed against his hard thighs, her lower back against the flagrant fullness of his sex. She gasped when he gathered her other wrist and restrained both of her arms in his hand. He leaned down, cupping her body with his long, hard length.

"It aroused you. Didn't it?"

A shudder of excitement went through her at the sound of his delicious voice in her ear.

"I . . . I hated it," she lied, fighting for the upper hand even though she knew she was losing . . . even though she increasingly didn't know what losing or winning meant when it came to Lucien. Her gasp turned into a moan of disbelieving arousal when he abruptly plunged a long finger between her labia and rubbed.

"Very warm. *Very* wet," he groaned near her ear, increasing her shudders of pleasure. "I'm going to cure you of this tendency for lying. I felt you submit there at the end, even if you are denying it now, and you were very brave in accepting your spanking. Here is your reward."

Her head fell back against his breastbone. It felt divine, the friction from his rubbing finger optimal. Her clit began to sizzle beneath his touch. Her hips ground against the pressure. He pressed her tighter against him, so that she could feel his cock throbbing against her lower back and hip. He'd been right about how wet she was—she could tell by the easy slide of his finger. She could even hear him moving in the lubricated flesh. How humiliating.

How *exciting*.

She subtly gyrated against him, growing wild with mounting arousal, her teeth clenched tight. She couldn't seem to stop it. He pleasured her more knowledgeably than she pleasured herself, something about his restrained strength and obvious skill creating a riot of bliss in her flesh. Her entire body grew rigid, and her nipples tightened almost painfully, making her wish he'd touch them, pinch them to ease the sharp pressure.

"Damn you," she muttered brokenly.

"Come," he demanded. The music swelled in her ears, cresting.

She clamped her eyelids shut and shook in delicious release.

"That's right," she heard him say, his voice seemingly both far away and so close it was like he was inside her head. "One day you're going to come like that while I'm buried in you, and it's going to feel so incredibly good."

His hand continued to work between her thighs, stimulating her until she sagged against him, panting. Her eyelids opened sluggishly a moment later when she felt his hand slow and stop.

For a moment, she didn't move or breathe as he cupped her outer sex in a possessive gesture and she felt his cock pulse against her, hard, heavy, and more than ready.

He released her. She whimpered at the sudden loss of his heat.

"Get dressed," he said, his voice sounding rough. She watched as he strode across the office to a closed door. When he jerked it open, she realized it was an entrance to a bathroom.

The door snapped shut behind him.

He came out a moment later as she finished fastening her pants. She studied him anxiously from beneath lowered eyelashes as she pulled down her smock. His short, thick hair looked sexily mussed. The strands at his temples and nape were damp, as if he'd splashed his face and neck with water. She felt as if she had suddenly been transported to a strange country and didn't understand the language. She didn't know how she was supposed to respond to him. None of her former experience with sex had prepared her for this.

"Why don't you go and wash up as well," he said, his tone softer than she would have expected, given his palpable tension level and obvious continued arousal.

Elise welcomed the opportunity for temporary escape from Lucien's disturbing, compelling presence. She didn't want him to know how stupid she felt, how inadequate. She rushed into the bathroom and shut the door behind her. The cheeks of the woman in the mirror shone red. Her eyes shone. It was another novel experience, seeing her reflection after she'd been so undone by desire.

How could she possibly feel so humiliated at what Lucien had just done to her and yet be so turned on by it? And why, despite her anxiety about what Lucien would do next, did she also experience a strange calmness after what he'd done . . . a newfound steadiness?

You can do this, Elise. You can handle Lucien Sauvage. You've talked dozens of powerful men into doing precisely what you want.

None so formidable as Lucien.

She clamped her eyelids shut, silencing the annoying self-conversation in her head.

What had occurred in Lucien's office was so alien to her, so powerful, the only way she could think to handle it was to ignore it. She would plow forward with her plan. Lucien had admitted to wanting her, after all. She wasn't entirely weaponless.

She washed and exited the bathroom, her chin up. He remained standing, his arms crossed, clearly waiting for her to return. He'd turned down the stereo in her absence. His eyes gleamed from beneath a lowered brow as he studied her.

"Are you all right?" he asked quietly.

"I'm fine," she said almost flippantly, glad to hear her voice sounded even. Let him think she'd been spanked dozens of times, just like he believed she'd fucked half the men in Paris. She would not tip her hand and reveal her vulnerability. She would not let him know that he'd just rocked her world, or that she had no idea precisely how he'd done it.

"Are you finished *keeping me in line*?"

"For the time being."

"Good. Can we talk about my job now?"

Her clear, melodious voice replayed in his mind again and again. He shook his head once as if to dislodge it.

"You haven't got a job," he said.

"Let me work here until you get another chef. You need the help, Lucien. You can't close the restaurant for days on end. Think of all the money you'd lose. If that doesn't matter to you, think of your disappointed customers."

His jaw ached when he unclenched it. It was a wonder to him Elise couldn't see his body shaking. He vibrated with barely contained lust. He didn't want to have a rational conversation with Elise Martin; he wanted to bend her over his desk and fuck her until every logical thought in his brain was incinerated by a glorious, explosive climax at her farthest reaches. Perhaps he shouldn't have punished her. The recollection of her courage in accepting it—the memory of her plump, pink ass—would undoubtedly drive him over the edge into madness.

No, he'd been *right* to punish her. He knew that on some gut level. He'd sensed a serenity to her, a strength, that was compelling to behold. She *did* require some kind of limit to her world. Lucien had understood that since he was twenty-one years old.

Still, she was right back to her bargaining and manipulation.

"What good would it do you to work at Fusion? You need a master chef to stage with and complete your training, correct?" he reminded her, frustrated by her tenacity over this topic.

"Yes, but I could continue to fill in until you find one. With any luck, the chef you hire will want a stage. Knowing the caliber of chefs you always choose in your restaurants, I'm sure he or she will be acceptable to my school so I can get my degree. I'm very good at what I do, Lucien. I have talent."

He closed his eyes briefly and glanced away. He hated the note of desperation in her tone. "You needn't sound so defensive. I know you have talent. Do you think I didn't sample selections of your lunch?"

"I hadn't realized," she said, her surprised tone sounding genuine.

"I wouldn't serve my patrons anything that wasn't up to my

standards. You surpassed them. You have an innate understanding of the French and Moroccan blend I'm looking for."

"Aha!"

His fierceness returned like a flicking whip at the sight of her smug grin. Perhaps she sensed his knife-sharp lust mingling with anger, because she forced her smile to vanish. For a few seconds, they just regarded one another in silence.

"I agree with what you said. I didn't have many friends in Paris," she said softly. "But you were my friend once, Lucien, when we first met in Nice when I was a child. Lend me a hand again. Please."

She was ruthless. He suspected she knew very well that he'd respond positively to a wide-eyed, sincere plea. Still, respect for her tenacity tempered his irritation.

"I am a fool to even consider it," he said after a billowing silence. "But I suppose it will allow me to monitor you even more closely."

She scowled at that. She really did delight him at times. When she noticed his fond smile, she smoothed her expression. "I won't disappoint you. You'll see. I *will* make this work."

He stepped toward her. "You will not tell your mother and father, or anyone of our common acquaintance in France, that you know of my location. You will not say a word to anyone here in Chicago that we knew each other previously. To everyone else in the world, we just met last night. You aren't to mention anything about our former acquaintance. Not. One. Thing," he said succinctly. "Am I making myself clear, Elise?"

"Crystal," she assured.

"You will follow my instructions in regard to your job without back talk and sass. The second you step out of line or try to manipulate me, you will know a consequence. I will not have you defying me day in and day out. If you can't agree to that, then you can't stay at Fusion. Those are my terms. I will put you on a salary until I can find a new chef. If and when you enter your official training again, your salary and official job here will end."

"I have enough money set aside to get me through the stage. If you pay me a salary until my training begins, I can stretch what I have to make it work."

He gave her a droll glance, his gaze sticking on the vision of her reddened cheeks and lips. No, it was not his lustful imagination. Little Elise Martin had been aroused by her punishment. *Very* aroused. It was going to be such a pleasure training her to his hand. His cock throbbed next to his thigh, as if in protest at being ignored. It only added to the boiling brew of emotion he experienced. He turned away from the intoxicating sight of her, worried that if he inhaled in such close proximity, he might catch her scent. He would snap then, for certain.

"Your papa would not see you starve," he said sardonically, moving around his desk.

"No. But I would starve myself before slithering back to him for another handout."

He lowered to his chair, glad the desk blocked his still-primed arousal. He found her quiet conviction appealing. Elise had what it took to make a success of whatever she attempted. It was her doubt in her strength, determination, and perseverance—in *herself*—that was her demon. Whether she could conquer that demon or not, Lucien was unsure.

He forced his mind to the practicalities at hand.

"I'll have Sharon bring you a job application. I'll have a contract drawn up for you as an interim chef. Saturday is market day," he said, picking up an invoice and studying it. "Since you're so adroit at driving a race car, I assume you can handle a four-wheel-drive truck?"

He glanced up when she didn't immediately reply. "You might have heard how much I value locally grown food in my restaurants. I want the freshest, most pristine, locally grown ingredients. It's one of my chef's duties to shop for the items he or she needs for the week at a farmers' market. There is more to being a chef than just cooking, Elise," he added when she continued to look amazed.

"Of course. I know how important marketing is," she said defensively.

He nodded. "But being new in town—in the country, for that matter—I'm sure you'll need some guidance through the process. Usually Javier or Evan will go with you to assist, but this Saturday, I will. We should get there early to get the best produce. Can you be ready by six?"

"Yes."

He studied her through a narrowed gaze, sensing her bewilderment. *Good.* She'd been throwing him off balance since her arrival last night. It was about time she looked a little tongue-tied. "I'll need your address in order to pick you up."

"I'll just meet you near the market if you tell me where," she said breathlessly.

He designated an intersection in the Gold Coast neighborhood for them to meet.

"I will set up medical exams for both of us tomorrow," he said.

"Medical exams?"

"Yes," he said calmly. "We should both know we are safe for sexual interaction. I know that I am, but I want to assure you of the same. Are you on birth control?" he asked levelly.

She nodded.

"Good. In the meantime . . ."

"Yes, darling?" she prodded when he faded off.

His gaze flashed to meet hers. *Darling.* The word sounded completely contrived, frequently practiced, and yet . . . undoubtedly alluring uttered from her flushed, ripe lips. Damn her. Always turning the tables. She waited, just a hint of amusement shining in her eyes.

"You are my employee. We'll keep our distance from each other, for the time being."

Her eyes widened in angry disbelief.

"You were the one who begged for the job," he reminded her mildly.

"But that has nothing to do with—"

"It *does*," he said sharply, shooting her a challenging look. "Remember? My rules? We'll go at my pace, or you'll feel a consequence."

Her hand flickered to the side of her bottom, as if she'd suddenly reexperienced the sting of his hand. He scowled; his cock lurched.

"Elise?" he prompted, waiting for her agreement.

"Oh, *fine*," she muttered, giving him a mutinous glance before she started for the door.

"One more thing."

She turned her chin over her shoulder, meeting his stare.

"Don't ever call me *darling* again," he growled softly. "I'm not one of your panting, disposable boy toys. I'm not even remotely the same animal."

He saw her throat convulse as she swallowed.

As he watched her scurry out of his office, his cock throbbing furiously, his emotional state raw, he wondered whether he'd just untied the first knot in his sack, or tied off and tightened the monster of them all.

Later that evening, Lucien stared out the floor-to-ceiling windows of his sixty-second-floor penthouse onto a gray, brooding Lake Michigan, holding a snifter of cognac in his hand. Originally, he hadn't planned to be alone tonight. He'd had a date following his match. He'd planned to spend the evening as he traditionally spent time after a polo match.

But then today had occurred. Then *Elise* had happened. And here he was, alone with a mess of unfinished business, a head full of doubt, and a hard-on that would not remit, no matter how much he distracted himself.

They had won the match tonight, despite his fierce Argentinean-bred polo pony's fouls. His teammates had joked that no one could handle Jax save Lucien, but it wasn't his horse that had been an unruly beast this afternoon. It'd been Lucien. Jax had just caught his surly mood and become too aggressive in his defensive bumps of other players, incurring fouls.

His temper had been unregulated when he was a child and young man. He'd learned control beneath the hand of an older lover at the age of eighteen. Natalia had sensed his need to master his emotions and desires, and had tutored him with BDSM sex, Natalia typically taking the role of master in the bedroom. It hadn't taken long for Lucien's dominant nature to assert itself, however, and the couple had decided to amicably part ways. Lucien would forever be thankful to Natalia for teaching him the value of control. At thirty-one, he didn't consider himself to be a hard-core dominant, and didn't require it in order to have satisfactory sex with casual lovers. When it came to Elise, however, he sensed the importance of immediately asserting his role as the sexual dominant. It would be such a pleasure to dominate her, but he intuited that it was important to Elise. She needed to learn the power of not only self-control, but of relinquishing control to another.

She needed to learn to trust. He *needed* her to put his trust in him. Perhaps it wasn't fair to ask it of her, given her history of fragile, impermanent connections, but he wanted it nonetheless.

How could he expect Elise to trust him when he harbored seeds of doubt about his very identity . . . about the fundamental *rightness* of his existence?

Don't think about that. It will get you nowhere but the bottom of a black pit of despair, he told himself irritably. What he'd told Ian Noble earlier had been true. A man chose his fate of his own free will. Lucien understood that he was more secure in that knowledge than Ian.

Still . . . the taint lingered, it's legacy a haunting self-doubt that Lucien absolutely refused to let overcome him.

He forced his brain back to the memory of the match this afternoon. Despite his typical discipline, he had allowed his foul mood—

not to mention his high-and-dry state—to get the better of him during the polo match, and that rankled at him.

He was as horny as a servicing bull. He'd been heavy and aching all afternoon—ever since he'd punished Elise. Pounding in the saddle during the match had only magnified the tight, uncomfortable pressure in his balls. The memory of Elise bending over his desk, of his warming the satiny smooth skin of her bare ass with his slapping hand, plagued him.

He always got worked up after a match, granted. It'd become a tradition for him since he'd first started playing polo as a teenager to have sex after time spent in the saddle. The aggressive, intense game had always primed him for play with a woman.

But tonight was unprecedented in his experience. He was coiled tight with sexual energy, but for once he had nowhere to spend his tension. He cupped his heavy balls through his pants and slid his hand along the rigid length of his shaft.

Lust rode him ruthlessly in that moment. The memory of Elise did. With an inevitable sense of resignation, he set down the snifter and walked to his bedroom suite. His fingers moved fleetly over his shirt buttons. Instead of removing the garment all the way, he merely opened the sides wide, baring his chest and belly. In the bedside drawer, he found a bottle of lubricant. He unfastened and lowered his pants, scooping his erection out from the confines of his boxer briefs, shoving the elasticized band beneath his heavy balls.

God he ached.

Hastily, he poured some of the lubrication into his hand and rubbed the silky liquid onto his straining cock. He clamped his eyelids closed at the friction against his overly sensitive flesh. He let go of restraint, and the floodgates of fantasy opened. Parting his legs and finding a stable stance, he gave in to primal lust, jacking his cock with a combination of precision and forceful, savage abandon.

What would it be like, to see Elise's dark pink, lush lips stretched around his girth, to see his straining cock plunging into her tight, humid depths while she looked up at him, the rebellion in her eyes trumped by desire, her gaze giving him permission to use and debauch her a little. Sweet, beautiful Elise . . .

Her eyes had always slain him.

He stood there before the floor-to-ceiling window and pounded the staff of his cock. His eyelids flickered open. The golden glow from the lamp provided a blurry reflection of his image. His chest and abdomen muscles flexed tight and hard, his cock looking enormous in his pumping hand.

But he was alone.

The image of Elise's shining, sapphire eyes as she'd turned and reached for his pants earlier in his office rose to haunt him.

He paused, prickly and edgy with unsatisfied lust. His hand wasn't what he wanted, but it was all he had. He would not jump into the flames with Elise immediately and wholesale. She would burn him to a husk.

He resumed jacking himself, groaning in undeniable pleasure. Masturbation, when all he wanted was to fuck Elise without mercy until he felt her shudders of pleasure and submission vibrate into his flesh.

Damn those bright eyes, the pink lips, the tight, lush curves that fit his hand perfectly. She lit up a room when she walked into it. She was so small, but so perfect. Her pussy would fit him like a second skin. To restrain her would be so satisfying. He would punish her for weakening him and then take her relentlessly, spend himself . . . empty himself of this tight, ball-aching, plaguing desire.

Leap into her flame and gloriously burn.

He grunted gutturally as warm semen spurted onto his lower chest, his climax so sharp it verged on pain. He pumped without mercy, milking every drop, ruthless in ridding himself of this unbearable tension.

His body shuddered one final time, his fist slowing on the shaft of his pulsing cock. Still panting, he cracked open his eyelids. From the reflection in the floor-to-ceiling window, he saw that his chest and belly glistened from his abundant emissions.

He wished he could have given it all to her.

Impossibly, desire tickled at his balls and moist shaft.

"Damn you, Elise," he muttered thickly, annoyed by his insatiable lust.

A heavy sense of the inevitable settled upon him as he used several tissues to mop himself dry. He stood next to the windows and stared out at the descending night.

It was not an option, for him to be at her mercy. She was too skilled at playing a man, too perfectly suited to Lucien's lust. She was an unacceptable risk. An infuriating temptation. An undeniable delight.

No. He wouldn't deny himself. Not this time.

The sun was just rising over the lake when Elise got off the bus on inner Lake Shore Drive and started walking west on Division Street. The slow ascent of the fiery orb seemed to match the inevitable rise of her anxiety as she neared State and Division . . . and Lucien. She'd seen little of him over the past few days as she was absorbed with her duties, and was nervous at the idea of spending one-on-one time with him. If only he'd suggested she go with Evan or Javier, she might have been able to disguise her relative ignorance on the topic of marketing. As things stood, she was bound to make a fool of herself in front of Lucien.

She sensed him watching her from where he stood beneath a storefront awning, sipping a cup of coffee.

"Good morning," he said when she approached. His gray eyes looked especially light in the shadow of the awning. They lowered over her appreciatively.

"Hello," she returned, feeling a little shy beneath his warm stare. He looked very sexy in a pair of well-fitted jeans and a dark red

T-shirt that showed off a lean, muscular torso and powerful arms to eye-catching effect. The casual apparel had the effect of making him seem a tad more approachable but every bit as appealing, reminding Elise of a sexy rock star instead of his typical businessman persona.

His T-shirt was partially tucked in to his jeans in the front, revealing a thick black leather belt with a silver buckle that rode low on his lean hips. She belatedly realized he was handing her a cup of coffee. Her cheeks heated. She'd been caught in the act of staring at his thighs and the way his jeans cupped his sex.

"Thank you," she murmured, grateful for the coffee at such an early hour. She immediately took a drink. Her eyes widened in pleasure.

"Café crème," she said, grinning. "You even remembered how I take it."

His smile made something hitch in her chest. "I remembered that you took it practically with equal parts coffee, cream, and sugar as a girl. Do you really still like it that sweet?" he teased.

She took another sip, her sigh of satisfaction his answer. He chuckled and put his hand on her elbow, urging her to walk.

"Did the cab drop you off in the wrong place?" he asked as they made their way toward the bustling outdoor market.

"What? Oh, no," she said, realizing he'd probably seen her walking toward him from blocks away. "I took the bus."

He blinked. "The bus?"

She dug into the pocket of her small backpack and pulled out a card. "My CTA pass. Do you have any idea how convenient these things are? Between buses and the L, I can go anywhere in Chicago," she said, the amazement in her voice genuine. Learning to navigate around had been an oddly liberating experience for her, invigorating to jump onto a vehicle and blend anonymously with the vibrant flow of humanity, to become a single cell in the lifeblood of the city.

His eyes gleamed in amusement. "You hold it up like it's a badge of honor."

"It is."

"*Étoile* would make quite the headline out of that," he murmured, referring to the French tabloid she hated with a white-hot passion for sensationalizing her life and using it as fodder to sell papers. "*Fair-Haired Heiress Caught Slumming It,*" he quoted an imagined headline.

"Screw *Étoile*," she said succinctly. She hitched her chin at the crowd of people bustling around them, intent on their marketing in the early morning light. "I'm willing to bet *they* don't even know what *Étoile* is, and nor would they care. They could care less about who my father is. They've never gobbled up the slop about my supposed love life. Most of them wouldn't remember my mother's movies—"

"Or have ever heard of my father's name, let alone his crimes."

She came to a halt, startled that he'd mentioned his father. He paused as well and touched her cheek, as if to erase her amazed expression. Her breath caught at the unexpected, tender caress. His fingertips lingered, warm and firm against her skin.

"We are both fugitives here, I think," he murmured.

"I prefer to think of myself as an adventurer," she replied in a hushed tone. His flashing smile was like an injection of adrenaline straight into one of her veins.

"You look beautiful," he murmured, his gaze lowering over the floral sundress she'd donned for the warm summer day.

"Thank you, but I'd rather just look like a chef."

"An adventuresome chef?" he asked, looking amused and . . . warm. She smiled, fully enthralled.

The delicate, charmed moment fractured when he began to dig in his jeans pocket, the motion distracting her. He withdrew a wad of bills and handed them to her. "Just get a receipt for whatever you purchase, please."

She nodded, eyeing the money with an appreciation she hadn't possessed for most of her life. It took not having something to really get the value of it. She'd learned that much in the past year.

She tucked the money carefully away in her backpack, and they continued walking, Elise staring with interest at the colorful vegetables and fruits and smiling at the vendors, suddenly feeling like a kid in a candy store. The smell of wild onion entered her nose, then a delectable, sweet fragrance that she inhaled deeply. A farmer had sliced one of his melons. Her mouth watered as they passed his booth.

You can do this, she told herself.

She'd been marketing with her fellow students and an instructor while at school, hadn't she? Of course this was different. Lucien was affording her the status of chef. She was in charge, she thought with a thrill of excitement.

"Do you have your list?" he asked.

Her eyes widened in panic as she stared at some brilliantly green Granny Smith apples. She was the chef. She should have made a list.

"I don't need a list. I've memorized the menu," she said honestly. "And I'll pick whatever is nicest and freshest for the special next week."

"All right," he said. She sighed in relief that he seemed to have accepted her reply. She wanted to convince him of her expertise at all costs. "We usually buy from Jim Goddard over there." He pointed to a booth with a thickset, gray-haired man sitting behind a table. "He's got a way with heirloom lettuce and arugula, and his peppers are usually good. If you trust me to do it, I'll pick up the avocado and snow peas from Mort Sanger over there. I'll rent a cart and bring it over when I'm finished."

Elise glanced to the booth where he pointed a quarter of the way down the block. She longed to see, touch, and taste the lovely produce there as well, but she thought it best to handle her bartering without Lucien coolly observing.

Twenty minutes later, she'd forgotten about her anxiety—and even Lucien, momentarily—as she chatted with Jim Goddard and sank her teeth into a fleshy San Marzano tomato.

"Délicieux," she exclaimed, eyes wide as the sweet, intense flavor flooded her mouth. She grinned widely at Jim. She took another bite and wiped the juice off her chin with the back of her hand. "I don't understand you Americans," she chastised Jim teasingly after she'd chewed and swallowed. "How can you put all that awful salad dressing on your salads when you have vegetables like *these*?"

"I don't make the salads; I just grow the vegetables," Jim said, looking a little dazed.

"And you do it extremely well. What's your price for these delectable gems?" she queried, holding up another pepper-shaped tomato near her mouth and eyeing it hungrily, all too aware of Jim watching her every move with stunned amazement.

Two minutes later, she had finalized the deal with Jim, and he walked away to pack up her order.

"You bargained for the tomatoes, but you were angling for a good price on the lettuce the whole time, you little minx," a deep, delicious voice murmured near her head, causing a tingling sensation to go down her neck. She twisted her chin and saw Lucien standing closer than she'd expected. His gaze was fixed on the back of her neck like he was considering taking a bite out of her there. Her nipples tightened against the tank top she wore beneath her sundress.

"How do you know that?" she asked innocently.

"Because I watched you eating one of those tomatoes a moment ago, just like Jim Goddard did." She watched his ungodly sexy lips move as if in a trance until she realized what she was doing and turned away. "After that display, the poor man probably would have thrown his farm into the deal in order to make the sale on those tomatoes. What's a few crates of lettuce to him, when he gets to witness you turning his vegetables into certifiable sex fruit?"

"You shouldn't complain. I saved you money," she said breezily, still not turning because she loved the feeling of his warm breath on her neck, the vibration of his deep voice in her ear.

"It's just a little hard not to feel for the rest of the helpless men on the planet when I see them so easily seduced by you."

"Seduced? I didn't do anything improper," she insisted, turning to face him.

He shook his head. "You *breathe* improper, Elise. You could make taking out the garbage an X-rated affair."

Her breath stuck and burned in her lungs when she saw the heat in his gray eyes.

Did she really know what she was doing, putting herself at risk with Lucien Sauvage?

She stilled, the question evaporating from her brain, when he reached up and carefully wiped juice off her chin.

They loaded all their purchases in the largest black pickup truck she'd ever seen. "These Americans do everything so *big*," she muttered as she helped him close the tailgate. She could just imagine what she was going to look like trying to peer over the dashboard of the enormous truck when she took over marketing next Saturday. The brutish truck hardly compared to the Bugatti Veyron she used to fly around Paris in. Oh well. At least she'd earned the right to climb behind the wheel of the behemoth vehicle. She'd never done any such thing for the cars her father gave her.

Lucien checked the platinum watch on his wrist. "Come on, we have time before the lunch preparations. I'll take you for something else the Americans do big."

"What?" she asked, her heartbeat escalating when he took her hand in his.

"You'll see," Lucien said elusively.

She gave him a doubtful look when he led her to a small restaurant nestled innocuously among expensive Gold Coast town houses.

"The House of Pancakes?" she asked dubiously.

Lucien just smiled knowingly and led her inside. The delicious aromas of ham and maple syrup made her mouth water.

"Is there a party going on?" she asked, bemused as she took in the crowded restaurant and rambunctious atmosphere.

"No. This is a typical Saturday or Sunday morning here. The

Americans love weekend breakfast. It's an occasion for them," Lucien explained quietly before the hostess greeted them cheerfully and seated them at a small Formica-topped table.

"Look at all the families . . . the friends," Elise said, examining the diverse crowd, everyone talking amiably or diving into mounds of syrup-drenched pancakes or fluffy omelets. In France, breakfast consisted of coffee and a croissant, and was hardly an occasion. The first meal of the day was the least important, and definitely the least social, in her opinion.

She opened the plastic-covered menu and stared in wonder at page upon page of decadently rich food. Lucien must have noticed her amazement because he was smiling when she looked up.

"It's like culinary Disneyland."

"I'm always telling people, when it comes to cooking, the Americans do one thing like no other: weekend breakfast. Look at them," he murmured. He grabbed her hand on the tabletop in a gesture that seemed entirely natural on his part but made her heart jump. She followed his gaze.

"And people say Americans will never understand the true meaning of a French meal," he murmured under his breath to her, eyeing the tables of happily relaxed people, friends and families talking about their week in an unpressured manner while they sipped steaming coffee or indulged in a doctor-prohibited meal for one precious moment during a busy week. She saw a teenage boy showing his dubious but interested grandfather something on his iPad, a man reading his *International Business Times* while his female companion perused a self-help book, their hands held fast on the Formica tabletop. Kids colored on the restaurant-supplied kid's menu, looking adorably like they'd just rolled out of bed with uncombed hair and sweatpants, shorts, and occasionally even pajama bottoms.

"I find," Lucien said quietly across the table, "they're at their best at breakfast."

She looked at him and they shared a smile.

"I admire the chef," she said.

Lucien chuckled. "I imagine it's more of a cook than a chef. It hardly compares to the complexity and nuance of what you do."

"Thank you, but I meant I admire him because he gets to bring all these people together. These families," she added, once again studying all the relaxed, happy people with longing. "You miss having family around, don't you?"

"I miss having a family. Period." She was surprised when he reached across the table and squeezed her hand. She saw something in his eyes—something she understood all too well.

We are alike, you and I. Both alone. Both misfits.

But not alone when we're together, she added in her head. A powerful feeling swelled in her chest.

"How is your father?" he asked quietly.

She grimaced. "He's growing more stubborn in his old age."

"He always could have used being a bit more stubborn when it came to you," Lucien said with dry amusement.

Elise rolled her eyes, even though she actually thought Lucien was right. She hadn't minded half as much as she thought she would have when her father cut her off financially. Maybe part of her had been waiting for someone in her life to show a little backbone; although, when it came to her father, she suspected he wouldn't hold out if she begged him hard enough. She'd just been tired, too worn out to exhibit the required amount of wheedling and bargaining to get him to relent.

"Other than his newfound cantankerous streak, he's much the same as always. Still gay and pretending to all the world that he's the Heterosexual Bull of All of Europe." She saw Lucien's small smile and matched it sadly. "Bless his heart. If only he realized it wouldn't matter a bit to most of us. It *hasn't* mattered to those closest to him for forever, if only he'd step outside of his brilliant head for a moment and notice. Although if he declared himself, my mother would be lost. How could she possibly justify all her affairs then?"

Lucien grunted softly in understanding. "A lie disguised by a mask wrapped in yet another façade. That's how I thought of my childhood."

"How is one ever to recognize the truth?" Elise replied softly.

Their stares met. She felt a little bereft when the waitress came and he released her, leaning back in his seat.

Nearly an hour later, she groaned in a mixture of discomfort and supreme gustatory satiation as they left the restaurant.

"Those carrot cake pancakes were soooo good," she said, rubbing her stomach as Lucien held open the door for her. "So was the bacon and cheddar omelet."

"Don't forget the hash browns or blueberry waffle," Lucien said dryly as they walked onto the tree-lined street, the sidewalk separated from the green lawns by a low, iron-gated fence. She saw his amusement and laughed. She'd asked to try far too many items from the menu, her culinary curiosity piqued by the cheerful, packed crowd and Lucien's description of American breakfasts.

"How could I forget them? All the ingredients were fresh, and it was so delicious."

He nodded in the direction of Division Street and the farmers' market. "They buy the produce right there."

"It was brilliant. This was a wonderful morning. Lucien, can we do a breakfast at Fusion?" she asked, enthralled by the idea. "I'll put a spin on it you'll never forget."

He glanced swiftly back at her and caught her dreaming about her breakfast. His expression went hard. He turned and she found herself in his arms.

It happened so suddenly, she didn't have a chance to exclaim in surprise. One second they were walking down the sidewalk and she was teasing and dreaming, and the next she was pressed against his hard body, her chin just below his nipple line, and he was lifting her face to his. She got a glimpse of the fierceness of his gaze before his mouth claimed hers.

His tongue pierced her lips, agile and possessive. His taste permeated her consciousness, and she melted against him, her body going soft and supple against his solid length, their tongues sliding together in a manner that made her forget where she was. Lucien's kiss on a Chicago sidewalk on a shiny new day was the most delicious thing she'd ever experienced in her life.

She moaned in regret when he lifted his head a sensuous moment later.

"You've already got me spinning," he said quietly against her lips, his intensity stealing her breath. His gaze moved over her face, narrowing.

"I'm sorry. I told you I wasn't going to do that. What kind of a model for self-control am I?"

"Don't be sorry. I liked it. A lot," she finished on a whisper, pressing her body closer to better feel his heat, his masculine contours. She grinned. "Who cares about self-control?"

His nostrils flared slightly. His expression went flat. He stepped away, keeping her hand in his.

"I do. Come on," he said. "We should get over to Fusion."

She hurried to keep up with his long-legged stride, disappointment swamping her. She didn't know what to say. He was obviously attracted to her, but he just refused to fawn over her like other men did. He'd said she had *him* spinning, but it was she who was struck completely off balance by his cool aloofness interspersed with moments of intense, entirely addictive, raw sexuality.

She glanced at his handsome profile and scowled. He'd said he wanted her to learn self-control, but it just wasn't fair how much control he wielded over her.

The following Tuesday, Elise waited nervously in the examination room of the Michigan Avenue medical practice.

She hadn't seen a lot of Lucien since they'd gone marketing on

Saturday, much to her disappointment. He wasn't avoiding her—or at least she hoped he wasn't—it was just that their paths didn't cross often at the busy restaurant. She'd been excited when Lucien had covertly pulled her aside this morning at Fusion, but he'd merely given her a few instructions and handed her a piece of paper with the address and time for her doctor's appointment. When he'd told her his appointment was at a different time, and that he wouldn't be accompanying her, she'd heaved a sigh of relief. She was highly anxious about this appointment, and she didn't want him witnessing her nerves with those cool, knowing eyes of his.

When the gynecologist entered a few minutes later, introducing herself as Dr. Sheridan, Elise was glad to see she was fairly young. Maybe she wouldn't laugh at Elise's questions or confessions.

"When was your last pap smear?" The doctor asked the inevitable question a few moments later as she did the interview portion of the exam.

"I . . . I've never had one before," Elise said.

Dr. Sheridan masked her surprise well. "Are you sexually active?"

"I've never had intercourse with a man. I know you must think it's odd, since I'm twenty-four."

"Not at all," the doctor reassured. "Lots of women are choosing to wait these days."

"But can you do an exam if I've never had intercourse?"

"Certainly. It's good that you told me, though. I'll use a smaller speculum. The vaginal muscles will be tight, but the chances of you actually having an intact hymen at age twenty-four are rare. You're in very good condition. Are you an athlete?"

"I run. I used to ride almost every day, even though I haven't had access to a mount for a year or so."

"More than likely, the hymen was ruptured long ago if you've ridden that long. We'll take a look."

"If the hymen is broken, then the man would never know, would he? That I was a virgin?"

Dr. Sheridan hesitated. "Is that important to you?" she asked quietly.

"Yes."

"Probably not. Not many men are all that experienced in gauging the subtleties. But I would encourage you to talk to your partner if you do become sexually active. It would be better if he could be as gentle as possible."

She nodded. Dr. Sheridan must have noticed her anxiety as she flipped back the cover on the tray that held the instruments for the exam. "Don't worry. I'll tell you everything I'm going to do beforehand."

The exam was slightly uncomfortable, but nowhere near as bad as she'd worried. According to the doctor, her regular horseback riding or some other activity had indeed long ago ruptured her hymen. Elise was relieved to hear it.

When the doctor had finished and told her to dress, Elise grasped for her courage. Lucien had arranged this appointment and was paying for it, after all.

"What I told you about not being with a man before, that's . . . that's confidential, right?"

The physician looked nonplussed. "Absolutely. I'll supply you with your records, and whom you choose to share them with is your business. But there won't be anything in the record but pertinent testing data."

Elise gave a heartfelt thanks and the doctor left the room.

Elise had had her share of men and exchanged sexual pleasure with some of them. But she wouldn't make herself vulnerable. The simple fact was, she was one of the wealthiest women in Europe. Men had tried to ingratiate themselves sexually and emotionally with her since she was fifteen years old. She didn't trust that there weren't males out there who would use her body against her. They might strive to impregnate her and use a child as an excuse to marry. That had happened to one of her acquaintances, a girl named Lucinda

Seacon. After Lucinda had gotten pregnant at seventeen by a worthless combination of skirt chaser and fortune hunter, Elise's mother had given her a pack of birth-control pills. For once, Elise had followed her mother's advice and taken them.

Better safe than sorry.

But a man might simply use intimacy to emotionally manipulate and gain the upper hand. In addition to all that, she had the example of her mother when it came to sex—not an example to follow, but an example to guard against. Any handsome man of any age was fair game to Madeline Martin, including many of Elise's boyfriends. Elise flatly refused to sleep with a man who had shared a bed with her mother. Sometimes that seemed like half the men in Europe. Her mother had even had the nerve to come on to her friend Michael Trent when she'd dragged him along for a visit to Cannes, begging him for support during a compulsory weekend spent with the sharks.

It hadn't even mattered to her mother that Elise had told her Michael was gay, she recalled disgustedly. Her mother thought so much of her beauty and allure, she'd believed she could lure a gay man to heterosexuality. It hadn't worked in the case of her husband, but that seemed to make Madeline all the more determined to try.

Classic Madeline.

For a variety of reasons, Elise had never felt secure or confident in romantic or sexual relationships. So she had been the one to maintain control. She grew skilled at giving a man what he wanted, of satisfying him sexually, while maintaining a safe distance. She hadn't planned to still be a virgin at age twenty-four, but she'd never encountered anyone in her adult years with whom she was willing to take the risk.

Until now.

Not only was she majorly in lust with Lucien, but she cared about him. She probably always would, after that summer they'd spent together. She'd believed him when he'd told her in his office that he cared about her as well. Some sort of invisible bond had been forged between them that summer, and it warmed her heart to know he felt that connection, too. She may frustrate him and she may infuriate him, but he cared.

Besides, Lucien had no reason to angle for her money. He had his own, and what's more, he was supremely aloof when it came to monetary greed.

Wasn't he?

There *was* that odd obsession he seemed to have with Ian Noble. But *no*, she scolded herself irritably, Lucien wouldn't do anything sleazy for financial gain. How many other people on the planet would abstain from a massive fortune that was their birthright?

No, Lucien was the one. She trusted him with her body and her well-being, despite all this bewildering domination business, not to mention her unprecedented sexual reaction to it.

Even though she'd agreed to this thing with him, she didn't want him to know about her vulnerability . . . her relative naïveté. Especially since he'd proposed such a sophisticated sexual arrangement. First of all, he'd never believe her, given all the hyped-up press about her. His disdain would hurt. Second of all, the idea of giving herself wholly when he knew of her weakness made her feel too raw. Too exposed.

Lucien had his secrets. It was only fair that she have one of her own.

Lucien stalked through the empty, hushed interior of Fusion, feeling particularly energized at the prospect of his upcoming meeting. A switch had been flipped in him recently. He'd discovered a new-found purpose here in Chicago, and it had nothing to do with Ian Noble.

He was considering buying a lovely vintage building ideally located in the South Loop near the once venerable, still atmospheric Prairie Avenue District. The location would make it the perfect spot for a restaurant and elegant boutique hotel. It was unusual for him not to have several new business ventures going at once. He'd restrained himself in the past year, however, unsure how long his business in Chicago would take. He still had several restaurants in Paris and one in Monte Carlo, along with four thriving European luxury resort hotels. He'd learned the hotel business firsthand from his father years ago. Each of the businesses he owned today had been acquired and cultivated completely on his own, however, without his father's money or assistance. The only debt he owed his father was the excellent training Adrien had provided by allowing him to manage several of his hotels. Lucien figured he'd repaid that debt amply in hard work and lucrative business decisions. Elise may have called him an heir the other night, but in truth Lucien had never touched a cent of his inheritance. He'd built a respectable fortune of his own, and he'd be damned if he ever pocketed dirty money.

The decision to begin a new business signaled a change was in the offing for him. It felt like a breath of fresh air flowing over the dark oppression of the past few years.

The thought of fresh air made his head turn toward the kitchen.

It was three thirty in the afternoon, the calm between the lunch and dinner bustle in the restaurant. In the distance, he heard the metallic sound of cookware and pictured Elise in the kitchen, her lovely face sober as she focused her entire attention on her culinary task. The memory of how she'd tasted when he'd spontaneously kissed her the other day sprung into his mind in vivid detail. The taste of maple syrup had lingered on her tongue, but the flavor of her—Elise—had been sweeter still.

It'd been a week since he'd caved and hired her as his interim chef, seven increasingly brutal nights since he'd come to a decision about her. He'd kept his distance with the exception of that regrettable kiss, all too aware that he must wait. She was his employee, after all.

For the time being.

He'd kept close tabs on her. All reports about her cooking from his staff and patrons had been stellar. Sharon had expressed her amazement yesterday when she'd come into his office, announcing the arrival of another chef candidate for Lucien to interview.

"Are you unhappy with Ms. Martin's work?" Sharon had asked.

"Not at all. Should I be?"

"No, everyone is raving about her food. And she's very pleasant to work with. Have you ever noticed everyone smiles when she's around? There's certainly a new pep to Evan's and Javier's strides."

"I pay her to cook, not perk up my male employees," he'd muttered dryly.

"It's not just the male employees," Sharon had continued, undeterred by his frown. It was one of the reasons he liked Sharon. She had a mind of her own. "She's a nice change for all of us. Do you know Maryanne won tickets to the symphony but couldn't go because of her kids?" Sharon asked him, referring to one of their waitresses, a single mother. "Elise volunteered to watch Allie and David so Maryanne could go. That meant a lot to Maryanne. It meant a lot to me, too," Sharon added thoughtfully. "And she's doing a marvelous job of cooking. Why do you need another chef?"

"Ms. Martin isn't a fully qualified chef yet," Lucien had said briskly as he cleared his desk in preparation for the interview.

"Tell that to your elated customers," Sharon had said wryly before she left to retrieve the chef candidate.

He'd pretended to be brusque, but in truth he'd been pleased that Elise had won Sharon over as a protector. Sharon was no pushover, and all of his employees looked up to her.

Another part of him was tense, however, waiting for the other shoe to drop. A calm atmosphere and Elise did *not* go together.

She was a storm waiting to break.

The thought flew into his head as he opened the smoked-glass doors of Fusion and saw Elise standing in the lobby of the Noble Enterprises tower wearing her chef's smock and talking to Francesca

Arno, Ian's lover. She was several inches shorter than Francesca, although he doubted most people would notice the inequity of the two women's heights. Elise was so vibrant and animated, like a flickering flame. As he watched, several casual passersby turned to look at her, and not just men. Her strength of character and palpable charm had always amazed him, even when she'd been a child.

Elise's expression shifted when she took notice of his approach, but she kept chatting amiably until he arrived by her side.

"Mr. Lenault! You know Francesca, don't you?" she asked, pink lips curving.

"Of course I do," he said, leaning down to give Francesca a brief kiss of greeting on the cheek.

"She just told me she's a runner," Elise said. "I'm going to start training with her for the Chicago Marathon."

"You run?" Lucien asked Elise, disguising his surprise.

"Yes. I started a year ago. It's good *discipline*," she emphasized, the defiant spark in her sapphire eyes meant solely for him.

"I hadn't realized you two had met," he added mildly, ignoring her stab at him.

"I introduced myself last night after experiencing the ecstasy of her Essaouira chicken and strawberry crepes," Francesca said, grinning up at him. "She's brilliant. Ian and I asked for you at Fusion last night, but they said you weren't in the restaurant. We had very important news to tell you."

Francesca was always a lovely woman, but he'd never seen her look quite so radiant as she did when she lifted her left hand. Lucien laughed and gave her a heartfelt hug. He reexamined the exquisite triple-diamond platinum ring on her finger after they'd stepped back from the embrace.

"Ian is a very lucky man," he told her sincerely. He bounced her hand teasingly. "Are you strong enough to handle such a heavy ring?"

"I'm strong enough," Francesca told him archly, and he knew she'd precisely understood his double entendre.

He smiled, pleased yet again by Ian's choice. "I believe you are."

"Thank you. Ian picked it out himself," Francesca said amusedly, her eyelids narrowing. "And if you know any different, don't tell me."

"He most definitely picked it out himself."

Francesca beamed at his steadfast answer. "We're throwing a little get-together at the penthouse Sunday night to celebrate. I hope that you'll come. You, too," she told Elise irrepressibly.

"Oh, that's so nice of you to ask, thank you. But . . . I don't think I can," Elise prevaricated, her hesitant, meek manner completely unbelievable to Lucien.

"Of *course* you can," Francesca insisted. "You told me just now that you hardly know anyone in the city. You'll love my friends Davie and Justin and Caden. . . . Well, Justin and Caden will love *you*, in fact, but they're relatively harmless. And Fusion is closed on Sundays and Mondays, so I know you're not working. Isn't that right, Lucien? Tell her." Francesca glanced at him for assistance. He held Elise's gaze as he spoke.

"Of course you should go, Ms. Martin. It will do you good to make some friends in a new city."

Elise's eyes widened in surprise at his agreeable tone. Clearly she'd thought he'd signal for her to decline the invitation, but Francesca's sincere request had blocked that option.

"Will you be there, Monsieur Lenault?" Elise asked, eyes wide and innocent.

"I wouldn't miss it for the world."

Her slight frown told him she'd understood his subtext. Allow Elise to run wild in the Noble penthouse without supervision?

Not likely.

The following day, Elise glanced up when Sharon walked into the kitchen.

"Lucien would like to see you in his office, Elise."

The knife she held in her hand stilled at the news. It took her a moment to recover, something she hoped Evan and Sharon didn't notice. It'd been a seemingly innocuous announcement, after all.

"You can take over here, Evan. You have it down perfectly," she said with a reassuring smile as she set down the knife. She'd been instructing and assisting Evan in the dressing of a capon. "I'm sure I won't be long," she added over her shoulder after she'd washed up.

She coached herself to ignore the butterflies she felt as she walked down the long hallway to Lucien's office. He couldn't be requesting the meeting because she'd done anything wrong. Her work ethic had been unquestionable. In fact, she was usually the first one there in the morning, eager to begin cooking. Part of that motivation might have been the depressing dreariness of her hotel room—not to mention a desire to pass Baden Johnson's room before he awoke from his nightly intoxication—she'd become an expert at avoiding her leering, malodorous neighbor at the Cedar Hotel. But the point was, she'd *been* here, ready to work.

Her stomach fluttered with anticipation as she knocked on the carved-wood door, graphic memories of her former meeting with Lucien in his office flooding her consciousness and mounting her anxiety.

"You wanted to see me?" she asked a moment later when Lucien opened the door. Today he was dressed in black jeans, a simple black crewneck shirt, and an ivory blazer that highlighted his broad shoulders and the smooth, beautiful color of his skin. He was such a sinfully gorgeous man, some rare, magical blend of unknown origins, the mystery of his existence somehow perfectly fitting the magnetic enigma surrounding him. She recalled how once during her fourteenth summer, she'd bluntly asked him about his ethnic heritage. They'd been fishing off the dock, a pastime they'd both gravitated toward that summer, a simple, wholesome activity that stood in such contrast to the complex machinations of their parents' business and social lives. It was obvious to anyone that Lucien couldn't be the natural child of his blond, painfully thin mother, and Lucien towered over his paunchy, balding father. Lucien hadn't taken offense, probably because he'd sensed her childlike sincerity and simple curiosity.

"I never knew or saw my biological parents. My mother and father adopted me when I was still a baby," he'd replied, nodding at her fishing line. She'd obediently lifted it, and sure enough, a fish had stolen her bait. He took it from her without comment.

"I'm adopted, too," Elise had told him. She'd thought it a thousand times before. It must be true. How else to explain how she felt as if she were interacting with a different species when she related to her parents? Lucien's smile had struck her as a little sad.

"You are the spitting image of your mama."

"I am?"

"Yes, but you will surpass even her beauty one day," he'd said as he rebaited her line. He'd glanced aside and noticed her expression. "You *look* like her. What is on the inside is whatever you make of it."

She'd stared at the sunlight dancing on the azure Mediterranean Sea, not wanting him to know how much his words meant to her. "Don't you ever wonder about your true mother, though? Don't you ever miss her?"

She recalled how he hadn't answered immediately.

"I wonder about her once in a while," he'd said, handing back her pole. "But it's hard to miss what you've never had."

What you've never had. Neither Lucien nor she had known much about what it meant to have a nurturing, available mother.

Lucien waved her into his office, snapping her back to the present. "Come in. Elise, I'd like you to meet Denise Riordan, Fusion's new chef."

Elise's startled gaze flew to the other occupant of the room. A tall, auburn-haired woman with a stern expression that was softened by kind brown eyes stood to greet her.

"I hadn't realized Lucien had gotten so far along in the hiring process. It's a pleasure to meet you, Ms. Riordan," Elise managed, despite her surprise.

"I understand from Lucien that you're a talented chef. I would be glad to take you on as my stage, if my qualifications are suited to your school . . . and to you, of course," she said.

"I'm sure that anyone Lucien would hire has the best qualifications," she said, glancing sideways at the distraction of Lucien's tall form when he approached.

"I've already taken the liberty of sending off Ms. Riordan's applicant information along with an explanation of the alteration in plans to your school in Paris. We should be hearing back quickly," Lucien said.

"Thank you," Elise replied, dumbfounded by the fact that he'd taken pains to smooth the path with her school.

"If you'll excuse me for a moment, I need to speak with Sharon. I'll just leave you two to get better acquainted," he said politely.

Denise Riordan and Elise sat in the chairs before Lucien's desk and got to know each other. By the time Lucien returned twenty minutes later, she felt certain she could work well with the older, knowledgeable woman. Two chefs in a kitchen was never an easy scenario, but Elise was eager to learn, and she had no problem with taking on the subservient role. It'd been what she'd expected when she came to Chicago, and she was convinced Denise Riordan had significant things to teach her.

"Please stay for a moment. I need a word," Lucien said to Elise after he'd returned and Ms. Riordan was saying good-bye.

Neither of them spoke for a moment after the new chef closed the door behind her. A prickly, electrical atmosphere descended.

"I received the medical exam results you left me," he said. "Did you receive mine?"

"Yes," she replied airily, as if she discussed such things all the time despite the heat of embarrassment in her cheeks.

"Do you like her? Denise?" Lucien asked quietly from where he stood near the door.

"Very much. I don't suppose there's a reason you chose a female chef, is there?"

"I chose the best qualified candidate."

She gave him a dry glance. "I wasn't going to fall into bed with any male chef that you hired."

He gave a small grin. She stilled at the appearance of the twin dimples, the flash of white teeth. "What about Mario?"

"What about him?" Elise asked, crossing her arms beneath her breasts.

"Wasn't that where things were headed on that night I caught you two here?"

"No. I had no intention of sleeping with Mario."

"What, precisely, were you doing here with him then?"

"He was going to supervise my training. When he asked me to dinner, I didn't really feel I had the option of saying no. I didn't know he was planning on trying to get me into bed."

He gave her a weary glance and walked toward his desk. "Right. That dress you were wearing screamed a practical day at the office. I hired the best candidate for the job, but I'm not at all unhappy that she's a female, the truth be told. I know the effect you have on men. They lose about forty points off their IQ in your vicinity. No need to light the fuse if it can be avoided."

"I resent your constant allegations that I'm promiscuous."

"That's funny," he said, unconcerned by her offended act. He lowered to the chair behind his desk. "Because *I* resented learning about your constant displays of promiscuity. I even witnessed them a time or two."

She stilled. "What do you mean?" she asked slowly, not sure she actually wanted an answer.

"Half of Europe saw that photo of you dancing nude on top of a cocktail table at the engagement party for the son of the archduke of Luxembourg," he said dryly.

"I was wearing a thong," she defended, chin up. Lucien's sharp, annoyed glance made her wilt on the inside, however.

"And how about the night I came upon you in a secluded alcove at the Opéra de Paris? You were busy demonstrating what was apparently your enthusiastic, *deep* affection for a married, middle-aged politician. I believe you were nineteen at the time. Do you recall?"

"I . . . You . . . *Wait*." Her heart squeezed tight and seemed to stop in her chest. "Was that *you* who interrupted when I was with Hugh Langier?"

His sarcastic expression was her answer.

Enthusiastic, deep *affection.*

Oh no. She shut her eyes, but Lucien's stare continued to score her. She hadn't seen who had walked in on her tryst with Langier; she only knew someone had. Knowing that *someone* was Lucien made her feel light-headed with shame. How could she have been so impulsive—so *stupid*—at times?

No. She wouldn't think of it. She *wasn't* that person anymore.

"I doubt you'd like what I did to your paramour when he came into Renygat two nights later," Lucien muttered. "Slimy sod."

"He *wasn't* my paramour," she bit out, but then she fully absorbed what he'd said. "Did you hit him or something?" Lucien gave her a bland glance. "You got in a fight with a *senator*?"

Over me?

He didn't comment further, but she saw the way his nostrils flared, a sure sign he was subduing his anger. What he'd referred to had occurred during the height of her careless self-indulgence. There'd been a time when she found life meaningless, when everything had been a joke. Her only concern was to have as much fun as she could, and damn the consequences. Acquaintances in

Paris—not to mention her parents—had looked the other way during her wildest, most desperate, period.

Wasn't it better that Lucien was angry versus uncaring?

"I know you believe in me, Lucien. Even if only a little bit. I know you're not so callous as you behave. I wish you'd quit putting on the act," she said, plucking up her façade of confidence.

"What do you mean?"

"Ms. Riordan told me that you specified that her job was provisional upon her taking me on as a stage."

A silence stretched between them. She'd been stunned and pleased when Ms. Riordan had revealed that morsel of information during their discussion.

"And I told you, if you are to live in this city, I'd just as soon have you nearby where I can monitor you. Speaking of which," he said, talking over the disgusted sound she made. She knew very well he'd just sidestepped her revelation that he'd done something kind for her. "I'd like to escort you tomorrow evening to Ian and Francesca's party."

Her heart leapt. Denise Riordan had been hired. Elise was no longer his employee. Lucien would feel freer now to act on his proposed relationship. A thought struck her, deflating her ballooning excitement like a dead-on torpedo.

"You want to supervise me, don't you? I told you I wasn't going to tell anyone that I know you from before. Don't you trust me?"

"Let's just say that I'd rather be in close watching distance so that I know where I stand."

"You don't, in other words."

"Trust is something that has to be earned, Elise," he said quietly. "And don't play the martyr. I know that you don't trust me completely, either. Not yet, you don't."

His intensity took her by surprise. She absorbed what he'd said, feeling unsteady.

"Where shall I pick you up?" he asked after a moment, his quick topic change only increasing her sense of being off balance. "At the address you put down on your application?"

"No."

She realized how abrupt she'd sounded. The last thing she wanted was for Lucien to see the rundown extended-stay hotel where she was living. It would only affirm his belief that she was scatterbrained and impulsive. She did some quick thinking when she noticed his narrowed gaze on her. "Can we meet here? In front of the Noble Tower building?"

His handsome face settled into an unreadable mask. "Of course, if you prefer it. Seven thirty?"

"That will be fine," she said, starting to back out of the office. "I'll see you tomorrow."

"Elise?" he asked sharply when her hand was on the door.

"Yes?"

"Your employment with me has ended now that I've hired Denise."

She held her breath.

"Just remember. My rules," he reminded significantly. "Denise being here means your salary will stop as well. You *do* have adequate funds to live here in the city, correct?"

"Of course. Didn't you tell me that Papa would never see me starve?"

He raised his eyebrows slowly. Not liking the suspicious expression settling on his features, she hurried out the door.

Chapter Four

Lucien remained seated and unmoving once the door closed behind Elise. He thought of how pale she'd gone when he'd mentioned catching her in flagrante delicto with Hugh Langier, illustrious member of the French senate and renowned womanizer. He regretted embarrassing her, but the memory was still volatile to him; it still made something hot and unbearable swell in his gut, not to mention what it did to his cock.

He'd been looking for her that night five years ago, having noticed her luminous face from a distance during the opera. It had been a year since his father had first mentioned the possibility of him marrying Elise. He'd flat-out refused to even discuss the idea, of course. No one was going to choose his future wife but him. But the idea had lingered in his consciousness: not heavily, but lightly, like a radiant, teasing smile, the prospect of a stolen summer day or a sip of the perfect champagne—light-filled and effervescent . . .

. . . like Elise herself.

He couldn't help but be curious about what sort of a woman that smart, funny, sad girl had become.

Still, his curiosity hadn't been so great that he'd sought her out when he'd moved permanently to Paris to open his first hotel and restaurant. It'd been completely by accident that he'd glimpsed her at the opera. Their boxes were almost directly across from each other. The curtain was about to go up when he noticed several faces in the audience flicker to the left of the stage. He'd followed their gazes idly, wondering what was causing the stir. His body sprung into instant alertness.

She'd stood and was making her way to the back of the box. The gown she wore was jaw-dropping. No, not the dress itself, but Elise in it. It was made of a pale ivory metallic material that clung to her ripe, svelte curves, the material giving off a pearl-like sheen that nowhere near rivaled the luminosity of her pale skin. She was completely covered, but the clinging fabric and its similarity to her coloring gave the impression of nudity. Her hair had been long back then. Lucien recalled that during that summer five years before, she'd forever worn her hair in a thick ponytail, tendrils increasingly escaping the band as the day wore on until by nightfall, her delicate face was surrounded by a riot of golden waves and curls. That night, she wore it up, but the casual twist gave a man the impression he could have the glory of it spilling down her shoulders and into his greedy hands with just a gentle tug.

He'd jerked up out of his chair, making a quick excuse to his companion.

Five minutes of searching later, he'd finally found the sweet, gawky girl he recalled, but that girl was no more.

She'd been on her knees in a velvet-draped alcove before an ecstatic-looking Hugh Langier.

The image haunted him to this day . . . killed him a little . . . aroused him a lot. When he'd whipped back the heavy drapery, Elise's lips had been clamped tightly around the base of Langier's cock. She'd slid her mouth back, revealing inches of slick, thick penis—not to mention the full extent of her talent for fellatio.

No wonder the senator had looked so ecstatic.

It had infuriated him that Langier had taken advantage of a young girl like that while his wife sat out in his choice box watching *Tosca*, unaware of her husband's lechery. The entire experience had infuriated him, period, when it should have been an eye-opening moment that he later considered with amusement.

Lucien shut his eyes, trying to vanquish the memory even though he knew by now it was an utter impossibility.

Take control of Elise Martin? Gain her trust? It was a challenge most men would fail. It was a dare the dominant in him could no longer resist, a trial he was anticipating unlike any other before in his life.

He'd have to willingly walk into the flames in order to control the fire.

She spotted him immediately from a block away, leaning against a limestone abutment of the super-sleek, modern-Gothic Noble Tower. Her stomach fluttered. She hadn't been familiar with the sensation for most of her life, but had experienced it far too much recently. She'd assumed since running into Lucien again that the uncomfortable feeling was anxiety due to his intimidating presence. No other man affected her like Lucien did. Maybe it was because of that idyllic summer he'd given her as a child. It might have been because of the way he kissed. Or perhaps it was simply because she knew he had no reason to manipulate her for her fortune.

Or maybe it was that he was the most powerful, sexiest man she'd ever met. By far.

Tonight, she had a sneaking suspicion the fluttery feeling was akin to that of a first date with a very attractive man.

Which was ridiculous. This wasn't a date. Hadn't he said he just wanted to be with her because he didn't trust her? She frowned, even though her gaze traveled over him covetously. Still . . . he'd said he was attracted to her, that he planned to have sex with her. They'd both dressed up and they were meeting at an assigned spot. The similarities to a date were not insignificant. Now that an official chef had been hired, how would he go about advancing this unorthodox relationship he'd proposed?

He drew glances from nearly every passerby, man or woman, even though he seemed completely unaware. His arms were crossed loosely beneath his chest. His looks were such a striking, unique combination of effortless elegance and raw male sexuality. He wore black pants that fit his long legs to eye-catching perfection, a starkly white shirt open at the collar, and a handsome tan and black herringbone blazer. He stared fixedly in the direction of the Chicago River. She admired his ability to stay so completely still, and remain so calm. Rarely had she observed such complete focus in a man. She recalled he used to quietly chastise her when they fished and she would fidget and sigh.

"You will scare the fish away."

"But it's so boring," she'd complained.

"If you can learn to handle your boredom, you will have truly mastered yourself."

"What's that mean?" she'd queried, puzzled but curious.

He hadn't answered her at the time, but she'd studied his calm, patient attitude while fishing or soothing an anxious horse or handling his drama-queen mother, and strived to follow his example. She'd failed for the most part, but she'd learned to respect that calm, steely strength in him.

"I hope I'm not too late," she said breathlessly when she approached him. "The bus broke down on the inner drive and I had to walk the rest of the way."

He straightened from his leaning position, his light eyes moving over her deliberately and making her skin prickle in awareness. "In those shoes?" he asked, the hint of a smile on his well-shaped lips.

She glanced down at the strappy high-heel sandals she wore along with a sack dress she'd belted at her hips. "This is nothing," she said as he took her hand and began to walk. "You wouldn't believe the miles I walked in heels while I was waitressing."

His eyebrows shot up. "Waitressing?"

She grinned, happy to have surprised him. "At La Roue, in Paris."

He hailed a cab.

"We can walk," she said. "I understand from Francesca the penthouse is very close, isn't that right?"

A cab snapped to a halt in front of the curb. He opened the door for her.

"You're getting a blister on your right ankle," he said deadpan when she gave him a questioning look. She glanced down. He was right. The skin around her ankle strap was abraded and red. When had he noticed? She sighed in relief a moment later when she settled in the air-conditioned cab and did a double take when she noticed his small smile as he studied her.

"What?"

"Tender feet," he said. She blinked at the unexpectedly seductive sound of his deep, resonant voice. "You were always getting blisters as a girl."

"My mother forgot to get me new shoes for the summer. I was growing like a weed that year."

Annoyance crossed his bold features. "All that money, all those resources, and yet she neglected you," he said. He noticed her blank expression. He shook his head slightly, banishing a bitterness that confused her.

"Can I ask you a question?" she said impulsively, hopeful at the sound of his disdain toward her mother.

"Yes."

"You never . . . you didn't sleep with her ever, did you? My mother?"

Her heartbeat quickened when he just stared at her for a moment. She'd wanted to ask him that very question for a long time, but also dreaded the answer.

"No. Absolutely not," he said with quiet forcefulness.

She exhaled in relief. She nodded, believing him completely for some reason. "Because I know she probably tried to seduce you that summer when we were in Nice. Probably other times, too. It's what she does. I'm glad to know she failed with you. She certainly never did with any of my other boyfriends," she laughed.

He closed his eyes briefly. "Elise, I'm sorry."

She shrugged, striving for an offhand manner. "We can't pick our parents. Unfortunately."

An awkward silence ensued. She suspected he was feeling sorry for her for having such a vain, substanceless mother and wished like crazy she hadn't brought up the topic.

"Have you really started running?"

She just nodded, thankful he'd noticed her discomfort and changed the subject.

"I'm proud of you. You need something to discipline your body, your mind . . . something to make you proud."

He held her stare. Her heart throbbed in her ears once . . . twice. Suddenly, he was looking out the window and the intimate moment had passed. She inhaled as if all the oxygen had been vacuumed out of the cab for a few seconds and abruptly replaced.

"It does make me proud," she said, regaining her balance. "So did waitressing. Why were you surprised I worked as one?" she asked as the cab zoomed down Upper Wacker Drive.

"Because you have one of the largest trust funds in Europe, perhaps?"

"They say yours is larger." When he didn't respond to her provocation, she sighed. She'd heard from her mother that Lucien hadn't touched the funds since his father's incarceration, but obviously it wasn't a topic he wanted to discuss. She knew he'd compiled his own fortune, so he had less reason than she to worry about trust funds. "I can't access my trust fund until I'm twenty-five," she explained lamely.

"What will happen to your newfound work ethic when that happens?" he mused, turning in profile to her, his light eyes reflecting the rays of the sunset off the flowing river. His mildly patronizing manner irritated her. Did he still question her ability . . . her drive?

"I'll be dutifully employed as a chef. That's my hope. Would you like to make a bet about my dedication to my career?" she teased lightly.

"What sort of a bet?" he asked. This, too, he considered a joke. Little did he know she had plans for what she wanted to do with her fortune and her life. *Good* ideas. Worthy aspirations that would pay tribute to a very special man's life.

She was just worried about having the clarity, the focus required to bring her plans to reality. She'd never done anything so . . . *big* before. What if, in the end, she really was like Madeline Martin— worthless fluff?

"Twenty thousand euros to me if I'm still gainfully employed as a chef one year after I have access to my trust fund and am leading a meaningful life. Twenty thousand to you if I've succumbed to the lures of wealth and am leading a wastrel existence."

He turned, his gray eyes sparking. *Ah*, now she'd gotten his attention.

"I'll take that bet."

"You're still doubting my dedication, aren't you?"

He shrugged, and her gaze flickered with interest to his powerful chest and shoulders contrasting with a narrow waist and flat abdomen.

"I just thought the potential loss of twenty thousand euros might strengthen that dedication of yours . . . just in case you should find it running thin," he said with a silvery sideways glance.

"I'm going to win," she challenged, suddenly completely confident now that she'd made the bet with Lucien.

"I'm inclined to believe you."

"You are?"

"Yes. I took the bet for good measure, though. I know how much you love to prove me wrong. It was a winning bet for me either way."

She remained silent for the rest of the trip—Lucien's low, delicious voice echoing in her head—turning over the unsettling fact in her mind that Lucien had known her reaction to taking that bet before she had.

Francesca and Ian entertained on a massive outdoor terrace situated on the roof of the dark brick art deco tower where Ian lived. The view was fabulous—the dark blue expanse of Lake Michigan to the east and the scarlet ball of the sun setting behind the cityscape to the west. Francesca had made the small area near a wet bar and fire pit intimate with paper lanterns that glowed a warm gold as darkness fell. It was a small party, consisting only of Francesca's friends Davie Feinstein, Justin Maker, and Caden Joyner; Ian's driver, Jacob; and Francesca's graduate school adviser, a friendly middle-aged woman named Anara Sloan. Also present was Lin Soong—Ian's executive assistant—Ian, Francesca, Lucien, Elise, and Mrs. Hanson, Ian's housekeeper, who kept trying to serve everyone despite Ian's and Francesca's frequent reminders that she was a guest. A built-in speaker system played a relaxed jazz mix. After an hour and a half of being there, Elise was feeling very content and mellow, even in the midst of Justin's and Caden's increasingly competitive flirtations.

"I hope they're not driving you crazy," Francesca apologized in a confidential tone when Justin went to open yet another bottle of champagne. Elise had occasionally noticed Lucien's gaze on her from across the terrace where he spoke to Jacob, Ian, and Davie. She strongly suspected that he was waiting for her to slip up and say something she shouldn't with all the alcohol that had been flowing, given the celebratory mood of the party.

"Not at all. They're really nice guys. Davie, Justin, Caden, and you are roommates, right?"

Francesca nodded. "Davie watches over us all," she said, smiling.

"You're lucky to have such good friends," Elise said feelingly. For a horrible moment, her throat tightened. Too late; Francesca noticed.

"Elise. Are you all right?" Francesca asked, sitting forward slightly, concern etching her features as she stared at Elise's face.

Elise slid her social mask back into place, only missing a beat. "Yes, of course. I'll bet you'll miss them, after you move in with Ian. Your friends, I mean. When will the wedding be?"

"We haven't decided yet. Probably next spring. I finish my classwork this fall at my program. Along with that, I just have a final project due before I can get my master's. I'll likely be finished by Christmas, so spring would be ideal. We're thinking of eloping to Hydra. Ian owns a place there."

"Oh, that'll be beautiful."

"You've been to Hydra?" Francesca asked, eyes wide.

"Yes, my parents own a home in Poros. I haven't been to the islands in ages, though."

Elise threw a surreptitious glance in Lucien's direction, but his attention was on Davie as they conversed.

"Ian and Lucien seem like good friends," she said in a hushed yet off-the-cuff manner.

"They are. Ian is very comfortable with him. He doesn't worry about his true intentions, like he has to with so many other potential friends he meets," Francesca said.

Elise nodded in understanding. "It's hard. A man like Ian has to always wonder about people's motivations. How long have they known each other?"

Francesca wrinkled her brow. "I'm not sure if Ian has ever said exactly, but I do know they were introduced by a common acquaintance in Paris several years back. Ian took to visiting Lucien in his restaurant whenever he was in Paris, and they discovered they both loved fencing. They started working out together when they got the chance. When Ian decided to open up his headquarters here in Chicago, he asked Lucien to open the restaurant in the tower as a personal favor."

"Hey, Ian," Justin called across the terrace, interrupting a conversation Elise found extremely interesting. Ian and Lucien paused in their exchange, turning toward Justin. Night had almost completely fallen. Elise noticed idly that Lucien's and Ian's shadows were exactly the same height, their profiles both stark and arresting. "Why don't you put on some real music? I might want to teach your fiancée how to dance," Justin called.

Francesca snorted into her champagne.

"I taught you how to dance, you braggart," she chastised.

"Just keep the gymnastics to a minimum, please. The last time I saw these two dance, Francesca left the floor with tennis elbow," Ian told Elise drolly as he passed them.

"Tennis elbow?" Elise asked, confused.

"Don't ask," Francesca said, laughing.

Elise thought she understood after Ian went behind the bar and changed the music selection to a dance mix. Justin immediately pulled Francesca into an athletic, exuberant dance that did, indeed, look potentially harmful to life and limb. She was enjoying watching the two friends dance beneath the stars when Caden approached her.

"Come on, we can't let these two steal the show."

Elise removed her high-heeled sandals and took Caden's hand. As she walked over to the designated dance floor—an open area behind the outdoor furniture—she noticed Lucien's eyes gleaming in the firelit darkness as he watched her. A thrill went through her for some reason. He'd been ignoring her all night—well, not *ignoring* exactly. She'd sensed his attention sporadically, his alert focus as he observed her. Why was he stretching things out now that she no longer officially worked for him and they'd both completed their medical exams? He was driving her mad with his elusiveness.

She definitely had Lucien's attention now, though, and she

gloried in that fact. Caden was a good dancer. She hadn't danced since her nightclub days and wasn't really sure if she still had what it took. Turns out, she found her rhythm just fine, if Caden's admiring grin and increasingly sexy moves in reaction to hers were any indication. She danced with Francesca's handsome friend, but she danced *for* Lucien. Even though she refused to look in his direction, she was acutely aware of his focus on her . . . of his increasing tension, like a powerful storm brewing in the distance. She laughed at Caden's comments and gyrated her hips, giving him a seductive look that turned his eyes hot. She glanced over her shoulder at Lucien and transferred the gaze to him, thrilling to see his stare trained directly on her.

She'd known it would be.

She'd stayed under the radar for the past year or so, but tonight, she felt the wild girl in her rattling at her cage.

When the dance came to an end, she and Caden shared a quick hug, both of them laughing and overheated. They began to walk back over to the seating area to join Jacob, Mrs. Hanson, Lin, and Anara.

"Aren't you going to dance, Lucien?" Ian asked pointedly as Elise and Caden passed their little circle, which consisted of Ian, Lucien, and Davie. Elise's cheeks grew even warmer than they had from the dance when she noticed Ian nodded in her direction, an infinitesimal smile on his sculpted lips. She realized Ian was teasing Lucien. "I don't think I've ever seen you dance before," Ian prodded.

"And you never will, if I have my way about it," Lucien said shortly. Caden and Elise drifted over to their group.

"Ah. As good at it as I am, I'll wager," Ian said, taking a sip of champagne.

"Lucien is a fabulous dancer."

Three pairs of eyes flickered over to her when she spoke; one pair flashed a disbelieving glance that seemed to burn right through her. She bit her lip.

Oops.

Ian lowered his glass. "When have you seen Lucien dance?" he asked, amusement tingeing his features. "I thought you two had just met recently."

"We did," Lucien said at the same time she did.

"What . . . does Lucien break into dance after last call every night at Fusion? I can't quite picture it," Caden asked, joking and doing a couple subdued dance moves, immediately stilling when noticing Lucien's impassive expression and glacial stare. She got the distinct impression that while easygoing Caden and Justin might have partially broken through Ian's reserve due to their friendship with his fiancée, Lucien was still considered a bit intimidating. Lucien transferred his gaze back to Elise, his manner seemingly calm, only his slightly flared nostrils betraying the fact that his hands were likely itching to stretch around her neck.

"Oh no, it's nothing like that. Sharon Aiken and a couple of the waitresses told me that Lucien stepped out for a few at the Fusion Christmas party last year," Elise sidestepped with a verbal sleight of hand to hide her error.

"I was at that party," Ian mused. "I don't recall seeing Lucien dance."

Lucien quirked a brow up at her calmly, as if to say, *I'll let you handle the lying, since you're the unquestioned champion.*

"You have to wait until the bitter end for the good stuff—or so rumor has it. *Thank you*," she told Mrs. Hanson warmly when the elderly lady brought Caden and her their drinks.

"Well, you learn something new every day," Caden said. Elise took a long drink. She felt a little light-headed, but she didn't think it was from the champagne. She pointedly ignored Lucien's stare.

Ian received a call and disappeared on the other side of the wet bar to take it. Lucien walked away to get another drink. Francesca begged off from Justin's manic dancing and went to follow Ian. Elise glanced over a few minutes later in the midst of conversation with Davie, Caden, and Justin and saw Francesca in Ian's arms at the far corner of the deck, her face reflecting in the moonlight as she looked up at him and they talked, their manner subdued . . . intense. Francesca nodded, as if in reassurance, and Ian leaned down to kiss her, his head lingering.

As a particularly boisterous song came to an end, Elise saw Ian walking toward the door to the penthouse while Francesca busied herself refilling guests' glasses, passing hors d'oeuvres, and chatting with Jacob. Elise watched from the corner of her eye, her curiosity mounting, as Lucien set his glass on the bar. His tall form melted into the shadows in the direction Ian had just taken.

Lucien stood with his back next to the wall, listening intently through the partially opened mahogany door.

"Those are my only two options?" he heard Ian's deep voice resonate from inside the library office. Lucien knew from his many visits to the penthouse that it was the room Ian used for business while he was working at home. He'd hoped that since Ian made the call inside, he'd use the house phone—Lucien could have more easily eavesdropped on the conversation then. Although Ian had sought out the privacy of his office, however, he still used his cell phone. There was a pause as Ian listened to whoever was on the other end of the phone speaking.

"I understand what you're saying, but surely there must be more choices than to either try this new medication or insert a feeding tube." Lucien's brow furrowed as he moved another inch inside the opened door, straining to hear. Ian sighed. "Fine. Let's do the medication, if it will make her eat. Yes, I understand," Ian said, sounding grim. Weary. "If she doesn't respond to the new medication, a feeding tube will have to be inserted. Damn it, it's so barbaric," Lucien thought he heard the other man hiss.

He froze when something drew his attention away from Ian's tense conversation. Elise stood several feet away from him in the hallway, her brows arched in amazement.

"I can't be there for a few days yet. Fax the authorization papers to my residence," Ian was saying. "We both know she hasn't been reacting well to the sight of me anyway," he said, his voice sounding hollow . . . barren. "If anything, I'd say *I've* been the trigger to her worst periods recently, Julia."

Elise opened her mouth. Before she could get off the first word of her demand to know what he was doing, Lucien lunged across the space that separated them. He cupped her face and covered her mouth with his own. He applied pressure, swallowing her tiny squeak of surprise, his entire focus on the man in the office.

Had Ian heard anything? he wondered distractedly.

Ian resumed his conversation with whoever was on the phone, but suddenly Lucien couldn't comprehend a word he was saying.

Elise's body was pressed against his, her breath coming in shallow, rapid gasps next to lips that had meant to silence, but now were molding . . . shaping. He leaned down and fit the tight curves of her hips in his palms, his cock jumping at the perfect fit. His fingers reached, digging into the firm, ripe flesh of her ass. He penetrated her lips with his tongue. Her taste surged into his awareness.

She was clean and delicious, tasting of strawberries and champagne . . . and Elise.

She gave a muffled cry, but this one of arousal, not shock. He knew, because her tongue began to duel with his, hesitantly at first, but as the friction built . . . energetically.

Yes, this was the Elise he knew. So eager, so sweet, so addictive; he was a fool to have ever taken a taste in these circumstances. Because she clouded his logic when he needed it most; she was a temptation that surpassed all others.

Elise didn't know what had happened to her. One moment, she'd been dumbfounded by what appeared to be the sight of Lucien eavesdropping—spying—on Ian Noble. Next, she'd been stunned at the feeling of his firm, persuasive lips moving over her own, spinning a spell of silence. Then she'd been luxuriating in his kiss and the sensation of his long, solid male body pressed against her own. She felt his cock harden next to her lower belly as their tongues slid and dueled and tangled together. Desire unfurled in her at the evidence of his stark arousal. She had touched, petted, and sucked her share of cocks, but this ripping, lightning strike of lust she experienced, this was different . . . a sharp, biting, imperative need. She had reached the age of twenty-four and never even glimpsed the edge of desire until Lucien.

She stared up at his shadowed, compelling visage a moment later when he sealed the electric kiss. His body throbbed next to her, hot, male, and primed. He lifted a long finger and pressed it fleetly against his lips before he grabbed her hand. She followed him without question, the luxurious fabrics and carpet of the penthouse muting their hasty tread. She would have followed him to the gallows after the shock of that kiss.

He opened a heavy door along an unfamiliar hallway and pulled her into a room. When he closed the door, it plunged them into complete darkness. Suddenly, her back was pressed against the door by his large, hard body.

"You never give up, do you?" he breathed out, the hint of anger in his amused tone thrilling instead of alarming her. "The only thing you were missing was the pole while you danced up there on the terrace," he said next to her mouth before he nipped at her lower lip. A ripple of excitement went through her.

"Were you jealous? Turned on?" she asked softly, plucking at his lips in return. He tasted wonderful.

"Wasn't that the entire point? I want you to know that I'm going to punish you for teasing me that way. Then you had your fun by almost giving me away about the dancing, didn't you?"

"I didn't do that on purpose."

"Of course you didn't. You never do."

"The slipup was an honest mistake," she said breathlessly as they nibbled at each other's mouths and her body seemed to liquefy from a rush of heat.

"Was it a mistake the way you were gyrating all over Caden? I felt like I was watching you two having sex with your clothes on. And what about just now . . . what the hell do you think you were doing in that hallway?" he asked, a new edge to his tone.

"I wasn't doing anything but looking for you!"

"You weren't doing anything but poking at the sleeping snake again. Some things never change," he muttered, shifting his hips so that his erection slid against her belly. She heard the dark amusement in his tone. He touched her jaw with caressing fingertips, then brushed her sensitive lips. "Now you're going to have to deal with the consequences, aren't you?" he asked, his voice a low, sensual threat.

Her heartbeat throbbed in her ears in the oppressive silence. Even though it was pitch-black in the room, she pictured his small smile . . . the glint of a dare in his eyes.

Pride warred with desire.

Desire won.

She reached between their bodies and outlined the contours of his erection. *Oh.* His testicles felt full—fuller than any man's she'd ever touched. It excited her, that evidence of his blatant masculinity. His cock rode down his left thigh. She stroked him through his pants, her eyes widening in the darkness. His low, rough groan sent tendrils of excitement through her lower belly and sex. Her fingers trembled as she unfastened his trousers. She wrapped her hand around his thick, tumescent staff a moment later and whimpered.

"That's right," Lucien said in a rough hiss as she stroked his warm, dense cock, completely spellbound. "Between that and my hand, I'll tame you yet, *ma chère.*"

Stark longing overwhelmed her. No retort came to her as he guided her to her knees.

Part III

When You Tease Me

Chapter Five

The feeling of her small hand sliding along his cock through his pants made his entire body coil tight with lust. He hadn't realized until that moment when she teased him with a touch that was both knowledgeable and hesitant at once—he would have said *shy*, but that term couldn't apply to Elise—how much lust he'd been trapping inside muscle, blood, and bone. Her touch liberated it. It roared in his veins, until even if Ian Noble had walked into the room at that very moment and accused him of some heinous crime, Lucien couldn't have stopped. Not while Elise's flavor lingered on this tongue.

His fingers sunk into her hair, thrilling to the silky feeling of the cool, loose waves caressing his skin, his breath stinging in his lungs as she unfastened his pants. He stroked the warm satin of her cheek and clamped his eyes shut at the sensation of her hand enclosing his shaft a moment later. Surely she didn't tremble? Then she stroked his naked flesh, and her caress was sure. Expert. He saw red behind his eyelids. His hand transferred to her shoulder, the thin material of her dress allowing him to feel her delicate bone structure and the heat of her skin. She flicked her fingers at the rim beneath the head of his cock—quick, concise. She wrapped her small hand around his girth and whimpered. The combination ripped through him like a blade. His cock lurched viciously.

He urged her downward. She sunk before him like a silent dream come true in the darkness.

She placed her hands on his thighs to steady herself. He cupped his balls in his hands, lifting them slightly and wincing in acute arousal, before he slid his hand below his shaft, lifting himself out of his clothing until he felt her warm breath mist the sensitive head. For a split second, neither of them moved, but he felt her focus on him, shared her tension.

Her warm, parted lips caressed him, making him shudder. She slid him into her warm, humid depths, her mouth eye-crossingly precise.

"Elise," he muttered roughly. He furrowed his fingers into her hair, spreading them until he palmed the back of her head. She bathed the straining head—such a ready, nimble tongue—and cupped his balls before she sucked him farther into her mouth. Her low purr of satisfaction vibrated into his flesh, making him hiss in pleasure. She gently molded his testicles to her palm and urged him with her touch and suck. Her clamping lips moved like a piston at midstaff, taking him deeper slowly . . . surely, sliding farther and farther down his shaft.

He wished to God he could watch her but was just as fervently thankful he couldn't. He recalled that brief flash of her sucking Hugh Langier so expertly and knew the vision of her doing the same to him would pull his trigger . . . end this nirvanic moment long before he was ready.

No, he wouldn't think about Langier now. Elise was all his for this stolen moment in the darkness. He wouldn't share her, not even with a memory.

She slid him along her tongue until he felt the muscular, rigid ring of her throat enclose the tip of his cock. His groan raked at his larynx, his fingers tightened on her skull. Suddenly she was ducking back and forth, treating him to a series of tight, fluid, rapid strokes. His eyes sprang wide. She took him farther this time, deeper, her palpable eagerness making him clench his teeth in raw lust. She gagged when he entered her throat, but immediately controlled the reflex, keeping him lodged deep.

He made a choking sound and slid out of her throat. Damn her, the little hellion . . . *always* pushing . . . *always* testing.

"Keep still," he said, his voice sounding rougher than he'd intended due to splintering restraint. He tightened his hold on her skull, preventing her from ducking her head forward when she tried. He slid the fingers of his other hand through her hair, immobilizing her when she tried to take him deeper. She whimpered, and he grimaced at the erotic sensation vibrating along his shaft.

He had given in to his desire for her, but she would *not* rule him in this. "I will control the movements until I say otherwise. Do you understand?"

Her tongue flicked along the underside of his shaft. He tightened his hold on her head. "You little tease," he muttered. He flexed his hips and fucked her tightly clamped lips for several delicious moments. Ah yes, this was what he needed: to gain supremacy over this clawing need, to give in to his lust at his own rate and preference. She hummed in pleasure, and he paused, gritting his teeth.

"I didn't tell you to hum, did I?" he challenged quietly.

For a moment, she didn't move, but then she twisted her chin from left to right, bringing his cock with her.

He was glad she couldn't see his small smile. She was exquisite. It was going to be such sweet agony to tame her. He began to pulse between her lips again while she sucked, sending spikes of sharp pleasure up his spine. "*Now* I'm telling you to, *ma fifille*," he said. "Hum for me."

She groaned along his shaft, and then softened to a satisfied purr as he flexed his hips, using her mouth for his pleasure. God, it felt good. Her fingertips moved along his hips. The waistband of his boxer briefs had stretched down over part of his ass. The sensation of her fingers sliding beneath the band and stroking his flexing buttocks nearly made him come then and there. Something about her stroking his ass so gently as he pumped with force struck him as potently erotic. He couldn't survive much longer in the midst of this taut, electric bliss.

"Use your hand," he instructed, lust ruling his tongue now, not reason. Her small, strong fist pumping the base of his cock while he fucked her mouth was a sinful heaven a man could survive in only for so long. "You little witch," he accused fondly, the words blistering his tongue as he gave himself to her. He flexed, once again feeling the exquisite sensation of her throat enclosing his cock. She flinched and he started to withdraw, but then she recovered and took him impossibly deeper.

"*Yes,*" he said in a strangled voice, feeling the tickle in his balls that signaled the end of this delicious torture. Then she was sucking him fast and shallow, her fist pumping in a perfect counter-rhythm, the sounds of a full-out pump—wet flesh moving tautly against wet flesh—ringing in his ears.

He thrust deep and held her steady as orgasm ripped through his flesh. Everything went black and dead silent for a moment. Somehow, he found the wherewithal not to roar.

He hoped anyway.

That must have been his low, guttural groan that pierced the bubble of his torrential pleasure.

He withdrew, sliding along her tongue. He continued to come, and come, the strength of his climax stunning him. Distantly, he became aware of the sucking movements and sounds of her mouth on his cock, of her fingertips caressing his ass tenderly while her other hand cupped his balls, milking him for all he was worth.

He sagged, gasping for air, clamping his eyes shut as her warm mouth continued to move, cleaning him, teasing him . . . arousing him all over again.

A light switched on in the hallway, illuminating a tiny crack beneath the closed door. His caressing fingers stilled in Elise's hair. Perhaps she felt his sudden tension, because the pulsing, sucking movements of her mouth ceased.

"Ian?" he heard Francesca say in the distance. Elise's lips moved against him, his penis remaining firmly in her taut hold. After a moment, the light switched out.

The reality of what had occurred struck him like a blow: where they were, what had just happened. It wasn't what he'd planned. Not in the slightest.

He slid his overly sensitive cock out of Elise's warmth, wincing in regret.

"Come here," he said quietly, his hands on her shoulders. He helped her to her feet. His fingertips caressed the smooth, dewy skin of her cheeks. He felt her heat and knew she was aroused. Again, regret flicked through him.

"I don't think they've noticed us missing yet," he said, hastily refastening his pants.

"Lucien—"

"Later," he said, his voice tense with unspoken words. The ringing silence was a remonstrance. She deserved more than that. He stepped toward her and took her into his arms. She felt small and warm and very feminine pressed against him. He kissed her, once on each warm cheek, then on her nectar-sweet mouth. His musk lingered on her tongue, the unique combination of their flavors compelling . . . drawing him deeper.

"You gave me great pleasure," he murmured honestly a moment later.

"I'm glad."

He paused for a moment, his mouth open, undone by her sweet, simple reply. His head lowered to kiss her deeper, and damn the circumstances.

In the distance, he heard a door close and froze. He found her hand and enclosed it in his own before he reached for the door.

"I'll take you to the bathroom so you can freshen up. Give it several minutes, then go back up to the terrace and rejoin the party until we can make a graceful exit."

The muted light from the hallway allowed him to see her golden beauty flushed with arousal . . . her puffy, reddened lips. A muttered curse blistered his tongue. Her dark blue eyes looked huge and glazed with desire. She looked stunning, radiating pure sex appeal. There would be those at the party who'd put two and two together and know she'd been sucking cock with that beautiful mouth.

"I'll bring some ice to the bathroom," Lucien muttered quietly, firming his hold on her hand and leading her down the hallway.

"Why?" she asked dazedly. Her brain was foggy. Bringing Lucien pleasure had left her lust-drunk. She wanted to do it again. She wanted to climb all over him. *Right now.* He opened a door and she distantly realized it led to a powder room.

She stilled when he touched her lips. "Because some bastard has been abusing your gorgeous mouth, that's why. The ice will bring down the swelling a bit."

She shivered at his touch and sexy tone. "Ten lashes to the perpetrator."

"Twenty to the victim," he countered quickly.

Her brows shot up in curiosity and interest. His gaze grew fierce.

He started to walk away, but she grabbed his hand. She purred with pleasure a moment later when she pulled him down to her and he covered her mouth with his, his rough moan a blessing.

Yes. She had him now.

"Forget the ice," she whispered seductively next to his lips a moment later. "Let's go to your place."

His gaze ran over her face. She felt his body stir and triumph soared through her. "It is what I plan, Elise. But later. I should try and smooth things over with Ian and Francesca, and we need to say our good-byes."

"Francesca and Ian are grown-ups. They know these things can happen. We'll apologize tomorrow."

"Just give it a few minutes. We'll go soon."

She arched her back and pressed her mons against his belly. "No, *now.*"

His nostrils flared as he stared down at her. She felt his body respond. Her heart dipped when he blinked and looked away. She sensed the spell was broken.

"My rules, Elise. Be patient," he said gruffly, kissing her cheek with lingering lips and leaving her arms.

"Do not walk away from me again, Lucien," she warned. God, she didn't think she could stand making herself vulnerable to him yet again and having him turn his back on her. Didn't he realize how much she desired him? Didn't he know now that Elise Martin had finally found the man to whom she was willing to risk it all sexually, he was supposed to fall in line and behave precisely as she imagined he should? Yes, that sounded selfish, but *damn* it. Was it really that much of a stretch to think he would be as impetuous and bowled over by lust as she was? Why was Lucien always so contradictory?

"I'm not walking away from you for good. This isn't easy for me, either. Don't be so melodramatic, Elise."

She stiffened. Is that what he thought? That her eagerness for him was silly? Hysterical? Childlike? Hurt gripped at her entire body.

"Elise—" she heard him say.

But he was talking to a closed door.

Fifteen minutes later, Lucien stood next to Ian and Francesca at the terrace bar, careful to keep his gaze from wandering toward the entrance to the penthouse. No one had made a big deal about his and Elise's earlier absence, either having not noticed or being too polite to comment about it. Ian likely had observed, but knowing his friend, he'd probably assumed it was related to sexual games that were none of his business versus being something to remark upon.

No great *obvious* harm had occurred with his hosts, but why was Elise taking so long in returning? He was starting to get worried. He hadn't meant to hurt her. If he'd been able to resist her in the seductive embrace of secretive darkness, this would never have happened.

Someone had altered the music selection to a more mellow pop mix. The dancing had ceased. Things felt flat with Elise missing. She'd always been the effervescence to a social gathering, the spice. The flickering flame. Perhaps her spoiled mother had noticed that from a young age and started requesting her only daughter be excluded from dinner parties and other gatherings, Lucien mused. Madeline Martin did not enjoy competition.

He, Ian, and Francesca remained in comfortable silence, Francesca in the curve of Ian's arm, Lucien leaning against the bar. When Ian glanced up and noticed Lucien studying his face for signs of how he was reacting to that phone call earlier, Lucien casually took a sip of his drink. As usual, Ian kept his emotions well hidden. Lucien wanted to ask if everything was all right, but resisted. He couldn't tip his hand.

He watched as both Caden and Justin again glanced toward the stairwell that led to the penthouse, their disappointed expressions informing him better than anything that Elise was nowhere to be seen.

"Elise is Louis Martin's daughter, isn't she?"

Lucien remained outwardly calm, even though his heart began thundering at Ian's unexpected question. It shouldn't have surprised him that Ian knew precisely who Elise was. Ian made it his business to know anything that concerned him, even remotely.

"Yes, Martin's only child," Lucien replied evenly.

"His heir," Ian clarified, watching Lucien closely.

Lucien nodded.

Francesca shifted in Ian's arms, perhaps noticing the sudden tension in the air.

"I think I'll go down and check on Elise," Francesca said, indicating she'd been thinking along the same lines as him. Lucien nodded, relieved. Elise would be more likely to allow another woman into that locked bathroom if she was upset than she would him. He knew that much about women.

In Francesca's absence, Ian refrained from asking him more questions about Elise, seeming to guess that Lucien wasn't inclined to gossip on the topic. Instead, they discussed the hotel Lucien was buying and his ideas for it. He straightened from his leaning position on the bar when Francesca returned five minutes later without Elise. He must not have been able to hide his worry, because Francesca spoke to him, not Ian.

"Elise wasn't feeling very well. I just put her in a cab."

"What was wrong with her?" Lucien demanded.

"She said she felt a little sick to her stomach, that's all," Francesca assured, her gaze on him.

"But you didn't believe her?" Lucien asked.

"I didn't disbelieve her, but . . . she did seem a bit upset," Francesca said cautiously. Ian waited silently, watching him. Lucien set down his drink. Well, there was nothing for it now. Ian and Francesca, at least, both clearly knew he'd been dallying with Elise in the penthouse earlier. He was uncertain what else they understood or speculated about Elise and him, but that much they knew.

"I'd better go after her," he said, buttoning his jacket. "Thank you for the evening, and again—congratulations. It gives me hope, seeing the two of you so happy," he said, shaking Ian's hand and giving Francesca a kiss. He left without bidding good-bye to the rest of the party. He didn't want to put it in Justin's or Caden's head that Elise had left.

He didn't want either young man to track her down, because that's precisely what he planned to do.

Elise warily left her room at the Cedar Home Extended Stay Hotel and locked her door behind her before she hurried silently down the long, dim hallway. Her ears were acutely pitched for the sound of the door of Room 16 opening, but the nuisance that was Baden Johnson remained absent.

She didn't breathe a sigh of relief until she hit the landing on the staircase. The elevator in the rundown hotel had been broken ever since she'd moved in. She flew out the door of the stairwell into the dark night.

Unfortunately, her father and mother had high hopes about her returning to Paris and conveniently marrying Erik Cebir, Swiss heir to the Cebir pharmaceutical fortune. When she'd continually refused to go along with their plans, her father had cut off all her credit cards. Her first and only paycheck from Fusion wouldn't come until next Tuesday, so she was barely scraping by. Consequently, when she hadn't had sufficient cash to pay the cab, she'd been screwed. The surly driver had been impervious to her charm, insisting she must go upstairs and get the money or he'd put in a call to the police.

"Here," she said, shoving her hand through the window of the driver's side.

"What's this crap?"

Irritation bubbled up in her. "It's a watch," she said fiercely. "It'll cover the cost of the cab ride. About a hundred times over," she added under her breath. It'd been one of the least valuable things she'd had in her jewelry box, given to her by her least favorite aunt who was renowned for regifting.

The cabdriver first gave her then the shabby hotel a skeptical glance and handed back the watch. "No thanks. I'll take the twelve bucks, plus tip."

"That's a Cartier, you idiot!"

"Right. Prince Charles himself has probably got one, but I ain't him. I want my money."

"But you don't understand! You could take that to any pawn-broker and—"

"What's going on here?" a deep voice interrupted. She swallowed convulsively when she recognized the steel-gray hair and the large, hulking form coalesce from the shadows. *Shit.* Baden Johnson had clearly once been a very strong man, but he was going to seed in middle age. That didn't mean he didn't carry the vestiges of massive, brute power, however.

"You her friend?" the cabdriver called through the opened window single-mindedly. "Your girlie owes me twelve bucks plus tip."

Elise backed away several steps as Baden approached. "What's this?" Baden asked, reaching for the watch.

She snatched her hand back, but too late. The platinum watch flashed between Baden's thick fingers. He held it up, examining it in the dim light. His gaze narrowed on her speculatively. She glanced up and down the dark street, but not another soul was in sight.

"It's . . . it's nothing, just a cheap knockoff. I'll just . . . I'll run back inside and get the cash," she prevaricated, longing for the relative safety of her locked room.

"Don't worry about it," Baden said, reaching into his pocket. He started to count off some crumpled, greasy looking bills. "I'll get your fare. I'm interested in seeing more of these *cheap knockoffs.*"

"No, please—"

"Hey now," he said, his teeth gleaming in the dim light, reminding her of dirty fangs. She'd discovered Baden was fond of what they called in the States *chew*. "I know you're good for it. You'll find a way to pay me back, right? I can think of a dozen or two things right off the top of my head," he said, his downward gaze over her body feeling like he'd smeared greasy slime on her skin.

Her thoughts started to come a mile a minute.

"Yes, of course. Thank you, Baden," she said. When he looked away, she turned and ran.

She couldn't think of what else to do. At least Baden was in the middle of finding the bills for payment. It would give her a few seconds to try to race to her room and lock herself in—better than waiting until he was unoccupied, the cabdriver had gone, and they were alone on the dark, deserted street together.

"Hey . . . hold up, you little—"

But Elise didn't pause. She reached the door to the stairwell, lunging to open it. Before she ducked into the musty interior, she glanced over her shoulder and yelped in alarm.

Big Baden was stalking rapidly toward her, just twenty feet away. He looked furious, not to mention determined.

She hurled herself up the stairs, cursing the fact that she hadn't yet removed her strappy high-heeled sandals. Through the pounding of her heart in her eardrums, she heard the metal door slam shut and the sound of Baden's heavy boots hitting the first stairs.

"Slow down, *French girl*. I'm thinking you're keeping some secrets from your neighbors. That's not too friendly, is it? Time you learned how to be a little nicer, seeing as you're a stranger in this country," he crooned, his quiet voice sending a shiver through her as it echoed in the empty, dark stairwell. Why had she ever exchanged a single word with him? She should have just avoided him, like any sane woman, instead of trying to charm away the threat of him. She heard his banging boots several steps behind her when she hit the landing and her heart jumped into her throat.

He was going to catch her.

Dear God. Was this it? All those years she'd partied indiscriminately with fools and drunks and remained unscathed. Was she to be raped or beaten *now*, when she was finally trying to take control of her life? No. The thought was unbearable. She reacted instinctively when Baden caught her arm, wrenching it behind her. She spun around like a whirlwind and whacked him hard at the side of his head with her fist.

"*Brûle en enfer.* Let go of me, you greasy bastard!"

Her unexpected move and fierceness temporarily set them both off balance. After a brief struggle, however, Baden steadied himself.

"You little slut," he hissed between ragged breaths. When she saw his face, terror tore through her like a tidal wave. She'd obviously hurt him, and he was as furious as a kicked junkyard dog.

"No—" she protested when he grabbed her hair, but her voice was cut off when he jerked back her head, stretching her neck, making it so that she couldn't see the threat of him. Her breath caught in her lungs as she instinctively braced for pain.

A jolt went through her, but it wasn't from Baden's fist. She staggered and tripped on the stairs, abruptly free of the restraint of Baden's hold. She glanced around in confusion at the guttural *oomph* of someone taking a fist deep in the gut. It was followed by the sickening sound of bone against bone. Baden sunk to his knees.

"*You fucking—*"

"Lucien," she muttered, interrupting Baden's curse, shocked and disoriented by his unmistakable tall shadow looming over both her and Baden.

"I'm assuming you live in this godforsaken place?"

"Yes," she replied shakily.

"Go to your room this instant and lock the door."

"But I—"

"Do as I say, Elise," he said with eerie calm when Baden started to struggle to his feet.

She scurried up the stairs on her hands and knees before finding her balance to stand. As she flew through the door to the hallway, she heard again the unmistakable *thud* of a fist sinking into flesh, followed by a vicious grunt.

An hour and a half later, Elise closed the door behind the two police officers that had arrived after she'd called 911.

"Lock it," Lucien said quietly from behind her. Only he and she remained in her room. Between Baden being taken away, and the police asking questions, she'd been too distracted to be embarrassed. It hit her now, full force. A flood of shame went through her as she considered him observing her shabby lodging firsthand. She triple locked the door and slowly turned to face him.

Baden was in police custody, although he'd been taken initially to Stroger Hospital for multiple contusions. Lucien, on the other hand, sported only a single cut over his right eyebrow. He wouldn't allow the EMT to see to the small wound, telling him to attend to Baden. Later, he'd allowed Elise to wash it and apply a small bandage, never speaking to her the whole time.

In fact, Lucien had said very little to her in the past hour and a half, talking mostly to the police officers as he gave his report and listening intently while she gave hers.

In a million years, she wouldn't have guessed the evening would end this way. What if Baden had pulled a knife or gun on Lucien, and he'd died out there in that stairwell? She shuddered at the horrible thought. Now they were alone together, and Elise wasn't sure what to say.

"Are you all right?" she asked him, studying him closely where he leaned against a chipped dresser, looking calm, deadly, and down-right gorgeous in his well-fitted pants and sports jacket. Somehow, the bandage above his right eyebrow appeared perfectly in sync with the rest of his appearance.

"I'm fine. It's you I'm concerned about."

"Like I told the officers, the worst I got was grabbed."

"You were lucky."

She gave a shaky laugh and walked toward him. "That you came? Yes, I was." Her gaze ran over his implacable features. "If I haven't thanked you yet, I will now. You have about a million more thank-yous coming." She swallowed thickly when he didn't respond, just continued to laser her with those light gray eyes. "I'm sorry I left Ian and Francesca's party like that. I was feeling . . ."

"Rejected?" he said softly when she faded off.

She swallowed. It did sound silly when she heard Lucien say the word. But why didn't he want to take her in a heated rush like other men? Was she not as attractive to him as she'd hoped when he'd first expressed his desire? She felt helpless about how to deal with him.

Manage him.

"Because I am controlling the pace of this doesn't mean that I don't want you like crazy, Elise," he said, seemingly reading her mind. He straightened and closed the distance between them. "I owe you."

Her breath hitched when she absorbed his low, ominous tone. "What do you mean?"

"What in the name of all that is sinful do you think you are doing living in a flophouse?" he asked succinctly, his nostrils flaring with what she recognized as contained fury.

"It's not a flophouse! It's a perfectly respectable—" She paused midsentence when they heard a door slam loudly in the hallway and the sound of a woman cursing loudly and a man talking in rapid Spanish. *Ms. Inga. One of her johns must have stiffed her.* Elise noticed

Lucien's frown as he glanced toward the hallway and quickly changed tracks. "I have to live within my means, Lucien. I am just doing the best I can."

"Your *means*? You're an extremely wealthy woman."

She sniffed and averted her gaze. "It just so happens my father doesn't agree with my plans for moving here. He's cut me off."

A tense silence ensued in which she found it difficult to meet Lucien's gaze.

"I specifically asked you if you had enough money to live in this city."

"I *do* have enough."

"I meant do you have enough funds to live in this city in a safe, reasonable manner. You knew exactly what I meant."

"How was I to know what you *meant*?"

"Because I *meant* what most sane adults would mean," he boomed, taking her off guard. She didn't step back or flinch in holding his stare, but it was difficult in those tense ensuing seconds. Something else entered his expression. Was it helplessness? He closed his eyes briefly and glanced away. "This is a dangerous neighborhood. I can't believe you've been living here."

"It's not dangerous," she said stubbornly, her glance bouncing away when he gave her an incredulous look. He reached into his jacket pocket. "I assume this is yours?" he asked, handing her the watch she'd tried to give the taxi driver for payment.

"Where did you find it?" she asked, her head lowered as she studied the watch, even though her entire focus was on Lucien.

"On the stairs. Baden dropped it. Why did he have your watch? Did he steal it from you?"

She stared sightlessly at the floor. She'd left out the part in her report to the police about her trying to give the taxi driver the watch for payment. Now she knew why she'd omitted that portion. She hadn't wanted Lucien to hear it. It was strange, but she honestly hadn't realized how potentially dangerous flashing around an expensive watch in this neighborhood could be.

Not until she considered her behavior through Lucien's eyes.

"Elise?" he asked pointedly. "Why did Baden have this watch? You weren't wearing it at Ian and Francesca's."

She blinked, but her surprise faded quickly enough. Lucien took note of the smallest details.

"I . . . I didn't have enough money for the cab fare," she said lamely.

An awful silence swelled.

"So you came up to your room to get something to give the taxi driver in lieu of payment, and you chose a designer watch worth several thousand dollars? Are you mad, flashing expensive jewelry like that around in this neighborhood?"

"It was the most reasonable thing I had to bargain with!"

"And Baden recognized that it was a valuable watch and took it?"

"Yes," she whispered, shame stealing her voice.

"Baden was smart enough to realize that if you were willing to throw away a Cartier watch, there was even more valuable treasure to be had," he said, glancing at the antique jewelry box on the dresser.

She closed her eyes in mortification. What might that lowlife have done to her if Lucien hadn't shown up?

Go home, a voice in her head taunted. *Get married. Let someone else take care of you. You always make a mess of doing it yourself.*

"What are you thinking, Elise?"

She met his gaze, chin tilted up proudly even though he had to see the irksome tears in her eyes. "The same thing you are, more than likely. That I should just run home to Paris before I cause some real damage."

His rocklike expression collapsed for a moment so brief, she thought she'd imagined it. He stepped forward and took her into his arms.

"That's not what I was thinking. Don't give up now," he said near her ear, his voice low and full of . . . regret? Concern? She couldn't say for sure. All she knew was that it felt like heaven to be in his arms. She put her cheek next to his chest and inhaled shakily when his long fingers threaded through her hair. He smelled so good—like clean soap, his addictive cologne, and just the hint of his former arousal. Her body stirred to life of its own accord as she recalled their illicit tryst at the penthouse. His hand moved. The back of her head seemed to fit perfectly in his palm.

"I'm sorry, Lucien. I would never want you to be hurt," she said in a muffled voice as she tried to control the full feeling in her chest.

"I know that," he said, his voice like roughened silk. "It's not me I'm concerned about. It's you. You are too impulsive at times. All you had to do was ask me for financial assistance."

"I didn't think I needed any."

She felt his fingers on her chin and looked up reluctantly.

"Well, you were wrong, weren't you?" He looked down at her with a hooded gaze. Her nipples pulled tight against his ribs. "I owe you a punishment for your impulsivity. I also owe you pleasure, for having pleased me so well earlier. Take off all of your clothes, Elise," he said quietly.

"*What?*" Her heart paused in its drumming to do a leap. Blood rushed into her cheeks.

"You heard me," he replied.

He'd done it. He'd made her completely speechless. Her fingers seemed to have gone numb as she began to unloop the rope of pearls from around her neck. What was this feeling that swamped her? Was it shame? No . . . it was shyness. Her—Elise Martin—shy and awkward.

She wouldn't have thought it a possibility. But it wasn't just any man.

It was Lucien.

Chapter Six

He'd told himself he wouldn't be consumed by her fires, but the slow burn began as he watched her remove the looped rope of cultured pearls from around her neck. The pearls interested him. They weren't an expensive item. In fact, he'd frequently been proud of her during the past week in regard to the fact that she wasn't flaunting her wealth with expensive jewelry, clothing, and designer handbags. Elise was a very beautiful woman, after all, not to mention the daughter of a renowned fashion designer. She was known for wearing the most expensive clothes in the world like they were her birthright. She'd been staying under the radar, though—as well as a blazing meteor like Elise Martin possibly could.

The belt at her hips came off next. He'd noticed the moment that she approached him earlier this evening that the blue fabric of her dress emphasized her flawless, pale skin and sapphire eyes. Beneath the dress, she wore a matching pair of silk panties and bra. Her dress had fallen off her shoulder earlier when she'd been dancing so outrageously with Caden. He'd seen that the strap of the bra perfectly matched the color of her dress as she'd gyrated her hips, her gaze directly on him—daring him.

Arousal and irritation spiked through him at the memory.

She was petite, but built for sin. Her waist was so tiny, he would likely come near to encompassing it with his opened hands. She was far from slight, though. The curve from her waist to her round hips taunted a man's hand, tempted him to touch smooth, satiny stretches of skin. Just looking at the pale expanse of her taut belly and the juncture between shapely thighs made him hard and heavy—ready from a glance. Her breasts were full for her petite figure. He'd idly wondered if they'd been enhanced before, but somehow he doubted it. Elise's mother had been a screen goddess and praised for her hourglass figure. Despite her more compact size, Elise shared a lot of her mother's looks. She was Madeline Martin's beauty distilled and perfected.

Another reason Madeline had envied her daughter.

"Take off the bra. I'll remove the panties," he told her gruffly.

His breath burned in his lungs as she unfastened the rear hook and her breasts spilled out of the cups. His cock lurched against his boxer briefs.

No. Most definitely the real thing.

Her lithesome arms fell to her sides, leaving her high, pink-tipped breasts exposed. Her eyes were still downcast. It was so strange to see her in anything remotely resembling a submissive pose. Unusual . . . and extremely arousing.

He closed his eyes briefly, blocking himself from the potent vision of her, and turned his attention to the grungy room where she'd been living. His mouth tightened when he again took note of the bars on the windows. He stepped over to the dresser and picked up the long-handled silver and enamel hairbrush he'd seen there earlier.

"Pick up your pearls and come over here," he said, waving toward the end of the sagging double bed. It was made. He'd give her this— she'd kept the room as neat and clean as she possibly could. Again, his heart squeezed in his chest at the thought of this gem of a woman living in such squalor.

He sat at the edge of the bed, making the springs squeak in protest. He noticed she still hadn't moved and was looking in turn at him, the hairbrush in his hand, and the heap of pearls she'd set on the desk.

"I'll tell you what I'm going to do with them. Bring them here." She scooped up the pearls and approached him, her gaze flickering from his face to his lap. His cock twitched as if she'd touched him.

He did his best to ignore the flagrant display of naked beauty just inches away from fingers that were itching to touch. He set down the hairbrush and held out his hands. She blinked, realizing what he wanted, and handed him the pearls.

"These pearls are valuable to you personally," he stated rather than asked as he held the creamy, heavy gems in his hands. She blanched.

"How did you know that?" she asked.

"Because while they are lovely, they're cultured and irregular in shape. You said the watch was the least valuable thing you could offer, but these"—he held up the pearls—"were a hundred times cheaper. More so."

"*Don't* call them cheap."

"I'm not casting aspersions on your pearls. I'm just pointing out, the cabdriver would have likely prized their value over the watch. It would have made more sense to offer them. Who gave you the pearls?"

He saw the mini-revolt spark in her beautiful eyes and something else . . . something he didn't like. "That's none of your business."

He examined her closely for several seconds, but she revealed nothing more. Anger flickered in him at her show of defiance. So did something else. Jealousy.

"I'm going to bind your wrists. Go like this." He held out his arms and put his wrists together, palms facing inward. For a split second, he saw panic flash across her beautiful face. Despite the outlandish reports of her sexual antics, this was not a woman used to being bound.

"What are you going to do after that?" she asked suspiciously.

"I told you earlier I owed you a punishment for teasing me the way you did. Now you're going to get something extra for living in this hellhole and putting yourself at risk." His eyelids narrowed when he saw her confusion . . . her desire. "Is there something you want to ask me?"

"No." Even though she said nothing else, her defiant expression said loud and clear, *I can take whatever you can dish out. It's all the same to me.*

"You are still pulling at the reins," he said softly. "When you stop it and submit, the time will have come."

He saw bewilderment shadow her features, but then her gaze met his. Her anxiety seemed to vanish. Slowly, she held out her hands to be bound.

He exhaled. Her show of trust aroused him even more than the vision of her gorgeous body. He resisted an urge to touch . . . caress . . . consume . . .

. . . possess completely.

"You're going to restrain me with *pearls*?" she asked incredulously from above him a moment later as he began to twist the gems around her wrists.

"If you struggle or try to get your hands free, you might break the silk." He glanced up into her now flushed face. "I find that something delicate can restrain better than metal if the wearer values what binds."

He determinedly focused on the task of looping the pearls around her wrists, making the long strand stretch snugly from lower wrists to forearms. Her thrusting breasts fractured his focus, trembling slightly as she breathed and he maneuvered the necklace. He could imagine in graphic detail how soft the skin of them would be sliding against his lips. When he'd finished restraining her wrists, he looked up at her face.

She was exquisite, her skin gleaming more luminously than the pearls. Her scent filtered into his nose—clean, light, extremely feminine. Her eyes looked large in her pale face, but they grew wider when he reached up, unable to resist, and stroked the under-curve of her left breast. He watched the rosebud tip darken and tighten. Blood pulsed into his cock.

For a second, a haze of lust fogged his vision, stealing his will.

"Lie down in my lap," he murmured after he'd steadied himself. She complied without speaking. He guided her, taking some of her weight since her wrists were restrained. He noticed how careful she was of not stretching the silk and pearl bond and felt a stab of irritation.

Who had given her the necklace? She clearly held it dear.

Her skin felt like warm silk as he grasped one hip, holding her steady. The fingers of his other hand trailed down her back. He felt her ripple beneath his touch, mounting his lust. She settled in his lap, the sweet pressure of her body taunting his erection.

"I didn't tell you last time, but it gave me great pleasure to punish you," he said, his hand flowing against her skin.

"It . . . it did?"

"Couldn't you tell?" he asked drolly. His cock lurched in arousal. She stilled beneath him and he knew she'd felt it. "Put your hands above your head," he instructed. She followed his command. Sensing her nervousness, he stroked her until she softened a little, her flesh becoming more malleable beneath his hand. Feeling the deep knots in her muscles, he molded and rubbed.

"You really are a tight little knot. I will work this tension out of you one day. You are so stiff," he said, listening to her soft, sexy moans as he massaged her back.

He'd always instinctively had an understanding of muscle, innately comprehended how stress, trauma, emotional and physical pain was stored and carried in the flesh. He'd learned to read a horse's tension from an early age by stroking muscle, seeing how an animal's body language altered with strenuous exercise, soothing words, and a touch . . . a concisely applied swat of the crop. Later, he'd learned to read his lovers' tension level, grew to understand how to build it with punishment, release it with an explosion of pleasure. . . .

Never had he touched a woman as tightly strung as Elise. He rubbed her shoulders and heard her exhale in a mixture of pain and pleasure. He winced. So much pain she carried.

"Is that better?" he asked, running his palm along her side, admiring her delicate rib cage and feeling her heart throbbing inside it.

"I think so," he heard her say. She lay with her forehead pressed to the bedspread, reminding him of a child who closed their eyes before a painful procedure, like getting a shot. He smiled and caressed her just above the elastic band of her panties. She shivered as he stroked the patch of skin along her spine.

"Then we'll begin," he said, using both hands to peel her panties down over her buttocks. She moaned softly, and he wondered if she'd felt his body's response to the vision of her, the decadent erotic feast she made, lying there nude and helpless in his lap. He worked the panties down her thighs in order to have full access to the lower curve of her plump buttocks.

He grasped one of her cheeks with his hand. "You knew you were teasing me, didn't you?" he asked gruffly.

"Yes."

He gave her a brisk swat. She jumped slightly in his lap.

"Stay still," he ordered, using his hands to palm both buttocks at once. She made a whimpering sound and settled in his lap. He released her and slapped each cheek again, grunting in grim satisfaction when she remained immobile. His cock swelled tight at the evidence of even that small submission on her part. He placed a flurry of spanks, letting her feel the burn. He watched in fascinated lust as her pale bottom began to blush pink.

She was a fantasy to spank, her ass plump and firm. He landed a brisk slap on each lower curve of a buttock, grimacing in lust at the erotic vision of her bouncing flesh. He shut his eyes and resisted an almost overwhelming urge to grind her body against his straining erection.

"I really didn't mean to say anything about our past association earlier tonight," she squealed a moment later when he slapped both ass cheeks at once. She clenched her bottom tight.

"Perhaps, but you are impulsive. You act before you think. Relax," he prompted, slapping very lightly several times at her ass until she released the contracting muscles. She continued her confession as if she hadn't been interrupted.

"And I only followed you because I was wondering what you were doing in the penthouse. Oh . . . *merde* . . . that stings," she moaned as he swatted her several more times. Her hips twisted feverishly in his lap, making him grunt in pleasure. He stilled her wriggling bottom, pressing her down against his straining cock. They groaned in unison. She was blushing pink now. He would have to be careful of her. Her skin was quite delicate, and he would never want to cause her any true harm. "Lucien?" she asked raggedly. "What *were* you doing, listening to Ian that way?"

"That's my affair," he said distractedly, molding an ass cheek in his hand and treating it to several focused slaps. Her ass was turning nice and hot.

"But why were you spying on Ian Noble?" she persisted.

He snarled in irritation and lust and slapped her one last time. Hard. He shoved her panties down her legs and whipped them over her feet. Unable to stop himself, he slid his fingers between her legs, touching her outer sex.

Ah, *bless* it. Warm wetness slicked his skin. She gasped at his touch and then wiggled her bottom down closer to his hand, tempting him.

"Stand up," he said sharply, his restraint a brittle thing.

Even though he commanded her, he helped her, mindful of her bound state. He rose. She stood before him, her luscious breasts plumped by her pearl-bound arms, her hair a sexy muss of golden waves and curls. Something about the six- or seven-loop strand of creamy gems around her wrists and forearms next to her naked skin really did it for him. Everything about her did it for him. He paused for a moment when he glanced at her face and saw the pink flush of her lips and cheeks.

He frowned. She ought to be outlawed for the things she inspired in a man—dark, dirty things . . . out-of-control things he'd surely later regret.

"What were you saying?" he asked, mouth tight, straining to recall why he'd been irritated.

"I . . . I didn't mean *spying* . . . like . . . like . . ."

"My father?" he prompted quietly.

She scraped white teeth over her plump lower lip, the damp drag spellbinding him momentarily, making him forget his anger.

"I don't think you're like your father, Lucien. At least I hope you're not. But that man in Paris, he mentioned Ian Noble. I don't understand—"

"I'm not asking you to understand," he said, touching her cheek and feeling her warmth. "I'm asking you to trust me. Do you?"

She nodded, but he saw the wariness in her eyes. He frowned and picked up the hairbrush from the bed. "Do you at least trust me enough to bend over for the rest of your punishment?" he asked.

Her eyes widened. "You're going to spank me with Grand-Mère's hairbrush?"

He smiled. "I like to innovate with whatever is available to me, and Grand-Mère will never know. It'll be our own little secret," he said, positioning himself next to her body instead of in front of her. "Now bend over."

Her lips curved alluringly. She held his gaze as she leaned over slowly—a nimble, sleek seduction—putting her bound hands on her knees.

"Witch," he accused. Her smile widened and he smiled back. He couldn't stop himself. She couldn't help it if everything she did was sex distilled. "Stare at the floor this instant. What did I tell you last time about seducing me during a punishment?" he asked mildly as he rubbed her firm, pink bottom. She stilled beneath him when his fingers brushed close to her thighs at the lower curve of her ass. He was so tempted to dip his fingers into the sweet, wet heaven of her.

"You said you'd give me more punishment," he heard her say. He blinked, his lustful trance fracturing.

"That's right," he murmured as he trailed a hand up her spine and felt her shiver beneath his touch. His cock swelled so tight, he didn't think there was room in his skin anymore. He wanted to ride her until the oblivion of climax shook him, abandon himself to her fires. But if he didn't maintain control, both of them would be lost.

He firmed his hold on her shoulder and drew back the hairbrush, the smooth, enameled, three-by-four-inch back of it facing Elise's ass.

"This will sting more than the spanking," he said. "Why in God's name couldn't you have asked me for help?"

"I couldn't," he heard her say in a muffled voice.

"But why?" he demanded.

A pause. He waited, his arm suspended in the air.

"I was too proud," he finally heard her whisper.

He swung the hairbrush. It hit her bottom with a brisk pop, the blow shivering through her taut flesh in a way that made his cock jump. He held her steady when she squeaked and lurched forward slightly.

He popped her bottom again and again.

"Ooh!"

"Is it too much?" he asked, palming a buttock and rubbing it.

She was growing hot. He listened, his ear cocked, ignoring his raging cock.

"No. It's bearable," she said after a moment, her shaky yet brave response making him close his eyes briefly, shielding himself from the glory of her.

He carefully examined her reddening ass, kneading the exquisitely soft, hot flesh. Yes, she could take a few more, but not much. He would never want to mark her, and she had a very tender, sensitive ass.

"You will take three more," he said, "but I'm not going easy on you for the last. Brace yourself." He saw her muscles tense in anticipation. Still holding her steady with one hand and rubbing her ass with the other, he examined her, his gaze catching on the delicious under-curve of her firm breasts suspended in the air as she bent over. Such sweet, tempting fruit. He let go of her shoulder and reached beneath her. She jumped and whimpered when he gently pinched a nipple.

"This nipple is hard. Are you aroused, little girl?" he growled softly.

Her breath froze on an inhale. "And if I am?" she asked warily after a moment.

"Then you wouldn't be the only one," he admitted, tweaking erect flesh. Her moan sounded feverish. "But this is still a punishment. I thought I'd have a heart attack, seeing that degenerate Johnson with his hands on your earlier."

"You . . . you did?"

"What do you think? He's lucky I didn't take his head off."

She gasped, but he thought it was because of what he was doing to her nipple more than what he'd said. "I saw him before they put him in the ambulance. You nearly did."

"The bastard will end up fine—unfortunately, for the rest of the world," he said, sounding bitter as he considered the possibility of Baden Johnson back on the street in months or weeks. He pressed her nipple to the palm of his hand and made a subtle circling motion. Elise made a choked sound. "My point was, this is a punishment," he said, reminding himself as much as her. "Your last three strokes *will* hurt."

He molded her entire breast to his palm before he reluctantly let go of her. He'd never felt such tender, responsive flesh in his life. Her heart had been beating frantically against his hungry hand.

He could so easily lose himself in her.

Your last three strokes will *hurt.*

His warning echoed in her brain, mounting what was already almost an unbearable anticipation. Would it really hurt that much? And what about after he was finished? He'd said he owed her pleasure. The sharp pinch at her clit made her instinctively clench her thigh and buttock muscles. She so wanted to touch herself and come in a hot rush of excitement.

"I need your legs wider. Here, come over to this desk."

He helped her stand. She followed him, wincing slightly at the burn on her bottom. She watched him move aside the desk chair and a few of her papers, clearing the surface. It humiliated her a little that she was completely naked, save the pearls and her sandals, her bottom more than likely red from her punishment, while Lucien was still immaculately dressed. He'd asked her to trust him. What better proof did she need for it than this?

Having cleared the desk, he approached her. She looked up, studying his handsome face as he carefully unwound the pearls, unbinding her. What was he thinking? How could he look so untouchable, so unreachable as he did these intimate things to her?

Her gaze slid down his taut abdomen to his crotch and thighs. No. He was far from cold when it came to her. His arousal was blatant and awesome to behold. Things were very full behind his crotch, and the pillar of his cock pressed against fabric in a mouth-watering fashion. She swore she could make out the shape of the thick, tapering crown. Her clit tingled, and again, she longed to touch herself, staunch the ache. She opened her mouth to . . . *what*?

Beg him?

Her lips closed, but her tongue and throat seemed to burn with the repressed plea. He paused in his task.

"Yes? Do you want to say something?" he asked quietly.

Her pride rallied. "No," she replied, jerking her gaze off his cock.

"Very well. Bend over and put your elbows on the desk," he said matter-of-factly when he'd removed the pearls and placed them on the bed. He took her hand and guided her, his touch gentle. "Fold your arms. Good, now rest your forehead on your forearm." She felt as if her lungs wouldn't work properly as she struggled to do his bidding. She had to bend over farther than she had previously in order to reach the surface of the low desk. The position left her thoroughly exposed. She stilled when Lucien placed his hands on her shoulders. "Slide back some," he said, his voice sounding thick . . . gruff.

She moved back on the desk and her breasts spilled over the edge. Lucien made a rough sound.

"Perfect," he said. He gently struck her inner thigh with the hard edge of her grand-mère's brush. "Spread your legs more."

She did so, suppressing a moan. He opened his large hand over her lower ass and lifted. Cool air kissed her damp, heated sex.

"Lucien," she cried out shakily, not sure if the single word was a plea for him to stop exposing her pussy or for him to touch what he'd exposed. She experienced his stare on her like a burning touch.

"God," she heard him mutter. *"Tu es belle."*

You're beautiful. Her heart felt like it'd explode from her chest. It jump-started when he released her ass and swung the brush.

"Ow," popped out of her throat. Her bottom smarted where he'd struck, but it'd been more surprise than pain that had instigated her response. He immediately replaced the brush with his hand, rubbing and soothing the stinging flesh.

"Two more like that."

"Okay," she managed shakily.

"Hold steady."

She couldn't stop herself. She turned her chin, still keeping her head on her folded arms, and watched him through a few curls as he swung, taut, powerful muscles flexing beneath his dress shirt. The brush made a cracking sound as it smacked her ass. She felt the burst of sensation and winced, gritting her teeth. Lucien's gaze was fixed on her breast. She saw his nostrils flare as the blow shook through the suspended flesh.

A groan burned in her throat. His stare leapt to her face. A spark of arousal seemed to leap between them.

"Tu es belle," she whispered between soft pants.

His expression turned fierce.

"Damn you, Elise." He placed one hand on the back of her head and turned her, so that all she could see was her folded forearms and the cheap wood veneer of the desktop. Her thighs quaked. He'd sounded so . . . *something* just now. Was he angry?

Suddenly, his hand was spread on her far hip and his body was on the other side. He pressed and rubbed the side of her ass against his cock, his actions frankly lascivious. Her eyes sprang wide.

No . . . not angry. Aroused to the breaking point.

She whimpered as he ground their flesh together, mounting the almost unbearable tension in their straining bodies. Her ass was trapped, sandwiched between his hard body and his strong hold. It was the tautest, most electrical moment she'd ever experienced or imagined in her life.

The hairbrush landed with a crack. A cry popped out of her throat. Oh, how her ass burned.

Something hit the desk. She lifted her head and saw the instrument of torture itself—the hairbrush—resting on the desk. Then his hand was rubbing her bottom, soothing her, even as his cock throbbed next to her hip. The moment was so full, so incendiary, she felt as if she couldn't take a complete breath.

"Your punishment is done. Stand up."

She tried to do as he'd said, but her flesh felt heavy and torpid with arousal. He moved back slightly to help her. She made a sound of protest in her throat at the loss of his primal heat resonating against her. But then he was helping her to rise, and his arms enclosed her.

"Lucien," she mouthed through numb-feeling lips, turning her face upward.

"I am here," he said, his warm breath brushing against her mouth. He pressed her closer against him, overwhelming her with the sensation of his solid, powerful body. "You were very brave, accepting your punishment as you did."

"I'll never let you do that to me again."

"Yes, you will."

"You're right," she whispered. Who was she kidding? It was very exciting, submitting to him. "I will."

He smiled and leaned down, covering her mouth with his, his kiss tender and passionate at once. His hands caressed her naked skin from flank to waist, weaving a spell she never wanted to escape. He cupped her bottom, leaning farther down over her. He was so tall, but she liked the way she fit against him. She shivered when she felt his fingers stretching at the back of her trembling thighs, then between them . . . seeking. He made a sound of dissatisfaction when they came up short.

"You are so tiny," he murmured fondly, lifting her in his arms in one fluid movement. Her feet came off the floor. She instinctively wrapped her legs around his hips and gripped onto his shoulders.

He seized her mouth with his. She purred. Her legs curled tighter around his waist. Her entire awareness swam in the power of his kiss, of his touch, of hard, straining muscle. He held her steady with one arm. His free hand cupped an ass cheek, parting her.

He pushed just a fingertip into her pussy and groaned roughly.

"You're tight," he muttered thickly, sounding a little crazed. He removed his finger. "And wet. God, you're soaking. You enjoy being punished, don't you?" he said against her lips. She whimpered as he transferred some of the juices from her slit to her outer sex. His finger burrowed between her labia.

"Answer me," he said harshly.

"*Yes.*"

He seized her mouth in another scorching kiss.

She cried out in stark arousal. He'd been too tall to easily reach her pussy while they stood, but now he had her exactly where he wanted her. She was completely at his mercy, she realized, holding her nude body against him, her entire weight held suspended with one arm. He pillaged her mouth while he palmed her outer sex and stroked her clit with bull's-eye precision.

Not that she was protesting. She was about to ignite.

She bobbed her hips eagerly, increasing the pressure of his finger and kissing him back for all she was worth. Oh, this was delicious. The friction mounted as she bounced in his hold, riding his hand. Her clit simmered. She was going to explode into a million pieces.

Her rabid arousal was interrupted by a smacking sound and a burst of pain. Lucien had spanked her sore bottom. She cried out into his mouth. He sealed the kiss. She blinked, trying to bring him into focus. When she did, she saw his rigid features.

"You do not ride me," he said gently. "I ride you."

"*Nobody* rides me."

Lucien's eyes flashed. She blushed when she realized what had burst out of her throat without thought.

"We shall see about that. Now hold still while I watch you come," he said through a tight jaw. She opened her mouth to soften her outburst, but then his long finger was sliding between very slick labia and he was rubbing her clit, giving her just what she needed.

She gasped as distilled, focused pleasure smacked into her awareness. Oh God . . . he was exceptionally good at what he was doing. Lucien watched her, his light eyes gleaming beneath heavy lids.

"Let go, *ma chère*. Submit to it," he whispered hoarsely.

She couldn't escape it. It wasn't like she really had a choice other than to follow his command to the letter.

She clung to him even as she let go, abandoning herself to pleasure . . . giving herself to Lucien.

Part IV

When I'm Bad

Chapter Seven

Watching Elise come, feeling her body tremble against his, hearing her excited cries, inhaling her unique scent—all of it made Lucien's head swim in a sea of lust. His hand continued to move between her thighs, his finger sliding with ease in the delightfully lubricated valley between her labia, playing with her clit, prolonging her pleasure . . . coaxing more shudders from her firm, soft body.

He was going to eat her alive, she was so sweet. He was going to take her like a rutting bull. For a blinding moment, he pictured exactly how it would feel to have that tight, wet pussy melt around his thrusting cock, her muscular walls clasping him, pulling at him like a hot little mouth. . . .

He needed to taste her even more than he needed to fuck her. He was intoxicated with lust, but still greedy for more sensation, starved for the pure essence of Elise on his tongue and in his throat. She whimpered in surprise when he leaned over the bed and placed her back on the mattress. He had a fleeting image of her eyes blinking open heavily. He touched her lips with his before he lowered himself, his knees on the floor.

"Lucien?" she murmured, her voice thick with satiation.

"I will taste you," he said without preamble, spreading her white thighs. He stared for a moment. Her pubic hair was well trimmed, looking darker gold near her slit and between her labia due to her abundant juices. Her sex was a lush pink flower, the color of it decadently erotic in contrast to her pale thighs. Entranced, he parted her lips, revealing her swollen clitoris. Her scent filled his nose. He gave a low, feral growl and inhaled deeply.

"This pussy is mine," he muttered, barely aware of what he was saying, guided solely by a primal need to possess, and hardly hearing his own voice, his heart throbbed so loudly in his ears.

He slid his tongue through the creamy valley, agitating her clit. Her taste permeated his awareness and he was lost. He turned his head slightly, stabbing her clit with his tongue, only distantly conscious of Elise's cries of surprised pleasure and her fingernails scraping his scalp as she held him to her. She was musk and honey and sunshine, golden sweet, the very flavor of sex. His sole focus became to get more of her taste, fill his mouth with it, his throat, his very being. With her juices as his reward, he learned her perfectly, discovering the optimal pressure of his tongue to pleasure her, the precise amount of suction she needed to make her cries go frantic.

He distantly became aware of several unwanted sensations battering at the edges of his rabid arousal. The sound of loud pounding on the door differentiated from the hammering of his heart.

"Oh, Lucien . . . *God* . . . someone . . . door," Elise gasped even as her hand tightened at the back of his head and she pushed him closer to her pussy.

"Shut it up in there!" a woman's harsh, cigarette-roughened voice shouted outside the door. "All that slapping and screaming and moaning, my customer is starting to get ideas that he can't afford!"

"Should . . . stop," Elise mumbled miserably. "I can't keep quiet. It's not . . . possible," she moaned.

But Lucien was too far gone to care about disgruntled neighbors.

He liked Elise's unguarded cries of excitement. He adored them. He continued to eat the sweetest pussy he'd ever tasted, determined.

"YOU! Don't act like you're not in there. Put a muzzle on it. Screaming like a banshee . . . giving my customers ideas . . . *French*," the woman added bitterly under her breath.

Elise began to squirm beneath him—he couldn't be sure if she did it out of arousal or if she was trying to get him to stop—but Lucien refused to be denied. He held her hips down on the bed and lashed at her clit ruthlessly while applying a firm suction. He felt her go rigid in his hands, a helpless whine ringing in her throat. He turned his head more and sucked her entire clit. The tension in her muscles broke. Her whine swelled to a sharp shout, quieted, then swelled again into a moan as another wave of climax hit her.

He soaked in the sensations of her hungrily: her desperate cries, her raking fingernails, her scent, her taste.

The woman pounded angrily on the door for the next several moments as Elise came and he drowned in her essence. By the time Elise sagged onto the bed, panting, and he took one last, reluctant lick between her swollen sex lips, all was quiet.

She lifted her head and met his stare. His rabid lust fractured for a moment from amusement. The dazed, vaguely bewildered expression on Elise's sex-flushed face was priceless.

"Was that Ms. Inga?" she asked him disbelievingly.

His hands transferred to her waist, his fingers delving gently into the muscles of her back greedily. He grunted in satisfaction. Her punishment and orgasms had made her flesh noticeably suppler.

"I have no idea if it was Ms. Inga. I've never made the woman's acquaintance, and have no desire to ever do so."

Still, what she'd said partially penetrated his brain. He glanced around the room, seeing the paint peeling on the walls, the rust stain from a leak in the corner, the threadbare carpet. He closed his eyes and willed the throb of his heartbeat in his raging erection to slow. He kissed a soft, pale thigh and stood.

What was he thinking? It wasn't time for this yet. He had coached himself not to become bowled over by her thousands of times, but the taste of Elise made logic a feeble thing.

"Get dressed," he said, purposely avoiding looking at the flushed, naked splendor of her as she lay there with her legs parted. She was a sex-mussed, unmade bed that he wanted to spend about a week in . . . for starters. He needed to gather himself. He'd almost lost control several times tonight, come *so close* to throwing himself wholesale into the inferno of her.

"I'll start to pack your things."

"Pack my things?" she repeated, shock ringing in her voice. She sat up slowly.

He glanced at her. His cock lurched against his trousers, the stab of arousal a sharp pain. He looked away, hiding his wince, and opened the closet door.

"Yes. You can't think I'd allow you to stay here," he said as he pulled a suitcase from the closet.

"I didn't think you had a say one way or another!"

"Again, you thought wrong. You're coming with me," he said, his tone brooking no argument as he tossed the suitcase on the bed and opened it. "Get dressed, Elise."

From the periphery of his vision, he saw her rise and move toward the dresser.

"Where are we going?" she asked, her incredulity now replaced by amazement.

"To my place."

When she didn't reply, he turned. She stood before the dresser, a T-shirt clutched in her hands, the material covering part of her belly and her mons, but little else. It took him a distracted moment to realize she looked utterly floored.

"You want me to move in with you?" she asked, her voice sounding hollow with shock.

"Yes," he said, his matter-of-fact tone belying his wariness about the plan. He began tossing the items on her bedside table into the suitcase. "You'll stay at my place until we decide what to do." He frowned as he picked up a bottle of her signature perfume from the dresser top—Hermès Perfume 24, Faubourg—and rolled it up hastily in a silk bathrobe. "It's an . . . unusual circumstance, but we'll have to make do."

"Where do you live?" she asked breathlessly. He glanced back and wished she'd put on the T-shirt.

"Near Lake Shore and Astor. Not far from where we met at the market the other day." He located a plastic bag and walked over to the closet, where he began scooping up loads of designer shoes and shoving them into it.

"That's a very nice area. But . . ."

"What?" he asked, his irritation growing when she continued to stand there, frozen.

Naked.

Lovely.

He raised his eyebrows in impatient expectancy when she didn't immediately reply.

"Well . . . don't you want to . . . finish?" she asked, staring at the bed and then down to his heavy cock.

His body leapt into full, throbbing readiness once again as he stared at her naked beauty and experienced the graphic fantasy of him laying her on that sagging bed and sinking into the glory of her. It was because of her uncertainty—what he could only call shyness— that he found his strength. How could such a flagrant wild child seem so naïve at times?

"I will not make love to you for the first time in this hellhole, but on my terms and in my place of choosing," he stated simply.

He saw her throat convulse as she swallowed.

"And Elise? The time *will* be of my choosing. Never think otherwise."

Rebellion flashed in her eyes, but she quickly cast her gaze downward, hiding it. Much to his surprise, she contained her pique sufficiently not to reply. She dressed fleetly before helping him pack up her belongings.

His condominium was everything Elise expected it to be, given it was Lucien's lair—sensual, rich, masculine décor set within the ideal backdrop of the lake facing the east and the labyrinth of sparkling high-rises to the north and the west. Of course, since it was Lucien, he was on the top floor of the building, occupying the premier penthouse.

When they first arrived in the hushed, luxurious residence perched high above the city, Lucien took the suitcase she'd been rolling along with the one he'd been carrying. "Why don't you relax for a moment here in the living room," he said, nodding toward the large, breathtaking expanse of space before floor-to-ceiling windows. "I'm going to get your room ready for you."

"*My* room?" Elise said, startled.

He studied her from beneath hooded eyelids. "I told you, we will do this at my pace. Are you willing to accept that?"

She bit her lower lip, trying hard to disguise her disappointment. She'd been hoping to lie next to Lucien's body, absorb his heat, his strength, tease him until he couldn't deny her the delicious explosion of his male power. She longed to be taken, to be claimed. She craved having her fill of him—of letting him take his fill of her—of falling into an exhausted sleep only to awaken and begin all over again. . . .

She'd never been so *hungry*, so starved for a man in her life.

When she noticed he waited, his eyebrows raised, she nodded reluctantly. Apparently, Lucien had different ideas as to how he wanted things to proceed.

"Say you accept that we'll do this at my pace," he said, and she realized he expected her to put the promise into words.

She vanquished her frown. "I accept."

"Good. Just give me a moment to get things set for you."

She murmured with pleasure a few minutes later when he led her into a large bedroom suite decorated with toasty brown shining antiques, beige walls, and decadently soft-looking ivory bed coverings and furniture. Silk and fine wool curtains draped elegantly from the floor-to-ceiling windows.

"It's a far cry from the Cedar Home Hotel," she murmured teasingly as she tossed her purse on the luxurious four-poster bed.

"I should hope so." She glanced up curiously when he paused a few feet away from her. What would he do now?

"There are fresh towels in the bathroom. My maid comes on Saturdays, Tuesdays, and Thursdays. If you have any special requests for food or other products, just leave her a note on the board in the kitchen. She shops on Tuesdays."

"Okay," Elise said uncertainly.

"I'll say good night. It's been a long day. I'd imagine you're tired."

"Lucien?" she called when he started to walk out of the room.

He turned.

"Thank you. I'll . . . I'll pay you back for this. Someday."

"You'll pay me back by being good."

But I want to be bad.

For a panicked moment when he narrowed his gaze on her, she wondered if he was practicing his mind-reading tricks again.

A few hours later, Elise cautiously turned on the light in the sleek, modern kitchen and padded silently across the white alabaster marble floor.

"Yes," she whispered triumphantly a moment later when she spied a pitcher of iced tea in the refrigerator.

After Lucien had left, she'd showered, read, and turned on the television in her suite and flipped distractedly through channels. Then, once she suspected Lucien slept, she had made a quick reconnaissance of the penthouse. It was larger than she'd thought, including a good-sized office, an elegant dining room, and a cozy, windowed breakfast area off the kitchen. She'd even discovered behind a closed door some stairs that led to a stunning private terrace on the roof of the building. The only room she didn't peer into was Lucien's, of course. She assumed his quarters were behind a closed, carved-wood door at the end of the hallway. The door reminded her a little of the one that led to his office at Fusion.

So like Lucien, to possess so many thick, elaborate closed doors in his life, she mused as she found a glass and began to pour herself some tea. The better to keep his secrets.

"What are you doing?"

She splashed some tea on her wrist when she jerked her chin around. She stared, her mouth gaping open. He stood at the entrance to the kitchen, wearing a scowl, a pair of ivory drawstring pants that hung low on his hips, and nothing else.

Very clearly nothing else.

"I . . . I was just getting some tea," she said, flustered by his unexpected appearance . . . by his appearance in general—the gleaming caramel-colored skin tightly gloving bulging muscle and cut, ridged abdomen. The ivory pajama bottoms set off his coloring to perfection. His chest was smooth, but there was a thin path of dark hair that began at his navel and disappeared beneath the waistband of his pajama bottoms. If she'd had to describe his physique with one word, she couldn't decide if she'd say *lean* or *muscular* because he was both—all sleek, coiled, primal male power.

"It's almost three o'clock in the morning."

"I know. I'm a night owl. I had trouble sleeping—I always have," she admitted when he just studied her with an incisive stare and didn't comment for several seconds. "Lucien?" she prompted.

"You used to have problems sleeping, even when you were a child," he said, as though he'd just remembered. "Your parents never gave you a bedtime. You were a law unto yourself in the nighttime hours, if I recall correctly."

She smiled and continued pouring her tea. "You used to be surprised that I would wait for you to come home."

"I'd come home from a night at the casinos in Monte Carlo in the early morning hours and find you curled up with a book in the parlor."

"I was just making sure you got home all right," she said, putting the pitcher back into the refrigerator. "I was quite jealous, you know. Of Monte."

"Of my gambling?"

"No," she said, picking up her glass. "Of the women who got to accompany you." She gasped in surprise when he approached her in two long strides and took the glass of tea from her hand. She watched in amazement as he matter-of-factly poured it down the sink. He glanced back and noticed her dumbfounded expression. He took her into his arms and she just looked up at him in amazement.

"It's not decaffeinated."

"What's that got to do with anything? I never drink decaffeinated tea."

He smiled as he looked down at her face. "It's time you started then, isn't it?" he asked gently. "Do you want some water?" he offered politely. She shook her head, too confused to speak. He took her hand and pulled her out of the kitchen.

"Lucien? What are you doing?" she asked when he led her into the room he'd designated as hers.

He paused next to her bed, her hand still held fast in his.

"Take off your clothes and get into bed, belly down."

She swallowed at the sound of his low, sexy voice. "Why?"

"I'm going to help you sleep. I can do it a fair bit better than that caffeinated iced tea would have."

He just stared at her following this disconcerting comment. She didn't know how to respond.

"You said you'd accept my rules. This is the chance to prove it," he said, his voice a quiet challenge. "Now, take off your clothes."

"All of them? Even the panties?" she asked a moment later as she peeled off her T-shirt.

"Yes."

For the second time that evening, she stripped in front of him, highly conscious of his stare on her.

"Are you going to spank me?" she asked shrilly as she drew her yoga pants down her thighs.

"No. I told you. I'm putting you to bed, in a very adult way."

She stood before him, naked and self-conscious, but he was busy drawing down the comforter and sheets. He waved at the bed. "Belly down, your hands above your head," he said. "Lie in the middle," he prompted when she sat at the edge of the bed. When she lay prone with her face in the pillow, he grasped one of her wrists. She jerked her head up and yelped in surprise when she felt him loop something over her hand. It was a thick black cloth cuff. He tightened it around her wrist. She pulled slightly and realized it was attached to a strap that appeared to be affixed somehow to the corner post.

"Do you often restrain people who stay in your guest bedroom?" she asked, amazed.

"I just put the restraints on this bed when we arrived, specifically for you." She stared at him incredulously. "I already have some on my bed."

She rolled her eyes, trying to disguise her anxiety. "Your maid must think that's pretty interesting every time she makes the bed."

"Maria is the soul of discretion," he replied levelly. "I will restrain you often. This will be a good opportunity for you to get used to being bound."

"But I thought you said you weren't going to punish me."

"I did. But I will restrain you for other things."

Her clit pinched in excitement. She resisted an urge to grind it against the soft sheets. "For what things?" she asked.

"For sex, certainly. For pleasure, frequently. When you find it difficult to submit, I'll use restraints, with your permission, to make submitting less of a challenge for you. You will have no choice but to accept what I give you. Tonight, I'm going to teach you to let go and relax . . . to begin to train you to my hand."

No choice but to accept what I give you.

Train you to my hand.

The phrases uttered in his low, decadently sexy voice reverberated in her brain and vibrated in her flesh. He sat next to her on the bed and she looked up at him in helpless excitement.

"I'm going to restrain your ankles and wrists. You will be at my mercy, but I will keep you safe, Elise. Always. If you let go and submit, I'll know it. I'll give you pleasure if you do. Do you trust me?"

"Yes," she mouthed.

He smiled and brushed a tendril of hair off her cheek. A shiver of pleasure went through her at his touch. "Then turn your face away from me and rest your cheek on the pillow. Your eyes have a way of undoing me. Try to relax. I'm going to finish restraining you."

Her heart began to thump uncomfortably against her breastbone as she lay there and allowed him to bind her naked body. When he got to her ankles, he flipped back the luxurious comforter and drew her legs toward each corner of the bed. It felt strange when he'd finished, to be spread-eagled, unable to move . . . vulnerable. He carefully covered her again with the sheet and comforter. By the time she felt his weight sink into the mattress next to her ribs, her breathing was coming erratically from nerves.

He drew back the bed coverings down to the top of her buttocks, exposing her back. He stroked the muscles deeply with a big, warm hand, and she shuddered in a release of anxiety and pleasure.

"That's right. It's time to give up control," he murmured. "Just relax."

He massaged her deeply, expertly for the next several minutes. She tried to resist, but his hands kneaded her rigid flesh into submission. Wherever did he learn the intricacies of pressure and release so well? She gasped when he swept his hand from her tailbone to her neck, applying a firm pressure. He repeated the movement, seeming to iron her anxiety and her resistance right out of her. She made a desperate noise in her throat as she tried to control an upwelling of emotion she couldn't comprehend.

"Let it go, Elise," he ordered, digging his fingers deftly into her shoulders. "Let go, period. I've got you. Just relax."

"No," she grated out when he grasped her rib cage, holding her completely at his mercy, and worked his thumbs along her spine. She had no idea why she was protesting. His massage was heavenly. It was the fact that he was telling her to let go of control.

"Yes," he said simply. He pressed his thumbs beneath her shoulder blades and maintained a relentless pressure. The air burned in her lungs. It hurt unbearably. It felt *so* good. She couldn't hold it in any longer. What was he doing to her with those devil hands? Something snapped in her.

She choked as emotion erupted out of her throat.

"That's right," she heard him say as if from a distance as he rubbed her back muscles, working the remaining tension out of her. She sunk into the mattress, gasping, every muscle in her body going limp, even though she never gave them permission to do so.

He continued to rub her—for how long she didn't know—occasionally murmuring to her in soothing tones, sometimes in English, sometimes in French. The torrential rush of feeling she'd experienced was unlike anything she'd ever known. She wasn't crying from sadness or anger, but from some kind of whirlwind of unnamable emotion that felt as if it'd been living in her body, residing in muscle and flesh without her permission.

The tears on her cheeks dried. A wave of sleepiness overwhelmed her, and her entire awareness focused on the sensation of Lucien's magical hands. He peeled back the covers, exposing her ass and upper thighs.

Her eyelids flew open. Tension sprang back into her muscles. His low chuckle and warm touch on her thighs reassured her anxiety, but did nothing to alleviate mounting excitement.

"Don't get worked up all over again. You did well. I'm proud of you. It's hard to let go, when you feel like the rest of the world could turn into an enemy at any moment. You come by your vigilance honestly. But you must learn to let down your guard with me," he chided. "Now . . . I'm going to give you a reward, something for especially sweet dreams."

His hand moved between her thighs, cupping her sex. Before she had a chance to say anything or respond, his finger deftly burrowed between her labia. She cried out, her arousal sharp, immediate, and unexpected. Had he done that somehow, built tension in her sex without her being aware of it? He rubbed and circled and pulsed, and she had no choice but to lie there with her legs spread wide, her spirit split open, and take every bit of pleasure he offered her.

She twisted her head on the pillow, desperate to see him while he touched her so intimately. Through several tendrils of hair, she saw him sitting at the edge of the bed, one knee on the mattress, his arm stretched between her thighs. With his other hand, he stroked his naked cock.

She stared, transfixed, her arousal mounting exponentially. She'd never actually seen his cock before. *God*, he was so beautiful. His pajama bottoms were bunched below the protruding shaft, hiding his balls, but his cock was large and thick, the crown shaped like a fleshy, tapering mushroom cap. She recalled how succulent it had felt next to her lips and tongue. Her mouth watered. He stroked himself as he stared at his other hand moving between her thighs. She watched, transfixed. Something about her helplessness, her inability to touch him, somehow sharpened her desire until it cut at her.

It was all too much. She dropped her head to the pillow as the pleasure crested and broke.

"Yes, that's right," he said gruffly from above her as she began to shake in delicious orgasm. "Now you're beginning to learn what it means to submit to me."

He nursed her through her climax, his fingers agile and knowing in the slippery flesh. The entire time, she kept her gaze pinned to his big hand moving like a piston over his swollen cock, faster and faster.

"Lucien," she cried out as he coaxed yet another shudder of climax out of her. He glanced at her face for the first time, both of his hands still moving . . . pleasuring them both. A convulsion went through his rigid facial muscles and she realized he was coming, too. Jets of white semen shot onto his flat, ridged abdomen as he jacked himself with a forcefulness that both stunned and aroused her. She felt his gaze on her as she watched him ejaculate.

It was an incredibly intimate, powerful experience.

His hands slowed. Their soughing breaths cut through the silence. Eventually, he reached for some tissues on the bedside table and used them to mop up his emissions, his manner matter-of-fact. Arousal prickled at her sex once again, but her climaxes had been so powerful she was mostly utterly satiated. By the time he stood and released her restraints, she was a muscleless mass of limp flesh. She wanted to turn around and look at him when she felt him sit on the bed next to her, his touch reassuring on her back, but she was too overwhelmed with heavy, warm drowsiness.

"Are you awake?" he asked quietly when he'd covered her, tucking the sheet firmly around her.

She made an incoherent sound.

"We will do this every night at eleven thirty until your body learns when it's time to rest and your mind learns to let go and relax. Do you understand?"

She understood and was more than willing. It'd been a delightful, wonderful experience.

Yes, she attempted to say. How frustrating. She was having trouble moving her lips. They weighed far too much. Trying to say the word out loud was the last memory she had until morning.

Chapter Eight

Four days later, Denise Riordan watched and instructed Elise as she put the finishing touches on a new dish they were doing for a special—smoked salmon terrine with mushrooms. Elise glanced up distractedly when the kitchen door swung open. She noticed Lucien's singular form and started, cursing under her breath when she poured some aioli sauce on the table instead of the plate.

"It's okay. Here," Denise said, taking the sauce from her and handing her a towel. "It looks marvelous," Fusion's new chef said with a smile before she handed the dish to a waiting server.

Elise glanced at Lucien skittishly. It had become rare for her to encounter him. She thought she might have seen more of him before she moved into his penthouse than she had in the past four days.

Of course . . . he *did* put her to bed every night, getting her used not only to falling asleep, but to the restraints. Not to mention his magical hands. The hard part wasn't accustoming herself to his touch. The difficult thing was not aching for his touch every second of the day and night.

Heat rushed into her cheeks at the compelling memories of

watching him masturbate, of him touching, rubbing, and pleasuring her until she was a mass of quivering goo.

That's all she really saw of him, those scant, decadently erotic moments when she was restrained and he masterfully coaxed her body to relax . . . let go . . . release. Last night, she hadn't even seen him, because he'd insisted on blindfolding her.

"You are refusing to cooperate," he'd said as he tied a silk scarf he'd found in her drawer around her eyes. "I tell you to keep your head turned, but you keep watching me, don't you? Greedy little thing," he'd murmured as he tightened the knot, his tone warm and amused.

It'd been worse—far worse—leaving things to her imagination, graphically picturing him stroking his cock while he made her shudder in bliss.

He said he was busy finalizing the details on the hotel purchase, and she supposed that was true, because he was rarely either at Fusion or the penthouse. She knew he occasionally went to his club for a polo match, but as of yet, he hadn't asked her to accompany him. The only hint of hope she had in that direction was that he'd alluded to the fact that he'd look for a mount for her so that they could ride together on the grounds.

She'd never felt so good as she had after so many nights of solid, deep sleep. Yet each morning, she woke up alone. All that extra energy was nice, but it was also leaving her with an unsatisfied edge. Not once had she been treated like this in her life. She was accustomed to men going too far in the other direction—bending over backward to please her, following her every demand to the letter, even pulling crazy stunts to get her to notice. Erik Cebir, for instance, the man her parents wanted her to marry, had asked her once if she liked fishing, and she'd idly replied that she did. Erik had responded by buying a brand-new yacht—complete with eight bedrooms—which he'd proudly dubbed *The Golden Elise*. He'd hidden his irritation quite well when he'd finally gotten her out in it to learn she knew absolutely nothing about, nor had any interest in, deep-sea fishing. When she'd told him she enjoyed fishing, she'd been referring to dropping a line off the end of a dock, like she had with Lucien during that summer of her youth. Despite her lackluster interest in hooking a gigantic tuna, Erik had rallied to please her in other ways.

She knew very well most men were doing it because of the lure of her status and wealth, and that it had absolutely nothing to do with her value as a person. They didn't really know her, and for the most part, none of them seemed that interested in discovering her character. But that didn't change the fact. It was what she had grown to *expect* from men, even if it wasn't necessarily what she desired.

Lucien had changed all the rules on her, and she suspected he knew perfectly well what he was doing. He knew her habits and her former lifestyle as well as anyone, after all. Her frustration was mounting by the hour. She couldn't possess what she wanted most— the gorgeous, insufferable, aloof man who stood regarding her now like she was about as interesting as the dirty pans stacked next to the sink.

"May I steal Elise from you for a moment? I need some clarification on her tax information from when she was under salary. I promise it won't take long," Lucien said to Denise.

"Of course; she's been working nonstop, and the lunch rush is almost over," Denise said as she ladled some steaming tomato bisque into a bowl and garnished it with goat cheese and freshly baked croutons. Elise respected Denise and was thankful that they got along so well. Compared to many chefs she knew, Denise possessed a very even temperament. She'd never learned better how to shut up and tamp down her pride than she had in cooking school, working with so many large personalities.

No, that wasn't entirely correct. She'd never learned better how to restrain her pride until she'd encountered Lucien in Chicago, she thought as she wiped off her hands and approached the tester of her temper himself. He tilted his head in a request for her to follow him. By the time he'd led her silently to his office and shut the heavy carved door, she was starting to get nervous. She hadn't believed him for a moment when he'd mentioned the tax information. Everything she'd given him had been correct and up-to-date.

She watched him as he went behind his desk and sat. He was wearing a pair of jeans today, the fit of them highly distracting, along with an open-collared white shirt and a black blazer that emphasized his wide shoulders. Behind his huge mahogany desk, he looked every inch the commanding, compelling lord of the manor.

"What's wrong?" she asked him shakily.

He blinked at her question. "Nothing is wrong. Why would you assume something is?" he asked, a smile pulling at his mouth.

"It's just . . . you don't usually call me back here." Her hand instinctively strayed to her bottom as she recalled him punishing her here in his office. His gaze flickered downward. His smile widened.

"Have you been bad, Elise?" he asked, his tone a low, sexy tease.

Damn those dimples of his. Realizing she'd been touching her ass, she pulled her hand away.

"Of course I haven't. Why did you ask to speak with me?" she asked curiously.

"I thought you'd like to know I have bought you a mare."

Her heart leapt. His smile widened as he studied her reaction.

"You bought me a horse?" she asked excitedly, approaching his desk. "Where is she? When do I get to see her?"

He held up his hands in a pause gesture. "I'll take you to the stables this evening after I close Fusion."

She made a frustrated sound. *Lucien had bought her a horse.* "I can't wait that long."

"You will, because you must," he told her with a pointed look that was softened by a fond smile. "You're going to love her."

"I know," she said irrepressibly.

"How do you know?" he said, chuckling as he stood and came around the desk.

"Because you bought her for me," she said. He looked surprised when she rushed him and threw her arms around his waist. When she glanced up after she'd given him a hug, she saw that he was also pleased. His arm slid around her back. He reached up and touched her cheek softly.

"You look radiant," he murmured, caressing her. "It's like holding on to sunshine, having you in my arms."

Warmth flooded her at his off-the-cuff compliment.

"It must be the beauty rest you're getting every night," he said.

"If it is, it's the beauty rest you give me," she said breathlessly, feeling light-headed at suddenly finding herself in his arms. She arched against him provocatively, pressing her breasts against his ribs and chafing the tips by rubbing back and forth an inch or two. She felt his body stir. A low sound of satisfaction purred in her throat.

His expression hardened. He gently peeled her arms from around his waist, ignoring her frown as he moved away.

"From a few things Denise has said to me, I gather you haven't told her about moving into the penthouse."

"That's right," she said. "I thought you'd want me to keep it a secret. Was I wrong about that?"

"Not at all. But we hadn't discussed it. I want to thank you for being discreet. You technically work for Denise, not me, but she is my employee. I wouldn't want her to feel uncomfortable, or that the situation is unfair in any way."

"I would never allow our relationship to interfere with my training," she said resolutely. He didn't reply for a moment, and she reviewed what she said. She blushed. "Not that we really . . . you know . . ."

"What?" he prompted

"Have a relationship," she said, glaring at him. Her scowl deepened when his smile returned.

"It's too bad you don't think so, as I usually don't ask women I'm not in a relationship with to move in with me."

"To the spare bedroom," she added under her breath.

"Pardon me?" he asked politely.

"Nothing."

"Is there something you want to ask me?" he prompted. His sudden intensity confused her. Why was he always asking her that? She shook her head stubbornly. She'd be damned if she begged him to take her completely . . . to claim her. He either wanted her or he didn't.

"All right, if there's nothing. There's something else I thought I should mention, even though I'm sure it's not necessary. You showed so much discretion with Denise and the other employees here at Fusion," he said as he picked up an envelope from his desk.

"What do you mean?"

He glanced up, and she sensed the tension he'd been trying to disguise as he rifled through his mail with seeming distraction.

"I spoke with Ian a few moments ago about our fencing practice tomorrow. He and Francesca are coming here for dinner tonight. Ian mentioned Francesca wants to speak with you about setting a time and date for a run."

The silence pressed on her eardrums. She was beyond grateful and excited over the fact that he'd bought her a horse, but something about this topic sent up a warning flag in her brain. Suddenly, she was absolutely certain that this issue over Ian and Francesca was the real reason he'd called her back to his office, not the gift of the horse—or at least the horse had been secondary.

"And you wanted to make sure I didn't spill anything about moving into the penthouse with you to Francesca, either tonight or when we get together for the run?" she clarified.

He shrugged. "It would seem odd, wouldn't it? For you to be living with me after such a short period of time?"

"You're worried that you won't be there during the run to monitor me with Francesca."

He gave her a bland look. "As long as we understand each other." He casually strolled around his desk as he opened a piece of mail.

"I'm not sure I *do* understand," she said slowly.

He froze and glanced back at her, his gaze hooded.

"What do you mean?"

"Why do you care so much what Ian Noble thinks? Why are you so . . . *interested* in Ian Noble, period? Does he have something you want? Are you maneuvering for something? Business-wise?"

"Of course not."

"Why can't you just tell me what you're doing? Maybe I could help you."

"Drop it, Elise."

She blinked at his sharp, quiet command. She didn't want to ruin this moment after he'd told her about the horse, but something uncomfortable fluttered in her chest and settled like lead in her belly. She'd grown up in an atmosphere of deceit and cunning. Every move her mother or father ever made was premeditated, designed for a specific result. She knew Lucien had grown up under similar circumstances. Worse ones. Lucien's father could have taught Machiavelli a few things.

"Ian Noble has got nothing to do with you—with us," he said.

She made a scoffing sound.

"I refuse to be blackmailed," he said. "If you feel that it's so imperative, go to Noble and tell him what you think you know."

"Oh, right. And then you'd toss me out on my butt," she said hotly. Had he just asked her to stay with him at his penthouse because he wanted to have something over her head to keep her quiet? Was it just more convenient for him to keep her under control if she was nearer to him?

"There's no question of me tossing you out. Don't get worked up over things that don't concern you. Not everything is about you, Elise."

"I know that!" she said, stung. "I just don't understand why you're being so secretive."

"It's not up for discussion. You either trust that I'm not up to something harmful, or you don't. I'll leave that up to you," he said, sitting down at his desk. He opened a leather-bound journal and a pen and began to enter some numbers.

She'd been dismissed.

She turned and stalked out of the office, feeling bewildered and irritated over the combination of his thoughtful gift and subsequent maneuvering for her silence. Her desperation mounted.

Lucien wasn't anything like his father.

Of course he wasn't.

So why did he behave so secretly at times?

Lucien was glad to see that she stayed late that night. He thought she might leave Fusion in a temper when her duties were done, refusing to accompany him to the stables after their earlier disagreement. He'd observed her interaction with Francesca and Ian earlier, and she'd done well with the possible exception that she'd pointedly omitted him from her warmth and charm. He could tolerate that himself, but Ian, at least, definitely noticed her giving him the cold shoulder.

"Are you ready to go?" he asked evenly as he entered the kitchen. Most of the lights had been turned down. She stood behind a wooden chopping table, stacking some plates. He saw that she'd changed out of her chef's smock and wore a pair of white Martin jeans, the flagship product of her father, Louis Martin's, famous fashion house. With the jeans, she wore a dark blue fitted T-shirt that emphasized her small waist and full breasts.

She merely nodded. He couldn't tell from her pale face if she was still angry or not. In fact, he couldn't read her mood accurately for the entire ride to his club. She was polite but quiet for most of the forty-minute ride.

The club was located in a forested area in a western suburb. The guard at the front entrance had been told Lucien planned a late-night visit to the stables. He opened the gate with a friendly wave. Once they cleared the lit clubhouse, the road that led through dense trees was shrouded in thick darkness. The grounds were desolate at this time of night.

"I can't wait to meet her," Elise broke the silence finally when they alighted in the parking lot. In the distance, the polo field was lit with a few floodlights, the forest surrounding it looking like a looming shadow. He heard excitement vibrating in her voice. He smiled into the darkness. The girl he remembered who had loved horses still existed inside her. "What's her name?" she asked.

"Kesara. She's still a filly. She'll be three in a few months."

"She's not a polo pony, is she?" Elise asked as they approached the dim stables. Stan, who lived on the grounds a half-mile or so down the road and who looked out for the thirty or so horses that were stabled there, was clearly not around.

"No. She's for riding. There are some nice paths and fields on the grounds."

"I'll bet it was hard to find a club that features polo in the States? It's not a very popular sport here, is it?"

"No, but it's popular among a few people in the area and becoming more so."

"You're the former member of the French national team. You must be a bit under-challenged by the quality of the competition."

"It's fine. We just do it for fun, and besides, I'm not a young man anymore," Lucien said, opening the door.

Elise snorted.

"It's true. My mount gives me enough challenge as it is. He's a firebrand."

"What's his name?" Elise asked in a hushed tone as they entered and heard soft whickers in the distance. The familiar rich, fecund scent of the stables entered his nose. They passed the tack room. A few of the horses' heads flicked up when Lucien turned on a light.

"Jax. This is him," he said a moment later. The huge, nearly black stallion jerked his head when he petted him, giving a harsh snort. Jax batted his hand in a rough gesture that Lucien recognized as gruff acknowledgment. The animal stilled when Lucien gave the corded muscle of his neck a deep rub.

"Oh my God, he's gorgeous," Elise enthused. She reached up to pet Jax, and the horse bared his teeth, whinnying irritably, the whites of his ebony eyes showing. Lucien hastily grabbed Elise's hand and led her away from Jax.

"He's no pet. Best to sweet-talk and coddle Kesara here," he suggested, leading her several stalls down to a sleek, brown filly who stood watching them, eyes alert and watchful. "Kesara, meet Elise," he said, glancing to the side and noticing Elise's gaze still lingering on Jax. She turned to look at the brown mare. Her eyes went wide.

It was love at first sight, he could tell, and the feeling was mutual. Kesara whickered softly as Elise petted and greeted her in a low, confidential tone. Kesara's ears flicked with interest. For a moment, Lucien found himself listening to the silky, soothing sound of Elise speaking in French to the horse, lulled just like the animal . . . charmed. The dulcet tones made his skin prickle, his body stir. His gaze lowered to the taut, sleek curves of Elise's hips and ass optimally outlined by the tight jeans and T-shirt. All the lust he'd been holding at bay suddenly flooded into his flesh.

Blood pumped into his cock, thickening it in a manner of seconds.

She turned, grinning with pleasure over Kesara. She paused when she saw Lucien, her eyes narrowing, her smile widening. His gaze was hot and wanting as he stared at her ass.

Damn him. She knew he wanted her. Why was he toying with her like this? She was sick of it. Why was he so intent on controlling her . . . on insisting she submit?

I'll make *him take me.*

She blinked at the raw intensity of her thought. Suddenly, she knew precisely what she was going to do to get what she wanted.

"Can we go for a ride?" she asked him eagerly.

He shook his head. "It's too dark. I'll bring you out on Sunday."

She used her eyes to seduce him. "I want to ride now. Please? She's so beautiful. We can just go around the polo pitch."

He paused, considering. She slicked her lower lip with the tip of her tongue, seeing the spark ignite in his eyes.

"All right," he conceded, removing his jacket. She was careful to hide her triumph. "Wait here while I saddle them up."

He'd finished Jax and had him tethered near the horse exit door when Elise asked for the location of the restroom. He pointed and gave her some instructions. She watched him enter Kesara's stall. Instead of going to the restroom, which she really didn't need to use, she quietly opened the stable door. Jax tossed his head up and gave her a defiant, one-eyed glare when she approached him. She smiled grimly and reached for the pommel.

A minute later, he heard what sounded like a door opening and Jax's disgruntled whinny.

A feeling of dread swooped through him.

No, she wouldn't.

He rushed out of Kesara's stall and saw the stable doors wide open, neither Jax nor Elise anywhere in sight.

The devil made me do it.

The words zoomed into her brain as Jax flew into the night and a mixture of terror and excitement made her heart leap into her throat.

She didn't mean the biblical devil. She meant the man who'd been bedeviling her for weeks. Lucien's angry shout pierced the night, but Elise was too preoccupied with staying on Jax's back to pay him much mind. She bent low, her chin just inches from Jax's flying mane, her thighs clamped on the saddle like a vise. She gathered the reins and pulled for all she was worth, but the large, strong animal had been startled when she'd crawled up onto his back.

Startled and pissed.

She was a good rider, but she hadn't been on a horse in over a year. Plus, she'd never been on a mount as strong or fierce as Jax. He shot across the dimly lit pitch, Elise clinging onto his back like a leech that was about to lose suction.

Maybe this hadn't been the wisest choice after all. But when had she ever been wise when she grew desperate?

"No, Jax, no," she pleaded desperately when the animal cleared the pitch and entered the forest. For a few wild seconds before darkness almost completely encapsulated them, she saw that it was a wide horse path. Jax was clearly familiar with it. He barely slowed with the dirt beneath his hooves instead of the grass. The animal bolted through the forest, Elise hanging on for dear life and beginning to panic over her decision to goad Lucien.

Damn him. If he only wasn't so insufferable—staring at her ass when she wasn't looking with those hot gray eyes, acting like he didn't want her when she knew perfectly well he did.

Her eyes were blinded by the patchy clouds and the dark trees. Jax pounded on the path, the sound of his hooves hammering into her ears and mixing with the terrified beats of her heart. The horse's footing was sure. If she just hung on, he would eventually tire.

Wouldn't he?

The boundless, raw energy she felt exuding from the animal made her doubt her self-assurance. At least he hadn't tried to throw her. Her eyes adjusted to the darkness. Very dim starlight helped her to make out the tops of the trees. Her thighs began to burn unbearably from the tight clamp necessary to stay on the horse's back. If Jax bucked or reared, she wouldn't be able to hang on.

Suddenly she became aware of the sound of distant hooves behind them.

Lucien.

Relief surged through her. Her increasing terror at being on the back of the out-of-control animal trumped the dread of his reaction.

"Jax!" Lucien shouted in a hard voice several moments later from behind her. Jax whipped up his head sharply and let out a throat-tearing whinny, the action and sound making her fear he'd rear.

"Hang on, Elise. Do *not* let go. Jax, slow down, you demon," Lucien bellowed from behind her, sounding wild with worry, not to mention furious. Could he catch up before she lost her strength and fell off? she wondered frantically. Elise could tell by Kesara's sleek form that she came from a family of racers, while Jax came from a long line of horses bred initially for the brute force and perseverance required on the battlefield, and in modern times for polo. But Jax was pitched into a frenzy.

She had herself to thank for that.

She heard the sharp cracking noise of a crop on horseflesh and had an image of Lucien back there, urging Kesara onward. For a crazy, brief second she hoped Jax would keep running.

"Jax," Lucien called sternly, his voice sounding closer this time.

Jax snorted loudly. At first, she noticed no change in the animal's pace, but it began to enter her awareness that he slowed. The sound of Kesara's clattering hooves drew nearer, mixing with the sound of Jax's ragged pants. He was tiring. He slowed to a fast trot. She heaved a sigh of relief, easing some of the brutal pressure she'd placed on her thigh muscles. She pulled on the reins and Jax finally responded, slowing even more.

The horse came to a halt. She remained bent over, panting, holding the reins in a death grip. She heard Kesara and Lucien come up beside them and come to a stop.

"Lucien?" she asked shakily a moment later when she felt his body brush her leg. She could just make out his tall shadow from the weak starlight. He put his hand in front of hers on the reins. Jax pranced and her heart again leapt into her throat.

"Whoa," Lucien said in a low tone. Jax calmed, and Elise wondered if Lucien wasn't patting his hindquarters with his talented hands, soothing him.

"Take your foot out of the stirrup," he said.

She did what he said. He grabbed ahold of the pommel, and the next thing she knew he was straddling the saddle behind her, his large body reassuringly solid and warm behind her. Without comment, he firmly took the reins from her and chirruped. Jax slowly turned in the path.

"Kesara?" Lucien prompted. Jax began to walk in the path in the direction of the stables. She heard Kesara's hooves on the path, following them.

"I'm so sorry," she began breathlessly. "I didn't mean to startle him. He bolted out of the stables before I could do anything to stop him. I only wanted to sit on him," she added lamely when Lucien remained intimidatingly silent behind her.

"You opened the stable doors," he said, his voice like frozen steel. She felt the tension coiled in his hard muscles as she leaned against him.

The fury.

Her heart quailed and then began to throb in her breast.

"Thank you for saving me," she said over her shoulder, part of her wishing she could read his expression, part of her glad she couldn't.

"Lucien?" she queried shakily when he urged Jax to a slow trot and Kesara followed.

"You would do best to be quiet. I'm furious enough as it is." He placed a hand on her belly and pressed back, forcing her into close contact with his crotch. Her eyes sprang wide when she felt the fullness of his flagrant erection, the heat of him seeming to pour into her body.

Oh no. He was a barely contained explosion.

"If it weren't for your white jeans, Kesara never would have been able to follow you in the dark. She doesn't know the trail yet. Jax could have easily broken your neck."

"I honestly didn't mean to—"

"I know exactly what you meant—to push both Jax and me into a frenzy, isn't that right?" he asked in a rough tone near her ear. She shivered uncontrollably against him. "Well, you've finally pushed hard enough, *ma fifille*. I'm going to give you precisely what you deserve."

She felt a long, rigid rod replace his hand on her belly. Dread and excitement pulsed through her when she recognized it was the crop. Well, this is what she'd wanted, wasn't it?

She must be out of her mind.

He held the crop firmly against her for the entire silent, simmering ride back to the stables, making sure her ass remained pressed tight to his cock . . . a constant, intimidating warning of what was to come.

When they reached the stables and dismounted, Elise nervously took Kesara's reins and went to unsaddle her and give her a rubdown.

"Just put a blanket on her," Lucien said sharply. "We'll give them a rubdown after."

After.

She knew after *what*. She avoided Lucien's gaze as she led the mare into her large stall.

"Come out here," he said a moment later.

She spun around in the process of covering Kesara with a blanket, freezing at the sight of him standing next to the closed half door of the stall. He rested one hand on the top of the door. In it, he held a length of leather tether.

She walked toward him slowly, her head held high, holding his stare. She wasn't afraid, necessarily. How could she be, when she'd been the one to instigate this?

She *was* almost unbearably excited. Not to mention worried she'd bit off more than she could chew.

He closed Kesara's door behind her and reached for her. The second before he seized her mouth with his own, her eyes sprang wide. He looked furious and wild with lust. His mouth settled on hers. He kissed her forcefully. Everything vacated her brain for a moment . . . evaporated to mist. There was no way thought could exist at the same moment as Lucien's hot, demanding possession. He'd kissed her before, but never like this. She felt sexually scorched by him. His hands came up to bracket her jaw. She went up on her toes, pressing her body against him, a willing, eager hostage to his mouth.

She whimpered, but he never broke their torrid kiss as he lifted her. Her legs wrapped around his waist, her hands went to the side of his head, furrowing her fingers through his thick hair and molding it greedily into her palms, inhaling his spicy scent, so hungry, so desperate to absorb every sensation of him.

A moment later, she blinked in disorientation when he set her down. Her gaze fixed on him. Every muscle in his body was rigid. She glanced downward and saw how full things looked behind the front of his jeans.

"That's just the way you wanted me, isn't that right?" he asked, his voice low, a menacing taunt. She realized he'd carried her over to a fenced-off pen. She'd seen something similar to it in other stables, where the groom hosed off the horses and the vet did examinations.

"Take off all your clothes," he said.

"But . . . do I have to?" she asked, glancing around the open area of the stables. His only reply was a fiery *What do you think?* glance. "What if the groom comes?"

"You should have thought of that before you climbed on Jax and pushed both of us to the brink, shouldn't you have?" he asked quietly through a tight jaw. "Why the hesitation? You must have known all along I'd do this. But you just had to push, didn't you. You just had to grab the reins." She noticed a flicking movement near his knee. Her gaze sprang to his face when she saw he held a crop. It was made of black leather and looked new in comparison to the worn, supple brown leather one he'd used on Kesara earlier. A flicker of anxiety and arousal spiked through her.

"All right," she said breathlessly, chin up. "But I'm only letting you do it because it sounds kind of interesting."

He exhaled a puff of air. His eyes looked crazed. "You nearly got yourself killed so that you could have a little sexual titillation?" She jumped at his sharp question. "God, I'm going to wear you out. Take off those clothes."

She began to undress hastily, draping the garments over the top rail of the fence. Dozens of horses were awake now, following the noise of their intrusion. It was ridiculous, but she felt self-conscious in front of the animals' gaze. Exposed. And what if the groom did drop in? It was late, true, but not *that* late.

"Do I have to take off my boots, too?" she asked, examining the stable floor. It was made of smooth cement so it could easily be hosed down and was straw strewn, but it looked clean.

"Completely naked," he said. Something about the edge of his voice made her glance up. He was staring at her bare breasts. Her nipples pulled tight. She jumped when he popped the leather slapper of the crop against his leg in an impatient gesture. That, and the dangerous glint in his eyes, made her hurry. A moment later, she stood before him nude. His nostrils were flared when she looked into his face, reminding her a little of Jax in a fury.

"Bend over the fence with your hands on the top rail," he said. She followed his instructions. Somehow she'd been expecting him to say just that. Expecting it . . . dreading it . . . anticipating it. A jolt of mixed excitement and anxiety went through her when he came up beside her. "Hold this between your thighs while I tie you up."

Elise looked up in confusion when he pressed the slapper of the crop at the top of her thighs, right next to her pussy.

"I . . . *What?*" she sputtered when he applied pressure and the slapper started to slide between her thighs.

"You heard me. Let the crop in, and then clamp your thighs around it. Do *not* let it slide down or drop it. Don't worry, it's clean. I just purchased it. I've decided to use it for riding you instead of a horse," he added darkly.

Her breath caught at that. She did what he said, bewildered, but instinctively reacting to the hard edge to his tone. After a few seconds of squeezing her thighs tight to hold the crop in place, she started to understand why Lucien had made the request. First of all, she'd had to clamp her legs like a vise to stay on Jax. Her thighs were very tight and sore. They started to burn under the sustained pressure of holding the crop in place.

Second of all, gripping the potential tool of punishment against her pussy felt dirty . . . illicit . . . *good.* Her already sharp excitement mounted. Her clit tingled against the tightly wound leather of the handle. She tightened her thighs to increase the stimulation and winced at the burn of the muscles.

She saw that Lucien had witnessed her grimace.

"Devil," she accused softly when she saw his almost infinitesimal smile.

"You have yourself to thank for that," he said as he lifted the leather tether and began to bind her wrists to the rail of the fence. When he'd finished and walked to the side of her, she blushed as she considered how she must look to him, stark naked and bound to a fence in a stable, the black leather crop handle sticking out just beneath her ass.

"How dare you put your life at risk that way?" She heard the distilled anger in his voice.

She twisted her chin, wanting to see his face. What she saw in his eyes made her flinch inwardly. It was as if he considered a threat to her life a personal affront. He lifted his hand and swung, giving her ass a stinging spank.

"Don't you ever . . . ever . . . ever pull something like that again, Elise," he seethed, smacking her ass for emphasis as he walked behind her. She strained to see him. Her heart started to pound in her ears when she saw that he was stroking the length of his cock through his jeans, his handsome face tight as he stared at her bound body. "I can't believe you did that. No other man on the polo team can handle Jax—strong, skilled men. What were you thinking?"

"I just can't stand it when you ignore me . . . discount me . . . act like I'm about as interesting as the hay on this floor. I did it to make you notice!"

"Is that what you think?" he bellowed, sounding equally amazed and infuriated. "That I don't notice you? That I could ever *possibly* ignore you when you're near? Or even when you're not? Impossible. I'm as likely to ignore you as I would a fire in the room." His gray eyes reminded her of a wild electrical storm when his gaze flashed up to her face. Oh dear. She really had unleashed a tempest.

"I'm sorry," she whispered.

His expression hardened. "No you're not." She muffled a cry when he grabbed the handle of the crop. He jerked up slightly on it, firing the aroused nerves of her pussy. Pleasure tore through her.

"Do you like that?" he asked from behind her, his voice tight with lust. He started to move the leather handle back and forth between her thighs, stimulating her pussy. When she didn't answer because she was so overwhelmed by the illicit pleasure he gave her, he peeled back her buttocks and moved the crop deeper against her tissues. She cried out excitedly when the rod buried between her labia and rubbed against her clit. Lucien made a low, rough sound, and she realized he could probably see how wet she was.

"Look at that," he muttered as if to himself. "Your juices are going to season this leather perfectly. You're really making it your own, aren't you?" She moaned uncontrollably. He pulled back on the crop and worked the two-by-three-inch leather slapper between her thighs in a subtle sawing motion.

"Unclamp your legs a little," he ordered, his voice sounding harsh. Tense. Was he as excited as she was? Her nipples pinched tight at the thought. She did his bidding, parting her thighs and crying out in pleasure when he rubbed the slapper directly on her swollen clit, back and forth, around and around in small circles.

"Lucien." The naughtiness of what he was doing spiced her excitement unbearably. She began to bob her hips against the delicious pressure. But then the crop was gone from her hungry pussy.

Smack.

He'd popped her bottom with the slapper. "Oh, it burns," she said, referring not just to the prickling nerves of her ass but also to the sizzling of her clit between her clamped thighs.

"You deserve it," he growled, smacking her once more with the crop, mounting her excitement.

"Please, Lucien," she moaned. Lust had vanquished her pride. An untenable, monstrous ache swelled in her, a clutching fist of desire that needed to be released.

"Don't worry. I told you you'd get what you were asking for," he grated out. She noticed the crop fall onto the floor.

"Lucien—" she began, wanting to apologize. She wanted this— she was so hot and tense with desire—but she regretted pushing him. He interrupted her by lifting her. She heard a scraping sound on the hay-strewn floor.

"I need to raise you," he said from behind her. She gasped when he lifted her with ease, settling her feet on a smooth carton made of hard plastic. When he set her down again, she was elevated by several inches, her bottom closer to the fly of his jeans. Jax whinnied loudly behind them.

Her eyes went wide at what she heard next: the sound of his zipper lowering. Her heart began to race faster than it had when Jax bolted.

"You've tried me enough, Elise."

He noticed her looking back at him and met her stare. She sensed how aroused he was, how rabid with lust. Sweat sheened his upper lip and his eyes looked wild. His breath was coming raggedly as he hastily worked at the fastenings of his pants and lowered his boxer briefs.

She gasped when he pressed the thick, engorged head of his cock against her entrance. She could feel his heat penetrating into her. *Oh.* She'd never felt a man so rigid with need, so huge . . . so primed. Panic fractured her arousal. What had she been thinking? She couldn't *act* her way through this. She wasn't sure the mechanics of what he was trying to do were even *conceivable.*

"I had planned to take you the first time in an exchange of pleasure you would remember forever, but a hard, rough ride here in the stables somehow seems more appropriate. Damn you for always getting your way, Elise," he said grimly before he held her hip steady with one hand and flexed his hips forcefully, grunting when he went nowhere.

"Spread your thighs," he ordered tensely.

She opened her legs wider, feeling the cool air of the stables lick at her damp, exposed tissues. The anticipation was unbearable. He widened her vagina with his fingers and pressed the thick, engorged head of his cock into her slit, stretching the delicate tissues. She whimpered.

He held her hips with both hands and drove his cock into her.

She cried out sharply at the abrupt invasion. Pain spiked through her. He froze. She panted for air, blinking the sweat out of her eyes. The pain segued to a burn. She moaned shakily.

"Elise?" Lucien queried from behind her, sounding incredulous. Angry. But she was too distracted to consider his fury.

No . . . it didn't burn after all, she realized as she panted for air, struggling to assimilate the foreign sensation of Lucien's flesh penetrating her own. The quick flash of pain had quickly cooled to a simmering sensation of fullness and pressure. He pried her wide. But was that his heartbeat pulsing along the shaft of his cock directly into her clamping flesh?

Incredible.

She tightened her vaginal muscles experimentally. His groan sounded harsh, disbelieving.

"Elise?" he repeated, louder this time, sounding desperate. "Have you ever?"

"No," she managed between pants.

"*Merde.* Why . . ." He trailed off, a hard edge to his voice. She couldn't reply. The ability for speech had left her. He moved, sliding his cock in and out of her a scant inch. He leaned down over, until she felt his taut belly expanding and contracting against her back as he struggled for breath . . . for control. It felt so strange to hold him so intimately in her body, his rigid shaft pulsing high inside her, firing nerves she didn't know she possessed. She clenched tighter around him, experimenting with sensation.

He exhaled like his lungs had deflated in an instant.

He tightened his hold on her and flexed his hips. She moaned. "I can't stop it. You feel so fucking good," he said brokenly.

She gripped the railing and pushed her pussy along his shaft. "I don't want you to stop," she said, bobbing her bottom against him. "This is what I wanted all along."

"You're going to get it, then."

He slid his arm beneath her belly, holding her to him, and began to fuck her.

Her eyes sprang wide, but she saw nothing. Sensation ruled. He drove into her with short, powerful strokes, their skin slapping together in a sharp, staccato rhythm. At first, she experienced discomfort. But then his free hand found its way between her thighs. He rubbed her clit, pressing and circling as if it were a magic button he coaxed and tickled in order to gain full entrance. It worked. A slow, delicious burn grew in her, every pass of his hammering cock making it amplify. Every time he crashed into her, he finished with a tight, upward jab of his cock that increased the pressure on her clit. The sensation of his heavy balls smacking against her outer sex fired her excitement even further, until she bobbed her hips back for each stroke, increasing the pressure . . . taunting him to take more.

He popped her bottom as she struggled to ride him. *Little hedonist.* God, she was going to kill him. The sharp cracking sound of skin against skin cleared the fog of lust momentarily from his brain. He held her hips with both hands, stilling her, then bumped her ass with his pelvis, fully re-sheathing himself again with force in the paradise of her pussy. She squealed at the impact. The rush of heat around his cock informed him loud and clear, however, how much she liked the demanding stroke.

He raised himself. His shirt stuck to the sweat that rose on his body as he stood there with his cock buried in her. "Hold still," he insisted roughly when she whimpered and twitched her hips in his hands. He withdrew slightly, wincing as he looked down at his cock.

She'd been a virgin. He'd never been with a virgin before, so he hadn't previously known if virginity was a state a man could discern or not. It seemed blaringly obvious, however, or at least it had in Elise's case. Then she'd confirmed it, and he'd been caught in the delicious, agonizing trap of Elise's pussy. He couldn't move forward.

He sure as hell wasn't going to back out.

She'd been a *fucking virgin*. He told himself that again and again, but all he could focus on was her pussy squeezing his cock. She shrink-wrapped him—hot, wet, clamping. To make matters worse, he wasn't used to being inside a woman raw. For some reason, it'd been imperative for the first time with Elise. He both relished and regretted that decision now. She had a pussy that could drive a man stark, raving mad.

Again she bobbed her hips, trying to take control. He snarled and held her immobile, spanking her lightly.

"Who will ride whom, Elise?" he muttered roughly, grasping for a thread of logic . . . straining as her heat emanated into him and her muscles clutched and rippled. He watched the beguiling sight of her slender rib cage's movement as she panted for air and absorbed his question.

"You will ride me," she said in a breathy voice.

His cock lurched in her tight sheath. "That's right. Now hold still while I fuck you." He groaned in rising agony and held her to him, flexing his hips, withdrawing and then sinking into the glory of her. She really was an inferno, and now he was submerged in her, hard and high.

No going back now.

He beat their flesh together, fucking her in hot, feverish bliss.

He watched, spellbound, as he withdrew almost entirely and saw her abundant juices clinging beneath the rim of his cockhead before he plunged back into her.

God, there was no going back ever.

He slammed into her and they groaned in mutual pleasure. Snarling, he reached, pulling at the leather strap, releasing her wrists. He pulled her up, plastering her soft, supple body against his front, and resumed fucking her in a slightly bent-over, upright posi-tion. He clenched his teeth together at the delight of the taut new angle. He caught her scent and the haze once again began to crowd out his vision. He filled his hands with her luscious breasts, using his hold on her to pump her body back and forth on his cock. She joined in the frenzy, flexing her knees, bobbing up and down on him.

"Ooh, that feels so good. *More.* Make me take it . . . hard. I've been *so* bad."

He saw red with lust. He gave her a swat on her ass. She was driving him berserk.

"You're going to pay for that dirty mouth," he informed her. Hell yes, she was going to pay. But he was going to be the one to burn in torment, having her taunt him so perfectly.

He plowed into her, forgetting everything but this vibrant, beautiful woman who was burning him from the inside out. He didn't allow her much leeway, but she managed to bounce against him, straining at his hold, racing for the finish line. He firmed his hold on her, his palms sliding across the silk of her skin, his thumbs sinking into her buttocks. She tightened around him and keened as climax hit her. He growled at the feeling of heat rushing around his cock.

He pushed her back down into a bent-over position. Her hands went out instinctively, bracing herself on the rail. Swamping pleasure eclipsed his consciousness as he took her with long, pounding strokes.

All sounds blended, creating a roar of lust in his ears: the sounds of Elise's sexy whimpers and cries as he drove into her, the erotic slap of skin against skin, the blood pounding in his ears, Jax's snort and whinny of excitement in the distance.

He loosened his hold on her hips sufficiently to let her take part in their frantic mating. She immediately joined the frenzy, bobbing her ass in a smooth, taut roll, absorbing his forceful thrusts with her soft, strong body, taking him for the ride of a lifetime.

Another rush of heat flowed over his cock, her muscles tightening. Her whine segued to a scream. Her vaginal walls convulsed around him. *Ah God*, she was coming again.

He drove into her and held her ass tightly to him, roaring as pleasure ripped through him, feeling the shudders of Elise's body quaking into his—both of them shaking and gasping from the same impact, burning in the same fire.

He'd forbidden himself from leaping wholesale into her flame. He knew regret would come.

But the first thought that penetrated his bliss as his climax waned was how *right* it felt, how inevitable . . .

. . . how indescribably sweet.

Part V

When You Submit

Chapter Nine

When Elise came back to herself, it was to the delicious sensation of Lucien's chest and abdomen heaving against her back. His head had fallen between her neck and shoulder, and she could feel the warm bursts of his breath on her perspiration-damp skin as he tried to catch his breath. She shifted slightly beneath him. His cock twitched inside of her and her eyes flew open.

Lucien was *inside* of her. He'd long been inside of her in the figurative sense. Now he was in the literal one.

He placed his mouth on her spine at the base of her neck. She shivered with pleasure, instinctively tightening around the novelty of his cock penetrating so deeply inside her. He grunted softly and tightened his hold around her waist.

"What am I going to do with you?" he asked, his low, resonant voice near her damp skin making her shiver. She heard the regret that had started to seep into his tone, and she experienced her own guilt. Why *must* she be so impatient?

"Are you mad at me?" she asked cautiously.

Somehow, she just knew he would understand she meant, *Are*

you mad at my not telling you I was a technical virgin? As embedded in her as he was, as deeply entwined as she felt with him at that moment, she wondered if misunderstanding was even possible. She'd prayed things would go like the doctor suggested they might, but Lucien wasn't just any man. Not only was he smart and knowledgeable about women, he wasn't . . . made like other men in the physical sense. Lucien was fashioned more like a god than a mere human, in her opinion.

"I'm not sure," he replied gruffly. He pressed his lips against her neck again. How could his warm mouth confer so much delight? "I should be. Why didn't you tell me that you'd never been with a man?"

"I have been with men. This part"—she squeezed his cock with her vaginal muscles and a puff of air flew past her neck—"was just semantics."

He grunted. She stifled a protest when he raised himself slightly, missing the solid weight of his chest and his warm breath on her neck.

"It *wasn't* semantics. It's not a 'sort of' or 'maybe' state of being. You were a virgin in the truest sense of the word." She cried out when he slowly withdrew and she experienced a sharp burning sensation. He turned her in his arms so quickly, she didn't have time to hide her wince of discomfort. His expression stiffened. "And here is proof of it. To think of how I—"

He cut off his own words, looking grim as he examined her face.

"Don't look so somber," she whispered. "I wanted it, Lucien. I wanted my first time to be with you."

"I wish you would have told me. Your first time still would have been with me, just not so rough and—" He paused, as if considering what had just occurred. She sensed his regret . . . his heat. "Why did you goad me that way?" he demanded. He closed his eyes briefly when he heard the edge of anger in his voice. "Jesus. I could have made it so much better for you."

"I thought it was wonderful," she said sincerely, thinking with awe of what it'd felt like to have him harbored so deep within her, their heartbeats melding. "It wasn't what I expected at all."

"I can only imagine," he said wryly. She hated the flat expression that entered his gray eyes. "We'll talk about it later. Let's get you home. You should rest."

When they reached the penthouse, Elise headed down the hallway, feeling raw and uncertain. Lucien had been so subdued on the drive home. She kept detailing the memory of her impulsive decision to climb onto Jax's back, the harrowing ride through the dark woods on the bolting horse's back, and Lucien's fury at her for putting her life at risk so foolishly. He'd known perfectly well she'd done it all to get his attention . . . to drive him into doing precisely what he'd done.

Elise couldn't regret their passionate lovemaking in the stables. It'd been an amazing, eye-opening experience for her. She only regretted pushing Lucien until his control had snapped. She regretted *his* regret. How long would he be furious at her for what she'd done?

He caught her hand as she started to head into her room. She turned to face him. His features were cast in shadow as he looked down at her.

"I'll help you get your things," he said, his voice so quiet that for a split second she didn't register what he'd said. When she did, her heart began to pound in her ears.

"Are you kicking me out?" she asked shakily.

His brows slanted and he tightened his hold on her hand. "No, of course not. But there's no going back. I won't be able to deny myself, now that I've actually been inside you. You'll sleep in my bed from now on. Come on," he said, pulling her into her room and flipping on a light. Neither of them spoke as they worked together to gather her things from the bathroom and bedroom. Lucien's mood was solemn, Elise's bewildered and wary.

She'd been the one to push this. So why now did she feel so much disappointment in herself for her lack of control? No—for her insistence upon *taking* control of the situation.

Lucien went ahead of her with her suitcase and an armload of items. Elise finished packing up her toiletries from the bathroom and followed him a few minutes later. That feeling came over her as she quietly walked through the partially opened door to his private suite and looked around for the first time, the feeling she'd never really experienced before beginning this thing with Lucien.

Shyness.

He glanced up from his task of placing a lacy camisole in an opened drawer of a massive wardrobe cabinet.

"Come in," he said. "This wardrobe will be yours. I have another in my dressing room where I've moved my things."

"Thank you," she said, feeling awkward as she stepped farther into the large suite. His addictive scent tickled her nose—a combination of his skin and his soap and his cologne, Clive Christian 1872. It was a masculine room, a luxurious delight to the senses. Maria, his maid, hadn't been there that day, with the result that his enormous king-sized bed wasn't made perfectly. Instead, Lucien himself had obviously pulled up the thick, feather-filled comforter and draped the sheet back over the top of it. The multitude of dark brown, caramel, and ivory colored pillows were slightly askew. She liked the hint of disarray. His bed looked sinfully soft . . . extraordinarily sexy. She pictured Lucien rising from it just this morning, gloriously naked, and fluffing and straightening the duvet absentmindedly before padding away to his shower.

He touched her upper arm, and she looked up at him, guilt rushing through her as if he could read her covetous thoughts about him.

"I'll show you the bathroom and you can put your things away. Perhaps you'd like to take a bath afterward?"

She searched his gray eyes but found no hint of how he was feeling about all this. She'd feel more comfortable with his anger than with this cool, aloof Lucien. Perhaps it'd always been that way. She'd been trying to peel back his distant façade since she was a child, so eager to connect with him.

So desperate.

Several minutes later, she stood alone in the huge bathroom, which featured a step-up marble spa bath in the center of it in addition to a steam shower. She set her bottle of perfume next to his cologne on the granite countertop, a surreal sensation going through her at the vision of the bottles sitting side by side. She was living in Lucien Sauvage's home . . . sleeping in his bed.

It had to be a dream.

"Do you want me to draw you a bath?"

She stared over her shoulder, awe spiking through her when she saw the man who came with that low, sensual voice. He leaned in the doorway, his hands bracing himself on either side of the frame, all lean, sexy male power. It really was him. This really was happening to her.

"I . . . I'll just get my things and take a quick shower," she said throatily.

He nodded once and was gone from the entry. Again, regret spiked through her. A tantalizing thought sprang into her mind's eye of bathing and scenting her skin . . . of walking into the suite nude and intent upon seduction, of goading Lucien into taking her again and again.

She could do it. The stables had proven that to her.

But it had been a hollow victory.

When she walked into the suite, Lucien was gone. She grabbed some items from the wardrobe he'd designated as hers and returned for her shower. Ten minutes later, she left the bathroom wearing a loosely fitted pair of soft cotton men's-style pajamas. They were serviceable, not sexy.

He stood by the far side of the bed wearing nothing but a pair of dark blue sleep pants that rode low on his hips, fully exposing his ridged abdomen and defined oblique muscles. He was so beautiful to her, it caused an ache to expand in the area between her chest and belly. It was overwhelming, this swelling, intimidating feeling. She had a ridiculous urge to turn and walk back into the bathroom. Instead, she just stood there awkwardly. He glanced up in the task of pulling back the luxurious comforter and met her stare.

"Come here," he said gruffly once his gaze had run over her from head to toe. He strolled around the bed as she approached. Confusion mixed with rampant longing as she watched his sleek muscles flex as he threw back the comforter and sheet. He nodded at the bed, and she got in, sighing as she sunk into the decadently soft sheets and feather-top mattress. He came down next to her, stretching his long body. Suddenly the light went out and he was rolling her into his arms against him.

It'd happened so quickly, she went from anxiety to amazed arousal in a manner of seconds. He must have gone and showered in another bathroom. His smooth skin smelled wonderful, and there was still the trace of humidity in it when she touched it with her fingers.

"Lucien?" she whispered into the darkness, her cheek pressed against a dense pectoral muscle.

"Yes?"

"Are you still angry at me?"

She felt his fingers move in her hair. Pleasure rippled from her scalp to her neck and lower, tightening her nipples against his ribs.

"No," his deep voice resonated into her when she pressed her ear to his chest. "I'm angry at myself. I always have prided myself on understanding you—reading you, even when you were acting at your finest. But I failed in this, *ma fifille*. I'm sorry."

She lay there, stunned by what he'd said in his quiet, deep voice.

"What do you mean?" she whispered. For a moment, he didn't speak. Ripples of sensation cascaded down her neck and spine when his long fingers moved in her hair.

"I had told myself I wouldn't flinch at anything you ever pulled. But this?" He laughed harshly. "I would have never guessed it—that you'd never been with a man."

Tears stung behind her eyelids. "I *have* been with men, Lucien. Plenty of them. I'm no innocent."

"Yes you are."

He sounded so starkly sure, she lifted her chin.

She felt him exhale.

"You're a paradox, Elise Martin. A virgin siren. I should have known not to make assumptions about you. I should have reminded myself that you wouldn't make things simple for me."

She turned her face into his chest, sighing as he ran his hand down over her back. Emotion swelled in her, as it often did at his deft touch. "I just wanted you so badly," she whispered, her lips brushing against his skin.

"You almost got yourself killed in order to show me," he said. "It would have been better if you'd just told me what you were feeling . . . what you wanted."

"But you already knew how I felt, how desperate I was getting. You were being cruel by withholding yourself from me," she blurted out against his skin.

He cupped the back of her skull. She lifted her head, even though she couldn't see him in the darkness. "I wasn't being cruel. I was waiting."

She stilled. "Waiting for what?"

"For you to tell me what you desired. What you needed."

"But I *have* been telling you!"

"Have you?"

His rich, quiet voice ran over her in the darkness, making her skin tingle. The question kept ringing in her head. *Hadn't* she been telling him? She'd made it clear she was sexually available. She'd agreed to this arrangement. Lucien couldn't possibly deny that, could he?

"I have specifically told you I wanted us to be lovers, even agreeing to this unorthodox relationship you've suggested."

"That isn't the desire I've been waiting to hear," he said, his fingertip rubbing the base of her skull in a manner that lulled her, despite her pique and confusion. She opened her lips to demand more information, but then he spread his large hand across her cheek and jaw, and his mouth was closing over hers in a melting kiss. By the time he lifted his mouth, her greatest desire was right on the tip of her tongue.

"Go to sleep," he said.

"But—"

He pressed her head back down to his chest and gathered her closer in his arms. She bit her lower lip when she felt his cock stir against her thigh. "You showed discretion by wearing these pajamas. You're respecting my wishes instead of flaunting yourself, when you know how difficult it would be for me to resist."

She just lay there, part of her brain busy absorbing his words, the other portion focused on the sensation of his growing erection.

"You're going running with Francesca very early, aren't you?" he murmured.

"Yes," she mumbled. With all the tumultuous events of the day, she'd forgotten about that. Suddenly, her muscles felt too weary to even consider moving, let alone running for miles. "I'll have to set an alarm," she said sleepily, nuzzling Lucien's skin with her nose appreciatively.

"I already set it for you."

"Thank you," she said, sincerely grateful. It was sweet of him, to have thought of her.

"Go to sleep. It's been a long day for both of us. I rode you hard and rough in those stables. Any woman would need a night to recover from that, let alone a virgin."

"A once-virgin," she corrected drowsily. "And I'm perfectly well."

He made a sound of rough irritation and amusement, which caused regret to soak into her awareness yet again. Despite his tone, his long fingers trailed down her spine, caressing her, making her limbs go heavy with exhaustion. How could he be annoyed and yet touch her so cherishingly?

"Good night, *ma chère.*"

It was the last thing she heard before she sunk into the rich decadence of sleeping in Lucien's arms.

The next morning, Francesca and she jogged side by side, Elise watching with wonder as the round, red ball of the sun crested the shimmering blue lake.

"I'm not sure I've ever seen a sunrise before," she murmured as they jogged.

Francesca gave her a surprised glance, sending the end of her rose-gold ponytail across her shoulder. They'd met up before dawn in front of the building where Ian's penthouse was located. Elise had left her backpack filled with things for work with the doorman, and Francesca and she had taken off together in the predawn light. This was their first time running together and they were well matched as partners.

"Really? The first time?"

"I've seen them before, of course," Elise said. She noticed Francesca's bewildered expression at her seeming contradiction. "Sorry. I guess I was sort of thinking out loud. I just feel really *awake* this morning. Good. It's like I've looked at a sunrise before, but never really *seen* it. Have you ever felt that way?"

Francesca's dark eyes had a faraway look. "Yes. I think I know what you mean. I remember one early morning in Paris when I was with Ian. It was like the sunlight was hitting the world in a way that made it shine. Everything seemed new." Seeming to realize how dreamy she'd sounded, she cast Elise a rueful glance. Elise gave her a reassuring smile.

"Funny, that you should feel more alive than ever before in Paris. It's where I felt most dead."

Francesca looked at her speculatively. "I've gotten the impression from some of the things you've said in conversation that you led a very . . . privileged life there."

"I also led a very empty one."

"And you're happier now," Francesca more stated rather than asked, her gaze steady on Elise's profile.

"Yes. Oh, yes."

Francesca turned to look at the sunrise. For a few moments, only the sound of the light waves, their padding tennis shoes on the pavement, and the muted traffic noise on Lake Shore Drive hit Elise's ears. "You're right." Francesca smiled. "That sunrise is spectacular. Thanks for pointing it out."

"You're welcome," Elise said, smiling back.

"You sound very taken with . . . Chicago," Francesca said. Elise raised her eyebrows in surprise at the other woman's knowing smile. "Does that mean you plan to stay here when your training is complete?"

"That's my goal, yes. I have an idea. Some plans."

"What plans?"

Elise hesitated, tempted to be honest by Francesca's sincere curiosity. She liked Francesca, instinctively feeling comfortable with her. Still . . . she hadn't had the nerve to reveal this to anyone yet. Her secret aspirations made her feel very vulnerable.

"I have this idea about opening a unique type of restaurant that caters to people recovering from addiction. Not just for them, of course—anyone can come—but with them in mind. And not just a restaurant—a coffee bar and a club that offers music, maybe live bands and dancing. It's really hard for people with substance abuse issues to go out and have a great time without being tempted by alcohol. Being surrounded by liquor is a real trigger, not just for alcoholics, but for all substance abusers."

"You sound very knowledgeable about it," Francesca said cautiously.

Elise flashed her a smile. "I'm not an alcoholic or drug abuser, if that's what you're wondering. Although I had my period of partying until dawn, I could walk away from the booze. But yeah—I know something about it." She inhaled for courage. "I had a very good friend die from a heroin overdose."

Francesca's step faltered. "I'm so sorry. How awful."

"Yeah. It was," Elise said, breathing through the sudden pressure that tightened her throat. "It's still kind of fresh. He died a little over six months ago. Michael Trent. That was his name."

"Were you and he . . ."

"No," Elise said, guessing what Francesca was about to say. "We were just friends. Really good friends. In fact, he was one of the few friends I've ever had in my life, I'm ashamed to say," she added shakily. She covered her discomposure with a bright smile. "I used to choose friends very poorly. Or they chose me unwisely. Maybe both."

"I'm sure that's all changing now."

"Thanks," Elise replied gratefully. "I'd like to think so, anyway. Michael really changed the way I looked at things. Not just his death, or the realization of how impermanent, how fragile life is. His life changed me. I know people have a preconceived idea about heroin abusers, but Michael wasn't a stereotype of anything. He was unique. Wonderful. I met him at chef's school. He was the most talented of us all—a true culinary poet—but he never hesitated to offer any of us support and help when we were struggling. He just had this demon. He did battle with heroin addiction daily. Hourly. He finally succumbed to that monster, but his life had meaning. He counted. To me, he did."

She swallowed thickly and blinked the bright sunshine out of her eyes.

"And so you want to create this restaurant as a tribute to your friend's life?" Francesca asked soberly.

"Yes. But it's more than that," Elise said quietly. "My life was going nowhere when I met Michael. I was a shell, empty on the inside. I might not have had as malignant of a demon as heroin abuse to conquer, but my life was spiraling out of control. He infused hope into me . . . meaning. I'll always be grateful to him for that."

"He must have been very special."

"He was," Elise said, striving to control her emotions and succeeding. "So that's why I came up with this plan for the restaurant. It'd be great. Family members and friends of people struggling with addiction often feel like they can't take their loved ones out anywhere for dining and entertainment, for fear of triggering a relapse. This would be a place where people could go without worrying. Michael told me that in rehab, they learn a lot about nutritious food and cooking. Their bodies get really run-down from all those chemicals. A lot of them turn into foodies—like Michael did—but have nowhere to go to celebrate their love of food and dining. It all sort of goes together really well."

She glanced anxiously at Francesca, worried one incredulous or condemning look would silence her idea forever. Francesca hardly seemed disdainful, however.

"What a fantastic idea. You know who else it'd be great for? Dieters. Or not dieters, necessarily, but people trying to have healthier eating habits. It'd have everything. They could dress up and show off their new bodies; they wouldn't have to worry about the extra calories of the liquor, and they could go dance off their dinners," Francesca said, grinning.

"I hadn't thought of that," Elise said.

"Overeaters are addicts, too," Francesca said, her knowing manner piquing Elise's interest.

"You say that like you have some personal knowledge on the matter," she said, echoing what Francesca had said earlier.

"I do," Francesca said matter-of-factly. "I was an emotional eater as a child. Very overweight. It's one of the reasons I took up jogging when I went to college."

"It helped you with your addiction?"

"It helped me take back control of my body. My life. Well, I love the idea. You know who you should ask for help with the idea? Lucien." When Elise didn't immediately respond, Francesca turned to study her. It just so happened they were nearing the tall tower where Lucien—where *she*—lived.

"Don't you think that'd be a good idea? He has a surprising amount of contacts here in the city. Ian always says he can't believe he just moved here last year, the number of people he knows. Ian also has mentioned Lucien was at the center of the entertainment and restaurant scene in Paris. He's well on his way to becoming a hub here in Chicago, too." Something seemed to occur to her. "Hey . . . did you ever meet Lucien before you came to Chicago? Did you ever go to his restaurant there? Ian says it's very popular with the late-night crowd."

"Renygat?" Elise asked. It would be strange for her not to be familiar with Lucien's landmark restaurant if she'd lived in Paris. It'd be okay for her to at least acknowledge its existence. "I think I went once," she said elusively, staring distractedly at Lucien's building. She was thinking about what Lucien had said last night about asking for what she wanted. She'd been thinking about that a lot.

Should she bring up her idea with Lucien? She hadn't yet because it made her feel far too vulnerable. It would hurt, to see doubt on his face in regard to her proposal. It was one thing to put herself on the line to Francesca. She was a new acquaintance.

Lucien, though—that was different.

"That's Lucien's building, isn't it?"

Elise blinked, rising from her thoughts. "Uh . . . maybe. I think it might be." She noticed Francesca's amused, wry glance. "What?"

Francesca rolled her eyes. "Come on, Elise. You really can't believe that I think you're so casually aware of the details of Lucien's life."

Elise's heart seemed to bound ahead of her feet. She almost faltered. "Why *wouldn't* you believe that?"

"Just an observation," Francesca said. "There's some pretty strong chemistry between the two of you." She glanced aside and saw Elise's open-mouthed look of incredulity. "He can't take his eyes off you whenever you're near. Ian has noticed it, too."

"He . . . he has?" *Oh no.* Lucien was going to be so irritated.

"Yeah. But it's no big deal, is it?" Francesca asked when she noticed her stricken expression.

"No, I just . . . We thought we'd been discreet."

"Don't worry about it," Francesca said confidentially. "I shouldn't have said anything. It's none of my business. But just so you know, I think it's fantastic. He's a wonderful man." Francesca gave her a gleaming sideways glance. "And sooo gorgeous. And that *voice* . . . the accent—so sexy. Well, you have the accent, too, so I guess you don't think it's as hot as we would here in the States, but—"

"I think his voice is sexy," Elise said before she could stop herself.

Francesca grinned. "We're in agreement, then. Are you going to speak to him? About your restaurant idea?" she urged.

Elise bit her lip. "Maybe."

"Well, if you decide to do it, good luck. I know Lucien can seem a bit intimidating—I used to feel the same way about Ian. They're alike in that way. But I happen to know Lucien is a very good guy."

"Thanks. And you're right about the intimidating part. I think I need more nerve than luck," she muttered under her breath.

Especially because she wanted to be honest with Lucien about more than just her business idea. She wanted to take his advice and tell him how much she desired him . . . how much she wanted to submit to him. Putting such a fragile, vulnerable desire into words felt like one of the most daring, difficult challenges she'd ever faced.

That night she left Fusion before Lucien, as soon as she'd finished her duties. She was waiting for him when he entered the penthouse past midnight. She sat up, peering over the back of the couch, watching him as he walked into the living room. He was checking messages on his cell phone, a slight frown on his face. It took him a moment to notice her. Elise took advantage of the opportunity to study him at her leisure.

She'd left his arms reluctantly that morning when the alarm sounded, all too aware of his solid warmth pressed against her backside as he spooned her with his long body. She'd risen from sensual dreams with his scent in her nose and the feeling of his heavy erection pressed against her bottom, a few layers of thin fabric the only thing separating them. It was a heaven almost too difficult to comprehend, the concept of waking up in Lucien's arms every morning.

He'd stirred when the alarm sounded but had fallen back into sleep when she'd shut it off. Once again, she'd had the vivid fantasy of touching him while he was vulnerable, taking his full cock into her hand, putting her mouth all over bulging muscle and smooth skin, kissing, licking, biting . . .

It was precisely the type of thing her mother might do to take advantage of a man—seduce him while he was sleeping.

He'd tightened his arm around her in an instinctive gesture after she'd shut off the alarm. Elise had had to use every ounce of her will to leave his embrace.

Now here she was with him again and he was fully awake, and she was the one who experienced acute vulnerability.

He looked up suddenly from his cell phone screen, pinning her with his light eyes. A small smile took the place of the scowl he'd been wearing.

"What are you doing sitting back there watching me, quiet as a mouse?" he murmured, coming toward her.

"I was waiting for you," she said, feeling a strange mixture of contentment and anxiety at hearing his familiar rich voice in the hushed room. He wore a European-cut, sharp-looking black suit today with a tailored, cuffed shirt and a silvery-blue tie. He looked crisp and exotic and so masculine, it made her ache. He briskly removed his jacket, loosened his tie, and unfastened several buttons before he sat on the cushion where her feet rested. She smiled when he picked up her feet and placed them in his lap. She moaned appreciatively when he began to rub them.

"Oh, that feels good," she said, watching his large hands on her feet, mesmerized by the sight. He looked so masculine in comparison to her, so strong, his veined hands striking in contrast next to her smooth, pale feet. "Why were you scowling?"

"Was I?" he asked, pausing momentarily to meet her stare.

She nodded, noticing his slight distraction in addition to his desire to hide it from her. "Bad news?" she asked, nodding at the phone he'd placed on the coffee table a moment ago.

"Yes, as a matter of fact," he said after a moment.

"Lucien?" she prompted, concerned by his worried expression when he didn't continue.

"I've discovered that the executive I hired to manage the Three Kings Corporation has been embezzling money," he said tersely, referring to the three luxurious hotels in Paris that had come under his reluctant control when his father had been sent to prison.

"Oh no," she said sympathetically. "What will you have to do?"

"Deal with it," he said brusquely after a pause. "Monsieur Leboeuf will be arrested as soon as I get there to provide concrete evidence of the embezzlement. But I'd rather not think about it at the moment. I'd rather hear from you why you were waiting up for me."

Her heartbeat began to throb in her ears. "Are . . . are you sure you don't need to leave for Paris . . . book a flight right now?" she asked nervously.

His eyes ran over her face. "Yes. I will have to leave. Very soon. It's my fault, what's happened to the Three Kings."

"How can you say that? You hired that man because you trusted him. You had no idea he was going to steal from you."

He closed his eyes briefly. "My father's property was not a responsibility I wanted. But it is mine nonetheless. I've let hundreds of employees down because of my refusal to take part in his businesses . . . because of my stubbornness."

"Lucien, that's not being fair. You know it's not. It's a complicated situation. You being repulsed by your father's fortune and properties, by his legacy to you, is very understandable."

"Understandable, yes. Forgivable? Given the possible consequences, perhaps not," he said, meeting her stare levelly. "Why were you waiting up for me?"

Something about his tone told her the topic of the embezzlement and his guilt at what had occurred was closed.

"I . . . I wanted to talk to you about something, but that was before all this happened," she said, waving at his phone. "I don't want to bother you with unimportant things."

His hands enclosed both of her feet at once, his thumbs pressing gently into her arches. "You're not bothering me, and I consider what you have to say very important. What did you want to talk to me about?"

She swallowed thickly. He seemed so calm, so expectant . . . as if he knew precisely how difficult this was for her. How did one begin talking about their hopes . . . their desires? She felt naked, despite the summer dress she'd donned upon arriving at the penthouse.

"I . . . um . . . I was talking to Francesca this morning, and . . . she encouraged me to talk to you about this idea that I have."

"Idea?" he asked. As he spoke, he began massaging her feet again. Did he instinctively sense her anxiety and was trying to relax her? She'd never known anyone who could read her the way Lucien could. "Elise?" he prompted when her words got clogged in her throat. A shadow fell across his face as he studied her closely. "Just tell me," he insisted gently.

It all spilled out of her. Everything she'd told Francesca about Michael, about their friendship . . . the trauma of losing such a unique man. She told him her idea about the restaurant she wanted to open, the words coming out of her in a pressured fashion. She couldn't meet his eyes the whole time.

"And so that's all of it, I guess," she said after several uninterrupted minutes. Lucien still held her feet in his warm hands. Through the reflection of the floor-to-ceiling windows, she could see that his head was turned, and that he stared at her face. "Francesca said something about mentioning the idea to you because you know so many people in the industry. I thought maybe you could . . ."

"What?" he asked gently when she faded off.

"Help me," she whispered.

"Elise, look at me."

Her throat convulsed. She dragged her gaze off his reflection and met his stare.

"Did Michael give you those pearls?"

She nodded, tears burning in her eyes. "For my twenty-fourth birthday, just weeks before he died. He didn't really have the money to buy me a gift like that."

"You really loved him, didn't you?"

"Yes. Not in the romantic way, but *yes*. He changed my life."

"He brought you to me."

One tear skittered down her cheek at his stark statement.

"Of course I'll help you, Elise."

"You will?" she asked slowly.

"It's a very good idea. Why wouldn't I help you?"

"I don't need money or anything. By the time I can open the business, I'll have control of my trust fund. I just need advice. Support."

"You have both. You have whatever I can offer."

The tightness in her chest and throat amplified. "It's that simple?" Her gaze glued to his small smile.

"Yes. It's that simple. All you have to do is ask. You don't have to manipulate, or seduce, or do something crazy or dangerous . . . or forsake your pride. Those are the tools of our parents, of a past I'd rather leave behind. If it's within my power, I'll give you whatever you need. But you must ask."

Whatever you need.

His nostrils flared slightly as he stared at her. Again, she experienced his patient anticipation. "Did you want something else?"

His quiet voice tickled her ear and caused her heart to throb.

"Yes," she whispered.

"Then tell me."

Her lips felt numb when she opened them. His gaze was both blazing and somehow compassionate, like a steady, strong flame. It gave her courage.

"I want to give myself to you. I want to submit to you . . . please you. I want to trust you enough to give you control sexually."

His nostrils flared slightly. His massaging hands stilled.

"You don't *want* to trust, Elise. You either do or you don't," he said, his gaze narrowing on her. "You undoubtedly have had good reason for the majority of your life to keep a tight rein on other men. Do you trust me enough to let go, or don't you?"

She searched his features, looking for any hint that she was making a mistake. She saw nothing but his rock-solid fortitude. Still, it was a frightening thing, to trust.

"I trust you," she said, hoping he didn't hear the tremor in her voice.

She was glad of her decision when she saw the flash of happiness and pride cross his features. She tucked that expression on Lucien's face safely away with other treasured memories.

"Come here," he said, putting out his arms. She swung her legs around to the floor, anxious, but also eager to go into his embrace, to begin to discover well and truly what he meant when he said he wanted to dominate her sexually, to find out what it meant to submit to desire.

His phone began to ring. Elise glanced at the screen as she moved into his arms.

"It's the Hotel Louis," she said, pausing next to the couch.

Annoyance flickered across his features. He hesitated.

"It's okay, Lucien," she assured. "It must be an emergency, for them to be calling at this hour." Still, he didn't reach to answer it, seeming undecided. Finally, he cursed under his breath and snatched up the phone.

Elise's concern rose as she listened to him speak in terse French to whoever was on the other end of the line.

"It sounds bad," she said when he eventually hung up.

"I had Monsieur Atale, the manager of the Hotel Louis—a man I trust implicitly—look into something for me. He's been working on it and reporting back to me every few hours. It seems our main accountant was in on the embezzlement scheme. Monsieur Atale doesn't have adequate funds to complete the payroll, and it's payday tomorrow."

"I'm so sorry," she said, hating the worry lines on his forehead.

He pinned her with his stare. "I can handle the technicalities of getting things back on track. I'm just furious at those sons of bitches for forcing the issue now. Just when you finally spoke your desire aloud to me."

She gave him a shaky smile and sunk down next to him on the couch. She took his hand. "It'll still be my desire when you get back."

He squeezed her hand and lifted it to kiss her knuckles.

"You're going to have to leave tonight, aren't you?" she asked.

"As soon as my secretary in Paris can book me a charter flight. She'll be calling back any minute. I'm sorry, Elise. It's rotten timing."

"I understand," she assured, ignoring the ache expanding in her chest. "Of course you must go. The employees of all three hotels have dependents . . . families relying on them. They need their paychecks and jobs."

"I'm glad you understand." He stood and took her into his arms. When she looked up at him, he cradled her jaw, his fingers caressing her tenderly. He glanced at his cell phone and then back at her. She heard him curse under his breath. The next thing she knew, he'd swept her into his arms and was carrying her toward the hallway.

"Lucien?" she asked, amazed.

"A few minutes isn't going to make that much of a difference," he said grimly.

A moment later, he lowered her onto his bed and placed his hands on either side of her hips.

"Do you own a vibrator, *ma chère*?" he asked, his face just inches from her own, his voice striking her as decadent and rich, making her skin prickle with awareness.

She swallowed thickly and shook her head.

He said nothing, but moved away from her. She watched, her breath coming in increasingly erratic puffs, as he turned and opened one of the bedside table drawers. He removed an unopened box and tore through the seal, tipping the contents into his hand. She saw a chrome, bullet-shaped object and several red elastic bands fall into his palm. He chose one of the bands and attached it to the vibrator. He secured the chrome bullet to his finger using the band and sat on the bed next to her.

"Take off your panties and lift your dress to your waist. I'm going to pleasure you, and you will return the favor. It's going to be quick, out of necessity," he said, his mouth twisting slightly in dissatisfaction, "but effective, and I want to explain something to you."

Quick but effective. Her pulse began to thrum at her throat.

She felt his gaze on her as she whisked her panties down her thighs and off her legs. "Sit in the middle of the bed," he demanded quietly when she started to raise her dress. She scooted to the center and leaned against the pillows, her breathing growing choppier by the second from mounting excitement. His gaze remained glued to her pussy when she lifted her dress to her waist.

"Now spread your thighs," he murmured, edging toward her on the bed, one knee bent, the other long leg left draped over the side of the mattress.

She watched with bated breath as he flicked a button on the vibrator and she heard a muted buzzing sound, like a bee had invaded the room. She gasped loudly when he matter-of-factly pushed the metal bullet against her labia. Delicious vibrations stimulated her clit.

"Oh," she cried out, her eyes going wide. It created a wicked tingling, and then an addictive, slow burn.

He studied her face and smiled. "Feel good?"

"Yes," she assured breathily. The metal was warming against her hypersensitive flesh. In the distance, she heard the insistent sound of his cell phone ringing. She opened her lips, but he spoke before she did.

"Ignore it," he said tautly. "This is your vibrator now. It's an expensive one—very powerful. I want you to use it on your little pussy every night at eleven thirty while I'm gone. I want you to think about what you told me, about how you wanted to submit to me in bed. Do you understand?"

"Yes," she replied. He'd pushed the vibrator deeper between her labia and was pulsing it ever so subtly with his finger. Her hips began to flex against the precise little instrument.

"And every time you are about to come, I want you to pull the vibrator away and stave off your orgasm. You may apply it again after you have cooled some. When you begin to crest again, you must pull the vibrator away. Picture me telling you that you must."

"How many times must I do that before I . . . come?" she gasped when he pulsed his finger against her with added pressure.

"Until you imagine me giving you permission to climax. Remember," he said, gray eyes glittering with arousal and amusement, "I'm a demanding master, but not a cruel one.

"When I call you every day, you'll tell me how successful you were—or how you failed," he continued. "I expect complete honesty. You know I could always tell when you were lying. Even when you were a girl," he reminded her as he watched his finger pulsing against her clit. "If you are successful in showing discipline, I will reward you. If you aren't, I'll tell you what your punishment is."

Liquid heat surged between her thighs at the potent combination of the vibrator on her clit and his illicit instructions. She could just imagine how erotic it would be, reporting to him her intimate moments of masturbation, anticipating his rewards and punishments when she next saw him. Yes, the punishments, because she knew she would fail miserably at the challenge. She'd never been very good at denying herself pleasure, especially such a delicious one. Her hips bobbed against the vibrator. It felt so good . . . so hot.

But suddenly Lucien lifted his finger. She whimpered at the deprivation.

"Do you understand, Elise?"

She swallowed the protest on her tongue. "Yes," she whispered.

"Good. Now, unbutton your dress and show me your pretty breasts."

Chapter Ten

Her chest was heaving against her fingers as she unfastened the row of buttons on her sundress. Lucien grunted softly in approval when she peeled back the fabric and he saw she wasn't wearing a bra.

"That's beautiful. I would prefer it if you didn't wear underwear here in the penthouse when it's just us, and we aren't expecting visitors. I will want you frequently, and it's best that you are prepared. Now, squeeze them and play with the nipples while I put the vibrator back on you," he instructed in a tight voice.

She gathered her breasts in her palms, squeezing the soft, firm flesh, growing more enthusiastic in her movements when she saw the way Lucien's eyes blazed as he watched her and the vibrator buzzed and stimulated her clit. Oh, she was starting to burn in earnest. She used her thumbs and forefingers to pinch at both nipples at once. She'd never done it before, not having much interest in her own breasts, despite her former male companions' avid fascination with them. It felt good. She pinched hard, the spike of pain spicing the stimulation on her clit.

"That's right. Do you like that?" Lucien asked, his finger pulsing against her clit more strenuously.

"So much," she said, bobbing her hips against Lucien's hand and the vibrator with more force.

"You're so beautiful," he muttered. "When I come back from Paris, I'm going to keep you in bed for days. That's right. Pinch those pink nipples."

She did what he said, her excitement mounting by the second. The bottoms of her feet began to tingle. The vibrator was extremely accurate and powerful.

"Oh, I'm going to come."

"Ask for my permission."

Her gaze darted to his face in surprise. His expression looked rigid with arousal . . . and entirely serious. "May I . . . come?"

"First spread your lips apart. Let me see your pink little jewel," he said, his voice an arousing combination of a purr and a growl. "Ah, that's right. Lovely," he muttered, momentarily lifting his vibrating finger to eye her glistening clitoris. "I expect you to use more discipline than this while I'm away," he said pointedly. "But since we are short on time tonight . . ."

She gasped and whined when he placed the vibrator on her exposed, naked clit.

"You may come, *ma chère.*"

A few seconds later, she shook in orgasm. She kept her labia spread wide with one hand and squeezed a breast with the other, her hips bucking in short jabs against Lucien's finger.

It felt so right, letting go in front of Lucien . . . giving herself to him.

"Very good," she heard him say a moment later as her shudders waned. She opened her eyelids sluggishly and watched in a daze as he removed the bullet vibrator, which looked glossy from her juices. He hastily grabbed for a different-sized elastic red band, and replaced it with the one that had been around his finger.

"Come up on your knees and kneel with your face over my lap," he demanded. She loved the sound of his lust-roughened voice.

"Like this?" she asked, breathless with arousal and confusion as she bent, and her lips were just inches above the fullness behind the zipper of his pants. Her mouth watered as she stared at the column of his erection pressed against his left thigh. His fingers moved fleetly, unfastening his pants. He stood momentarily and unceremoniously jerked his clothing down to his lower thighs. She only had a covetous glimpse at his muscular ass and thighs before he sat again, and she was staring down at him.

It was the first time she'd really been this close to his cock with the light on. He wouldn't let her touch him while he masturbated and pleasured her at night, and the restraints ensured she couldn't get closer to all that glory. His cock was long, thick, and straight, the color a rich caramel cast with a blood-flushed, rosy hue. There was some dark hair clipped very close at the base of his cock, but his balls were shaved. Her clit pinched tight at the image of the full, round testicles. When they'd hung free that night in Ian's penthouse when she'd sucked him, they'd been a delicious weight in her palm. He looked awesomely lush and virile and masculine, teeming with life and raw power. She licked her sensitive lips, longing for the hard pressure of his cock.

"You're the most beautiful man I've ever seen in my life," she told him sincerely, glancing up at him. He looked extremely sober and formidable as he stared down at her. "May I suck you? Please?"

A muscle jumped in his rigid cheek.

"How do you do it?"

She blinked, unsure what he meant. "Do what?"

"Play the submissive so perfectly at times that even I believe you."

"Because I'm not acting, Lucien. I do want to please you. So much," she whispered, wonder lacing her tone as she realized what she said was 100 percent true.

His nostrils flared slightly as he looked down at her. He placed his hand on the back of her skull, his fingers delving into her hair. Then he was reaching for something. Confusion swept through her when she saw he'd grabbed the vibrator again. She gave him a questioning look.

"Open your mouth."

She parted her lips wide without hesitation, even though her bewilderment amplified. She tried to say something but couldn't, because Lucien had gently grabbed the end of her tongue and was sliding the band of the vibrator over it. A moment later, the little bullet vibrator rested in the middle of her tongue, her own taste soaking into her awareness. He turned it on again, sending a pleasant pulsation through her flesh. When he removed his fingers, she closed her mouth to contain her saliva and swallowed while the vibrator buzzed away happily on her tongue.

Her eyes sprang wide in understanding when he fisted the base of his cock and held it at an upright angle from his lap. He noticed her amazed expression and smiled.

"I've learned firsthand just how talented you are with that mouth of yours. I can't stop thinking about it, to be honest. It haunts me. You hardly need any assistance in giving me pleasure, but since we are tight on time . . ."

He faded off and gently pushed her toward his cock with the hand at the back of her head, but Elise was already on her way. Once she understood the rules of the new game, she was eager to play. She could tell by the pressure of his hand on the back of her head that he wasn't in the mood for a tease or a trial, so she went straight for the kill, taking his cockhead into her mouth. He stretched her lips wide as she slid down over his staff, pressing the vibrator against first the fleshy crown and then the stalk experimentally, gently buzzing him, before applying a firm pressure that made him growl, deep and guttural, and tighten his fingers in her hair.

It felt so strange, having the vibrator tingle against her flesh, knowing he was feeling that same energy pulse into his sensitive skin. She bathed and massaged the first half of his penis with her mouth and tongue before pumping him between her tightly clamped lips and pulsing him with the vibrator.

"So eager, so lovely," she heard him murmur from above her, his tone gruff and strained. It excited her to think of him watching her as she swallowed his cock. *Yes*, she was eager all right. She was also curious about the benefits of the little bullet. She slid her mouth off the tip of his tapered cockhead, feeling his fingers tighten in protest. Before he could say anything, however, she twisted her head, fitting him between her lips in the opposite direction. He seemed to understand her intent, because he altered the angle of his cock with his fist. She took the first few inches of his flesh into her mouth and used the vibrator against his supersensitive slit.

He gasped. "You clever little minx," he groaned. "God, that's good. You really are going to make short work of me."

A flash of sadness went through her at the reminder he would soon be leaving her. Still, she wanted to give him his due. She lifted her mouth and turned again, sliding him deep at the more hospitable angle.

"No. I will hold it," he said roughly when she tried to replace his hand with hers in order to pump his cock while she sucked. He groaned when she sunk him deep and bumped her lips against his forefinger. "I should turn your bottom red for being so blessed good at this."

She glanced up at him in a startled query, her mouth full of his throbbing flesh, her cheeks hollowed out from sucking so hard.

"*Fuck,*" he said savagely, urging her with his clutching hand until she bobbed up and down on his cock at a rapid pace, her jaw and lips aching from the sustained pressure. "I can take almost anything, but not your eyes," she heard him mutter darkly.

She felt him swell impossibly large a few moments later. He began to come, ejaculating on her tongue. It was difficult to keep up. The vibrator made controlling even her own salivation a challenge, and now she added Lucien's copious emissions. Still, she loved it: the feeling of his cock throbbing against her tongue as he came, his singular taste filling her mouth, his grunts of sharp pleasure, the sound poignant to her somehow. Beautiful. He was the definition of power to her. She loved that moment when his strength swelled and broke, and she held him close while he shook in bliss.

"No, *ma chère*. No," he mumbled in a tight voice a moment later as she licked and sucked him clean. "It's like stimulating a raw nerve doing that."

She blinked, coming back to herself. Reluctantly, she began to slide him out of her mouth. His penis was already overly sensitive in a post-climactic state. The vibrator combined with the enthusiastic cleaning with her lips and tongue was too much for the nerves in his satiated flesh. Much to her surprise, he halted her, however, holding her down with the hand on the back of her head. His expression was amused and self-deprecating when she met his stare.

"It feels like too much, but it feels *good*, too," he said. "You could probably have me coming again in the underside of five minutes. A man doesn't stand a chance with that mouth of yours, Elise." His cock twitched between her smile. She tickled him lightly with the vibrator and his eyes flashed.

She was more than game, if he was.

His phone rang again in the distance. Lucien closed his eyes briefly in regret and released his hold on her head.

"I should go, as much as I might wish otherwise."

Elise slowly, reluctantly slid her mouth off him. She bent her head to remove the buzzing vibrator and set it aside. He put his hands on her shoulders and pulled her to him. Elise's throat tightened as she breathed his scent and luxuriated in his embrace.

"It meant more to me than you know, the way you expressed your desire," he said near her skin as he kissed her temple. "You are always difficult to resist, but when you're open and honest? Impossible."

A strange mixture of feeling rushed through her: embarrassment that she'd made herself so vulnerable, but also gratefulness that he'd recognized how difficult it'd been for her . . . and pleasure that she'd pleased him.

Out of sheer habit, she opened her mouth to say something like,

It was my pleasure, or worse yet, *It wasn't a big deal.* But no, she wouldn't diminish either the challenge she'd faced or the gift she'd given Lucien.

She just looked up at him, her heart in her eyes. He blinked. The next thing she knew, he was kissing the daylights out of her and all rational thought vacated her brain.

"Why do you always have to make things so hard, Elise?" he said next to her lips a moment later.

"Because you always make things such a challenge for me?"

His mouth curved into a smile.

"I never knew walking out a door could be so difficult until this moment," he said soberly. He dropped his hands, frowning. "You will do what I said? Every night at eleven thirty?"

Her cheeks heated. "Yes."

"Good. I will enjoy picturing you, knowing you are testing yourself with only my voice in your head to instruct you. I hope in addition to what I said, you'll also hear me saying how lovely you are," he murmured, stroking her cheek. "How irresistible. It'll make me feel as if we're together, knowing you're hearing me in your mind, even if we are an ocean apart," he said before he stood and pulled up his clothing.

She pulled her dress up over her breasts, all the while thinking to herself that she heard his patient, guiding voice in her head with increasing frequency even without his instructions tonight. She'd begun to internalize his steadfast reassurance. He was cultivating the courage and confidence in herself that she so craved.

Elise was beginning to suspect that was what Lucien had intended all along.

The next night she returned to the penthouse late. Thursday nights were often packed with late-nighters at Fusion. Although the kitchen closed before the bar, they still prepared dishes later on Thursday, Friday, and Saturday nights than they did earlier in the week. Denise had needed to leave early, and Elise had volunteered to stay. She didn't mind. She enjoyed her work, and it kept her distracted from Lucien's absence.

The penthouse felt depressingly empty when she entered a little after eleven. She'd already eaten her dinner at Fusion, so she headed straight back to the bedroom. On the way to the bathroom to change, her gaze lingered on the large, three-drawer nightstand next to Lucien's bed. He'd put the vibrator she was supposed to use at eleven thirty in the top drawer, she recalled, her cheeks flushing with heat at the memory of his instructions. She edged toward the polished mahogany cabinet.

What other instruments of torture and pleasure did he keep in there?

The top drawer slid open. Her gaze ran over several boxes and implements, some of which made her heat with excitement, some of which puzzled her. There was an unopened box that appeared to hold several rubber plugs, the larger sizes making her eyes go wide. There was a long, slender, mechanized dildo that made her frown. It hardly compared to Lucien's gorgeous cock. She picked up a short-handled, highly polished wooden paddle and felt heat rush through her sex. Why did she get so excited over the idea of Lucien using it on her bottom? She opened a lovely velvet box and stared at an assortment of chains with clips and tweezers at the ends. Her nipples tightened. Without thinking, her hand flew upward and she pinched lightly at a crest to staunch the sharp ache.

She'd never used nipple clamps, but she knew what they were. Something about the delicate beauty of the jewelry-like ones in Lucien's possession aroused her. They were nothing like the heavy, brutish, sadistic things she'd imagined when she'd heard about them. She flicked one of the gold ones experimentally, wondering what they would look like on her nipples, aroused as she considered Lucien's expression at seeing them on her, fascinated by whether or not she could endure the tiny clamps. . . .

She pinched harder at her nipple, the mixture of pain and pleasure bringing her out of her fantasy. She glanced at the clock on the bedside table and replaced the box before she rushed into the bathroom to prepare for bed.

Lucien had told her eleven thirty, and she wanted to follow his instructions precisely. She thought of the thrill of the little vibrator and hurried through her bedtime routine hastily.

She wanted to follow his instructions *very* much.

At precisely eleven thirty, Elise was naked and lying on top of the comforter, her thighs spread and the vibrator strapped to her finger. She pressed the little bullet between her labia and sunk into the pillows, sighing with pleasure. Why had she never bought one of these little gems before? She rotated her hips, getting better pressure on her clit. Oh, it was divine.

She recalled how Lucien had taken her so completely that night in the stables, riding her so masterfully, his big, pulsing cock pounding into her flesh, his hands holding her immobile while he took his pleasure in her flesh, his bold possession making her scream.

Oh yes. It'd been so *hot*, so glorious to hold him inside her, to hear his grunts of primal satisfaction, to feel his balls slapping against her with each thrust . . . so delicious, to know she was pleasing him so well.

She gritted her teeth and writhed against the precise pulsations of the vibrator. Oh, how she missed him. She couldn't wait to have him fuck her that way again, to have him take her any way he pleased, to submit to him while he abandoned himself to erupting lust. . . .

Discipline, ma chère.

She gasped raggedly. Her hand thumped on the mattress, the vibrator continuing to buzz on her finger, teasing her . . . taunting her. She panted, trying her best to ignore the acute ache at her pussy.

Gritting her jaw together tight, she ran her open hand over her heaving belly and cupped a breast. Her hips twisted on the mattress as she pinched a nipple. It felt good, but it wasn't enough.

Her clit simmered, begging to be touched.

She wanted the vibrator. She *needed* Lucien.

"You devil," she muttered, perfectly seeing the glint in Lucien's gray eyes, his small, sexy smile in her imagination. She writhed in discomfort and arousal . . . burning . . . straining to ignite. Slowly, some of the unbearable tension started to dissipate from her muscles.

Now, again.

The warm, hard vibrator was back, pulsing her clit at Lucien's imagined permission. She whimpered with pleasure. This little thing could get a girl into real trouble, Elise thought dazedly as ecstasy swamped her and she burned in bliss. She was going to come.

No, ma fifille. *You don't have my permission yet.*

She growled in acute frustration and slammed her hand onto the mattress. For a few seconds, she just lay there panting shallowly, her body coiled tight, every muscle straining, her nerves shouting in protest. She waited for her flesh to cool. She prayed for it.

Breathe through it, Elise. You are so lovely when you show control. You may come very soon, I promise. Endure just a moment more. Don't give up. I'm with you.

"No, you're not," she grated out in supreme frustration. She was alone. And she was missing him. And he was thousands of miles away.

He would never know.

Within seconds she was shaking in climax, moaning, drowning in forbidden pleasure, her hips gyrating against her hand and the vibrator.

She sunk into the mattress moments later, her flesh deliciously limp and satiated following her explosive orgasm. It'd felt so good. So decadent.

You've been the very embodiment of self-indulgence.

Her eyelids flew open. This time, Lucien's voice hadn't been a product of her imagination, but a memory of something he'd once told her. Guilt and regret slinked into her awareness. She should have done better. She *could* have, but she'd chosen not to, feeling sorry for herself because Lucien was gone and not with her.

Her phone began to ring. She sat up, startled. She stared at the device on the bedside table, seeing the number on the screen. Panic flickered through her.

No. It couldn't be. He couldn't possibly *know* that she'd failed.

"Hello?" she asked shakily.

"Are you all tucked into bed?"

She shivered at the sound of his low voice tickling in her ear.

"Yes," she said too matter-of-factly. "And what of you? How did things go with the police?"

"As good as can be expected," he said with a sigh. "We presented the evidence. Leboeuf and the accountant have been arrested."

Concern overrode her earlier panic when she heard the weariness in his voice. "Have you slept?" she asked, knowing that it was early morning in Paris.

"No, I just arrived at my apartment. I thought I would sleep on the plane, but I ended up working with my banker to ensure the transfer of funds from my private accounts to the Three Kings. Everyone received their paychecks, right on time. I also had to work on hiring a private investigator to see if he can trace the embezzled funds. Perhaps a good portion of it can be recovered. I've just come from an all-night meeting with Monsieur Atale. I was a fool not to hire him as the executive director of the Three Kings right off the bat. He's a good man. But I was wary of people that had worked for my father previously. I thought it was best to bring in an outsider."

"That's hindsight, Lucien. I know that you wouldn't hire someone who didn't have excellent qualifications. You can't see the inner workings of a criminal's mind and heart."

Her breath hitched when he didn't respond.

"You should rest," she said, sensing his tension at the topic of his father and trying to turn the subject. "You sound absolutely exhausted."

"I'm in bed right now."

Her thighs clamped tight. She realized her instinctive reaction had come from the quiet, seductive quality of his voice.

"It's ten until midnight in Chicago," he murmured. "Did I catch you in the midst of your discipline lesson?"

"Yes," she said impulsively, her brain starting to leap into panic again. Did she imagine that short pause on his end?

"Are you aroused?"

"Yes. Incredibly so," she lied breathlessly.

"You're lying."

Irritation spiked through her at his quick, confident reply.

"How do you know that?"

"Because I know what you sound like when you're edgy with lust, and I know what you sound like when you're relaxed. Aside from seeming a little nervous, you sound to me like a woman that's just had a nice, hot orgasm."

Her typically glib tongue went uncooperatively numb.

"I told you I would know if you were lying," he said mildly, a thread of humor in his tone. "How many times?"

"How many times *what*?" she asked, irritation at his confidence in her failure and regret at her lack of control making her tone snappy.

"How many times did you pull your hand away and try to cool off?" he clarified evenly.

"Twice," she admitted after a pause. Her cheeks heated in embarrassment, but for some reason, another wave of lust went through her, so powerful that she placed her hand on her outer sex and pressed to staunch it.

"That's more than I expected."

"It is?" she asked, amazed.

"Did you imagine me telling you that you could come?"

"Well . . ."

"Elise?" he asked sharply.

She grimaced. "No. I . . . imagined that you told me I had to hang on just a bit longer."

"But you put the vibrator on your little pussy and came anyway?"

His voice had dropped a decibel, sounding sultry in her ear. Her hand moved between her thighs. "I tried hard, Lucien. But the vibrator is very powerful. It made me think of . . ."

"What?" he asked sharply when she faded off.

"The stables. How you rode me so hard. How much I liked it."

A rough groan made her ear and neck tingle.

"You little minx," he mumbled tightly. "How will I ever convince you that you were wrong to goad me that way when you were inexperienced, if you keep shoving it in my face how much you liked it?"

Her pussy was growing very wet. It excited her, playing with herself as they spoke so intimately to each other while they were leagues apart.

"I can't help it that I liked it. Do you wish I was different?"

"Don't pout," he chided. "You know I think you're perfect, and you love shoving *that* in my face every opportunity you get as well, don't you?" She smiled. He'd sounded amused. And extremely aroused. "I believe I told you I would punish you if you failed."

She rubbed her slick clit with the ridge of her forefinger more rapidly.

"What will you do to me when you get back?" she asked, trepidation twining with the excitement in her voice.

"Oh, you won't have to wait. You'll receive your punishment now."

That made her pause in her self-pleasuring.

"What do you mean?" she demanded. "You're in Paris."

"I know that. So you will administer the punishment in my place."

He really did have an uncanny way of making her speechless.

"Open the top drawer of the bedside table. There's a round,

wooden paddle in there with a short handle. Perhaps you noticed it earlier."

"Lucien," she said, disbelieving at the hint of mirth she heard in his voice. "Do you have a camera set up in here? Are you spying on me?"

"Of course I don't," he said sharply. "Do you honestly think I'd record you without your permission?"

Her mouth fell open in surprise at the edge to his tone.

"*No,* I don't have a hidden camera," he said, exhaling and leveling his tone, as if he'd sensed her surprise. "I knew you had to get in the drawer to get the vibrator. I know what a curious thing you are. Did you see anything else in that drawer that interested you?" he asked quietly.

"No," she replied stubbornly as she opened the drawer, stung by his effortless ability to read her.

He chuckled. "Do you have the paddle?"

She swallowed thickly as she wrapped her fist around the handle and withdrew the instrument of punishment.

"Yes."

"Then put me on speakerphone and place the phone on the mattress near your hips." She did what he'd suggested, her trepidation and excitement rising. "Now lie on your left side on the bed. Curl up your knees, little kitten," he murmured, his seductive voice resonating throughout the still room. "Is the paddle in your right hand?"

"Yes," she whispered.

"Twist your hips a little. Present your bottom to the paddle."

She bit her lower lip to prevent a whimper of arousal from escaping her throat. She now knew for a fact that the rumors of Lucien seducing from his voice alone were 100 percent accurate. The polished wood felt hard and exciting next to her buttock as she pressed it there while she drew up her knees toward her waist and twisted her hips.

"Are you in position?" came Lucien's voice in her ear.

"Yes."

"Are you comfortable?"

"Yes," Elise answered honestly. She lay on her side, her bent knees near her chest, her right thigh higher than the left in order to better expose her buttocks.

"You were correct in what you imagined me saying while you pleasured yourself. If you thought I was demanding that you continue to abstain just a bit longer, than you should have complied. But I'm pleased, as well, that you succeeded in pulling your hand away twice. Because of that, you may touch yourself at the same time you give yourself a good spanking. I give you permission to come, if you are so inclined."

"Oh . . . okay," she said, experiencing a strange mixture of shyness and arousal at his words. Instinctively, she ground her thighs together tightly to get pressure on her pussy. "May I begin now?"

"You may begin touching your pussy once I hear how hard you land the paddle. I will know whether or not you are going easy on yourself. Is the phone near your bottom?"

She scooted the phone nearer to her ass and lifted the paddle.

Smack.

"Hmm, that seemed adequate. You tell me. Was it hard enough to fit the crime?"

"Perhaps I was a little easy on myself," she said in a quavering voice.

He laughed. "Elise, you please me so much."

Her heart bumped against her breastbone at the sound of arousal tightening his voice.

"You will paddle yourself ten more times. Count out loud, so I can hear you. I expect it to sting. If I notice the smacks weakening, I will tell you how many more you must take when you finish. Do you understand?"

Arousal flashed through her, electrical in its intensity. Could there be anything more exciting than hearing Lucien instruct her in self-punishment, anything more stimulating than his utter confidence that she would do *precisely* what he demanded?

"May I . . . may I touch myself now?" she asked, unable to disguise her breathless eagerness.

"You may begin."

It was excruciating, the anticipation. She was having trouble catching her breath as she propped her upper body on her left elbow so as to better see the profile of her curved, naked bottom. She plunged her hand between her thighs and rubbed slick, hungry flesh. Her phone had never seemed remotely sexy before, but knowing Lucien was listening while she spanked and pleasured herself made the mundane technology incredibly erotic.

She lifted the paddle over her ass.

Smack.

She jumped slightly. In her excitement, she'd landed the paddle more briskly than she expected. Her buttock prickled with mild pain. Her hand moved more strenuously between her thighs. "One," she called out, remembering what Lucien had instructed.

She paddled her ass again and grimaced. "Two."

At five, her bottom was starting to burn. Surely Lucien would be pleased, wouldn't he? She rubbed her clit more rapidly in mounting excitement.

"Are you turning pink?" he asked, his voice sounding slightly hoarser than before, like a rough seduction.

"Yes," she panted, inspecting her right buttock.

"And hot? Touch your bottom."

She skimmed two fingertips over the taut skin with the hand that held the paddle, feeling the heat.

"Yes," she told him, her hand moving even faster between her thighs. He gave a harsh groan.

"Continue," he said, sounding much less calm than he had earlier.

"Six," she said between pants as she paddled her ass again. The protesting nerves sent prickles of excitement along her anus, sacrum, and sex. Her pussy was aflame and drenched. She was going to come . . . very soon. She landed the paddle again with an even louder cracking sound. A puff of air flew past her lips.

"Seven."

Lucien was masturbating while he listened to her punishment; she suddenly just knew that for a fact. She imagined his fist moving up and down on his thick stalk in a rapid, powerful, pistonlike motion from just below his fleshy cockhead to his full balls, his facial muscles rigid, his eyes hot. She'd seen him do it enough to have the image burned into her brain for an eternity.

She felt herself cresting at the erotic image and moaned out loud. She paddled her bottom briskly again, the flash of pain and the subsequent burn feeding her arousal. "Eight," she grated out before popping her ass again in quick succession. "Nine . . . *oh* . . ."

Orgasm loomed. She struggled to stave it off by paddling her smarting ass extra hard, but the burst of sensation only served to send her over the edge.

"Ten," she managed through a desperate, quaking voice before she groaned in delicious anticipation. She fell back onto the pillows and dropped the paddle heedlessly. Orgasm crashed into her. Her entire arm jerked back and forth as she pressed her hand between her thighs and pleasure swamped her consciousness.

A moment later, she gasped to catch her breath and her sawing arm movements slowed. Distantly, she became aware of Lucien's voice emanating from her phone.

"Pick up the phone, damn it," he bellowed.

She followed his instructions dazedly, instinctively drawing the phone near her ear even though it was still on speaker. He must have heard her ragged breathing because he immediately began issuing orders.

"Put the phone right next to your pussy. *Quickly*, Elise," he hissed tersely, his breath sounding nearly as erratic as her own. She rolled onto her back and spread her thighs, then did what he'd said.

"I heard you coming," he said roughly. "Are you wet?"

"I'm soaked," she admitted starkly.

"Run your fingers over your pussy. Play with yourself. Let me hear how wet you are."

She followed his orders. Sure enough, she was so intensely aroused a wet sound could be heard as she moved her fingers against her satiated, lubricated flesh.

"I can hear you," Lucien said, and Elise knew he was nearing orgasm by the ragged sound of his voice. She pictured his flexing muscles as he pounded his cock . . . straining. "God, I wish I was there to suck and swallow *every drop of you*," he said so quietly but so fiercely that her eyes sprang wide.

She went completely still and listened, enthralled. He grunted, as if he'd just been stabbed by a knife of pleasure. Slowly, she raised the phone to her ear as a taut second of silence was shattered by his sharp shout. Turning the speaker off—feeling closer to him with his voice directly in her ear—she absorbed his every gasp, his every groan as he climaxed.

Every time she was with him, he introduced her to yet another height of pleasure and intimacy. He'd done it again, in spades. How did he do it so effortlessly? So precisely?

She waited, completely satisfied listening to his pants as he recovered from what must have been a powerful orgasm.

"Do you think you'll sleep well now, Lucien?" she asked quietly when his breathing slowed.

He gave a bark of laughter. "I expect I won't have any other choice. You wore me out."

She smiled. "Who knew? I've heard of phone sex, but never thought it could be so . . . fulfilling."

"It never has been before. I suspect you set some kind of world record," he replied thickly.

"*You* did that. I was just an innocent victim," she muttered, her pique just a limpid act. She felt supremely relaxed and satisfied.

"You are about as much of a victim as Attila the Hun."

"I resent that," she purred, grinning like the Cheshire cat.

"You had better improve on your lessons by tomorrow at eleven thirty."

"Or *what*?" she postured.

"You know what. You've met your match. Even the Huns were conquered."

She heard the hint of steel in his sensual purr and swallowed thickly. His tone had gentled when he called her name again across countries and an ocean, and it felt to her as if his head were on the pillow next to her.

"Elise?"

"Yes?" she answered groggily.

"Get under the covers. I don't want you to catch a chill," he said. "And Elise?"

She paused in fumbling with the comforter and sheet, doing what he'd said.

"Yes?"

"You'll do better tomorrow with your self-discipline. I have faith in you."

A rush of feeling went through her. "Thank you," she whispered.

"Good night, *ma chère*. Sleep well."

"Good night, Lucien."

A choking loneliness overcame her as she hit the disconnect button, set the alarm, and turned off the bedside lamp. She snuggled into Lucien's bed, struck by how enormous it seemed . . . how empty without him.

Despite the pang of loneliness, Lucien had trained her body well—not just for pleasure, but for health. She was asleep within three minutes of hanging up the phone.

Two days later, Sharon peeped through the kitchen door while Elise was stirring a thickening béarnaise sauce.

"Francesca Arno stopped in. She was wondering if you had a moment to speak?"

Elise winced. "I can't right now. I can't leave this—"

"I've got it," Evan said, coming up behind her and reaching for the whisk. Elise glanced at Denise, who nodded to her with a distracted smile as she prepared a roast duck. Elise washed her hands and walked through the swinging door, looking for Francesca.

"Hi," Elise said, glad to see Francesca standing in the bar area, a glass of club soda and lime on the bar in front of her.

"I'm sorry; I know how busy you must be. I promise I won't take long. It's a bit of an emergency."

"What's wrong?"

"Oh." Francesca looked contrite when she noticed Elise's anxiety. "I should have specified. Not a *real* emergency. A *bride's* emergency."

Elise laughed. "My father used to say there's no catastrophe in the universe larger than a bride's, because she makes her panic everyone else's."

Francesca joined her in laughter. "It's so funny you mentioned him. He's the reason I stopped by. Or one of them, anyway."

Elise's amusement vanished. "My *father*?" she asked, stunned.

Francesca nodded. "Yes. Louis Martin."

Elise just stared, her mind racing. Lucien had specifically told her he didn't want anyone here in Chicago to know of their former connection. She'd made a point of not talking about her family or her past because she didn't want people to start to see the possible previous connections between Lucien and her. Lucien's desire for anonymity coincided with her own desire to start a new life.

How was she supposed to respond to Francesca?

"Your father is Louis Martin, right? The famous fashion designer?" Francesca prompted.

"I . . . He . . . How did you know that?" Elise sputtered.

Francesca's expression fell. "I'm sorry. Did you not want people to know?"

I don't know what I want, Elise thought anxiously. She wasn't sure what secrets Lucien wanted her to keep and what he didn't. Why was he always so infuriatingly vague about all that?

"It's just that I hadn't told anyone here. I'm trying to start out fresh in a new place."

Regret went through her when she saw Francesca's crestfallen expression. "I'm so sorry. I shouldn't have brought it up—"

"It's okay, really," Elise assured. "I just don't understand how you knew Louis Martin was my father."

"Ian told me," Francesca admitted. "He knew that I was obsessing about the perfect dress for a beach wedding—casual but elegant, simple but classic—all the characteristics your father is known for. Ian suggested I speak to you about the possibility of contracting your father for a design."

"He did?" Elise asked numbly. Lucien was *not* going to like this. Plus, knowing Lucien, he'd think it was somehow her fault that Ian and Francesca knew about her family.

"How could Ian have possibly known I was Louis Martin's daughter? Is he that involved in French fashion?"

Francesca studied her face anxiously. "Not specifically, but Ian is very aware of the goings-on in the European business community. He spends a lot of his time in Europe. And Ian just has a way of . . ." She blushed. "Finding out things about people," she finished, an apology in her eyes.

Of course. For a business mogul like Ian Noble, knowledge was power. She'd been admitted into the realms of his private penthouse. If he was smart—and Ian was reputedly brilliant—he wouldn't have done that without having at least a minimal check done on her background to assure she wasn't a thief or spy.

She was processing all this when Francesca spoke again. "I'm sorry, Elise. I didn't realize you were trying to keep your background secret. I knew you didn't offer a lot of information, but I just thought it was modesty on your part. Even at the engagement party, I heard

Ian ask Lucien if you were Louis Martin's daughter, and Lucien confirmed that you were."

Elise blinked, shocked anew. Lucien hadn't made a secret of her past to Ian? She was bewildered. Precisely what was it he had been warning her to be circumspect about all this time? She thought he didn't want her bringing up things that would create any suspicion on Ian's part, but he clearly didn't think her background or family or status qualified. Irritation flickered through her at his refusal to open up in regard to this Ian Noble business. If Elise did screw up, it was no one's fault but Lucien's for not being more specific about what he wanted kept secret. He was leaving her to walk around blindly in a landmine.

She shrugged and smiled at Francesca, determined to do her part to keep the waters smooth for her and Lucien.

"It's not a big deal. I'd be happy to talk to my father about it. I'm sure he'd be thrilled to design something for a friend of mine. When he sees you, he'll be inspired."

Francesca's dark eyes went wide. "That's so sweet of you," she said quietly. "Are you *sure*, Elise? I really didn't mean to be so tactless about a . . . a sensitive issue. I should have realized you want to be recognized on your own merits, that you're trying to make a life for yourself outside of the shadow of your family. I'm forever sticking my foot in my mouth," she mumbled under her breath.

"Don't be ridiculous," Elise said, stepping forward and touching Francesca's elbow in reassurance. "I was just surprised you knew I was Louis Martin's daughter, that's all."

"I'll explain to Ian how you feel about a fresh start, and we'll be sure not to mention your family to anyone. He'll understand," Francesca assured. "But that's not all—I also wanted to ask if you and Lucien would come over to Ian's penthouse Monday night for dinner."

"That would be lovely, but I owe you an invitation first. You asked us last, for the engagement party. I'm sorry I haven't reciprocated. Things have been so busy with work."

"Nonsense," Francesca said, waving her hand. "There's no reason to be so formal about a casual dinner, is there?"

"Well, if you're sure," Elise said hesitantly.

"Of course I'm sure. Please say you'll come. Ian has been under a lot of stress lately. To be honest," Francesca added quietly, "I'm concerned about him. He works so hard, and it's been necessary for him to spend a lot of time away from home recently. It would do him good to relax with friends, and Lucien always seems to have such a good effect on him."

"I'll ask Lucien, then," Elise assured, seeing how much the dinner meant to Francesca and wanting to make that shadow of worry on her features fade. "I'm not sure if he'll be back from Paris by Monday. I'll call you when I know. And I promise to make you and Ian a special dinner very soon."

"You do every time we come to Fusion," Francesca said wryly as she stood.

"That hardly counts," Elise said, giving a sunny smile. Inside, though, a storm was brewing. She was angry at Lucien for leaving her to feel so vulnerable and clueless. But she was infuriated that his refusal to prepare her might be the thing that betrayed him. She truly didn't believe he was up to something criminal, but he was up to something that could land him in trouble. She just knew it.

He had some explaining to do. And this time, some vague half-truths weren't going to cut it.

Part VI

When You Trust Me

Chapter Eleven

Elise grimaced as she glanced at the bedside chest at midnight. Part of her regretted not opening that drawer this evening. Part of her longed to do a replay of the past two nights and experience such intense pleasure . . . such intense *intimacy* with Lucien. They hadn't just had mutual climaxes for the past two nights; they'd made love while they were half a world apart. He really was magical, the way he could pull off the impossible. Part of her wished she could just ignore her irritation.

But she couldn't.

She picked up her ringing cell phone.

"Bonjour," she said crisply into the receiver.

There was a pause. *"Bonsoir.* Don't we sound businesslike," Lucien said, sounding amused and wary.

"I am in the mood for business. And not the business of the past two nights," she said pointedly. It was technically a lie. She *was* in the mood for the business of gushing in pleasure and hearing Lucien's voice go rough and sexy with lust as he instructed her and she did precisely what he commanded. But she had more crucial business at hand. "How was your day?"

"Productive," he said. "Atale and I are still getting the books in order for the Three Kings. It's tedious work."

"I can imagine," she said, compassion seeping into her awareness. No matter her annoyance at him, Lucien was going through a rough time right now. He sounded exhausted. "Don't tell me you were up again all night?"

"I'll catch some sleep this morning," he said, the hitch in his voice making her think he'd just fallen into bed. A sharp longing went through her to be there with him, to feel his arms around her—She interrupted her own thoughts before she sabotaged herself.

"Francesca stopped by Fusion today. She asked you and me to come to dinner at Ian's Monday night. Do you want to go?"

"I should be back in town by then. Yes, if you do." There was a pause and Elise simmered in the silence. "You might as well get to it," he said.

"Get to what?"

"Whatever you're pissed about. I assume there's something, because you clearly haven't been following my instructions," he said levelly.

"With good reason. Do you know what else Francesca asked me?" Elise demanded, launching into her attack. "If I would ask my father to design her wedding dress. *Ian* told her to ask me."

"Okay," Lucien said slowly. His cautious confusion at her anger only amplified her irritation.

"Why didn't you tell me that Ian knew who I was?"

"Was it important to you that he didn't know?"

"No," she exclaimed heatedly. "It's not important to me. I thought it was important to *you* to keep my family and background hushed up. I thought you were trying to keep people from asking questions about our past connection!"

Lucien sighed. "If it's any consolation to know it, I never told Ian specifically about your family. He found out himself. He knows everything about people that are in his life, even in the peripheral sense. It's not only a precaution; it's in his nature to know as much as he can in any given situation. He's not the most trusting type, Ian. I imagine he comes by his paranoia honestly."

Elise's mouth fell open. Her annoyance segued to outrage.

"By your logic, Ian Noble would know everything about you and *your* past, then." The silence rung in her ears. She threw caution to the wind. "He would know all about your father's prosecution and imprisonment."

"He *does* know all about it. I confided in him after my father's arrest. He supported me during the trial, just by listening. I never told you anything different," he added when she remained silent in disbelief.

"That's because you never said anything to me *period*. Besides, you've told me from the beginning you didn't want me screwing up and spilling the beans about your father and your identity."

"I never said that about my father. You just assumed it."

Hurt swamped her at his cool response. Her throat grew tight. For a few seconds, she couldn't speak. Lucien made a sound of frustration.

"When you stormed into Fusion that day pretending to be my chef, and Ian walked in on us, I just thought it would be easiest and cleanest to say that we didn't know each other. I couldn't make things too complicated, given the situation."

"You couldn't make your *lie* too complicated. Isn't that what you mean?" she seethed.

"If you prefer to put it that way. Yes."

"Did you know that Ian and Francesca realize that we're lovers?"

"I suspected they did, ever since the party at the penthouse."

"And you didn't think it was important to tell me? *No,* no one can tell Elise anything," she shouted into the phone. "She's too much of a loose cannon. Just leave her in the dark and let her stumble around like a fool. That's the best way to deal with a wild child."

"I don't think you're a loose cannon," he said in a tight voice.

"That's precisely what you think. You even told me you needed to keep an eye on me . . . keep me in line—isn't that what you said?"

"Elise—"

"Here's a crazy idea," Elise interrupted, her voice going high. "Why not just tell me why you're being so crazy about Ian Noble, and then you won't have to worry about me unintentionally setting off an explosion?"

"I can't do that."

"Why not? Because you don't trust me enough to tell me." She answered her own question, her hurt turning to a burn in her chest. "You still think I'll impulsively say something wrong . . . or worse, try to blackmail you with the knowledge."

"I don't *really* think you'd try to blackmail me," he said, frustration in his tone.

"You said you did before."

"What if I did?" he said abruptly. "You were thinking about how you could use something against me to get what you wanted. I could see it in your eyes that day in my office. Do you deny it?"

She opened her mouth to do just that but bit her lip, halting her lie at the last second.

"I didn't think so," he said after a charged pause. "That doesn't mean I truly believe you'd do something underhanded to intentionally hurt me."

That admission let the pressure in her chest and throat remit enough to allow her to take a painful inhale, but she was still furious. And confused.

"I wasn't worried that you would intentionally undermine me, Elise," Lucien repeated, suddenly sounding weary. "I just thought it'd be easier all around if you could be quiet about our past. I realized that I wasn't giving you enough guidance and information on that. That's why I said I wanted to keep an eye on you. It wasn't because I don't trust you."

The silence seemed to swell in her ears and in her throat.

"If you believe that, then why don't you just tell me the truth? Tell me what's haunting you, Lucien."

Inexplicably, tears swelled in her eyes. She realized her reaction was because on some deep level, she recognized the truth of her words. He'd been behaving so inexplicably since he left Paris. Something was haunting Lucien, plaguing him. His secret was eating him alive from the inside out. Of *course* it was. Why hadn't she understood that before?

"I can't," he replied quietly. "It's not my secret to tell. Not entirely, anyway."

"You don't trust me," she whispered, hurt strangling her voice . . . and panic, as well, that he wouldn't let her in far enough to help him.

"That's not it," he said edgily. "Look, we'll talk about it more when I get home."

"When will that be?" she asked dully after a moment.

"I'm not sure. The day after tomorrow, most likely. Elise?" he prompted when she didn't speak.

"Yes?"

"I'm sorry for leading you to believe that it was my father's crimes that I was trying to keep from Ian. It was just more . . ."

"Convenient to keep me quiet that way?" she asked when he faded off. It felt like there was a handful of marbles in her throat. "You knew how much I care about you. You knew that if I believed you were feeling vulnerable about Adrien's incarceration for corporate espionage that I would keep quiet in order to protect you. You used my feelings for you against me to gain my compliance."

"I never did that intentionally."

"You don't have to. It comes naturally, to maneuver to get what you want. You and I are alike. Haven't you said that before?" she reminded him quietly. "You've accused me of learning manipulation at the cradle, but you're no different. You did whatever was convenient to keep the fuse from being lit. You even suggested this relationship to keep me under control."

"I suggested our relationship because I care about you," he said in a hard voice. "I know how proud you are. If you didn't believe that I truly care about you, you wouldn't have agreed to any of this between us. You wouldn't be in my bedroom this very moment."

A silent spasm of emotion went through her. She thought of denying that she was, indeed, sitting on his bed as they spoke, just to spite him for his smugness. But what was the point? She *did* care about Lucien. She knew that he cared about her.

He didn't trust her, though. And that was what burned like acid.

"I'll be home soon," Lucien said quietly. "We'll talk more when I get there. Try to get some rest, *ma chère*."

"Good night," she said with as much calm dignity as she could muster.

The next morning she arose before dawn and drove out to the stables for a ride on Kesara. Lucien had been kind enough to purchase her a membership at the club, but she wasn't in the mood to think generous thoughts about him at the moment.

It helped, the fresh, early morning air and brisk gallop clearing some of the frustration and worry about her conversation with Lucien. Afterward, she returned to the city and showered. When Sharon came to open Fusion, Elise was waiting at the front doors. She poured all of her agitated energy into her work. By the time nine thirty p.m. came around, she was starting to drag.

"Why don't you take off early and get some rest?" Denise suggested. "You look dead on your feet."

"It's Saturday night," Elise reminded her as she arranged some greens on a plate.

"We're completely prepped for the post-theater crowd, and Evan and Javier are both here. Go on, Elise. You worked like a maniac today. I don't want you to get sick. I need you too much."

Elise gave the older woman a weary smile. "Maybe I will get some rest," she conceded.

"Good. There's no time like the present," Denise said briskly, taking the knife Elise was holding in preparation to slice a juicy loin of pork. "Have a wonderful weekend."

The penthouse was dim and silent when she unlocked the front door that evening, so she wasn't sure what caused her to go still in the entryway. She listened intently, curious as to what had made her pause and go wary. All was quiet, but then she heard a scraping sound, as if a chair had been pulled a few inches across a wood floor. Her heart jumped into her throat. With her pitched hearing, she heard a man's voice. It was too muffled to interpret what he'd said, but it sounded guttural and unfamiliar to Elise's ears.

There was someone in the penthouse.

Chapter Twelve

She fumbled in her backpack for her cell phone, starting to back out the door. She'd call the police and wait with the doorman downstairs until the authorities went up to check things out and hopefully arrest the interloper. Her cell phone screen flickered on. She'd missed a text from Lucien, she observed distractedly as she started to close the door behind her.

She halted the door when it was an inch from closing. Lucien's message said that he'd rushed to finish his work and would be on a plane by six p.m. Paris time. Given the time difference, he'd have been in Chicago now for hours.

She warily reentered the penthouse and moved down the hallway, her tread silenced by the thick carpeting. A flicker of relief went through her when she heard Lucien's voice, although she couldn't make out exactly what he said. A moment later, she stood outside Lucien's closed office door.

"I can't believe he's dead," she heard Lucien say clearly.

"The prison lifestyle isn't a healthy one."

Elise's mouth went dry. She'd been wrong to think the voice of the man Lucien spoke to was unfamiliar. She'd heard that German-accented voice once before, in Paris. It sounded like the same man Lucien spoke to that night she'd eavesdropped at Renygat.

Were they talking about Adrien Sauvage? Dear God, he wasn't dead, was he?

She should back away. It was wrong to eavesdrop again. But what if she could learn something about Lucien's secrets . . . about what was plaguing him? She held her breath, listening.

"I'll say this for him. He never tried to blackmail any of you, and that's twenty in all. The bastard hinted there was more, both to me and the police, although he was always coy and clever about offering anything of substance, lest it bring him to trial again."

"Your powers of interview and interrogation must be huge. He opened up to you like no other."

"He was vain. I was someone to brag to. Besides, it gave him a chance to learn about you. He soaked up that information."

"And yet he refused to speak to me in person."

"Perhaps he possessed a sliver of a conscience. His guilt wouldn't let him face you."

"That man didn't know the meaning of guilt. What a sick fuck."

Elise started at the amount of venom in Lucien's usually level tone. He sounded intimidating in that moment. Frightening.

"Well, he's gone now," the man said.

"Too bad he couldn't take his twisted legacy with him." Her heart began to pound in the ensuing silence. What could make Lucien sound so bitter? Was Lucien truly that angry at his father that he would speak of him this way if he died? No . . . there was something about that possibility that didn't fit somehow.

"What of the other matter? Do you think you'll be able to locate the stolen funds?"

"The signs are good. I think I'll have something to report to you by tomorrow afternoon."

"Good," she heard Lucien say, something about his brisk tone making her think he was concluding the meeting. "Herr Schroeder, thank you again for coming to Chicago. As always, your thoroughness and quick execution is appreciated."

"Not at all. I was in the States when you called, so it wasn't difficult to meet with you. I'll leave for Switzerland to continue the investigation and call you as soon as I know anything—"

Elise jumped when she heard a totally unexpected sound—a quick, light tread on the stairs that led to the rooftop deck. She hastened guiltily from her spot in front of Lucien's office toward the master bedroom.

"Elise!" Maria Oronzo, Lucien's maid, squeaked when she saw Elise standing in the hallway. Elise had met the friendly middle-aged woman several times before and got along well with her. "You startled me. Lucien told me you wouldn't be home until later."

Elise smiled, trying to look calm even through her heart was racing. "I was due to come home later, but—"

The door to Lucien's office snapped open.

"Elise?"

She turned, her breath burning in her lungs. Lucien stepped into the hallway, his gaze boring into her. "You're home early," he said.

"So are you," she murmured, unable to keep her eyes off him. He looked tall and awesome in the shadowed hallway, his white shirt and light eyes a contrast to his dark gray pants and black blazer. Stubble shadowed his jaw, giving him a dark . . . slightly dangerous air. Someone cleared their throat and Elise blinked, realizing it was Maria and that she'd been staring at Lucien and he'd been staring back.

"I must be going," she heard Herr Schroeder say from just inside Lucien's office. "The plane you have ordered for me will be waiting."

"I'll be going, too," Maria said, giving Lucien a nod. "Everything is ready, Lucien."

"Thank you. Thank you both," Lucien said, pulling his gaze off Elise and glancing into his office. "Maria, would you mind seeing Herr Schroeder out before you go?"

"Of course," Maria said, smiling at Herr Schroeder as Lucien stepped aside and the other man walked out. Elise caught a glimpse of a silver-haired, elegantly dressed man of about sixty before Maria was leading him down the hallway. Lucien and she stared at each other without speaking. A moment later, Maria called a good-bye and the front door closed.

"Come in," Lucien said. He nodded toward his office. Elise stepped inside the luxurious, masculine, leather-clad room. "Have a seat," he murmured, waving at one of two leather wingback chairs that faced each other, a toasty brown walnut table between them. Lucien sat across from her. Elise searched for what to say. Would he suspect she'd overheard part of his conversation with Herr Schroeder?

"He's a private investigator." Lucien spoke before she had decided how to broach what had just happened. "Herr Schroeder is looking into the location of the embezzled funds for me. As you likely already realize, he's worked for me on several occasions in the past."

"He's the man I overheard you talking with in Paris years ago. Lucien, what's going on? The man you mentioned dying in prison, it wasn't Adrien, was it?" she asked, anguished.

He blanched. "No, of course not. I was referring to a man you don't know. A man you have no connection to whatsoever, and never will."

"Then what has that man—Herr Schroeder—got to do with Ian Noble? You two were discussing Ian in Paris years back, and then you came here to Chicago. *Please* tell me," she added softly when she saw how glacial his stare became.

"How will I ever cure you of this proclivity for eavesdropping," he mumbled after a moment.

"You seem to have a talent for it yourself," she returned quickly, referring to catching him listening to Ian while he'd been on the phone. He frowned. She heard the brass clock on his desk ticking quietly in the ensuing silence. Lucien remained unmoving, his arms reclining loosely on the arms of the chair. His gaze on her didn't waver. She sensed his tension despite his relaxed pose, sensed him studying her with that laser-like stare. Suddenly he stood.

"I need a drink," he said, walking toward a sideboard with several decanters and glasses set on a tray. "Will you have a glass of cognac with me?"

"All right," she said, even though she didn't really want a drink. She was anxious to hear what Lucien would say. She watched him as he deftly poured the golden-brown liquid from a crystal decanter into two snifters.

"Do you remember years ago, in Nice, when you asked me if I was curious about my biological mother?" he asked a moment later as he came toward her with the glass in his hand.

She started in surprise before she accepted the snifter. "Yes. Of course. You said that you didn't think about her often. That you had nothing to miss, never having a devoted mother figure."

His smile struck her as poignant. "And you informed me you were adopted as well—just as confident and sure of yourself as a princess."

"You told me that I was the spitting image of my mother. I was so hurt by that," she said softly. "But then you reminded me that it was what was on the inside that counted . . . that I could choose who I wanted to be. I've always remembered that."

He sat again and took a sip of his cognac. "Now here you are, creating a meaningful life, proving that there's more to our destinies than our biology."

Her cheeks heated in pleasure at his compliment. "You're the one who first taught me that lesson."

"And do you believe it?" he asked, his intensity mounting her confusion over his puzzling manner.

"Yes. I do. I think our parents influence us, but as human beings, we can choose what we want our life to mean. Lucien, what's this all

about? What does it have to do with that man—Herr Schroeder—
and Ian Noble?"

He seemed to hesitate. For a moment, she thought he wasn't
going to answer her. He finally took another sip of cognac and set
down his snifter on the table.

"During that same conversation in Nice, I told you that I didn't
think much about my biological mother. I wasn't being completely
honest with you."

Something squeezed tight in her chest. "You *did* think about her,
didn't you? You wondered," she said in a hushed voice.

"It wasn't an easy topic for me to discuss. Then or now. Of course
I wondered about the woman who bore me. What had made her
give me up? What were the circumstances that she needed to? Did
I have other family? Brothers? Sisters? Aunts? Uncles? Did I look like
them? I wondered. Incessantly. I've been trying to find her for eight
years now," he admitted starkly.

"You have?"

He nodded slowly. Something about his rigid expression made
compassion flood through her. She sat forward in her chair. "Have
you found anything yet?"

He exhaled and shut his eyes briefly. She sensed his frustration.
"Most leads have been dead ends, for one reason or another. I know
a few things. I know that my mother gave me up for adoption in
Cabourg, and that she was of Moroccan descent. Apparently, she
worked as a domestic in northern France."

"Moroccan. Moroccan and French. Fusion," she muttered, her
mind whirling. He'd been thinking of his ethnic heritage when he'd
named his restaurant and designated the type of food to be served.

His hard mouth softened a fraction. "Yes. A moment of fancy on
my part."

"What else did you find out about her?"

"Bloody little," he replied bitterly. "Herr Schroeder was unable to procure any helpful documents. We only found out what we know because of his careful, painstaking investigative work and interviews with people in Cabourg who worked in the hospital where my mother gave birth, in the adoption agency . . . and around the vicinity. The name she gave them at the hospital was an alias. My mother's Moroccan accent was still very strong, leading the people who remembered her to believe she hadn't been in France all that long. She spoke Arabic and English, but apparently very minimal French. She made an impression on many of the people she encountered, though. Apparently, she was very beautiful."

"Of course she was. Look at you," Elise said with a tremulous smile.

"Two of the nurses formed attachments to her. They remembered how frightened she was. How alone. She was very young."

"How terrible for her. She must have been so afraid, with her homeland and family so far away. Do you . . ." Elise hesitated, studying every nuance of his face. "Do you have any indication she's still alive?"

"The chances are, she is. She was likely in her late teens when she had me. She'd still be in her forties . . . fifty at the oldest."

"Lucien, I can't believe you've been going through all this." She set down her snifter and stood, going to him. She sat on the edge of his chair and hugged him. He returned her embrace, tightening his hold until she slid into his lap. Her cheek pressed against his chest. He kissed the top of her head and stroked her upper arm.

"Is Herr Schroeder still trying to locate her?" Elise asked after a moment, not lifting her head from his chest.

"His investigation is ongoing," she heard him say, his deep voice reverberating from his chest into her cheek. She sat up slightly when he brushed his fingertips beneath her chin and applied a slight pressure. She met his stare, sensing he was about to tell her something important.

"We do have one lead. A crucial one."

"What?"

"One of Herr Schroeder's most important witnesses told him that there is a single individual who could likely give me the true name and background of my mother. That person is Helen Noble, Ian Noble's mother."

Elise's mouth fell open. "But . . . wasn't Ian's mother the daughter of the Earl of Stratham? I met the earl and countess once at a charity function in London. I thought I'd heard that their only child had died, and that Ian's grandmother and grandfather raised Ian."

Lucien nodded. "That is what Ian tells people. Helen Noble is still alive, though. I first suspected it from some cryptic comments Ian made after we became friends in Paris. I sensed his sadness when he spoke of his mother, his bitterness . . . his grief, as if his feelings for her and what had happened to her were fresh emotions, not the far-distant memories of a ten-year-old boy. Between Herr Schroeder and myself, we discovered that she is, indeed, alive. I came to Chicago to see if I could uncover anything else about Helen and her fate. We've located her whereabouts in London."

"But . . . why would *Helen Noble* know about your biological mother?" Elise asked.

"She worked for Helen. She was her maid. Apparently she only left her service when she discovered she was pregnant with me."

"Have you spoken with Helen, then?" Elise asked, thoughts racing through her head. "And *why* would Ian and his grandparents say that Helen was dead?"

"She's very ill," Lucien said quietly. "Very fragile. The hospital where Ian has her being cared for is private, with very high security. In fact, Ian owns the facility. It's impossible to get inside unless you're staff, family, or an invited guest. As for why Ian says his mother is dead, I don't believe it was he who first fabricated that story. He was only ten years old when he went to live with his grandparents. His grandparents must have told him his mother was dead to save him the anguish of seeing her so unwell. I don't know when Ian found out the truth about her."

"So Ian doesn't realize that you know all this?"

"No," Lucien said, briefly closing his eyes.

"Can't you just explain the circumstances? *Ask* him if you can speak to Helen Noble?"

"At one time, I considered it. But it's . . . a very complicated situation, Elise," he said, looking away.

"In what way? Lucien?" she asked when he remained turned in profile to her. He met her stare.

"I believe that Helen Noble's health has taken a downturn. Ian seems worried lately, and I've overheard a few conversations. If his mother is so fragile, he won't want me there asking her questions about her past."

Elise frowned. "That's understandable, but surely it wouldn't be too taxing on Helen to have you ask her a few questions about a woman she knew thirty-odd years ago."

"No," Lucien said with finality.

"But finding your mother means so much to you," she said in a pressured fashion. "You've altered your entire life in order to find her. You can't give up now."

A shadow of frustration crossed his features. "I'm not giving up. Far from it. But other people's lives are complicated and difficult, too. I can't force or trick Ian into acting in compliance with my wishes. I don't want to. He's a friend. He has his own concerns. He has a family that he worries about as well."

"If he is a friend, he'd at least want you to tell him the truth."

"He's likely to think my purpose is completely mercenary and selfish." He exhaled and rubbed his eyes. "And in fact, it *was* in the beginning. I specifically asked a common acquaintance to introduce Ian and me in Paris because I hoped to find out more about both Ian and his mother. I've come to care about him since then, but if Ian knows the truth, he'll likely discount all that. He'll just think I've used him."

She studied his face soberly, sensing the weight of his burden. She could tell by the well-practiced way he said the words that the logic had been replayed in his mind again and again. How hard it must be for him, to feel so close to the source of his mother's identity and yet have it remain just out of reach.

"God, Lucien. I had no idea finding your birth mother was so important to you." Realization struck her and her facial muscles convulsed with emotion. Of course true family was important to him. He'd always insinuated he felt like an outcast in his adopted family. He'd even commented on that similarity between Elise and him.

"I *should* have known," she said shakily.

He opened his hand along her jaw, cradling it. He was so large in comparison to her. She always felt so encompassed when he touched her . . . so cherished.

"Why should you have known? I wasn't comfortable speaking my wish aloud. I told no one, save Herr Schroeder, and only then in a business sense."

"You . . . you've never told anyone else about your search for your mother?"

He shook his head, his silvery-gray eyes steady on her. She experienced a sense of humbleness that he'd opened up to her.

"I'll help you find her, Lucien. I'll do whatever I can. I know how important family is to you," she whispered through a swollen throat.

"You have no idea how important," he said, his gaze running over her face. "But I want you to promise me you won't do or say anything in regard to this business. I have it all under control. Trust me."

"I do, but—"

"Come here," he interrupted gently. His tone was in stark contrast to his embrace. He crushed her to him, his arms surrounding her, holding her tight against his body, almost as if he wanted to absorb her. She clamped her eyes shut as a rush of emotion went through her. What was that powerful feeling that kept rising in her, stealing her words and her wits? She'd felt the seed of it toward Lucien, even as a girl. It'd sprouted since they'd come together again, mounting and growing and flowering. Tonight, it'd seemed to swell and bloom at his honesty, at his willingness to trust her with his vulnerability. Whatever this feeling was, it felt as if it'd suffocate her if she didn't release it.

Love. It's love.

She clenched her eyelids together tighter, as if she could vanquish that knowing voice. It frightened her, to think of it being true. She would be so weak, so helpless if she admitted to that need. But she couldn't keep it locked inside her much longer. . . .

Lucien's warm lips moved against her hairline and nuzzled her ear, the sharp shivers of excitement shooting through her making her forget her anguish . . . making her forget her unanswered questions.

"Let's forget about Helen Noble for now. I have a surprise for you," he said, his low voice in her ear making her shudder with pleasure. She shifted her hips ever so slightly, feeling his cock swell beneath her bottom and thigh. It seemed like ages since she last felt his embrace.

"What is it?" she whispered, tilting her chin and finding his jaw. She rained tiny kisses over his whiskers, thrilling to the abrading sensation against her sensitive lips.

"It wouldn't be a surprise if I just told you, would it?"

She pressed her mouth against his moving lips, fitting their contours together delicately. He growled softly at her teasing and seized her mouth in a voracious kiss.

She gave herself to that kiss wholesale, sensing how much he wanted to forget his anxieties and unanswered questions. His heat melted away her doubts as well, her insecurities about losing control . . . about falling in love.

"I'd like to go and shower after the trip," he muttered next to her lips a moment later. "I'll clean up in the spare bedroom bath so you can bathe if you like. I'll come and find you in a few minutes."

"Will I get my surprise then?"

"You'll get it then all right," he replied in a hard, dry tone that made her eyebrows go up. "You'll get your surprise and something extra for eavesdropping again," he said, the grin pulling at his lips intoxicating her.

"I wasn't eavesdropping. . . . I mean . . . not necessarily. Just because I was passing in the hallway and overheard you doesn't necessarily equate to eavesdropping."

He shook his head. "When are you going to learn I read your lies like a neon sign, *ma fifille*?" He cut off her protest with his mouth and tongue. She whimpered into his mouth and clutched his shoulders when he gathered her to him and stood, bringing her along with him. His kiss was so hot, so all-consuming, she thought he'd throw his plans to the wind and get into the shower with her. Instead, he set her down on the master suite bathroom floor and pressed his lips to her nose.

"Hurry up," he said succinctly when he backed away.

Even though she was disappointed when he walked out of the bathroom, leaving her alone, she liked his rough insistence for haste. She liked it a lot.

While she showered, she thought about the other things she'd overheard Herr Schroeder and Lucien discuss. Who was this man who had died in prison and toward whom Lucien expressed such bitterness? Herr Schroeder likely had worked on several different cases for him over the years. Still . . . surely a business concern wouldn't have made Lucien sound so disdainful.

She would ask Lucien about it, but not tonight. Tonight was special between them. She'd sensed it ever since he'd opened up his office door earlier, said her name, and pinned her with his stare. He'd come back early from Paris. He'd been honest with her about his search for his mother.

That meant more to Elise than she could put into words.

Ten minutes later, her curiosity and desire overcame her. Instead of waiting in bed, she walked out of the master suite in search of him, clean and fragrant from her shower. All the fatigue she'd experienced earlier that day was a mere memory. He came out of the extra bedroom almost at the same moment she left the master suite. They turned toward each other, half of the length of the hallway still between them. Her gaze lowered over the length of him covetously. He wore only a pair of black lounge pants, the drawstring tied several inches below his belly button, leaving his taut, ridged abdomen exposed. His smooth skin still looked moist from his shower. His muscles gleamed in the soft lighting from the hallway sconces.

She saw his gaze dip over her, and again that strange feeling overcame her . . . that shyness she'd never known until Lucien.

"You look beautiful," he said, walking toward her. She couldn't quite interpret his small, enigmatic smile. "Did Maria pick out that gown for you?" he asked, nodding at the short sapphire-blue nightgown she wore.

"*Maria?*" Elise asked, surprised. She laughed. "Of course not. Why would she?"

He shrugged, still looking amused. For the first time, she noticed he wore something she'd never seen before. A platinum chain looped around his neck. Attached to it was a small key.

"What's that?" she asked curiously, eyeing the key resting in the valley of bulging pectoral muscles.

"You'll see," he murmured.

"Is that my surprise?" she asked mischievously, eyeing the black velvet pouch he carried in one hand. He stepped nearer to her, so that the tips of her breasts were mere inches from his ribs.

"Part of it," he said, reaching up to tuck a tendril of hair behind her ear. Pleasure rippled through her at the caress of his fingertips.

"Where is the rest?" she prodded, laughter in her eyes and a small smile pulling at her lips as she looked up at him.

"Greedy little thing," he chastised at the same moment he bent and swept her into his arms. She was still laughing in pleasant surprise when he opened the door that led to the stairs.

"We're going up to the terrace?" she asked breathlessly as he strode up the steps rapidly on long legs. "But I thought . . . the bedroom," she said, unable to keep the disappointment from her tone. He carried her onto the massive deck that encompassed almost the entire rooftop. It was a warm June night. The sultry, pleasant lake breeze tickled her cheek. Lucien turned. She gasped at what she saw.

"Oh . . . oh, it's . . . how did you *do* that?"

She stared at Lucien wide-eyed and then back at the lushly romantic scene before her. "I bought the essentials and helped out, but mostly we have Maria to thank for the niceties," he replied as he carried her toward the east parapet that overlooked the expanse of Lake Michigan. He set her down at the foot of a bed.

And *what* a bed.

Elise twisted around, taking in her surroundings with amazed delight. She felt like she sat in the midst of a sensual, glowing lantern. She perched on a four-poster canopy bed, the tall posts made of a light bamboo composite that looked relatively easy to maneuver and manipulate for a temporary bed. But there was nothing makeshift about this decadent creation. White, opaque silk panes hung from the cross posts, shifting delicately in the gentle lake wind, the fabric blocking the view of the city behind them. The top of the bed was open to the night sky, and the east-facing portion was left exposed to the lake. Crisp white sheets covered the mattress and were folded down over a midnight-blue satin duvet. White rose petals had been sprinkled on the cover, as if to mimic the starlit night sky above them. One perfect white rose had been laid against the cushions at the head of the bed, the color of it a contrast to the dark blue of the pillowcases. Dozens of candles flickered and glowed in small glass holders that had been set along the four-foot-high brick parapet and all around the perimeter of the bed. A bucket stand had been set up next to the bed and filled with ice and a bottle of champagne.

A small smile shaped Lucien's mouth when she looked at him. She shook her head in disbelief.

"You're a romantic, Lucien Sauvage."

"Would you like some champagne?" he asked as he sat down next to her.

She shook her head, unable to pull her gaze off him. "Maybe later," she whispered. Something caught her eye. "My pearls," she exclaimed in surprise, seeing the long rope coiled on the far side of the bed.

"I had Maria bring them up. I hope you don't mind," he said huskily. Elise swallowed, guessing he probably planned to use them again to restrain her.

"It's a good thing you pay Maria so well," she mumbled, blushing. "I can just imagine the stories she could tell about you, given some of the things she sees around here."

"There's nothing scandalous about pearls."

"I'm willing to bet there is with what you plan to do with them."

He chuckled and prodded her with a hand on her upper arm. She scooted over the mattress with him. The delicate scent of rose petals filtered into her nose by the time they leaned back together on the pillows. The building where they perched was the tallest in the near vicinity. With the silk drapes blocking the city, they were in their own private little cocoon, even with the bed being open to the sky and lake. Lucien reached behind her and set the rose in her lap.

"Is all of this to make up for the fact that you kept me in the dark for so long about your mother and Ian?"

"All of this is because I missed you," he said, his nostrils flaring slightly as his gaze ran over her face. "And because I've wanted you for a long, long time and circumstances have prevented it."

"Circumstances? Such as my lack of discipline?"

"Such as my inability to maintain my own discipline when you refused to attempt to control yours," he said with a pointed glance. His head lowered. Her breath caught when he brushed his lips across hers and she inhaled his clean, spicy scent. "And because until the night I had to leave for Paris, you refused to tell me what it was you wanted. What you needed."

She placed one opened hand against a smooth pectoral muscle, wondering at the solidity of him, the strength. "To submit to you?" she asked shakily.

He nodded, his gaze unwavering.

"In bed. To submit to you in bed," she clarified breathlessly. "Because I don't know that I can submit to anyone—even you— elsewhere."

"You will," he said softly, the hint of a smile on his mouth when he felt her backbone stiffen. "Whenever I want you, you will submit. It will often not be anywhere near a bed."

She swallowed thickly and nodded. "You know what I meant. Sexually."

"I know what you meant," he said, his voice a velvet caress against her skin. He toyed with the strap of her gown, watching himself, his actions and stare highly distracting to her. "And yes, submission sexually is what I meant. What I expect."

"All right," she whispered, her pulse beginning to throb at her throat. What was he going to do with her, now that she'd agreed to submit and they were face-to-face? Liquid arousal surged between her thighs. She pressed them together to staunch the sudden ache. The rose fell away, unheeded.

His gaze shifted to meet her stare, but he kept playing with the strap of her gown, his fingertips flickering against her shoulder making it difficult for her to concentrate.

"Would you like your gift now?"

"What?" Elise asked, his hot eyes making her forget the velvet pouch he'd carried. She recalled it sluggishly when he placed the pouch in her lap. She stared down at it dazedly.

"I had them made specifically for you."

"You did?" she asked with restrained excitement. His long fingers moved in her lap, flipping back the flap of the pouch and sending prickles of pleasure through her. He tilted the pouch and two exquisite bracelets fell onto the silk of her gown.

"Oh, Lucien," she whispered. The bracelets were a pair, although not identical. Candlelight made the sapphires flicker as though they contained trapped fires. The gems were interspersed with tiny, perfectly detailed platinum charms. Her eyes wide, she studied and took delight in each one in turn: a spoon in commemoration of her love of cooking; a horse in midstride that very much resembled Kesara; a tiny lock; a miniature flag with the English Union Jack on one side and the French tricolor on the other—the only painted charm—a homage to her heritage; and . . .

"Oh," she exclaimed, grinning happily when she recognized a platinum fishing rod—a memento of that golden summer spent with Lucien so long ago. "Thank you," she said fervently, beaming at him. She'd received some of the most expensive gifts in the world before, but never anything so intimate. So personal. "I love them. They're so beautiful. So unique."

"Like the wearer," he said. She flushed with pleasure. He lifted his arm. She watched in amazement as he drew the chain and key off his neck. "Other charms may be added. You can wear them on one wrist when you go out in public. But when we're together like this, I'd prefer you wore one on each wrist. I will use them to cuff you."

"What?" she asked breathlessly, thinking she'd misunderstood him. Her eyes widened when he matter-of-factly lowered the straps of her gown down over her arms, causing the fabric to slide down her chest and drape at the tips of her breasts. "But . . . the bracelets are so delicate."

"Do you value them?"

"So much," she assured.

"Then as you learned with the pearls, you will take care not to pull at your restraints. Don't worry," he said, picking up one of the bracelets and releasing the clasp. He slipped it around her right wrist. "If I ever feel you are losing control, I will restrain you with something more durable. But it will please me to see you bound by restraints that pay tribute to your beauty." He met her stare as he fastened the second bracelet around her other wrist. "It will please me to see you exhibit a little control, even in the midst of letting go."

Elise swallowed thickly, both intimidated and aroused by his words. She *would* take care of the bracelets. They were an exquisite gift from Lucien. He would also drive her to mindless ecstasy. She knew he would. She watched as he used the key to unfasten the tiny platinum lock. He replaced the chain back around his neck, then bent his head to insert the lock through a metal loop on the opposite bracelet. The lock clicked shut. Her wrists were bound together now. Could she keep the priceless cuffs intact? she wondered anxiously. A pressure grew in her as Lucien regarded her, and she knew this delicious friction is what he'd intended all along by his gift of precious restraints.

"Put your arms above your head and lean back against the pillows," he instructed gruffly, his hand warm on her upper arm. She raised her bound wrists over her head. He pressed closer to her, his crotch brushing her hip. At the same moment that she slid against the slick surface of the bedding, reclining on the pillows, his hand glided downward, tugging her nightgown down over the peaks of her breasts, then down over her belly and hips and off her feet. She was naked, completely exposed to the night sky and the candlelight. Her nipples stiffened, not from the cool lake breeze but from Lucien's hot stare. He groaned softly as he looked down at her.

She bit her lip as he reached for the pearl rope. She watched him, her heart starting to thrum at her throat as he looped the creamy gems around her ankles. The pearls clicked gently together as he manipulated them, adding to the voluptuous spell he spun around her. When he ran out of rope, and there wasn't enough slack in the silk to loop around her entire foot again, he carefully looped the pearls around the two largest toes on both her feet.

"It's very . . . secure," she said when he scooted up on the mattress to sit next to her again. Her ankles were bound surprisingly tight together. He smiled as he looked down at her.

"You are well and truly trussed by jewels," he murmured, his gaze skimming over her belly and mons and lingering on her ankles. "Do not climax until I remove the pearls, do you understand?"

"Why not?" she asked, confused by the sternness of his voice.

"First, because you don't have my permission to do so. And second, the feet flex during climax. It's an instinctual response. You will likely break the silk if you come."

Her eyelids narrowed on him even as her clit throbbed in arousal. "You truly are a devil, do you know that?"

"You tease me about being a devil, but you know I would never truly harm you, don't you?"

"Of course I do," she exclaimed, her brow creasing at his sudden intensity.

He just nodded, seeming reassured. "Now . . . tell me again what you desire," he said gruffly, his gaze fastening on her breasts and then flickering to her face.

"You. To submit to you."

"I'm so proud of you," he said gently. He palmed her jaw. "I know how hard it is for you to willingly forsake control. Trust me," he said.

"I do," she whispered.

She felt his cock harden next to her and wondered what he was thinking as his gaze roved over her face with an expression of fierce possession. "You haunt me, night and day. Don't ever worry that you can't please me, Elise. If you are honest about your desires, you'll please me every time."

He leaned closer. His addictive scent tickled her nose—a combination of his skin and his soap and his cologne. It mingled with the fresh breeze and the scent of rose petals, making her dizzy.

"I want to please you, Lucien. Tell me what to do," she said.

His nostrils flared slightly as he looked down at her.

"You're doing it, in spades."

She repressed a whimper at the sound of his low, sexy voice and the blazing quality to his eyes. He caressed her, running his hands along her sides and over her hips, massaging her back muscles . . . shaping a breast to his palm. No one touched her like Lucien. She felt owned beneath his touch, cherished like she never had in her life. She also sensed his restrained hunger, his mounting excitement.

He plucked at her stiffening nipples and she moaned, twisting slightly on the luxurious bedding. She felt the pearls pulling taut and forced herself to stop. He moved, straddling her body, holding himself off her with his knees and flexing arms. She looked up at the glorious sight of him framed by the starlit night sky. How she wished she could press up against him, rub her breasts next to the hard, muscular wall of his chest, slide their bellies together, stroke his awesome erection.

"Do you have any idea what it does to me to see you restrained and helpless to resist?"

The platinum key hung from his neck. It wasn't the only thing hanging over her. She noticed how huge his cock looked, suspended in the air between them and barely covered by the thin layer of his pants. She slicked her tongue over her lower lip in nervous excitement.

"Elise?" he prompted.

"I'm guessing you like it?" she asked, still staring at his erection.

He chuckled. "Yes, you make me stiff as stone. But that's not what I meant entirely," he murmured. She held her breath, watching him as his elbows bent and he lowered his head. She whimpered when he inserted a tight nipple between his lips and lashed at it with a warm, wet tongue. He drew on her and she felt that tug all the way to her womb.

"I meant that it does something to me to see you willingly give yourself," he said a moment later, his warm breath brushing against her damp, erect nipple. She opened her eyes and made a whimpering noise of protest at the absence of his mouth on her nipple.

"I would have given myself willingly anytime you asked," she said.

"I know," he said, shifting his body so that he was kneeling over her. "But I wanted you to ask." Perhaps he noticed the flash of irritation that went through her at his words, because he added pointedly, "Not beg, *ma chère*. *Ask*. There's a difference between asking and begging. There is no desperation in asking—only courage."

Her lips closed, her complaint forgotten. He smiled. Her womb contracted. *What a beautiful man.*

He put his hands on the outer and under curves of her breasts and lifted them, plumping them in his palms. She moaned when she saw the way he stared at them so greedily.

"I have been dreaming night and day about your breasts. They've become the focal point of ridiculous amounts of masturbation."

A vivid image popped into her mind's eye of him fisting his formidable cock, his muscles flexed and rigid, stroking . . . pounding. . . .

She gasped at the powerful image. "I didn't think you ever noticed them," she said in a choked voice as he shaped her breasts to his hands, causing the nipples to poke between his thumb and forefinger. She'd never seen a more erotic sight in her life than the vision of her pale breasts in his dark, masculine hands.

"When I'm finished with you, you'll have little doubt about how much I think of you. And know that everything I'm about to do to you I've thought about in vivid detail more times than I can count," he growled softly before he leaned down and took her mouth in a scorching kiss. She kissed him back eagerly, her awareness eclipsed

in its entirety by his delicious taste and skilled, sensuous tongue, by
the feeling of his hands massaging her breasts in a manner that
struck her as firm . . . lascivious. He wasn't treating her with kid
gloves. He wasn't harsh, by any means, but he was making his desire
baldly evident. Had she really once thought that he was cold toward
her? Ridiculous. He was rabid with lust. His control was just as
strong, but tonight, he liberated it.

Sensing his naked, unmasked desire freed her own.

His mouth was hot and demanding on her neck. He took a small
bite out of her shoulder muscle and she squirmed in arousal in her
restraints.

"Keep still," he soothed at the same moment that he gathered her
breasts in his hands, pushing them together until the nipples were
just inches apart. He ran his thumbs over both peaks, staring at her
heatedly, before he scooted back farther over her thighs, leaned
down, and slicked his tongue over both nipples.

"Oh!" she cried out sharply, her pelvis flexing upward, the action
purely instinctual to alleviate the sharp stab of arousal that shot
through her pussy. Her bottom came up several inches off the bed.
Her thighs brushed against his heavy cock and balls. He continued
to massage her breasts in his hands and lick and suckle her nipples.
She watched, spellbound by the image of him sucking on the tip of
one breast, then the other. She twisted against the delicious weight
of his cock and moaned in a fever of lust, all the time distantly aware
that she must be careful of her fragile bonds.

Still, she writhed in restrained bliss.

"Put your beautiful ass back on the bed or I will punish you," she
heard him say as if from a distance. The edge of his tone penetrated
her arousal. She sunk back onto the bed, missing his heat and heavy,
rigid cock. He continued to play with her breasts for the next several
minutes, his actions deliberate . . . ruthless, driving her into a frenzy
of excitement. Her nipples grew exquisitely sensitive and swollen

with his relentless ministrations. By the time he inserted one deeply into his mouth and sucked hard, lightly pinching the other one, she was desperate.

"Oh, please. Please stop it, Lucien," she moaned, grinding her ass against the mattress. He'd been right before. She didn't crave pain, but this sort of hurt was a heady rush. Despite her plea, he continued to suck and pluck at her nipples and squeeze her flushed breasts until she thought she'd scream. She thrashed on the mattress. "Oh, I'm going to come," she muttered, sounding as incredulous as she felt. She hadn't known it was possible to come by having a man treat her breasts with such rough, sweet love.

"You don't have my permission," he said gruffly, his mouth less than an inch from an erect nipple. "You must be still. I'm preparing your breasts, making the nipples ready."

"For *what*?" she asked in a strangled voice.

But he ignored her and continued with his task, sucking at her nipples until the cool lake wind had no effect on her fevered body. She grew mindless with excitement, twisting and moaning beneath him. She gasped in protest when he raised himself slightly, his lips damp and his expression rigid.

"You have to be the most sensitive, hot-blooded . . . irrepressible female in existence," he muttered thickly.

"You make that sound like a bad thing."

"It is. You are going to break your pearls," he replied curtly, his gaze flashing to her face. His expression softened. "It's also a blessedly good thing."

She smiled, panting softly, watching him dazedly as he grabbed for something on the mattress. It took her a moment to recognize the velvet pouch. It had slipped out of her lap when he removed her gown. She'd felt the weight of it earlier and knew there was something else in it besides the bracelets, but had been too preoccupied with Lucien's lovemaking to comment on it.

Lucien tipped the bag and more sapphires and a platinum chain spilled into his large hand.

"Oh . . . it's *beautiful*," she said, her eyes glued to the unique piece of jewelry. He opened it and held it up for her avid gaze. The top part looked like it went around the neck—an exquisite necklace of filigreed platinum interspersed with dozens of gleaming, half-carat sapphires. She'd known she was correct about her assumption when Lucien knelt over her and looped the necklace portion around her throat, fastening it. The unusual part was the two chains that dropped vertically six or seven inches below the necklet. Another chain was looped between the two suspended metal ropes, and several sapphires were suspended from it.

"What *is* it?" she asked, bewildered as she watched him pinch a tiny, flexible loop that was attached to the chain.

"The necklace has a nipple chain attached. You can remove the chain and merely wear it as a necklace," he explained. She moaned softly when he slipped a stiff nipple into the tiny loop. "I just have to twist this sapphire—like this—and the loop tightens." Her eyes sprang wide when the metal loop narrowed, pinching at her nipple. Lucien studied her face raptly. "It should pinch, but not be unduly uncomfortable. Is it too much?" he asked quietly. "I can loosen the loop."

She shook her head, too amazed and aroused to speak. She couldn't stop staring at the erotic sight of her pink nipple surrounded by the metal loop. It was tight enough to create a focused, mild sting. The pressure and slight abrasion was highly exciting. She felt her pulse began to throb in her nipple. She experienced an overwhelming urge to feel more friction on the highly sensitized crest. Her breathing started to come erratically as she watched him attach the joined chain to her other nipple. When he was finished, the delicate chain hung in an arc between her nipples.

Lucien sat back and inspected her, his face rigid and shadowed.

The dark pink tips of her breasts were very erect, but they seemed fatter than usual, the loops causing increased blood flow, plumping them. She bit her lip to stifle a moan when she saw his cock lurch against his cotton pants.

"Here, let me help you," he said, putting his hands on her back and lifting her from the pillows. "Sit up slightly. Let the chain fall free between your breasts," he commanded.

She moaned in stark arousal when he repositioned her so that she leaned partially upright against the pillows and the chain hung free between the tips of her breasts. The sapphires attached to the nipple chain acted as erotic weights, pulling gently at the taut peaks. Her clit twanged sharply. She whimpered and jerked her hands in the delicate wrist restraints, wincing.

If she hadn't been bound, her hand would be on her pussy, trying to staunch that stabbing ache.

His stare leapt to hers, and she knew he'd noticed her reaction.

"It feels good?" he asked huskily.

"In a weird way, it feels fantastic," she whispered, bewildered by her powerful response to the nipple chain.

A smile flickered across his lips. "You have no idea how beautiful you look." He reached up and gently plucked at one of the center sapphires. She cried out at the tug on her nipples, clenching her thighs together tight. Lucien appeared rapt by her reaction. He gently knocked at another sapphire.

"*Lucien,*" she groaned feverishly. Her hips twisted on the mattress. She was desperate for pressure . . . for release from this sweet torture.

"Yes?" he asked quietly.

"I need to come," she said, her face clenched tight with arousal. She licked her upper lip and tasted salt. *"Please."*

He muttered something terse under his breath and scooted her body back into a reclining position. She panted, feeling disoriented as she watched him rapidly unwind her pearls from her ankles and set them aside, liberating her feet. He lowered over her, straddling her with his arms holding himself off her, his muscles bulging. She cried out when he matter-of-factly ground his hard, swollen cock against her pussy.

He looked fierce as he stared down at her and circled his hips, his actions stunningly precise. The key hung from his throat, just inches from her lips. "I can feel how wet you are," he grated out. "You're like an inferno. I'm going to fuck you so hard and melt in that hot little pussy."

Her facial muscles clenched tight in cresting pleasure. She craned up her head off the pillow and stilled the swaying key with her seeking lips. Lucien groaned gutturally and thrust extra hard.

She exploded in orgasm against the delicious pressure of his throbbing cock, her cries flying past the little key that had fallen against her tongue.

Much to her disappointment, he lifted his cock from her pussy almost immediately when her shudders of pleasure waned. He flashed a sexy smile at her as she panted on the pillows.

"You got that excited? You have the most responsive breasts. I'm going to have so much fun with them. I'm going to treat your nipples to such sweet torture," he murmured, still watching her with fiery eyes as he again rose to a kneeling position over her. Her ragged breathing came to an abrupt halt when he shoved his hand beneath the waistband of his sleeping pants. She watched, mesmerized, as he extricated the thick column of his cock. He remained kneeling over her for a moment, stroking himself.

"Let me, Lucien," she whispered longingly, and her desire was so sharp, she knew that he knew precisely what she meant.

"You are sweetness itself, but your mouth makes things too easy," he said, dark amusement in his tone. "It's tempting, but I'm going to ravish you right now. This is another thing I imagined doing to your pretty breasts."

She watched as he came toward her on his knees. He brushed

the flaring, velvety cockhead against a hypersensitive nipple and she gasped. She bit her lower lip to stifle a scream when he batted teasingly at the nipple chain with his heavy erection. He swung the thick column of his cock against the outer curve of her left breast, gently flogging her.

"Devil," she whispered shakily when she saw his small smile.

"Another time I will have you hold them together and I'll fuck them until I come on your nipples. Will you like that?"

"Yes. God yes," she said, thrashing her hips on the mattress, rapidly rising up the slope of renewed arousal. What he said in combination with what he was doing to her was going to have her shuddering in orgasm again within minutes. Maybe it was because he was typically so restrained, or maybe it was because of the thick lust in his smooth, rich voice, but hearing Lucien talk dirty was a potent aphrodisiac.

He backed up slightly and leaned down, placing his mouth against the side of her ribs. She shivered at his hot kisses. It felt like his lips and teeth and tongue were everywhere at once. Her trembling continued as he charted her ribs and belly. All the while, she was tortured by the vision of his heavy penis hanging over the waistband of his pants.

"Why don't you take off your pants?" she asked between gasps as he ran his tongue along the strip of skin above her pubic hair, lifting his head when she tried to raise her pelvis to his mouth and get him just where she needed him.

"In good time," he murmured, flashing her an amused, sardonic glance that she interpreted as a warning for patience on her part. By the time he began torturing her thighs with his consuming mouth, she was squirming once again in full arousal. It was incredibly erotic to watch him, knowing she had no choice but to lie there and accept his every caress, kiss, and tease.

"Oh, please," she whispered a moment later as he licked the inner part of her thigh. She gave a quivery whimper when his tongue flicked within an inch of her pussy.

"Your juices are running down your thigh. Hmm, delicious," he said thickly before he tasted her again.

She clamped her eyelids shut, overwhelmed by the image of his dark head between her thighs. She keened in growing frustration as his tongue flicked over her moist skin yet again. Her toes curled.

"Tell me what you want," he murmured.

"Put your mouth on me and make me come," she begged through lips that felt swollen and overly sensitive.

His nostrils flared slightly at her bald plea. "Since your desire is in accordance with mine, I'm more than willing to grant your wish."

He matter-of-factly bent her knees and spread her legs. He rolled back her hips, fully exposing her pussy. She yelped a moment later when he knelt before her, his knees bracketing her hips, and lifted her lower body off the bed, his hands open on her buttocks. She'd never get used to how easily he took her weight.

He sat on his haunches and brought her pussy slowly to his mouth, biceps bulging hard. The anticipation seemed to cut at her from the inside out.

She detonated a moment later as he whipped at her clitoris with the firm, wet lash of his tongue. He continued to eat her as she moaned and shuddered in orgasm, covering her outer sex with his lips and applying a firm suction that left her flying in the sexual stratosphere for an unprecedented length of time. He lifted his head after he'd worked a final shudder out of her. He lowered her and she sagged into the mattress, utterly wrung out. She noticed that his facial muscles were rigid and his lips were gleaming with her juices.

"You're delicious. I'm going to shave you sometime soon. Nothing is going to interfere with me getting my fill of this pussy."

Her vagina contracted tightly at his stark, unrelenting tone.

"Yes, all right," she whispered, even though she knew he hadn't said it for her agreement. He seemed single-minded in his lust. She gasped when he lowered his head again, tilting it at an angle. He plunged his tongue into her slit and ladled out her juices, sucking them into his mouth. Oh God, it was a decadent, sybaritic delight to have him pleasure her with such skill, to feel his sexual hunger penetrate every pore of her being. She had never felt herself to be the object of such concentrated, burning desire in her entire life. She wanted to touch him so badly. Her palms itched with thwarted desire.

"I want to touch you. Why do you have to restrain me?" she asked in frustration as he continued to dip his tongue into her pussy.

He lifted his head. "It's exciting, knowing that you're at my mercy, that you'll have no choice but to accept whatever I give you," he said gruffly, rising to his knees and once again straddling her supine body.

"You mean like for punishment?"

"Not just that. For pleasure. You can't escape any of it. No matter how intense it gets."

"I don't really like pain," she said weakly. "I'm not a masochist."

A small smile shaped his gorgeous mouth. His gaze flickered over her flushed breasts wearing the nipple chain. "You like small amounts of it. Nothing too harsh. Don't worry, I've noticed. I'm getting used to what excites you. I look forward to finding out more." When she didn't reply because she was too busy absorbing the fact that he'd been reading her on their other times together, gauging her, he added, "You've become aroused when I've punished you before, or when I instructed you to punish yourself, haven't you? And that hurt, didn't it?"

"Not much. It stung—especially the paddle and the hairbrush— but I was more . . ."

"What?"

"Excited," she whispered.

He nodded in understanding. "And you like the pinch on your

nipples, don't you?" he asked gruffly, touching a crest with his fore-finger. Her nerves were so exquisitely sensitized she shuddered in pleasure even from that soft caress. "If things ever become too intense between us, though, all you have to do is say 'End it.' That's all. And I will. But you must say *that*, specifically. If you scream for me to stop or curse at me or beg me, I will continue according to my aim. *End it*. That's what you must say, and I will. No questions asked. Do you understand, Elise?" he asked sharply.

She swallowed and nodded her head. Her vagina had clamped tight when she thought of begging him to stop and him continuing with whatever he was doing. Why was that? Perhaps because he'd also given her the power to truly stop him? It was like a secret key, a get-out-of-jail-free card she had forever at her disposal.

"I understand," she whispered.

His gaze lingered on her lips even when she no longer spoke. "You have come to me and been honest about your desire. Now I'll be honest about mine. You goaded me into taking you like an animal that night in the stables. But tonight, I'll take my pleasure of you because you have offered yourself, and I have been burning alive from wanting you." He caressed the underside of her bound arm, then her chest, finally cupping her breast. She choked off a moan when he gently tweaked at a sapphire. "I have been holding back, chaining myself. But tonight"—he glanced at her, his expression fierce—"I'll feast on you and I won't come away hungry, Elise. I will take you hard . . . maybe a little savagely."

He studied her reaction, candlelight glinting in his eyes. His pants were still gathered beneath his cock. It jumped when he said those words. She clamped her thighs together, his rich voice echoing in her head: *hard . . . maybe a little savagely.*

"If you want me to stop at any time, remember what I told you to say?"

She nodded. He really had been holding himself back when it came to her. Tonight, she was going to be the recipient of all that trapped passion. She craved it, but how could she not be intimidated by being the target of all that raw, pent-up sexual power as well?

"Say the words I told you to speak if you want me to stop. I want to know you remember them," he said grimly.

"End it," she repeated. "But I won't want you to. I want you to fuck me hard. I want you to use me for your pleasure, Lucien."

His eyes flashed and a small snarl shaped his mouth. He opened her legs wide and took his cock into his hand.

"Then you will have your wish, *ma chère*."

Part VII

When I Need You

Chapter Thirteen

ucien had told her he'd been burning alive with need for her, and he'd meant every word he said. As he spread her pale thighs and positioned himself to take her, he indeed felt as if a fire were burning beneath his skin, racing in his blood, hollowing out his insides until there was nothing left in him but pure, blazing, cutting desire. He propped himself up on one elbow, watching as he inserted the tip of his cock into the center of her glistening pink slit, willing her to bloom for him . . . to accept his monstrous need.

They both gasped at the sensation of him stretching her delicate tissues and embedding his cockhead in her clamping, sultry embrace. He lowered his other arm, holding himself off her, and focused on her rapt face as he pushed his cock into her body. He'd been obsessed by the idea of her pussy for the last several days, haunted by the idea of being submersed in her again. It was a sweeter agony than he either recalled or imagined.

A moment later, he bumped his testicles against her damp tissues and caught her shaky cry with his lips. He immediately began to fuck her with short strokes, examining the way her face tightened every time he jabbed at her clit on his forceful downstroke. He groaned in ecstasy. She was too small and feminine for his big, masculine body. Yet she took him without complaint. In fact, if her sublime, rapturous expression was any indication, she liked the way he filled her. The sounds of the waves hitting the breakwater and the distant hum of the city were drowned out by the throb of his heartbeat in his ears. He matched his rhythm to it, so that the pounding in his ears fell into tempo with the slap of his pelvis and balls against Elise's skin. He withdrew his cock farther and slammed into her harder, grimacing in pleasure. She whimpered and he felt her muscular walls convulse around him. He drove deeper, harder, faster, until a cry popped out of her throat and her nipple chain jumped with each intense thrust.

"Your pussy is perfect," he grated out, rearing over and pounding his cock high inside her. "Tell me it's mine. Say it."

"My pussy is yours," she said shakily.

Her eyes sprang wide and she keened when he rocketed into her.

"That's right. Mine," he uttered savagely, feeling the unbearable, untenable fire rising in him. Fucking Elise truly was like throwing himself wholesale in the flames. He rolled back her hips and came up on his knees. She cried out when he pressed her knees to within inches of her chest and plowed into her. His growl of primal satisfaction twined with her scream. He rode her like that for blissful moments, the flex of her hips providing the perfect counter-rhythm to his demanding strokes, the friction divine . . . too optimal for him to exist in this taut ecstasy for long.

When he felt his balls tingle with impending climax, he forced himself to still high inside her squeezing, hot channel. He gritted his teeth at the sensation of the back of her womb pressing against his cockhead. She squealed. He leaned down and inserted a nipple between his lips. They were swollen from the clamping loops, blood-flushed and red. He lashed at the tender flesh with his tongue, wincing at the delicious sensation of her shuddering around his cock as she came. When he bit tenderly at the sensitive morsel, adding the abrasion of his teeth to the clamp, she jerked her bound arms from over her head and scraped his scalp with her fingernails hard enough to draw blood.

Climax seized him at the sensation. He erupted while pressed deep inside her, pleasure blasting through him like a firebomb. When it relented slightly, he fucked her shuddering pussy with short, hard strokes, still coming, still burning alive, wondering how she could satisfy him so completely, and yet he already wanted more.

He slowed, gasping for air, still planted deep inside her. She quieted by degrees, until her fingers in his hair caressed instead of clawed. She looked sublimely beautiful when he met her stare.

"Don't get too relaxed," he said. "I plan to fuck you again in a moment."

Her fingers paused. "Already?" she asked incredulously.

"I have been waiting for this for a long time," he said, stroking her clamping channel with his satiated cock and feeling the embers of arousal flicker and smoke.

A small smile shaped her lush mouth. He was uncommonly fond of her curving lips, that sparkle of mischief and fun she got in her sapphire eyes . . . everything about her. He leaned down and touched his mouth to her smile at the same time he withdrew and thrust deep again. She moaned. "I hope you didn't have any other plans this weekend, because I plan to spend as much time inside you as is humanly possible."

"I'm here to please," she murmured, looping her bound wrists behind his neck and squeezing his cock with her vaginal muscles. He gasped and began stroking her again. She spoke the absolute truth.

Did she ever.

Elise had thought he'd been speaking figuratively when he'd said he planned to spend as much time inside her as possible, but he spent a good portion of the entire night doing just that. When he wasn't inside her, he was making love to her in other ways and making her scream in pleasure. He finally removed her nipple chain and jeweled cuffs, and they drifted off into an exhausted sleep an hour before dawn.

She awoke to the sensation of Lucien nuzzling her ear with his nose.

"The sun is up. It's getting warm up here," he murmured in her ear. "Let's go downstairs and shower."

Elise blinked sleepily and sat up in the luxurious bed. The sun was well above the shimmering blue great lake. It must be ten or eleven o'clock in the morning. She closed her eyes and absorbed the sun's golden warmth. Memories from the magical night replayed in her mind's eye. She turned to smile at Lucien. He reclined against the pillows naked, a decadently handsome sybarite, watching her through a narrowed gaze. He reached up and caressed her naked shoulder, trailing his finger over her skin.

"Every time I think you couldn't look more beautiful, you make a liar of me," he said.

She laughed. "I must look like a wreck."

"You're exquisite. You shine brighter than the sun itself."

Her smile faded at his simple, stark declaration, once again bewildered by his intensity . . . his depths. She could tell he'd meant what he'd said, but he was thinking of something else, as well, something that didn't match the gilded sunshine and their glorious night of lovemaking.

"Lucien? Is there something wrong?" she asked quietly.

He just stared at her a moment, blinked, and seemed to come to himself. "Of course not. Here, put on your gown," he instructed, handing her the discarded garment and finding his pants, which he pulled on. He gathered up her jewelry and clambered off the bed. "Come on. Time to cool off in the shower."

"But what about the bed? I think it's supposed to rain this evening," Elise mentioned dubiously as she followed him.

He nodded toward a locked ten-by-fifteen-foot structure in the center of the roof. "I'll call someone from building maintenance and ask if they'll break it down and store it in there. It's an airtight enclosure. I think the bed will fit in there."

"You've never stored it in there before?" she asked, studying his profile closely.

He gave a sideways glance and smiled knowingly. She blushed, suddenly certain he'd guessed at the reason for her question. "I just purchased that bed. For you."

She grinned, unreasonably happy at the knowledge that he didn't typically treat women to the decadent fantasy of being made love to by Lucien beneath the stars.

They showered together in the master bath, taking their time, washing each other with caressing fingertips, finding ticklish spots, laughing, and kissing each other's smiles. Her nipples were still slightly swollen, flushed and sensitive from the nipple chain. Lucien played with them gently while they bathed, his gaze hot and admiring. She loved seeing Lucien like this, relished his unguarded manner, sultry stares, and fond teasing, and she treasured the knowledge that he'd loosened his self-restraint enough to show her more of his true self.

That required trust, didn't it? she speculated hopefully.

When she noticed how full and firm his penis became as they showered, she reached to stroke him, but he halted her with a hand on her wrists.

"We'll let it build," he said, softly cupping an aching breast and tweaking a nipple before he released her. Something about his husky voice and steamy stare sent a thrill through her. At one time, she would have taken his response as a rebuff, but not anymore. He'd proven his desire for her exceeded her wildest dreams. His methods of restraint only served to mount the friction so that the final release was all that much more explosive.

"I'd like to take you somewhere," he said as he dried her off with a towel a while later.

"Where?" she asked.

"You'll see," he replied quietly. "Dress in riding clothes. We'll go see Jax and Kesara afterward and ride."

Her curiosity piqued, she dressed in dark brown jodhpurs, boots, and a cream-colored short-sleeved blouse. As she buttoned up the shirt in the bathroom, she noticed that her nipples were still very sensitive, the material of her bra abrading them slightly. It was a pleasant, welcome sensation, a constant reminder of her night spent with Lucien. When she glanced at herself in the mirror, she saw that the peaks protruded from the fitted shirt, showing even through the light padding of her bra. She brushed her fingertips over a stiff nipple. Wincing, she pressed her hand between her thighs to staunch that sudden, sharp ache.

It was as if her body had sprung a billion more nerve endings beneath that starlit sky and Lucien's touch.

She let her hair dry in natural waves, combed it, and pinned back her bangs with a white and yellow daisy clip. The decoration matched her sunny mood. They shared a smile when they rejoined in the bedroom after dressing, Lucien's gaze running down over her appreciatively . . . possessively. He cradled her jaw and brushed his thumb over her cheek. He looked outrageously handsome in a pair of khaki-colored breeches, a light blue cotton shirt, and scuffed, supple, dark brown leather riding boots. What Lucien did to a pair of riding pants ought to be considered illegal, in her opinion. She was about to tease him by saying so but paused, her lips parted, when she saw the intent way his gray eyes ran over her face.

"You've bloomed overnight," he murmured, kissing her so softly, so persuasively, she closed her eyes and lost herself for a moment. He finally lifted his head and took her hand, and they left the penthouse together. He said little once they'd gotten into his sedan, but Elise was divinely relaxed and happy as he maneuvered smoothly through the busy city streets. It was strange, this elevated feeling, this contentment. Her whole life she'd chafed a little inside her own skin, always longing, always striving for the electricity of the perfect moment, maneuvering and pushing herself without really understanding where she wanted to be, or precisely what she wanted to be doing.

So amazing to realize that she'd arrived, that she was precisely where she wanted to be in that precious moment. She glanced at Lucien's classic profile and told herself to savor every delicious second as it came . . . and not think about tomorrow.

Lucien pulled in front of a nineteenth-century redbrick building with beautiful, stone-carved ornamental decoration. It was about fifteen stories, built in the French-chateau style. The street on which they'd parked reminded her more of Paris than Chicago, with its brick townhomes and trees that created a canopy over the street. The way Lucien stared at the building to the left of them made her lean forward and gaze at the structure.

"It's lovely. So is this entire area. Where are we?" she asked, never having seen this atmospheric neighborhood on the Near South Side of Chicago that spoke of another era.

"In the Prairie Avenue Historic District," he said. He turned the keys in the ignition. "Do you want to see inside?"

She smiled as realization hit her. "Is this the building you bought for the new hotel?"

He nodded. She flipped open the door and sprang out of the vehicle. "Let's go," she said enthusiastically.

"You have *got* to be kidding," she said, utterly stunned ten minutes later when they walked into the building's kitchen. It was enormous, and even though it was ancient and had fallen into disrepair, all the hallmarks of the classic European great kitchen remained: the large alabaster-topped center island, the exquisite handmade cabinetry complete with intact lead-crystal panes, three large serviceable but still elegant copper chandeliers.

"It's pretty amazing, isn't it?" Lucien asked, looking around the interior. "It was the preferred hotel for guests visiting Chicago during the late eighteen and early nineteen hundreds. After the district fell to manufacturing, it became an administrative building for a local hospital. This kitchen hasn't been used for its original purpose in almost a hundred years."

"It's perfect," she said, meaning it. It was every chef's dream to revamp a classic kitchen like this one, stock it with all the new culinary accessories, and yet keep all the elegant nuances of days gone by.

Lucien turned. "Do you want it?"

It took a moment for her to absorb the meaning of his quiet question, but even then, she was confused.

"Want it?"

"Yes. With proper redevelopment and remodeling, will these premises suit your purpose for the restaurant you told me about?"

She blinked and looked around her stupidly.

"Of course they would. It'd be fantastic. But you bought it for your restaurant and hotel," she exclaimed.

"I know. I'm offering you the position of comanager of the establishment, if you'd like it . . . along with that of executive chef, of course." When she just stared at him, speechless, he added, "I was very impressed by your idea, Elise. I had a market-research firm do the statistics for me. This entire area is undergoing a massive redevelopment, but there aren't enough restaurants and clubs to keep up with the growing population. There isn't one boutique hotel within two square miles. Plus, there's almost a dozen new upscale condo buildings within a half-mile, not to mention a high-end workout facility patronized by members of the Board of Trade. The idea of healthy, fresh gourmet food without the temptation of alcohol will appeal for several reasons. I think it'd be a good opportunity for your concept. We might consider marketing lunch for an 'in,' and using that hook to expand to dinner."

"Lucien, I just wanted your advice on how to get started. You don't have to offer me all of this."

"I know that." He took a step toward her, his gaze narrowing. "If you don't like the idea of having your restaurant here, just say the word. We'll find the right location for you."

"No, it's not that!" she exclaimed, once again staring around her in disbelief. "I've never seen premises more ideal in my life. But . . . this was your project. I don't want to horn in on it."

"You're not," he said simply. "I told you. I really liked your concept. If anything, I'm the one horning in on your good idea."

She swallowed thickly. "You really thought it was good?"

"I've said it several times, haven't I?" he asked, a slow smile spreading across his mouth.

She stepped toward him hastily and threw her arms around his waist. When she lifted her face, he leaned down, his grin widening when she kissed his jaw and lips fervently.

"Does this mean your answer is yes?" he asked, his laughter deep and rich.

"No. I want to talk about it more," she mumbled, plucking at his mouth with her lips. "*This* is because you believed in me."

His smile faded. He cradled her jaw with his hand. "I've always believed in you," he said. "I just wanted you to believe in yourself. When you expressed your idea to me, when you told me what you wanted, I knew that you were starting to do just that."

Her heart seemed to swell to two times its normal size, making it difficult for her to speak. She was glad when he lowered his head and kissed her with barely restrained passion, making speech an utter impossibility.

Lucien took her to lunch at his club, where they talked almost non-stop about the exciting possibilities for the restaurant and hotel. He had thought things out carefully, laying out several potential plans for a partnership and assuring her she could choose whichever one she wanted and change her mind at any time. In essence, he was giving her carte blanche to be anything from a full, invested business partner to merely a well-paid employee with 50 percent of the right to make decisions. When she dryly pointed out to him that all the odds were in her favor for the venture, he merely shrugged unconcernedly.

"It's such a good idea, I would have risked more to be a part of it," he said levelly. Despite his assurance, Elise couldn't help but feel that he was doing this as a very special favor to her . . . giving her the priceless gift not only of the unique, excellent location and opportunity, but of his vast experience. No other entrepreneur would ever offer her a tenth of what Lucien proposed. His belief in her was like a charm stored safely away in her heart, a talisman that was forever within her reach.

His belief in her had magically segued into a belief in herself.

After a light lunch, they rode on the grounds, Elise enjoying the physical activity and glorying in spending exclusive time with the man with whom she'd fallen in love.

It seemed pointless at this juncture to keep denying it.

They dismounted at a wooded lake and tethered the horses. She sat next to Lucien on a nearly horizontal branch of a low-lying oak tree, leaning back against his strong thigh. He put his arm around her, opening his hand below her waist, and they stared out at the peaceful surface of the mirrored lake.

"Lucien?" she asked after a moment. "Have you spoken to your father at all since he's been in prison?"

"No," he replied, moving his chin idly in her hair.

"Are you angry with him? For what he did?"

"Yes. Not as much as I used to be, but still . . ." He paused and kissed the top of her head. "He took advantage of a lot of people because of his own greed. The company that he stole the industrial patents from was publicly owned. His actions could have potentially driven the stock down to nothing. Thousands of people would have lost their investment savings and jobs."

She sighed, sensing his bitterness over the blind depravity of his adopted father's greed. "And then he embroiled you in it all," she murmured. "The police questioned you. He was sent to prison, leaving you his tainted empire. No wonder you never wanted to touch any of it."

His hand moved below her belly, stroking her, creating a heavy, pleasant feeling at her core. "I'm going to have to stop running from his legacy, no matter how tainted it is. It's my responsibility."

She turned to gaze into his sober face. "You're going to accept your inheritance?"

"Not the money, no. But I can't keep ignoring the responsibilities my father left me. I would be no better than him if I kept ignoring all the people that rely on the businesses my father created."

"The embezzled funds at the Three Kings made that clear to you, didn't it?"

He nodded.

"Do you . . . do you plan to return to Europe?" she asked. Her pulse had begun to throb at her throat and a sick feeling swept through her stomach.

"No," he said, sunlight reflecting in his eyes as he studied her. "I can manage things from here as well as anywhere. But I will have to dig in for the short run and make sure I hire people I trust in Europe. It will require more travel than I've been doing as of late."

She nodded, relief sweeping through her at hearing he had no immediate plans for leaving permanently. His gaze sharpened on her and he cradled her jaw.

"Did you think I was planning on leaving you?" he asked.

"No, of course not," she said too quickly. When he raised his eyebrows in a sardonic gesture, she blushed and lowered her head, a feeling of shame seeping into her awareness. He lifted her chin, forcing her to meet his stare.

"Why are you always convinced you will be rejected?"

His words cut to the quick. She twisted her chin out of his gentle grasp and stared blindly at the still lake, unwanted tears filling her eyes. What could she say without sounding melodramatic and foolish? *Because every time I feel close to someone, they end up leaving me? Because no matter how hard I tried to please the people in my life, they would rather I wasn't around?*

Never. She'd never say those stupid, weak things.

She couldn't stop a tear from spilling down her cheek, however. Lucien leaned down and caught it with his lips. He made a rough soothing sound. Suddenly, his arms were around her, and he was lifting . . . urging her onto his thighs. He turned her, so that they were face-to-face, and her legs straddled his hips and fell over the tree branch. His arms closed around her until her breasts were crushed against his chest. He held her there, heartbeat to heartbeat, his hand massaging her back in that deft, knowing manner.

Elise pressed her chin between his shoulder and neck, shielding herself. She cried silent tears, warmed by dappled sunlight, filled by Lucien's embrace.

"Because your parents didn't prize you doesn't mean that you're not a precious, priceless jewel," he said gruffly near her ear minutes later. "It only means that you have to learn to prize yourself. And you are, *ma fifille*. Aren't you?"

She swallowed thickly and inhaled for courage. She leaned back and let him see her damp cheeks.

"I am," she whispered.

His eyes glinted between narrowed lids as he looked upon the gaping weaknesses and uncertainties she'd run from her entire life . . .

. . . and she'd never felt so whole.

She kissed his mouth softly, and he plucked at her parted lips with his own. For several golden, sunlit moments she melted in the cocoon of Lucien's acceptance. Her flesh grew torpid, her sex damp.

She felt him harden against her and knew he shared in her arousal. But it was more than just a sexual embrace.

It was so much more.

She wasn't sure how long they remained like that, but eventually Lucien cradled her face with both hands and waited for her to open her eyelids sluggishly.

"Come on. Let's head back to the city. I'm going to take you for dinner. Where would the chef like to go? Everest? Savaur's? Tru?" he asked, referring to some of the finest restaurants in the city, all with world-renowned chefs.

She leaned her forehead against his and stroked his back. "To be honest, I wish I could go to Fusion. I've never been there to dine."

He chuckled appreciatively. "We're closed on Sundays."

"I could cook for you," she murmured languidly near his mouth.

"Absolutely not. You're not working tonight. I want you focused on one thing: pleasure," he said gruffly before he kissed her once, brisk and thorough. He stood and cupped her ass, letting her body slide against his hard length sensually before he set her boots on the ground. "But that gives me an idea."

"What?"

"You'll see soon enough," was all he said as he led her toward the grazing horses and she stumbled after him, her mind still fuzzy from arousal and Lucien's all-encompassing embrace.

When they returned to the penthouse, Lucien left her to attend to a few things in his office. She was so relaxed and content following the sunlit ride on Kesara that she took off her boots and curled on top of the made bed, almost immediately falling asleep.

She awoke to the sensation of Lucien's lips skimming along her hairline and the sound of running water in the distance.

"Wake up, beauty," he murmured, the sound of his rough, low

voice in her ear making her shiver with pleasure. "We have dinner reservations to make."

She blinked her eyelids open sleepily and brought him into focus, her gaze glued to the sexy shape of his firm, curving lips.

"How long did I sleep?" she asked, disoriented.

"Two hours," he said, his white teeth flashing in his shadowed face. "You needed it, no doubt. After you kept me up all night," he added, pulling on her hand until she rose alongside him.

"After you kept *me* up all night, you mean," she muttered drowsily, letting him lead her to the bathroom.

"Your bath awaits," he said with a flourish once they'd entered.

She purred in satisfaction at the vision of the large Jacuzzi bubbling away on the center island, steam rising off the surface.

"Will you get in with me?" she asked huskily when Lucien turned her and began to unbutton her blouse.

"That's the plan," he replied, slipping her blouse over her shoulders.

Once they were both naked and submerged in the bubbling water, Lucien leaned against the side of the tub and pulled her into his arms, her back against the front of his body. She moaned softly as he began to run his hands over her, caressing and massaging, his touch decadent in the midst of the hot water.

"You could make a woman into a slave with those hands, Lucien Sauvage," she mumbled, her head resting on his chest, her eyelids fluttering closed in sensual pleasure. She sensed his smile near her cheek.

"I can't see you being a slave to any man. Could you?"

She went still, the back of her neck prickling.

"Perhaps," she breathed. "What if I wanted to experiment with the idea once in a while, at my discretion . . . with you?"

"That would be your decision. But after you consented to this enslavement, your freedom of choice would end for an agreed upon span of time. You would be at my mercy until the period ended."

She inhaled sharply when he began finessing her nipples with his thumb and forefinger, and she felt his already semi-erect cock stiffen into full readiness along the crack of her ass and her lower back.

"How long would this span of time last?" she asked, stifling a moan when he cupped her breasts from below and squeezed them gently at the same moment he tweaked her nipples.

"Hypothetically?" he asked right next to her ear, his rich voice causing a shiver to run down her neck.

"Yes."

"Well, for an example, if you agreed to be my slave tonight, it would last until I had my full pleasure of you or until morning came . . . whichever comes first."

A thrill went through her. She bit her lip and pressed down subtly on his erection, shifting her hips. "And you could do anything to me that you wanted during that time period?" she whispered.

"Of course. And you would have to accept it. It would require a great deal of trust on your part to allow it," he said, opening his large hand over her belly and stroking her, his hand looking dark and masculine against the pale expanse. He pinched an aching nipple, the sharp sensation a contrast to his languorous caresses on her belly.

"I do trust you that much," she declared heatedly. She twisted around and met his stare. "I do. I will be your slave . . . for tonight," she added with a small smile, shyness unexpectedly crashing into her at the realization of what she'd just said.

"You will do whatever I command?" he clarified, gray eyes gleaming.

"Yes."

He studied her closely. "You could truly submit to that degree? You would have to do everything that I insisted you do. You would have to make my pleasure your highest priority, knowing that it would please me if you followed my demands without question. This is what you agree to for the night?"

"I agree to it," she said without hesitation.

He looked amused . . . and aroused by her daring.

"Then wash me, little slave."

She moved away from him momentarily, turning off the whirl-pool. She wanted to be able to look down into the clear, still water and see his body perfectly. Her smile was supposed to be seductive as she turned to face him and reached for the soap and a washcloth, but when Lucien's eyebrows went up amusedly, she suspected she'd looked more mischievous than anything. She put her knees on either side of his hips, kneeling and lathering up her hands before placing them on his chest. She relished the opportunity to touch all that lean, hard muscle and smooth skin without restraint. He said nothing while she cleaned him, but she felt his gaze on her, watch-ing her every movement. The sound of the water trickling from the washcloth onto his skin and back into the water struck her as highly sensual. Elise couldn't help noticing that his cock was becoming stiffer and more swollen with every pass of her lathered hand and the cloth.

Excitement raced in her blood. She would clean his belly and thighs, torturing him as he had tormented her last night, and then finally touch his cock. She had just slid her hand against his flat, ridged abdomen, however, when he reached up and grabbed her shoulders.

"Lucien," she murmured, frowning at the thwarting of her mis-sion when he firmly pulled her down against him, her knees bent as she knelt over him, her belly sliding against his delicious erection and hard torso. He shifted, so that she lay against him, her belly and breasts in the water while her ass and pelvis were above the surface.

"Give me that," he demanded softly, reaching for the soap in her hand.

"But I was washing you," she protested a moment later when he lathered up her back with large, soapy hands.

"I'm clean enough," he murmured. He firmed his hold on her

waist and slid her higher up his body, her legs straddling him and her face just inches from his. So she was looking directly into his eyes when he matter-of-factly slid a finger between her ass cheeks.

"Lucien?" she whimpered when he touched her anus with the tip of his finger, rubbing against the sensitive area firmly.

"Hush," he soothed before he penetrated her with the warm, slippery finger. Her mouth fell open, and she gasped against his lips and the foreign invasion. Beneath her, she felt his cock lurch next to her skin.

"It feels . . . odd," she whispered dazedly. "Do you have to do that?"

A small laugh fell past his lips. "Yes. I suppose I do," he replied as he began to slide his finger in and out of her asshole. It felt shamefully good having him touch her so intimately while he watched her every reaction so closely. Her cheeks flamed with a strange mixture of embarrassment and arousal.

"And I suppose I have to let you," she said. "Because I'm your slave for the night?"

"That's correct."

He used his other hand to push her face down to him. He kissed her for several minutes passionately while they lay in the hot water and he continued to thrust his finger in and out of her. It felt almost unbearably intimate to her . . . untenably exciting. By the time he sealed their kiss she was panting softly and her sex was aching and ready.

"Finish washing up and get out of the tub," Lucien said next to her mouth. She moaned softly when he withdrew his finger from her ass. She began moving her hands over his slick body hungrily, but he caught her wrists. "Do as I say," he said, his voice soft but with an edge to it that matched the hard glint in his eyes.

She washed cursorily and left the tub, reaching for a towel. She watched in the large vanity mirror behind her as Lucien, too, finished washing and rose from the water like a gleaming, rippling god.

"I'll finish up in my dressing room," he told her a moment later as he stood next to her, the vision of him with the white towel draped low across his hips distracting her. "Don't get dressed yet."

"Why not?" Elise asked, forcing herself to look away and tucking the towel between her breasts.

"Because I will choose what my slave wears for dinner," he said, his tone implying his reasoning couldn't have been more obvious. He responded to her incredulous glance with a small smile before he left the bathroom. Elise could tell from that knowing look that he had something in mind—the devil's work, no doubt.

When he knocked and reentered the bathroom ten minutes later, she'd tamed most of the damage caused by the humidity of the bath to her hair and applied her makeup. She glanced around in interest at the sight of Lucien looking drop-dead gorgeous in a dark gray suit that had been perfectly tailored to his tall form; a cuffed white shirt; and a black, white, and silver tie. She rotated on the vanity stool she sat on when she saw he carried one of her blouses. He draped it over a second vanity stool and turned to her.

"Stand up, please," he said.

She rose slowly, a little mystified by his manner, a little wary . . . increasingly excited. He reached for the edge of the towel she still wore and tugged. She stood before him naked. The smell of his cologne filtered into her nose and she inhaled deeply. It wasn't until then that she saw he held the black velvet bag in his other hand.

The black velvet bag.

"Lucien . . . you're not going to make me go out in public wearing those . . ." She faltered when he withdrew the exquisite necklace, and then the attachable nipple chain.

"Yes," he said simply as he put the necklace around her throat, the metal and jewels feeling cool against her heated skin. He set the velvet bag on the counter and placed the nipple chain on top of it.

Her confusion mounted as he sat on the vacant stool and put his hands on her waist, pulling her between his long, spread thighs.

"But . . . people will see, won't they?"

"You must trust that I wouldn't expose or humiliate you," he said, his gaze fixed on her breasts. He looked up at her. "You do, don't you?"

"Yes, but . . . *Lucien*," she exclaimed in surprise when he inserted a nipple into his warm, wet mouth and began to lash at her with his tongue. Liquid heat surged at her sex, as if he'd demanded the wholesale reaction with his sucking mouth. She clutched onto his head and moaned in sharp pleasure spiced with just a dash of pain for the next minute as he moved his head back and forth between her breasts, making her nipples stiffen and redden.

She was so wet by the time he moved back his head, she might as well not have bathed. He picked up the nipple chain and methodically attached it to the necklace. Her mouth went dry when he slipped the loop between his fingertips and shaped it around her swollen nipple. She moaned shakily. He twisted the sapphire bead, narrowing the loop, as he watched her face closely. When she winced slightly, he stopped.

"Can you handle that?" he asked quietly.

She nodded. The pinch was abrasive on the sensitive flesh, but the sensation was a highly erotic one as well; one that she couldn't escape. She truly would be a slave to the experience all night . . . a slave to Lucien and her desire to please him.

He attached the chain to her other nipple and stood, his gaze glued to her breasts. Unlike last night, this time Elise could see herself in the mirror. Even she had to admit that the jeweled combination of the necklace and nipple chain was stunning to behold. As in all things, his taste was immaculate. Her clit twanged with arousal. She experienced an almost overwhelming desire to touch herself, to rid herself of this plaguing ache.

Lucien picked up the white blouse and held it up for her to put on. She met his stare in amazement.

"That's a sheer blouse. I can't go out in public without a bra and camisole on under it . . . let alone wearing this thing," she said, pointing to the swaying nipple chain.

"I told you I wouldn't expose you. You will wear a jacket and button it until we are alone together. No one will know." He jerked up the blouse an inch, a hard look on his face. She had no choice but to turn and slide on the blouse. He buttoned it for her. When he reached the button covering the sapphire weights on the chain, she gasped at the tug on her nipples.

"Okay?" he murmured, his long fingers pausing.

"Yes," she managed. For a moment, she could perfectly feel her heartbeat in the swollen crests, causing a pleasurable throb. His fingertip brushed ever so lightly against a nipple, teasing her. Heat rushed through her at the erotic sensation and the primal flash in his gray eyes. If only he'd touch her pussy . . . make her come in that magical way of his. . . .

"You're so lovely," Lucien muttered thickly when he'd finished. He turned her so that she could see in the mirror. The dark blue sapphires shone against the pale skin of her throat, mimicking the shine of arousal in her eyes. The placket of the sheer white blouse was double thick, making it more opaque than the rest of the garment. It mostly covered the dipping nipple chain and center sapphire weights. But the fabric over her breasts was whisper-thin and fairly tight. Her nipples looked fat, dark pink, and stiff against the blouse.

An involuntary whimper left her throat.

"I'll be back in a moment," Lucien said, moving back her hair and brushing his lips against her hairline, making her shiver in pleasure.

He left the bathroom, and she told herself to put the finishing touches on her makeup. Instead she just stood there, staring at the image of herself wearing nothing but the necklace and nipple chain and a blouse that covered nothing, and only made her breasts appear more exposed and lewd than they would completely naked. She touched one of the vividly pink tips experimentally. A sharp pain of arousal tore through her.

This is what Lucien would do to her all night. Play with her. Tease her. Make her mad with arousal.

Her hand moved between her naked thighs, her finger agitating her slick, swollen clit. Oh, *yes* . . . if she hurried, perhaps she could bring herself relief before Lucien returned. Her body tightened as she raced for the finish line, her hand moving faster and faster—

The next thing she knew, her wrists were pinned behind her and her back was pressed against the length of Lucien's body. She met his gaze in the mirror and saw that he was amused, but also vaguely annoyed.

"Little hedonist. I can't leave you alone for a moment, can I?"

She made a frustrated sound and pulled at her wrists, but he held firm. "It's only natural," she defended. "You've got these instruments of torture attached to my breasts."

He leaned down, his chin brushing the side of her head. "It's not natural to all women to become so turned on by a nipple chain, lovely. That it does arouse you pleases me. But you aren't allowed to come until I give you permission, are you?" he asked quietly near her ear in a hard voice. "You're impulsivity does *not* please me. I will have to punish you for it."

His low, rough voice made her nipples prickle against the sheer blouse.

"Finish dressing and put on your bracelets, one on each wrist. They are in the bag," he instructed, freeing her hands. For the first time, she realized he had more of her clothing slung over his forearm. He placed a black pencil skirt and matching blazer on the stool. "Then come out into the bedroom. I will give you your punishment before we go for dinner. And if I discover you touching yourself again," he added dryly as he began to leave the room, "I will make you regret it."

Her ragged breathing hitched in excitement at his threat. She reached for her skirt, overly careful in her movements so as to prevent the sway of the chain and tug on her nipples. "Lucien," she spoke to his retreating back. "There're no panties here."

"You won't be needing them," he said before he walked out the door.

"Of course not," she muttered sarcastically under her breath as she pulled on the fitted black skirt and ever so tenderly straightened her blouse. As a slave, it was her responsibility to make things as convenient for him as possible.

The jacket helped a little, stabilizing her breasts and the wicked, swaying chain. She looked at her reflection in the mirror before she walked out of the bathroom. She'd buttoned her jacket. If it weren't for the vivid color in her cheeks and lips, not to mention the brightness of her eyes, her look might have passed for chic conservative. The shimmering sapphires at her throat and wrists winked at her in the mirror, as if they shared a secret.

Lucien straightened from the bedside chest when she walked out. He glanced over his shoulder.

"You look stunning," he said slowly. He blinked, and then nodded toward the foot of the bed, where she saw a black pair of Christian Louboutin pumps resting.

"Put on your shoes," he instructed. He turned once she stood in her heels. She glanced downward to what he held in his hand. Her expression flattened in disbelief when she saw the box of butt plugs she'd discovered in the drawer while he was out of town.

"Don't panic," he said. "If it helps you to know it, this isn't part of your punishment. I would have put one of these in you whether I found you masturbating or not. I will make this as comfortable for you as I can, but that will take some time and patience. On both of our parts," he added wryly under his breath. "Fortunately, we do have the gift of time tonight." He opened the seal on the box and withdrew the smallest, narrowest of three rubber butt plugs. "Now, lift your skirt up over your ass and bend over the bed," he said so matter-of-factly. It took him a moment to notice her incredulous, defiant glare.

"Do as I say," he said, a trace of steel in his soft tone. "I would not ask anything of my little slave that I didn't think she could take."

Her chin went up at that, but so did her skirt. Her fiery glance over her shoulder before she leaned over and placed her hands on the mattress told him loud and clear that she could take it all right. She kept her head turned, wariness and excitement pulsing through her in equal measures when he set down the box of plugs and extricated the wooden paddle from the drawer.

"Look down at the bed," Lucien said.

She turned her head slowly, painfully aware of her throbbing nipples and the cool, air-conditioned air tickling her wet pussy.

Smack.

She moaned softly at the stinging pain on her ass. A surge of liquid warmth dampened her sex even more. He paddled her again.

"I expect you to ask my permission to come, especially tonight," he said from behind her. He landed another spank and her ass began to burn in earnest. "Tonight, you are my slave, so everything about you is mine, including your pleasure. Do you understand?"

When she didn't immediately respond, he placed his hand on her shoulder and paddled her again, steadying her when she lurched forward slightly. She squealed.

"I asked you a question."

"Yes, I understand . . . you devil," she added under her breath.

She got another hard one for that.

She bit her lip but couldn't stop her moan of arousal when he parted her ass cheeks with one hand and paddled the flesh just over her asshole. Her anus tightened reflexively and tingled at the illicit blows.

By the time he stopped and replaced the paddle in the drawer, the surface of her ass burned. She watched over her shoulder with a mixture of curiosity, anxiety, and excitement as he lubricated the black plug. She noticed that it was tapered at the end and then grew wider, but then it narrowed again to a thin stem at the base. Lucien glanced up at her face as he walked toward her, plug in hand.

"The narrowed stem will keep it secure once it's inserted," he said, obviously noticing her trepidation and curiosity.

"You mean . . . while we *go out*?" she asked shakily as he used one of his hands to part an ass cheek. She shivered when he pressed the tip against her anus. It felt cool against the nerve-packed tissue, the pressure stimulating.

"Of course while we go out. No one will know but you. And me, of course. I'm assuming by your reactions that you are a virgin here?"

"If I was a virgin in the other location, do you really think I'd not be one for this?" she asked, exasperated. His low chuckle caused goose bumps to rise along her neck.

"You give head like a seasoned professional, Elise. How am I to know what sexual escapades you got yourself into? I am pleased, though," he added gruffly, "that you saved this for me."

His voice rang in her head. *That you saved this for me.*

He pushed the tip into her ass and her eyes sprang wide.

"Lucien, I don't think—"

"Stay still," he instructed harshly when she shifted. He put his hand on her hip, immobilizing her.

"Oh," she gasped as he gently sawed the slick plug back and forth for a moment, pushing the thicker part farther into her ass with each pass. She moaned uncontrollably. He pushed, and finally the rubber plug was submerged, the base pressed snugly against her buttocks. Lucien caressed a hot ass cheek and she glanced back at him.

"It feels so strange."

His hand slid around her hip. Her lower lip trembled when he casually flicked his forefinger against her swollen clit. Her ass muscles clenched around the clamp as pleasure stabbed through her.

"Strange?" he queried.

She wondered if he noticed the flush of heat that rose in her cheeks. "Strangely good," she admitted grudgingly.

He smiled and removed his hand. He started to pull her skirt down over her ass.

"Stay still," he said sharply when she tried to stand and assist him. He lowered the fabric down slowly over her stinging buttocks, his actions striking her as highly sensual. She remained bent over the bed as he smoothed the fabric around her hips and ass, the movements applying a subtle pressure to the butt plug, exciting her further.

"Ready?" he asked her when he raised her to a standing position and brushed a tendril of hair off her heated cheeks. She watched, going very still, as he removed the medium-sized plug from the box and slipped it into his jacket pocket. He placed a small bottle of lubricant in the other pocket. Her gaze darted to meet his stare.

For this?

"Not really," she whispered.

He took her hand and kissed a knuckle, even that small gesture sending off fireworks in her overly sensitive body.

"Don't worry. You will be," he assured in a low voice that felt like knuckles gently rasping her spine.

Chapter Fourteen

ucien unlocked the back door of Fusion and opened it for Elise to enter.

"Are we picking something up?" Elise asked him as she trailed him down the long hallway past his office a few seconds later.

He glanced back to answer and his gaze remained glued to the sight of her. He'd never seen her lips and cheeks so pink. She was the very image of a stunning, intensely sexually aroused woman. He had to force himself to look ahead before he stumbled over his own feet. He'd seen her slight wince when she'd sat down in the car earlier, and had worried the plug was causing her discomfort. By the time he'd pulled out of the parking garage, however, her color had deepened, and he'd recognized her arousal. If her vivid cheeks and lips hadn't told him, the teasing hint of her erect nipples visible even through the barrier of the fitted jacket would have informed him loud and clear what Elise experienced.

"No, you said you wanted to dine here," he reminded her quietly as they entered Fusion's empty, hushed dining room. "I arranged for the kitchen to be opened and a meal to be served just for us."

"You didn't call Denise to cook on her day off, did you?" Elise asked, clearly perplexed as she noticed the light on in the distant kitchen.

"No," Lucien assured, leading her to a secluded private booth he reserved for his own use or for special guests when they requested it. He nodded toward the circular booth. Elise carefully sat and inched toward the middle of the candlelit table, draped with a white cloth.

"Then . . . who is cooking?" she asked when she'd settled and Lucien scooted in next to her.

"I think you'll approve of the chef. He used to live in Paris. He and his partner, Richard St. Claire, owed me a favor, and they seemed very willing to even things up between us. Ah . . . here is Richard now."

A very handsome dark-haired man with the slender build and light step of a dancer approached their table carrying a bottle of wine, his fingers twined around the stems of two wineglasses. He set down his burden on the table, smiling broadly. Lucien stood and the two men exchanged a warm greeting in French, shaking hands. Richard took Elise's hand when Lucien introduced her.

"I hear tonight is a special occasion. So Lucien has finally found someone worthy of him," Richard said, grinning slyly before he brushed his lips across her knuckles. "Emile and I have said forever that no such creature exists. I will be glad to tell him we were wrong."

"Emile?" Elise asked, politely bewildered.

"Emile Savaur," Richard said as he began to uncork the wine, not noticing Elise's mouth fall open in amazement. "We chose this one out of your private stock to suit the meal, just as you suggested," Richard told Lucien as the cork slid out of the bottle. "Emile was green with envy over your selection, but he personally chose this for the oysters." He held up the bottle of muscadet.

"Excellent choice," Lucien murmured, glancing at Elise as she studied the wine label. "I once met an adorable little girl in Nice," he said, referring to the fact that he'd handpicked the wine from Bellet Vineyards, near Nice.

Elise gave him a small, knowing smile.

"And please tell Emile that he should take another Bellet wine before he goes tonight," Lucien said.

Richard glanced sideways as he poured the wine. "You can tell him yourself. Here he is," Richard said. An older man with gray-streaked hair, a high forehead, and patrician features approached the table and set down an iced platter with a flourish.

"Tomales Bay oysters and mignonette sauce—my mother's own recipe. I serve it only to family and close friends," the world-renowned chef said briskly. "And I heard what you said about the wine, and you know you owe us nothing, Lucien. Richard and I would come and cook and serve for you ten times over for all you did in getting us that property in Paris years back. And who is this blooming rose?" Emile said, ignoring Lucien's outstretched hand and turning to Elise.

"Elise," she said simply, and Lucien was sure she didn't want to be recognized as the wild-child, spoiled heiress of Louis Martin. And why should she, he wondered, studying her as Emile took her hand, when she had grown into so much more than that . . . when she *was* so much more than that stereotype? He'd once been foolish enough to try to squeeze her into that narrow role, but of course Elise could never be pigeonholed.

"I've been wanting to meet you for years now," Elise said, staring up at Emile with an amazed, starry-eyed expression. "I went to your restaurant in Paris several times. Your cuisine took me to a higher state of consciousness."

Emile beamed at her stark, completely sincere-sounding compliment. "You're referring to the very restaurant where Lucien found us ideal premises. It was no small favor on his part. That is why Richard and I are here tonight."

"How is your mother?" Lucien asked Emile quietly as he released Elise's hand.

"As opinionated as ever. You should hear the way she harangues the cook at her assisted-living facility."

"And you wonder where you get it," Richard said smugly.

Emile gave his lover a sly smile. "At your every command, Lucien. Come, Richard, I need some help with the quail."

A few seconds later, Elise turned and stared at him. She still looked slightly startled.

"You got *Emile Savaur* to come and cook for us?" she asked hollowly.

"Yes. You know he's opened a restaurant in town, don't you?"

Her stunned expression told him that was hardly an explanation.

"I didn't want a Fusion employee to come and do it, and you said you wanted to eat at Fusion," he said, shrugging and unbuttoning his jacket. He handed her a glass of wine.

"He's my absolute idol."

"Then you prove what I already knew: you have excellent taste. I tried incessantly to get Emile to cook for me at one of my restaurants, but he prefers a self-owned establishment. He and Richard work exceptionally well together. I understand why he doesn't want to change a perfect recipe. Emile's mother lives here in the area, and has been unwell. That's why they moved here and started a new restaurant."

Elise still looked dazed following his explanation. He nudged the bottom of her glass. When she sipped some of the light gold fluid between her lips, he took her glass and set it down.

He placed his hands lightly on her rib cage and kissed her, catching her tiny gasp on his tongue. Her scent filled his nose—her familiar perfume mingling with the intoxicating smell of her arousal spicing her skin. He could never get enough of the fragrance of her.

"I love that wine, but it takes on a whole new dimension of deliciousness on your tongue," he said a moment later next to her lips. He slipped the button of her jacket from its hole and lightly trailed his fingertips over the buttons of her sheer blouse, feeling the heat emanating off her skin, relishing the small shudder that went through her. He unfastened the top button of her blouse and reached into the opening. His cock lurched in excitement when he flicked his finger over a nipple. It was hard and swollen from the metal loops. They must be exquisitely sensitive.

"How are you feeling?" he asked in a hushed tone as he lightly tugged the nipple chain and a burst of air flew past her puffy, pink lips.

"Breathless?" she asked, panting slightly as she sat there motionless and he returned to tweaking her nipple.

He studied her somberly. "You are being a very good little slave, letting me play with you without protest. Don't you want to tell me to stop?" he purred as he lightly pinched just the very end of the center nubbin of a crest, making it even more defined than it already had been. She dragged her front teeth across her lower lip when he turned his attentions to her other breast, and he knew she was trying to prevent herself from groaning.

"No. I know I agreed to this. But I am uncomfortable," she gasped. "Because I'm afraid Richard or Emile will return while you're . . ."

"Don't worry," he said when she faded off. "Richard and Emile believe in the intimacy of the dining experience. They won't return until it's time for the salad. They would want us to enjoy the wine and the oysters. And each other," he added in a low voice as he leaned back and unbuttoned her blouse farther.

"Lucien," she began, but she paused when he spread back first her jacket and then her thin blouse so that he could see her delectable breasts. Her nipples were a dark pink contrast to her pale skin, fat and erect and mouthwatering. The nipple chain trembled slightly between them. Perhaps she noticed the awe in his gaze combined with the sheer hunger, because she didn't further her protest. Leaving her breasts exposed, he reached for the iced platter of oysters. He spooned on just a dash of the mignonette sauce and lifted one to her mouth. She kept her eyes on him as he placed the shell next to her mouth.

The oyster slipped between her lips.

She closed her mouth and her eyelids fell shut. His cock throbbed at the rapt expression of sensual pleasure on her face. He ran two fingers over the sweet swells of her upper breasts. Her mouth moved as she enjoyed the flavor of the fresh oyster to its fullest, squeezing the fragrant juices onto her tongue. He wanted to do that to her: savor her until he was drunk on her, ravish her until her taste filled his mouth and ran down his throat . . . absorb her into him.

"You're exquisite. I have never wanted another woman more," he murmured, running his lips over her flagrantly pink cheeks even as his fingertips did the same to the skin of her breasts, feeling her heat. *You won't ever want another woman as you do her.*

The sound of a pan hitting a metallic surface jarred him from the unexpected, powerful thought. Elise jumped, her moment of rapt pleasure fracturing.

"Shhh," Lucien soothed, kissing her temple. "Have you never dropped a pan before?" he asked, running his hand along the bare skin of her ribs and feeling her tremble. He loved how delicate she felt in his hands, how responsive.

"Lucien, we shouldn't. Not when they might see us."

"They won't," he assured, glancing into her face and seeing her anxiety. "But if the choice is worrying you, I will take it away from you. It is my desire to play with you while I feed you this delicious food and wine. And as my slave, you will fulfill my every desire without protest." His tone was gentle, but he made sure she heard the edge to it as well. He would not be denied the smallest thing when it came to Elise tonight—not her sweet sighs of pleasure, her body trembling next to his hand, her wide-eyed look of surprise when she shocked herself by surrendering completely to him.

He removed the key from his neck. Her eyes grew large now with that mixture of amazement and arousal that he prized. He drew her wrists together. After he'd locked her bracelets together, he reached beneath the table and began to inch her skirt up her thighs. He felt her gasp against his neck.

"Lucien, must you?" she asked in a strangled voice when he lifted the hem of her skirt just above her mons, giving him access to her pussy.

"I must, and so you must allow it," he said simply before he flipped the edge of the tablecloth over her restrained hands and her lap. "Now," he said, reaching again to touch a plump nipple, "it's time to enjoy this delicious fare set before me."

Her body trembled and vibrated like a plucked harp string as Lucien played with her breasts and tugged gently on the nipple chain, pausing every once in a while to feed her the creamy oysters spiced with a dash of the piquant mignonette sauce or to lift her wineglass to her lips. The combination of flavors on her tongue was sublime, what he was doing to her body the sweetest agony. She swam in a bright sea of vibrant sensation. She grew so wet, she knew there would be a damp spot on the fabric of her skirt just beneath her pussy. Had Lucien chosen the color black for her skirt because he'd known how aroused she'd become?

Another oyster slipped between her lips and Lucien bent to kiss her as the flavor filled her mouth. Once she'd swallowed, he plucked at her lips with his own, and then caught the lower one between his white teeth, abrading the flesh gently.

"Your lips are turning as red as your nipples," he murmured.

She groaned softly. "If you keep biting them, they will turn redder."

"Then I will keep biting them," he murmured before he nibbled at her more, his pinching fingertips on her nipple and his sensual kisses making her desperate.

"Lucien, please touch me," she begged softly.

"Where?"

"On my pussy. It aches so much," she whispered as she slid her lips feverishly against his. She followed when he leaned back slightly, her mouth seeking out his.

He examined her face. "I will not touch you there yet," he said, avoiding her lips until she made a sound of frustration at being deprived the heaven of his mouth. He pinched at her swollen nipple and she moaned in rising agony, her hips shifting on the leather seat. "But you may come, if you can, while I play with your breasts."

"Oh," she gasped in a mixture of frustration and intense arousal when he tugged on the chain, and pleasure spiced with pain tore through her. "Do you require a little help in that mission?" she heard him say as if from a great distance.

"Yes," she hissed.

She felt his hands on the chain, and saw he was loosening the bead below her right nipple. She gasped. Pain tore through, thousands of nerves firing at once at the sudden release of the taut clamp.

"Shhh," he soothed roughly before he bent his head and took the nipple into his mouth. At the same moment, he lifted her bound hands an inch off her lap, making it impossible for her to press on her pussy from above.

A sharp cry fell past her lips as he drew on the throbbing nipple, and she began to shudder in climax. It hurt. It felt so good she could barely stop herself from screaming. Her hips bucked on the leather seat, but she couldn't get the full friction she needed on her sex, giving her orgasm a tight, cramped quality.

She was disoriented when he lifted his head a moment later and hastily reattached the loop to her nipple, Elise wincing at the familiar pinch. He just as quickly fastened her blouse. Richard appeared a scant second after Lucien buttoned her jacket. Elise watched as if through a heat haze as Richard served them a lovely white-asparagus and mushroom salad. Richard opened his mouth to speak when he was finished, then glanced at Elise and closed it again. He quickly refilled their wineglasses.

"Enjoy your salads," he said with a small smile before he walked away.

"Lucien?" she asked breathlessly when Richard was out of ear-shot.

"Yes, *ma chère?*" he said as he picked up his knife and fork and began to cut her asparagus.

"I will not survive until the main course if you keep this up."

She saw his small smile. "You will survive, because I demand it of you," he said simply before he lifted his fork and slipped it between her swollen lips.

Elise was beyond eating by the time the main course arrived. It wasn't possible to exist in the sustained, white-hot fires of arousal and think of anything but release from the glorious torture. When Lucien noticed her turn away from the forkful of quail with chorizo, spring onions, and clover that he offered her, he kissed her lips softly. His gaze flickered over her face. She could feel a slight sheen of per-spiration on her upper lip and gathering between her breasts. She panted, but gently, so as not to agitate her overly sensitive nipples against the buttoned jacket.

"Poor girl," he murmured compassionately. He set down the fork and reached for a glass of ice water. He pressed it to her lips, and she drank thirstily, knowing all along the cool liquid would never quench her inner fires. Lucien set down the glass when she'd fin-ished and began to eat. His free hand slipped beneath the tablecloth.

"Oh" popped out of her throat a second later as his finger found her clit and rubbed firmly. Her eyes sprang wide. She stared sight-lessly at the beautiful presentation on her dinner plate and shook in climax. Perhaps it was the inserted plug that made her climax so

sharp, or maybe it was just the long period of sustained sensual stimulation, but her orgasm was explosive. She moaned in a mixture of misery and bliss as she tried to contain the detonation occurring in her flesh, thrashing her hips against Lucien's finger.

"Better?" he asked her quietly a moment later as he ate, his hand still moving in her lap, working the last shudders of pleasure out of her.

Elise gasped, trying to catch her breath. She slumped in the seat. The blast of sheer pleasure had left her dizzy.

"Why do you like torturing me?"

He gave her a sharp look before he took a bite of quail, then chewed and swallowed. "Do you think this isn't torture for me as well, sitting next to you while you tremble helplessly beneath my hand, inhaling the scent of your pussy, knowing your entire body is alight with arousal and that soon . . . very soon, I'm going to incinerate high and hard inside you? You're the most desirable woman in existence, and yet here I sit," he said in a stark tone. His hand moved again demandingly in her lap and she bit her lip at the fresh friction. "I am not as cruel to you as I am to myself," he added before he took another bite of quail, his face rigid with arousal and determination.

"I'm sorry," she whispered. "I know this isn't easy for you, either."

"Would you rather I stopped?"

"No. *God*, no. Your brand of discipline is teaching me things about my body I didn't know existed. I want to learn control."

"Take your pleasure now and savor it," he said quietly, setting down his fork and taking a sip of wine, his hand still moving in her lap, coaxing another orgasm out of her. "Because when we return to the penthouse, it will be my pleasure that must be your priority."

She moaned softly and shifted her hips against his hand. What he'd said had aroused her. "Even if I don't take pleasure in what you demand?"

"Yes, even then." He leaned down and pressed his lips to hers, his kiss somehow both tender and demanding. She felt herself melting beneath his mouth and hand, and she was soon quaking in climax once again.

Elise had no choice but to sit there while Lucien ate his meal and to come repeatedly beneath his hand. After her third climax, her clitoris became almost painfully sensitive. Further stimulation left her limp and gasping as she experienced what was almost like a constant low-level climax. It was delicious, but it was like dripping water drop by drop onto the tongue of a person dying of thirst.

Lucien finally set down his fork and removed his hand from her lap. He placed his napkin on the table.

"Come with me for a moment," he said, taking one of her bound hands.

She followed him out of the booth. He pulled down her skirt for her. Elise was so drunk with lust, she hardly had a passing thought about how embarrassing it would be if they ran into Richard when it was clear that her hands were bound in front of her. Richard and Emile were at the front of the restaurant, however, in the kitchen, while Lucien led her down the back hallway to his office.

He closed the door behind them and hit a switch, lighting the room.

"Go bend over the desk."

His sharp command penetrated her dazed state. She blinked. "But what—"

"Just do as I say," he said, and Elise caught the edge to his tone that betrayed his arousal.

She went to the desk and placed her bound hands on the smooth wood. She bent over, just as she had that first day in this very office weeks ago when Lucien had shocked her by telling her he would punish her . . . show her the limits of her self-indulgent world. Tonight, she felt no less excited than she had that first time, but she'd grown more confident in Lucien. In herself. Her certainty allowed her to experience less anxiety and more arousal in challenging sexual scenarios than she ever could have in the past.

"Are you going to punish me again?" she asked shakily when he began to work her skirt over her thighs and then her ass.

"No. This won't take long. I don't want to be rude and miss Emile's dessert course. Spread your thighs."

She repressed a gasp when he matter-of-factly spread her lower ass cheeks, exposing her pussy.

"I've never seen you so wet," he said, his voice rough with arousal. "Your clit is swelling past your lips." Air whooshed out of her throat when he flicked at the swollen flesh. She moaned loudly when he removed the butt plug, firing the nerves in her anus and sex. She twisted her chin around, curious and wary, and saw him applying lubricant to the larger plug he'd brought in his pocket. It looked intimidatingly large.

He caught her staring at him a moment later as he pushed back a buttock. He held her stare as he inserted the lubricated tip into her ass.

"Push back on it," he ordered when she winced.

She did what he said and the larger plug slid into her with relative ease. She exhaled at the sharp flash of pain that went through her, but it passed almost as quickly as it came, leaving an arousing, forbidden sensation of fullness and pressure.

She couldn't escape the exciting knowledge that she was being sexually penetrated, even when Lucien pulled down her skirt and helped her to stand. She stood there waiting, her nipples, clit, and anus throbbing, while Lucien went to the bathroom to wash up. When he returned a moment later, he looked possibly even tenser than he had before. He took her hand and led her back to their table. They were seated just in time for Richard to come and serve them coffee, brandy, and a splendid Venezuelan chocolate custard.

This time, Elise managed several bites of the delicious dessert. Lucien, on the other hand, didn't eat a thing.

* * *

She felt the tension building in him as they said their good-byes and gave their thanks to Richard and Emile later. She sensed it mounting as they drove home, brewing and coiling tight until it felt like the very atmosphere on the inside of the sedan pressed down on her skin and made breathing difficult.

It thrilled her to know she would be the target of all that awesome passion, but it intimidated her as well. Lucien never ceased to excite and amaze her sexually, but his challenges frightened her a little as well.

Was she worried she would fall short somehow, and not meet his demanding expectations?

If you are honest . . . you'll please me every time.

The recollection of what he'd said to her last night gave her courage when Lucien led her back to the bedroom immediately upon their return to the penthouse. His face looked like it'd been cast from stone it was so tense, as he turned and began to undress her without preamble. He'd unlocked her bracelets before they'd left Fusion. When he'd removed her jacket and blouse, she stood before him wearing only the skirt, her shoes, the necklace and nipple chain, and her bracelets.

He moved to take off her skirt and looked at her face. He paused.

"Are you all right?" he asked, his eyelids narrowing.

She nodded. When he continued to stare, she said, "I'm a little afraid."

"Of me?" he asked, his eyebrows slanting.

"No. I'm afraid I won't be able to please you."

His mouth fell open. He stepped closer and cradled her jaw. "That's not even a remote possibility. Trust me on that. Do you?" he asked intently.

She looked into his eyes and nodded.

"You've already pleased me more tonight than I've ever been in my life." He bent and touched his mouth to hers, his kiss a quiet reassurance he'd take her safely through the storm. He lifted his head a moment later.

"But that doesn't mean I'm going to treat you with kid gloves," he said, his tone reminding her of velvet-covered steel.

"I don't want you to," she assured. Now that she'd spoken of her insecurity, and heard Lucien's response, she experienced a sense of mixed regret and reassurance. She shouldn't have been afraid. Of course he would keep her safe. Of course he wouldn't demand anything of her she couldn't give.

But can he keep me safe if he doesn't share in the love that's threatening to burst out of my chest? You'll be all alone, then, even if Lucien is right by your side.

Her thoughts were so volatile, she longed to distract herself from them . . . make her fear a distant memory.

"Good," Lucien murmured. "Because you drove me to the brink of madness tonight."

She touched his jaw and brushed her body against him, the slight abrading of her erect, tender nipples against the fabric of his suit coat thrilling her. She tilted her head back and met his gaze. "I will help you stave off madness. I am your slave. Use me for your pleasure," she whispered, letting him read the dare in her gaze. She saw something spark in his light eyes. His nostrils flared as he looked down at her.

"You needn't offer yourself. I would have taken what I wanted anyway, because you are mine to do with as I please."

Fresh arousal spiked through her at his stark dominance. He reached behind her and unfastened her skirt, pushing it down her hips and thighs until she stepped out of it. She stood before him naked except for her heels and jewelry. When he gently released the loops on her nipples, she bit her lip to halt a cry at the quick, sharp pain resulting from the sudden release of pressure.

"I'm sorry," he whispered hoarsely. He set aside her necklace and the nipple chain and leaned down to brush his lips against hers. The pain faded as quickly as it came. He ran his hands over her hips and sensitive sides. He gently caressed her sensitive nipples. She shivered uncontrollably beneath his touch and blatantly possessive stare.

"Your nipples are so large now, so pink. So beautiful," he said, his fingers worshiping.

"Lucien," she said, her desperation rising.

"I will not draw this out any further," he said with sudden decisiveness. He led her over to his large bed. "Put your hands on the railing and bend over." Excitement built in her when she took the position, her hands bracing her weight on the mahogany rail that ran between the two end posts, her heartbeat throbbing in the tips of her suspended breasts.

"Stay put," he said.

She craned around and watched as Lucien walked into his dressing closet. When he came out a moment later, he wore nothing but his suit pants, his delineated muscles gleaming in the soft lamplight. She couldn't help but notice how full his cock looked behind the fly of his trousers and riding along his left thigh. She yanked her gaze off the compelling sight, frowning in puzzlement at what she saw in his hands.

One of the items she recognized immediately: the black leather crop he'd used on her the night in the stables when he'd taken her virginity, the one he'd said was now hers . . . not hers to use, but to have used *on* her. A thrill went through her. A shiny wooden shoe-polish box was tucked under his arm. The third item had her completely puzzled, however. Hanging from his left hand was something made of incredibly supple black leather. Two straps hung loosely, swaying.

She was still staring at the leather item when he approached her and let the wooden shoe-polish box drop to the floor. He placed the crop on the bed.

"Lucien . . . what is that?" she asked through a tight throat, referring to the leather thing with straps.

She wasn't expecting his small smile when he turned to her, or that familiar, devilish gleam in his eyes. He'd been so stern and tense all evening that his playfulness took her by surprise.

"It's a leather corset, of sorts. Very strong. Very durable. I thought it would look extremely sexy, next to your white skin," he said, holding up the corset. Elise gasped when she saw the two thin leather straps sewn to the back of the soft leather, one on each side of the zipper.

"Are those . . . ?" she muttered in amazement.

"Reins," he said, a hint of mirth in his tone. "It's your ad hoc saddle. I had it made for you. Inhale," he murmured as he fit the corset around her ribs and zipped it in the back. She understood why he'd said to inhale. It fit very tightly. The leather stopped an inch or two below her nipples, plumping the flesh above it until it spilled over the edge. "It seems to fit," he murmured, running his fingers over the fulsome flesh squeezed above the leather. A shudder of pleasure went through her at his touch. "How does it feel?"

"*Extremely* tight," Elise blurted, still stunned by what was occurring. She didn't know whether to be irritated or pleased by his gift. *An ad hoc saddle?*

He straightened, regarding her and undoubtedly noticing her slight pique. "If you recall, you once told me in no uncertain terms that no one rode you."

"And you thought to prove me wrong?" she exclaimed heatedly.

"I bought this to make it clear to you that there is one person on this planet whom you will submit to," he growled softly, running his hand over her ass. "And yes, there is one man you will allow to ride you. Who is that?"

For a moment, she just stared back at him, her heart beginning to pound in her ears.

"You," she finally admitted softly.

Her gaze remained glued to the small, god-awful-sexy smile that shaped his lips. He walked over to the bedside chest and extricated another bottle of lubricant . . . and the last plug in the box.

The largest one.

Her muscles tightened instinctually around the plug already inserted. He set down the lubricant and the plug on the tabletop. She watched in avid lust as he methodically stripped off the rest of his clothes. Her mouth went dry at the profile vision of his muscular ass, his powerful thighs, and his erect penis, the heavy weight of it making it fall at a horizontal, slightly downward angle.

Her sexual hunger mounted exponentially.

He walked toward her, the bottle of lubricant and the last plug in his hand.

"You're going to . . . fuck me in the ass, aren't you?" she asked, flushing with embarrassment, even though it had seemed obvious to her all night that was precisely what he was preparing her for.

"Yes," he said, flipping open the cap on the bottle of lubricant. "And you will submit to it. But first, I will ride your hot little pussy."

A whimper of pure arousal leaked past her lips. The paradox of her feelings created an untenable friction. She *didn't* want to be ridden. And yet . . . she *did* want to be ridden. By him. She wanted the rebellious, empty, hot-blooded wild child she'd been her whole life to find her limit. Held in check.

Held secure by Lucien.

He came toward her, his cock and balls swaying slightly between his thighs as he stalked. Her gaze flicked nervously to the largest plug in his hand. Her breath started to come choppily as Lucien moved behind her. She moaned as he removed the plug in her ass. She clenched her eyelids shut and clamped her jaw a moment later when he inserted the new lubricated butt plug. It hurt a little going in, but once it was fully inserted her ass throbbed around the rubber intruder.

She should have been humiliated, bending over with a large plug in her ass and wearing a corset with reins that Lucien would use to control her. Instead, she was almost overwhelmingly aroused. It grew worse when Lucien came next to her and picked up the crop from the bed. Her arousal was so acute, she looked away from his stare. His hand caught her chin, preventing her avoidance.

"There is no shame in submission," he reminded her softly. "Only pleasure. And trust. And a desire to please."

"I *do* want to please you."

"I know you do. Even if you doubt. And that pleases me more than anything."

She bit her lower lip, the anticipation cutting at her, as he walked behind her.

"Step up on the box," he said, scooting the smooth shoe-polish box near her feet. She shifted and stepped onto the box, still leaning against the horizontal rail at the foot of the bed, putting her body at a more hospitable angle for Lucien to penetrate her.

He impaled her pussy with his cock in one long, forceful stroke. She shrieked at the burst of pressure and pleasure. She was filled to the brim—*over*filled—with the plug in her ass and Lucien plunged to the hilt in her vagina. He caressed a buttock as if to soothe her, even as he immediately began fucking her demandingly, his pelvis and balls slapping against her ass. The dual combination of pressure in her ass and pussy was almost too much for her to bear. And he wasn't being gentle. He drove into her again and again, and Elise strove to keep herself steady for his onslaught.

"You're so *hot*," he grated out, and she gloried at the thick lust in his tone. He withdrew almost entirely, only the bulbous head of his cock submerged in her, and flicked the side of her ass with the crop.

"Ooh," she squealed, and bucked her hips, sinking her pussy down over his rigid length and bobbing eagerly. He popped her ass harder for that with the leather slapper and gripped her hips in his powerful hold.

"I ride *you*," he reminded her, his tone a strange mixture of harsh arousal and fond amusement.

"Yes. Yes, all right," she conceded in a muffled voice.

This time, he gathered the reins in one hand. It was shockingly exciting to have him control her movements with the taut reins as he fucked her, pulling back on her body until it smacked against his pelvis in a heady, naughty rhythm she loved and responded to wholeheartedly. Her nipples throbbed as her breasts bounced from his forceful thrusts. Her ass tightened around the plug, sending a dark thrill through her. As his pace increased, he popped her bottom with the crop, urging her on . . .

Oh yes. She was made to ride free . . . but she was also made to submit to this man. *This* man.

She heard Lucien's blistering curse a moment later as she shuddered in orgasm. She howled in protest when he jerked his cock out of her body.

"Irrepressible," he muttered thickly as he pulled the butt plug out of her and she yelped at the interruption of her orgasm. She squeaked in surprise when he landed the crop several times on her ass and thighs. "I didn't give you permission to come," he said starkly.

"I couldn't help it," she moaned as he continued to swat her bottom and upper thighs, making her skin sting and smart.

He tossed the crop onto the bed. Her eyes widened when she felt him spread back her ass cheeks and present his lubricated, hard-as-steel cock to her ass a moment later. "How would you feel if I was continually telling you I couldn't control it, that I couldn't help myself?" he asked her darkly.

"I . . . I wouldn't mind," she replied defiantly. "I could take it."

He pushed his cock into her ass and she squealed.

"You're such a little fool if you think that," he said before he firmed his hold on her hips and slowly penetrated her.

It was the purest, most distilled version of sexual torture he could ever imagine, let alone endure. Her ass was on fire, magnifying the burn in his blood and brain and balls, making him feel like he'd melt like candle wax from unadulterated lust.

It was difficult going. Even with all the preparation he'd given her, her ass resisted him. He spanked her bottom gently, but his tone was rough with arousal.

"Push back on me. It will help," he demanded.

She did it, and of course, being Elise, she didn't do it halfway. She plunged her bottom backward, making both of them groan in agony. Lucien knew enough, however, to recognize that her moan was not of the sexual variety.

"Are you all right?" he grated out. Holding still with half his cock submerged in her clamping channel was like telling himself not to draw air with deflated lungs.

"Yes," he heard her moan. "It hurt for a moment, but no more."

"Stay *still* this time, then."

He slowly began to pump back and forth a scarce inch in and out of her while she moaned. When she began to bob her ass against him, he swatted her ass.

"Stay still, you little minx." He reached around her and found her clit, rubbing the slick flesh strenuously. With his other hand, he kept her hip immobile and pushed his cock farther into her.

"Ohhh," she cried out, sounding aghast. This time, Lucien could tell she experienced excitement, not pain. He growled savagely as he entered her to the hilt and his balls pressed tight against her buttocks. He rubbed her clit hard and felt her buckle. Catching her weight, he stood there holding her against him, his cock buried in her ass while she shuddered in orgasm.

She was going to kill him. No doubt about it.

When he could endure no more, he tightened the reins on her leather corset and spread his hand over a hip. "You have had your pleasure many times over. I will have mine now. Take me for a ride, little filly."

He began to fuck her, using his hold on the reins and on her ass to control her completely.

"That's right. Now you are submitting to me, aren't you? And it feels *so* good," he muttered through a snarl as he pounded into her.

Even though he mastered the movements, she still took him for the ride of a lifetime. She bounced her ass in perfect rhythm to his demanding strokes, her sharp cries of excitement every time his pelvis and balls slapped against her ass mounting his lust until he finally could take no more. He lifted her lower body, utterly controlling her, serving her to his cock again and again, ruthless in his possession. She shouted, but he couldn't tell if her cry was from arousal, surprise, or discomfort. He was too busy peaking over the crest into nirvana.

He dove into it.

A roar erupted from his throat. He began to ejaculate deep inside her, howling as the sharp talons of pleasure ripped through him mercilessly.

Pain brought him back to himself. His biceps had locked in a rigid flexed position as he held Elise to him and climaxed. He hissed in discomfort as he released her, carefully setting her feet back down on the shoe-polish box. He remained bent over her for a moment, panting, trying desperately to get control of himself.

He was surprised that orgasm hadn't ripped his head clean off him it had been so powerful.

"Are you all right?" he asked her. Yes, he'd told her he would take his pleasure of her and that she must accept it, but he hadn't really planned on his need growing to the cataclysmic level that it had.

"Yes," she murmured. She sounded okay—worn out . . . satiated. Had she come again, there at the end? He'd been too tied up in the twist of his own pleasure to tell. She moaned shakily when he withdrew his cock. He quickly unzipped the corset and encouraged her to stand. He took her weight, lifting her off the shoe-polish box and brushing his mouth against hers, his kiss every bit as tender as his earlier possession had been demanding. She trembled in his arms, feeling so warm, so feminine. It stunned him that he could want to cherish her so much, soothe her, and yet still desired her to the point of near savagery.

He carried her to the bathroom where he set her down and removed her bracelets. She flipped off her heels.

Then he turned on the shower and pulled her in next to him. He gently washed her, as if he thought he could clean away the residue of his blazing, raw hunger, all along knowing it was a helpless cause. He would want her again soon enough, and all he could do—all he could ever do—was tame the savagery, regulate the taint inside him as best he could.

It was a daily mission. Elise made it an hourly one, a battle he fought minute by minute. But because it was her—because he cherished her—the fight was not only worthy, it was sanctifying to his spirit.

Twenty minutes later, they lay in bed, their limbs entwined, Elise's head on his chest.

"Are you sure you are well?" he murmured, stroking her upper arm.

"I am so good," she answered groggily. "But hungry."

"Hungry?"

"I hardly ate anything at dinner. Emile will think I'm so unappreciative. If he thinks poorly of me, it's all your fault," she told him, pressing a small smile to his skin.

"I hardly think Emile and Richard are ones to judge the idiosyncrasies of two people . . . so involved with each other."

Her warm breath seemed to cease at his pause.

"Lucien?"

"Yes," he said, stroking her back now and once again wondering at her softness.

Another pause.

"Have you ever been in love?"

His caressing hand slowed.

"Why do you ask?"

"I don't know. I mean . . . I wouldn't know for sure if I was."

"I'm no expert on the matter," he said, kissing the top of her head. "But I do believe a person knows it, deep down, if they are. It's just a matter of trusting that feeling, isn't it?"

For the next minute, he couldn't be sure if she slept or was thinking. She didn't move as he caressed her, and her breathing was warm and even on his chest.

"Who was the man who died?" she asked suddenly, her clear voice startling him from his private ruminations about her earlier question.

"What?" he asked, bewildered.

"I heard Herr Shroeder tell you that someone was dead last night. He implied he'd been in prison, and you called him a sick fuck," she mumbled, sounding very sleepy. "I just remembered that I wanted to ask you about it. I'd forgotten with everything you told me about your mother, and the terrace . . . and the restaurant," she added lamely.

Her ear was pressed against his chest. He hoped she didn't feel his increased heart rate.

"Remember I told you that a very important witness had informed Herr Shroeder that Helen Noble likely knew details about my mother's identity and possible whereabouts?"

"Yes."

"The man who died was that witness."

"And he was in prison?" she asked, sounding a little less sleepy now.

"Yes."

"What for?"

When he didn't immediately respond, she lifted her head from his chest. "Lucien?"

"Rape." He expelled the word bitterly. "Worse than rape."

He felt her mounting concern swelling in the silence.

"Did that man . . . *rape* your biological mother?" she whispered.

He winced. He put his hand on the back of her head and guided her back down to his chest. He'd tried to prepare himself for it. But when he heard the thick dread in Elise's voice just now, he knew he was a fool for thinking he could accustom himself to such an ugly truth.

"I'll never know for certain, until I find her . . . or until I speak with Helen Noble."

"Oh, *Lucien*—"

"Not now, Elise. Please," he whispered hoarsely when she tried to lift her head again. "Let me enjoy this moment with you. Let's not ruin it."

He felt her open her lips, but perhaps she registered a hint of his pain, because her lips closed again next to his skin. He hugged her tighter, and she reciprocated. Something swelled inside him, thick and hot, when he felt how she squeezed him with an almost desperate strength.

"I want to help," he heard her say in a strangled voice.

"You are," he assured her gruffly, trailing his hand along her spine, pressing her to him even more tightly. "Your being here with me is all the help in the world."

Part VIII

When We
Are One

Chapter Fifteen

Elise raised her eyebrows in delighted surprise the next evening when she accompanied Francesca into the kitchen and saw "Ian's favorite meal" being checked by Mrs. Hanson.

"Roast beef and vegetables and Yorkshire pudding," Mrs. Hanson said with an impish grin when Elise leaned over the roasting pan and inhaled deeply of the delicious aroma.

"I was expecting something much more chic, given we're talking about Ian Noble. I'm pleasantly surprised," Elise said, grinning. Francesca laughed behind her and Mrs. Hanson smiled.

"Well, perhaps I should have specified that it was Ian's favorite when he was a twelve-year-old," Mrs. Hanson said.

"It still is. And it's quickly becoming mine," Francesca said. "Mrs. Hanson is a wonderful cook."

"Will you call me when you start to prepare the pudding? I'd love to watch you, and help out if you'll let me," Elise asked Mrs. Hanson, her mouth watering. She was suddenly famished. Ian had called Lucien earlier and asked if it was all right if they arrived an hour later than their original plan. In addition to the later hour, she never really had caught up on her eating since last night. Lucien had gotten an emergency call from Monsieur Atale in regards to the Three Kings hotels in Paris this morning, and Elise had gone for a long run along Lake Michigan while he worked. When she'd returned, her body had been too overstimulated and overheated to eat. Lucien had been too busy with the Three Kings accounts to take a break as well. Besides, she'd sensed his preoccupation, his somberness, and wondered how much of it had to do with what he'd said last night just before they'd fallen asleep.

A sense of familiar uneasiness went through her at the thought.

Was he withdrawing from her, by chance? Flinching away from the intimacy they'd shared, and the truth he'd *almost* revealed to her, the truth she suspected related to his mother? Every time she thought of the thread of pain in his voice, her heart seemed to squeeze in anguish. Why didn't he just end his painful wait and speak to Ian Noble to find out where his mother was once and for all? It must be torture for him to be so patient when his prize was so close. It was increasingly becoming unbearable for her, this cautious waiting.

"By all means." Mrs. Hanson's voice pulled Elise out of her thoughts as the housekeeper returned her gorgeous roast to the oven. "I'll come and find you in a little bit. But it's really nothing special. I hope you won't be disappointed."

"I'm a chef. My nose is as much an expert as my tongue, and I can already tell this is going to be *very* special," Elise assured.

Francesca hastened to the refrigerator, where she extricated two bottles of club soda. Elise had turned down a glass of wine when they'd first arrived, explaining she was a little dehydrated from her long run.

"Come on," Francesca said. "I think Lucien and Ian went into Ian's office—Lucien is showing Ian some online photos of the new property he bought in the South Loop—and there's something I want to show you in there," she added as she twisted off the cap from the soda and handed it to Elise.

"What?" Elise asked, following her out of the enormous kitchen and down a wide, gallery-like hallway.

"You said you wanted to see more of my paintings? There are several hung in Ian's office—including *The Cat That Walks By Himself.* Remember, I mentioned that one to you?"

Elise recalled how Francesca had told her about unknowingly painting Ian on a desolate city street years before she'd ever met the elusive billionaire entrepreneur in person. She recognized the paneled door Francesca led her through. This was the room where she'd come upon Lucien listening to Ian on the phone that night. They entered a large room lined with stained walnut bookcases filled with volumes. Two comfortable-looking leather couches faced each other. A large desk and a long, conference-like table had a laptop on it along with a decanter of wine and a glass. Ian sat in front of the computer screen while Lucien stood looking over his shoulder, a glass of bloodred wine in his hand.

Elise had noticed that Ian had seemed preoccupied and tense when they arrived, but he currently laughed unrestrainedly at something Lucien had said. Francesca gave her a quick, pleased smile before she led her over to the fireplace mantel. Elise stared with wide-eyed wonder at Francesca's painting.

"I can't get over how talented you are," Elise praised sincerely. "And to think . . . you painted Ian all those years before you ever even met, and he recognized himself and bought the painting without knowing you. Talk about fate, the way you two ended up together. It's very romantic."

"A more unlikely couple you wouldn't find anywhere. And yet . . . once we got together, nothing could have been more right," she said for Elise's ears only.

"I suppose you could say the same of Lucien and me," Elise said, looking back at the two men as they chatted. Lucien glanced up and caught her staring. He gave her that small, secret smile that always made her cheeks heat and her heartbeat escalate.

Oh Lord. She really did have it bad.

"You and he actually have similar backgrounds, though," Francesca pointed out quietly.

"Yes, but he's the most disciplined man I know. And I'm about as controlled as a tornado," Elise murmured before she took a sip of soda.

Francesca laughed warmly. "Somehow, I suspect that's precisely what Lucien loves about you. Sometimes oil and water really do mix for the best results."

Elise blinked at the word *love* but she quickly hurried to hide her discomposure. "In Lucien's and my case, the more apt analogy is more like a match and dynamite," Elise muttered under her breath.

Francesca chuckled, but her gaze was fixed on Ian across the room. She wore a worried expression.

"Is Ian doing all right?" Elise asked delicately.

Francesca sighed. "He's had a lot on his mind lately. I told you Lucien has a good effect on him."

Elise glanced at the men, glad to see Ian lean back in such a relaxed manner and nod in interest. She and Francesca walked across the large room to the long, oval table.

"I understand Lucien has already found himself a very talented executive chef for his new restaurant," Ian said with just a hint of a smile as they approached. Elise was learning that for Ian Noble, that ghost of a grin was the equivalent of beaming for the average person.

Francesca looked around, a delighted expression on her face. "You?"

Elise nodded.

"Really? How exciting. Why didn't you say something?" she said accusingly.

"Well, we're still in talks," Elise said, meeting Lucien's warm gaze. "And I still have to finish my stage. But I think all the details can be worked through. I'm no fool, to turn down such a wonderful opportunity." His eyebrows arched slightly as if in interest at what she'd said. She hadn't been so forthright with him but had hedged, worried she was taking advantage of his generosity. Elise broke into a smile.

Lucien shrugged negligently, bringing her attention down to his broad shoulders draped in a bluish-gray button-down shirt that did marvelous things for his eyes. "I'm the one who took advantage of a wonderful opportunity."

"Lucien's been telling me about your concept for the restaurant. Sounds very interesting," Ian said as the phone on his desk began to ring. He made no move to answer it. "I have a friend from my college days who is a recovering alcoholic, and he's told me point-blank he finds the sight of alcohol and people drinking challenging. I worry at times, meeting him out at restaurants. And as you can see"—he nodded toward the well-stocked sideboard against the wall that contained several crystal decanters of cognac, brandy, and bourbon—"this is hardly a safe meeting environment, either. I have to ask Mrs. Hanson to move all the alcohol before I have him here."

"Speaking of Mrs. Hanson, she must be busy. I'll get the phone," Francesca said.

"No, no, I've got it," Ian said, standing. He caressed Francesca's shoulder warmly as he passed. Lucien came around the table as well, and the three of them sat down on the facing sofas, Francesca across from them.

"When do you think you'll be able to open the new hotel?" Francesca asked.

"Probably not for at least a year. It requires extensive rehab," Lucien replied, draping his arm over the back of the couch and skimming his fingertips across Elise's upper arm. Her skin prickled beneath his touch and she met his gaze. It seemed so strange—and wonderful—to have him touch her in public so comfortably.

"Plus I have to finish my training—"

She cut off short at a sharp question from Ian, who stood behind his desk, the phone pressed to his ear. Alarm swooped through Elise when she saw his fixed expression of shock. His face had gone very pale next to the contrast of his dark hair.

"But how did this happen, Julia? She was stable when we spoke yesterday," Ian said loudly.

"Oh no . . . ," Francesca whispered, standing and staring at Ian. Elise glanced at Lucien anxiously, but he was also looking at Ian, his brow furrowed.

"Was it because of this new medication? Is that what's causing her liver to fail?" A horrible pause. "Of course you can say definitively. What else could have caused it?" he demanded. "I'll be there as soon as I'm able," Ian said tensely after a moment. He hung up the phone. Lucien slowly stood and Elise rose next to him. Francesca remained frozen in place, a wide-eyed stare of anxious dread on her face as she watched Ian approach. Ian's gaze bore into Francesca, and it was as if Lucien and Elise weren't even in the room.

"My mother is experiencing acute liver failure," he said, the stark, hollow quality of his voice indicative of shock. "Julia told me she likely only has days to live."

"Oh my God," Francesca whispered, reaching for him. Ian stepped back, though. Francesca's hand fell in the air before his chest. He looked like a man who had just had his soul stripped from him . . . a man who thought he didn't deserve the solace of his lover's touch. "It's my fault. I agreed to that godforsaken medication."

"Ian, don't say that. You had no choice. She was refusing to eat," Francesca implored.

Ian's gaze flickered over to Lucien and Elise. Elise felt like an interloper on an intensely private moment of grief.

"I'm sorry, Lucien. You must think this is all odd. I led you to believe my mother was dead—"

"That's the last thing you should be concerned about right now," Lucien said. "Besides, I suspected she was alive."

Ian's gaze narrowed. For some reason, Elise's pulse began to throb at her throat. The atmosphere of the room suddenly felt charged by the unexpected turn of events.

"Why would you suspect that?" Ian asked slowly.

Lucien looked entirely calm, but Elise sensed his rising tension. Her thoughts were coming a mile a minute as she stared at his stoic profile. What must he be thinking? The one link to his mother was about to be silenced forever. . . .

"Lucien?" Ian prodded.

"Just tell him," Elise said. "It might be your only chance."

Elise's eyes widened in horror when Lucien looked over at her, a startled expression in his eyes. Had those pressured words really come out of her mouth?

"Just tell me *what?*" Ian said, taking a step toward them.

A muscle jumped in Lucien's cheek.

"Lucien? Tell me *what?*" Ian prompted, louder this time.

Lucien inhaled slowly. "I have good reason to believe that your mother knows the identity of my biological mother."

For a terrible moment, the silence rang in her ears. Francesca looked startled, but Ian and Lucien seemed eerily calm.

"Why in the world would you think that?" Ian asked.

Lucien gave the other man a searching look before he spoke. "I learned it from my biological father," he said evenly. "A man named Trevor Gaines. I hired a private investigator years ago to discover the identity of my biological mother, and the trail led him to where Trevor Gaines resided—Fresnes Prison."

Elise's heart felt as if it stopped beating for several seconds as she stared at Lucien's profile, aghast. This isn't what she'd expected him to say.

Ian's reaction was possibly stranger than Elise's. His cobalt-blue eyes looked like glowing slits between narrowed lids. He reminded her a little of a sleepwalker as he took a step toward Lucien. All the color had left his face, but his expression was strangely focused and rapt upon Lucien, almost as if he existed in a particularly lucid dream . . . or a nightmare that was unfolding fully for the first time.

"What has Trevor Gaines got to do with my mother?" he asked, a sandpapery quality to his voice.

"We can discuss it at another time," Lucien said after a moment. "You don't look well. You're in shock, and I'm sure you want to make arrangements to go to London."

"How do you know my mother is in London?"

Francesca stepped forward and put a hand on Ian's arm. "Ian, Lucien's right. This isn't the time—"

"How do you know?" Ian repeated harshly, his gaze still locked with Lucien's. There was a strange paradox to him of wild desperation covered by a steely armor of complete control. Only his blazing eyes and pallor betrayed his internal battle. Lucien seemed entirely calm as the target of that focused torment—almost as if he thought he deserved it. For a moment, he just stared at Ian, not saying anything, seeming to gauge his options given the unexpected turn of events.

"I know all about Helen," Lucien said finally. "As I said, I hired a private investigator years ago to discover the identity and whereabouts of my mother. Helen Noble was identified as being a key to the answers I was seeking. I've known where she was since last year—"

"You were spying on me," Ian said.

Elise glanced from Lucien to Ian and back to Lucien again. A shivery feeling went through her, as if someone had poured ice water over her, starting at the top of her head. She'd noticed it before, but idly—their height and build, their self-containment, the similar nuances of their profiles.

"Ian, please," Francesca urged. "This hardly seems like the time or place. You're in shock over your mother."

"You were spying on me, weren't you?" Ian demanded.

"Yes. I admit it."

"I ought to call the police right now," Ian hissed. "Why? Why were you doing it?"

"For two purposes only. Whether or not my reasons seem mercenary and selfish, you'll have to be the judge. One, I needed to discover the whereabouts of the woman who might provide be the key to unanswered questions. I didn't think you would easily open up to me about your mother if I just asked. Two, I wanted to get to know you better personally."

"Why would you want to get to know me better?" Ian asked angrily, looking offended.

"Because family is very important to me," Lucien replied. "And for better or for worse, you're the only blood family I know of at this point. You're my half brother, Ian."

Chapter Sixteen

an collapsed heavily onto the leather couch. For a moment, all four of them didn't speak. The silence seemed to press on Elise's chest, making breathing difficult. Ian looked like he'd just been clobbered, but Elise also sensed his mind working . . . churning . . . sifting for answers.

"Trevor Gaines?" he finally asked Lucien.

Lucien nodded once. Elise had never seen him look so sober.

Francesca went and sat down next to Ian. Ian numbly took her hand and squeezed it.

"What was Gaines in prison for?" Ian croaked.

"I'm not sure you want to know that right now," Lucien said.

Francesca's face looked ashen. Something flashed in her dark eyes as she stared at Lucien's solemn face.

"I agree. Of course we'll have to hear more about this, but later. We need to go to London, Ian."

Ian looked into Francesca's face. Elise saw the sleety misery in his eyes when he gazed upon his fiancée . . . the dawning emptiness.

"I want to know," Ian said. "I've wanted to know about the son of a bitch that was my father for most of my life. You *know* that, Francesca."

"Whoever your biological father was won't change who you are," Elise heard Francesca whisper in a pressured fashion.

"It was for rape, wasn't it?" Ian rasped, seeming not to have heard Francesca. "Trevor Gaines was a rapist."

A wave of dizziness struck Elise in the short pause that followed. She didn't know if she swayed or not, but suddenly Lucien was staring at her, his hand on her elbow. She sat automatically when he lowered her to the couch.

"He was indicted on two counts of rape, but by all accounts he was probably guilty of more. It was only the two they had sufficient evidence on to prosecute. But there's something else. I might as well tell you," Lucien said. "Now that you know his name, you'll find out soon enough. In addition to being a rapist, Gaines was a serial reproductionist."

"What's that?" Elise asked when no one spoke. Lucien glanced down at her. What she saw in his eyes made her want to weep: a hopeless sadness, a bitter disgust that could never be purged.

"A serial reproductionist has a sick obsession with impregnating women. He does it by seduction and craft—by discovering women's cycles and sabotaging birth control, perhaps weakening a condom to ensure it breaks during intercourse, increasing the likelihood of impregnation. He might compulsively give sperm for insemination. When his means fall short, he might resort to rape. Trevor Gaines used all three tactics, and quite possibly others that we aren't aware of. The police suspect that he impregnated close to twenty women, although Gaines often bragged to Herr Shroeder—the private investigator I hired—that there were more. Many more. We were like trophies to him."

Nausea struck Elise when she realized the *we* Lucien referred to was all of Trevor Gaines's offspring.

"Until you understand the psychological profile of such a man, it's very difficult to comprehend his motives and actions . . . and even then . . ." Lucien shook his head.

"I think I remember reading something about him. The Gentleman Rapist—or something idiotic like that. Isn't that what the English newspapers called him?" Ian asked.

Lucien nodded. "He was a wealthy man, with supposed noble blood, as well as being a brilliant scientist and inventor. He was also one of the sickest fucks ever born. He wanted nothing to do with his children. He just got some twisted, narcissistic satisfaction out of knowing he proliferated so greatly, planted his seed far and wide. It was all a twisted game to him, the selfish bastard," Lucien added bitterly under his breath.

"Lucien, this all seems so far-fetched," Francesca said suddenly. "How can you possibly know that this man is yours or Ian's father?"

"In my case, I know because he agreed to a blood test. Trevor Gaines definitely is—or was—my biological father."

Elise made a shaky sound at his barren tone. She hated seeing his pain exposed, and she had no one to blame but herself for what she so unexpectedly witnessed.

"Was?" Ian asked sharply. "Don't tell me he's dead."

"He just died several weeks ago, of a sudden heart attack while in prison."

"He'd better be thankful from hell that he died naturally," Ian muttered viciously, his sudden blaze of anger sending a chill through Elise. Francesca's eyes widened in anxiety as she studied her lover's profile.

"I've had similar thoughts ever since I discovered what he was," Lucien said, and Elise heard the edge of bitter fury in his tone as well. "Unfortunately, Gaines must have realized his progeny might feel that way, because he refused point-blank to see me. I assume it would have been the same for you. As I've learned, a prison can keep people out just as effectively as it keeps people trapped inside." He paused, holding Ian's stare. "I've wanted to tell you. For a long time now. But how does one go about revealing something like this? It's not as if it's happy news. I wasn't sure how you would take it. I'm still not sure, but after tonight . . ." He paused, glancing at Elise. Her heart plummeted in her chest. "It seemed impossible to keep the truth from you anymore."

"But again," Francesca said desperately, "why are you convinced in Ian's case? Are you only going by Trevor Gaines's word that Ian was one of his biological children? *Surely* his word isn't to be trusted."

"He knew a great deal of intimate information about Helen Noble. He met up with her first in England. She'd apparently had her first psychotic break there." Lucien said the last quietly, his gaze still locked with Ian's. "She had run away from home, and Gaines took her under his wing in Essex. He could be quite charming when he chose, as many sociopaths can be, and your mother was at the beginning stages of schizophrenia, and very vulnerable. He brought Helen back to the north of France, near where he lived, installing her in a small house about fifty miles from his estate—the house where you spent the early years of your life, Ian. He claimed Helen and he were lovers, but if they were, he abandoned her after she became pregnant, despite her increasing illness and disorientation."

"We never knew how she ended up in France," Ian said dully. "My grandparents searched far and wide in England and all over Europe. The village where we lived was so remote, though. He must have understood who she was . . . her status. Gaines probably knew it was unlikely anyone would ever find my mother there."

"My mother was Helen's maid. Apparently, Helen had hired her during a moment of lucidity, while she was still in England. It was several months after she'd fled Belford Hall," Lucien explained, referring to Ian's grandparents' estate in East Sussex. "He had a penchant for impregnating women that were related somehow. For instance, one of the women he raped that he was finally successfully prosecuted for was one of three sisters. He'd seduced two of them, unbeknownst to each other. He attempted to seduce the third, but when he failed, he resorted to rape. He couldn't have anything—including a woman's right to refuse him—stand in the way of his sick goal of having all three sisters pregnant with his children at once. He also had a proclivity for videotaping both his seductions and his rapes. It's that which finally landed him a guilty verdict without a doubt."

In the awful silence that followed, Elise noticed Ian's gaze flash to Francesca. His features were impassive, but Elise thought she saw pure horror in his glance. Francesca shook her head, looking utterly helpless.

"No," Francesca said with quiet forcefulness, her meaning lost on Elise, but her desperation clear. Ian turned back to Lucien.

"What else?" Ian prodded doggedly.

"He pulled something similar with our mothers. Not the video-taped rape," Lucien said quickly when Ian's look grew wild. "I mean his desire to impregnate women who were associated with one another. Apparently, Gaines was having relations with both of our mothers at once, whether by force or seduction, I don't know. We're only six weeks apart in age, I believe."

Ian just stared.

"But still," Francesca interrupted. "That's hardly proof. What makes you so sure Ian is definitely this criminal's biological son?"

Lucien seemed to hesitate.

"Lucien?" Ian asked.

"You'd find out now anyway," Lucien muttered. He turned and walked over to the oval table, retrieving the laptop. He returned, sitting next to Elise on the couch. She watched as his long fingers moved fleetly over the keyboard. A black-and-white photograph appeared. She stared in numb disbelief.

Ian took the computer when Lucien handed it to him. Frances-ca's hand flew up to cover her mouth.

"Jesus," Francesca muttered, sounding like she was about to be sick as she stared at the photograph along with Ian. Elise knew precisely what she meant by her horrified exclamation. The newspaper caption beneath the scanned photograph said it was of Trevor Gaines when he was in his thirties, looking extremely handsome and charming with a small, mysterious smile on his lips—the exact opposite of what one might imagine a rapist and conniver to look like.

Ian Noble was the spitting image of Trevor Gaines.

"That's why she always got scared of me when she was psychotic," Ian said with an eerie calmness that sent shivers down Elise's back. He looked at Francesca's shocked, puzzled face. "My mother. That's why she sometimes acted afraid of me—all my life, she'd wince and cower at times at the very sight of me. I never understood why, but I sensed something. Something bad. That's why my presence could trigger a relapse for her . . . still to this day. Because I looked so much like him. Because I had the face of the man who took advantage of her. I had the face of her rapist." He looked at Lucien. Lucien looked back, every bit as grim.

Every bit as sad.

Francesca's mouth hung open. Elise could almost hear the inner workings of the other woman's mind, sense her searching for words of comfort . . . and finding none. She understood because she herself had gone numb with helplessness.

Ian set the computer on the couch and stood.

"Ian," Francesca said sharply. He paused and looked back at her. She stared at him . . . mute . . . shattered. He held out his arms and Francesca flew into them, hugging him. He crushed her to him, his eyes clamped tight, every line of his body conveying unspeakable pain.

"You are the best of me," he muttered. "The very best. But there's so much more ugliness. The balance is uneven."

"No," Elise heard Francesca whisper heatedly.

Ian kissed the top of her head, his lips lingering as he inhaled her scent. He wore a death mask as he gently extricated her from his arms and strode out of the room.

Francesca just stood there for a moment, stunned.

"I'll go after him," Lucien said, standing. "I know what it's like to find out—"

"It's his worst nightmare made a hundred times worse," Francesca said bleakly as if to herself. She roused and glanced back at Lucien. "I'll go," she said, hurrying from the room.

In her absence, Elise just looked up at Lucien, dread making her shrink within herself. He stared at the closed door where Ian and Francesca had just exited. Why hadn't he told her the full truth? What must he be thinking?

Elise herself couldn't put into words what she was feeling: Misery for Ian, Francesca, and Lucien for such a harsh, soul-tearing truth. Shame that she had been the one to reveal it out of her ignorance and her damnable impulsivity. Lucien had always wanted family. He hadn't just been spying on Ian for the purposes of discovering the whereabouts and circumstances of Helen Noble.

He'd wanted to get to know a blood brother. To love him, despite the foulest of circumstances. And they *had* grown close . . . so comfortable with each other.

Elise had changed all that now. Ian was confused. Furious. She'd perhaps robbed Lucien of the only blood family he would ever know.

"Lucien," she whispered, wild to apologize . . . to ask him why he hadn't told her everything, but fearing his answer. Why should he tell her anything important, when she'd betrayed the truth the way she had? But the door suddenly opened and Francesca stepped into the room, her face as white as a sheet.

"He's gone," she said blankly.

Again, that frightening shiver of inevitability rippled through

Elise. Somehow, those two words seemed to signify more than a short absence on Ian Nobel's part.

"I've never seen him so upset—" Francesca broke off as a convulsion of emotion went through her.

"This is my fault. I'll find him," Lucien said when Francesca faded off. "I'll call when I do."

Elise just sat there, watching as Lucien walked away from her, all the while thinking that if anything, tonight had been her fault, not his. After the way she'd inadvertently exposed Lucien, perhaps he was walking away from her for the last time.

After the panel door closed with a snap, her dazed glance landed on Francesca. She rose swiftly and went to her. The other woman looked completely shell-shocked, and let Elise lead her to the sofa without protest. Francesca blinked when Elise handed her a snifter of brandy a moment later.

"What's going to happen now?" Francesca wondered hollowly.

"Lucien will find him. It's going to be all right," Elise said with a certainty she was far from feeling.

Earlier, Elise had felt like an interloper during an intensely private moment, but as she sat there with Francesca waiting to hear from either Ian or Lucien, she couldn't shake the feeling that it was like waiting at a deathbed. For half an hour, they sat in near silence in the office, both of their cell phones on the coffee table in front of them. Francesca cursed under her breath at one point and tried to contact Ian.

"He's not answering," she said a moment later, hanging up the phone.

After a while, a tap came at the door and Mrs. Hanson poked her head in.

"Elise? I'm about to start the pudding."

"Mrs. Hanson, I'm sorry," Francesca said, standing. "I should have found you. There's been a change of plans, I'm afraid. Lucien and Ian had to go out."

"Would you like me to serve you and Elise in the dining room, then?"

"No . . . I couldn't eat . . . I'm too . . ."

Elise stood when she saw Francesca so flustered. "Perhaps I could come with you and bring a little something for Francesca to eat now. I'm sure she could use the food, but she's waiting for a call."

"Of course—the beef is done enough. I'll slice some off for you," Mrs. Hanson assured her, looking politely puzzled and concerned for Francesca. Knowing Francesca was in no state to answer questions, Elise escorted Mrs. Hanson back to the kitchen and helped her make a tray.

Francesca barely swallowed two mouthfuls of the aromatic beef before she pushed her tray back and picked up her phone, checking for messages.

"Do you know Ian's mother well?" Elise asked when Francesca gave up and set down her phone. Francesca shook her head.

"I've only visited her a few times. Other than the first time I met her, she's usually fairly sedated."

"I can't imagine how hard it would be for Ian to see her that way."

Francesca nodded. "Sometimes I want to tell him not to go, although I know that's awful to think. I'd never say that about his mother. Still . . . it seems to take away a bit of his soul every time, to see the mere shell of someone he loves." There was a pause. "What Ian said there at the end . . . that's true," Francesca said in a bereft tone. "Helen does shrink away from him sometimes, when she's least in contact with reality. Perhaps Ian was right. Maybe she is reminded of . . . that man."

Elise understood Francesca's hesitance to say Trevor Gaines's name. No wonder Lucien looked like he'd just eaten something foul every time the topic of Gaines was broached.

Several minutes later, Elise's phone rang. She checked the caller identification and quickly hit receive.

"Lucien?"

"Yes. Ian's fine. I'm with him."

"Ian's fine," Elise immediately conveyed to a wide-eyed Francesca. "Where are you?" she asked Lucien.

"We're on our way to London."

"What?"

"I took a guess and followed Ian to the airport in Indiana where he keeps his jet. I thought if I couldn't find him, I could charter a plane there. I figured he'd want to get to his mother's side as soon as possible," Lucien added under his breath, something about the hushed quality to his voice making her think Ian wasn't far away.

"Are you . . . are you going to try and see Helen, too?" Elise asked shakily, suddenly wondering where she stood with him. She couldn't read his mood. Was he furious? Worried? Preoccupied? Elise sensed mostly the last, but she couldn't be entirely sure.

"It depends upon her state. I assured Ian I wouldn't push the issue." Guilt washed through her at his words. She recalled how he'd insisted that day in his office that he wouldn't force things with Ian when Ian was dealing with his own private anguish. But Elise just had to be the one to push . . .

"Please tell Francesca that Ian said he would call her later," Lucien was saying. "He's . . . tired at the moment."

"Lucien . . . " she began, glancing anxiously at Francesca. She desperately wanted a private word with him. She longed to apologize for her faux pas.

"Can you tell Sharon that I'll be out of town indefinitely as well?"

"But Lucien, can't—"

"I'll be in touch when my plans are settled."

"Lucien," she blurted out, desperate lest he hang up before she got the opportunity to apologize. "I'm so sorry. I didn't know. . . . I didn't do it on purpose."

"Of course you didn't. You never do."

Shame swept through her at his words. He'd said something similar to her before, when she'd offered up a lame excuse for her impulsiveness.

"It's done now. Try not to worry," he said.

The line went dead. Elise pulled the phone from her ear, feeling numb all over again.

"What is it?" Francesca asked sharply.

"Ian is with Lucien. They're on Ian's plane, flying to London."

"Ian left without me?" Francesca asked, her voice ringing with shock.

"He says to tell you he'll call later. Lucien said he was tired," Elise said soothingly, even though she was quite sure that Lucien was using *tired* as a euphemism. She sincerely doubted Ian Noble was sleepy at that moment.

Francesca stood and picked up her phone, paging for a number.

"What are you doing?" Elise asked.

"Booking a flight to London," Francesca replied grimly.

Helplessness gripped at Elise. She envied Francesca's position as Ian's fiancée that she could make such a decision. She—Elise—felt like a powerless outsider. She couldn't go storming into the private hospital, demanding to see Lucien. Not after what she'd done.

No, she was worse than an outsider. It'd been her impetuousness that had created all this anguish tonight.

Twelve days later, Elise rode the elevator up to Ian Noble's penthouse, her heart feeling as heavy as a lead weight in her chest. Francesca was waiting for her in the foyer when the elevator slid silently open. Francesca had lost weight in the past week, with the result that her dark eyes looked larger than usual . . . haunted. Without saying a word, Elise walked over to her and they hugged.

"The funeral was *today*," Francesca said while they still embraced.

"Anne, Ian's grandmother, just called to tell me right before I called you at Fusion. I can't believe it," she said shakily. "I'm still in shock. Ian *promised* me he'd give me time to get there."

"I'm so sorry," Elise said. She and Francesca had been in contact since that night the truth had come out. Francesca had immediately flown to London while Elise stayed in Chicago, ritualistically going through her routine to keep herself distracted from what she couldn't control. Lucien had called Elise the day after he'd left, but after that he had resorted to text messages with updates on Helen's status. He'd corresponded with Francesca ever since she'd been forced to return to Chicago because of her graduate program's demands. Lucien's regular contact with Francesca reaffirmed Elise's anxiety that he was too angry to speak with her.

Elise had been so guilt-ridden on the phone with Lucien on the one occasion he'd called that she'd stumbled over what to say. He seemed distant as well . . . perhaps cold? Clearly, he hadn't come to terms with what had happened. True, he'd told Ian that night that he'd suspected his mother was alive, further prying open the door to the secret, but it'd been Elise's impulsive statement that opened the lock in the first place.

"Thank you for coming over so quickly," Francesca said, releasing her.

"It wasn't a problem. Denise is covering things at Fusion," Elise assured. Elise took Francesca's hands in her own when they broke apart. "I can't believe there's already been a funeral."

"It was a memorial service more than a funeral. Apparently, Helen had made a request during one of her more lucid periods to be cremated. I had just heard from Lucien early in the morning that Helen had passed away, and before I had a chance to make some last-minute plans at school and pack, Anne was calling to say they'd already held a service and not to come."

Elise's heart leapt at the mention of Lucien's name. Elise repressed an urge to ask a slew of questions about Lucien. She knew from those messages he'd visited Helen Noble in the hospital with Ian, but she had no idea about the outcome of those meetings. Once again, she experienced that terrible feeling of being an outsider.

Alone.

"Don't you see, Elise?" Francesca asked her miserably. "Ian didn't give me a chance to even get to the service because he doesn't *want* me there. Why is he avoiding me this way?"

Elise shook her head, determined not to show her worry about Ian's actions regarding Francesca. Although Francesca had immediately flown to London when she'd heard Ian was there, she'd only stayed for three days. After learning that a professor refused to extend a deadline for a project, Ian had insisted she return to Chicago, assuring her he'd contact her when things got worse with his mother. Apparently, Ian hadn't done that, however, and that's what Francesca was so upset about.

"He's confused and grieving. Give him time," Elise assured, taking Francesca's hand and leading her to a salon that led off the main gallery hall. "Sit down. I'll get you something to drink," she said, spying a pitcher of water and some decanters on a sideboard.

"But I'm his fiancée, aren't I? I'm supposed to be with him while he's going through something so terrible. When Anne called and said I shouldn't come, she said Ian had to leave for an important business crisis in Germany. She was being elusive on purpose. I know it," Francesca said shakily as Elise handed her a glass of water.

"Ian doesn't strike me as the type of man who would want you to see him while he's vulnerable."

"Well too bad!" Francesca blurted out. "You can't have a relationship with someone and avoid that person just because you feel vulnerable. Of course he feels bowled over after his mother's death . . . after what Lucien told him. Who wouldn't? All the more reason I should be by his side right now. But he's barely said two words to me since he stormed out of here that night, even while I was in London. He kept insisting I shouldn't come until Helen had passed. But when Helen did go, he never told me! I'm furious at him," she said, her voice breaking in anguish. "And I'm sick with worry. What in the world is he thinking?"

"I wasn't defending him, Francesca. I just meant, it's not too shocking that he's throwing up some walls at this point."

"I have this awful feeling he's going to leave me."

Elise's mouth fell open in surprise at Francesca's stark declaration. Francesca had never struck her as being prone to hysterics. "Ian leave you? No . . . never. He adores you. He worships the ground you walk on."

Francesca shook her head as if she couldn't adequately convey her fear. She set down the water on the coffee table untouched.

"You don't know Ian. You don't know what a nightmare this all has been for him. It's bound to send him into a crisis," she said hoarsely. She blinked and brought Elise into focus. "It's been awful for you, too. You knew more about Lucien and Helen than Ian and me on that night, but the rest of it—the part about Trevor Gaines—was a shock to you as well."

Elise nodded grimly. "And Lucien has been just about as uncommunicative with me as Ian has been with you. Lucien has a good excuse, though. He's got to be furious at me for forcing the issue that night. He's always considered me impulsive . . . a loose cannon. I had to go and prove him right, didn't I?"

Francesca patted her hand where it lay on her knee. "Lucien made a conscious decision that night to tell Ian. You didn't force him to it, Elise. You acted from the heart. That's not a bad thing. You were worried Lucien would never get a chance to find out about his biological mother with Helen so ill." Her expression lightened slightly. "Oh . . . and Lucien told me good news about that when I spoke to him early this morning. Has he told you, by chance?" Francesca asked delicately.

"No. What is it?" Elise asked, the back of her neck prickling with awareness.

"Helen Noble was able to give him his mother's name. At first, she couldn't. She was barely conscious when they first arrived. But she rallied just a bit before she passed and became somewhat lucid. Ian and his grandparents got to say their good-byes." A sad expression settled on her face. "Apparently, even though she was so weak, and so easily disorganized by her psychosis, she seemed to recognize something about Lucien. It sounds as if she'd been very fond of Lucien's mother, because she smiled and reached for him, and said his mother's name. It's funny, the memories that can linger so sharply, even in a mind that was so ravaged like Helen's."

"That's amazing that she connected him to his mother without ever seeing him before . . . like a miracle," Elise breathed. "He must look so much like her. And what is it? What's her name?"

"Fatima," Francesca said. "Fatima Rabi, I believe he said her name was. Helen Noble was even able to give him the name of the town where she'd grown up in Morocco. With that, and her name, there's a good chance he'll be able to find her . . . or at least other members of his family."

Elise's heart leapt and then throbbed as she thought of Lucien getting his prize. "He must have been so happy . . . so relieved to get that news. All these years, he's waited for it. He's waited for family. I know it came at a heavy price, with Helen passing, but . . ."

Francesca tightened her hand on Elise's.

"Lucien's search had nothing to do with Helen Noble's illness or death. Absolutely nothing. He may not see it right now, Elise, but if it hadn't been for you setting off that chain of events, he would never have his mother's name. He would never have had even the remotest opportunity to meet her. Helen Noble was the last link. Because of you, he's been given that chance."

Elise made a show of smiling. She was ecstatic that Lucien had a clearer path to his biological mother. But she couldn't help feeling bereft as well, knowing he was likely on his way to Morocco even as she and Francesca spoke.

Not knowing when she'd see him again . . . if ever.

She returned to finish her duties at Fusion after talking to Francesca. When she arrived at the penthouse late that night, she stood in the opened doorway to the bedroom suite. Since Lucien's absence, the room had taken on a funereal feel. His elusive scent remained like an insubstantial ghost, haunting her.

A pang of longing went through her—so sharp, it stole her breath. God, she missed him.

She should leave. Of course she should. She'd been engaging in wishful thinking by remaining at all, hoping for that opportunity to meet with him face-to-face . . . to beg for his understanding. But what was the point? She'd proven to him that she deserved his lack of faith in her. She'd illustrated precisely why he shouldn't trust her. In fact, she'd ended up behaving in the precise manner he'd always accused her of.

Impulsive. Impetuous. Self-indulgent.

Tears stung her eyes as she pulled out her suitcase. It hadn't been long ago that Lucien had packed it for her there in that run-down hovel where she'd been staying. Where would she stay now? She knew she should make plans, but a pressure seemed to be pushing down on her chest, a weight of grief, making the ability to make such a huge decision seem like an utter impossibility.

She tossed item after item into her suitcase, straining to keep control, but increasingly seeing the interior of Lucien's luxurious suite through a film of tears.

Impulsive. Impetuous. Self-indulgent. The words kept repeating in her head like a bully's chant.

She sunk onto the edge of the bed and shuddered with grief. It was the first time she'd wept since Lucien had left Chicago. She'd even been reckless in falling in love, doing so deeply. Irrevocably. Now she'd done it, and there was no going back—only forward, into a future that looked bleak and lonely without Lucien.

But she'd learned something about herself since coming to Chicago, hadn't she? She was a hard worker. She had a passion for cooking. And despite everything that had happened recently, she still felt that newly found kernel of strength in herself—impossible to deny or ignore.

She wouldn't fold. She would endure. No matter how difficult that might be.

Wiping off her face with the back of her hand, she stood and continued with her packing, determined to proceed one minute at a time. One second, if need be. Plans needed to be made, and they would be. No matter how hollow she felt on the inside.

The penthouse had a flat, lifeless quality to it when Lucien opened the front door the next day. It was early in the morning on a Sunday. He hadn't slept except for a few hours on the plane, and his eyes were gritty from exhaustion. It'd been a heart-wrenching past few days, watching Ian and his grandparents at Helen's side, seeing her fade from this life ever so slowly.

He'd left as soon as he'd assured himself he'd done everything he could. He had an overwhelming desire to look upon Elise's luminous face . . . to find solace in her vibrant presence.

If he had to guess, he'd say the penthouse was empty. Perhaps she'd gone for a run?

Anxiety built in him as he walked back to the bedroom suite to check and make sure his assumption was correct. Sure enough, the large bed was empty and made—a very depressing sight after his increasingly frequent fantasies of finding Elise in it, warm, soft, and pliable from sleep.

His brow furrowed as he examined the master suite. It looked entirely too neat. Elise wasn't messy by any means, but she usually left signs of her presence—a magazine or book on the bedside table, a scarf tossed across a chair . . .

. . . her grand-mère's brush on the vanity cabinet in the bathroom.

He strode to the bathroom in search of that telltale evidence. He saw no brush, nor did he see Elise's bottle of perfume that used to sit next to his cologne. *None* of her personal belongings to which he'd become accustomed were there.

Alarm rushed through him, potent and jarring.

"Elise?" he bellowed. He quickly checked the living room, kitchen, dining room, extra bedroom, and den. All empty.

She was gone. An icy chill went through him. He'd half worried that she might be disgusted by what she'd learned at Ian's penthouse the other night. She'd certainly seemed awkward and uncomfortable when they had briefly spoken on the phone, and she hadn't called him once while he was in London. He knew they needed to talk, but he felt the uselessness and hollowness of doing it via the phone, so he'd just sent her messages to keep her updated. They'd talk face-to-face once he returned.

He hadn't believed things were so bad that she'd *leave*. But maybe it wasn't her discomfort about Trevor Gaines? Maybe she was angry because he hadn't confided the full truth to her?

He'd always preached to her about honesty after all, he recalled grimly.

He pocketed the keys he'd set on a table in the living room and headed for the front door, already drawing his phone out of his jacket. He'd find her, he thought, his moment of panic giving way to grim determination. If she didn't answer her phone, Francesca probably knew of her whereabouts . . . or Denise and Sharon were good possibilities, although Fusion was closed today. . . .

His hand was on the front door when he glanced aside at an entryway table and paused.

Elise's purse rested on it. A powerful feeling of relief swept through him, stealing his breath. Trepidation was close on its heels.

He realized fully for the first time that he was colluding with Elise in their distant, impersonal communication. He wasn't sure what to say to her.

He thought of how he'd encouraged her to be honest, how he'd told her he'd never be disappointed in her if she was. She'd deserved the same courtesy, but he'd deprived her of that. Yes, he'd had a good reason. The truth about Trevor Gaines was not only his ugly story, it was Ian's. Lucien had decided it was only right that Ian be the first to hear the facts. He truly believed in that decision, but his secrecy had come from more than just respect for Ian. He knew that now. His rationale had given him the excuse he needed to keep a distance from others for years. The women he'd dated, his adoptive mother, his foolish adoptive father . . .

From Elise.

It'd been Lucien who had been too insecure about the truth. He'd been so disgusted by it, he'd guarded the ugliness of it even from her.

Especially from her.

Which was the same thing as putting up a wall against his own heart.

Elise stood at the east-facing parapet, a cool, pleasant, early morning lake breeze brushing against her cheeks and fluttering her hair. Scattered clouds occasionally blocked the sun, so that she stood in bright light one moment, shadows the next. She was on the roof terrace, but she had the strangest feeling she was at a symbolic crossroads.

Her plans were in place. It was time for her to leave Lucien's residence for good. He couldn't want her there. He wouldn't.

Her bags had already gone ahead of her. Instead of having to return to Paris, her tail between her legs—as she'd feared—Denise had been her savior. The chef had insisted last night that Elise stay with her.

Elise had called her mentor and told her an edited version of her reasons for needing to leave Chicago, not wanting to betray Lucien to his employee. It turned out she needn't have worried. Being the perceptive woman Denise was, she'd already guessed at Elise and Lucien's relationship, and was sympathetic to a breakup, wisely not taking the side of either party. Elise had assured the older woman she would pay her back the rent money as soon as she was able, but Denise hadn't been concerned.

"With your talent, you'll have your own restaurant very soon. You can pay me back then if you choose, but the most important thing is that you finish your training," she'd said.

Elise inhaled the fresh breeze, praying for inspiration. Insight.

There's a difference between asking and begging. There is no desperation in asking—only courage.

The words Lucien had once spoken to her on this very terrace beneath a midnight-blue, star-studded sky echoed around her brain. Was she perhaps being a coward by leaving? Was she giving up too early, without giving herself the opportunity to speak to Lucien . . . to ask for his forgiveness?

Was she still being impulsive, even if she wasn't being selfish?

"You're not leaving."

Elise jumped in alarm at the sound of the familiar quiet yet determined voice.

She spun around, her eyes wide. He stood not ten feet away, wearing a pair of jeans and a white T-shirt, his scarlet button-down shirt flapping slightly in the wind around his lean torso. Stubble surrounded his usually neat goatee, his cheekbones looked more prominent than usual, and there were shadows beneath his eyes.

Yet he'd never looked more beautiful to her.

"Lucien," she mouthed.

"Why are none of your things in the penthouse?" he asked, his face rigid, his eyes blazing as he stepped toward her.

"Because they've been sent on to Denise's. She said I could live with her while I finished with my stage. That is"—she licked her lower lip nervously—"if you allow me to finish my training at Fusion."

"Why wouldn't I allow you to finish your training at Fusion?" he asked, his nostrils flaring slightly, his eyebrows slanting in a dangerous expression.

Elise shrugged and gave a desperate, gasping laugh. "Oh, I don't know. Maybe because I betrayed your trust, and made you tell Ian Noble the truth before you were ready? Maybe because it blew up in not only my face, but Ian's and Francesca's? Maybe because, as usual, I didn't have a clue what I was doing, and screwed everything up. Even if I never mean to harm, it seems I'm fated to do it inadvertently."

He gave her a long, searching look and shook his head slightly, casting a wild glance to the lake.

"You didn't do anything that isn't in your character, Elise. It was me who shouldn't have kept you in the dark. If I had opened up in the beginning about why I was in Chicago . . . well. Things would have been different."

A car horn beeped in the far distance. The wind rushed past her ears.

"Why didn't you?" she asked, not at all certain she wanted to know the answer. "Is it because you didn't trust me with the truth? Did you think I was going to hold it over your head somehow or maybe . . . blurt it out the way I did?" she finished hopelessly. "You ended up being right about that."

"No," he said scornfully. "That's not it. At least that hasn't been a concern for a long time now. And besides, you didn't blurt anything out. You may have set the stage, but I was the one who decided to tell Ian the truth that night in his office. You didn't force me into anything. It just seemed . . . fated or something, me telling him at that moment. I'm not the only one who has said so. Ian mentioned something about it as well."

"He must hate me, for bringing it all to the surface when he was so vulnerable."

Lucien shook his head. "He doesn't. Not in the least. He told me that the whole experience had an uncanny feeling for him, as if he'd been waiting for a good part of his life for that moment. He dreaded it, but he longed to know the truth about his origins. About himself."

She just stared at him, speechless.

"I thought you were angry. When I apologized and said I didn't do it on purpose, you said, 'Of course not. You never do.'"

His brows slanted as if he tried to recall exactly what she meant. "I wasn't being sarcastic."

"What?" she asked, bewildered.

He closed his eyes briefly and exhaled. "I know I was distracted. Ian was a wreck and he wasn't far away while we spoke. I only meant that while it's in your nature to speak from the heart, I know you never intend to harm. You're very kindhearted as a rule. I know you aren't capricious. You're never more yourself than when you speak the truth."

"Oh," she said, eyes going wide and warmth flooding through her. She recalled Francesca saying something similar about her motivations. It seemed too good to be true that Lucien had felt similarly. "Capricious, no—foolish at times, perhaps."

He shook his head. "No. I felt it too that night. It happens sometimes in life, when you feel a moment unfolding and you see your path clearly, when you understand that the time has come. That's how I felt that night when Ian got that phone call. As I said, Ian felt the same way."

She recalled the random thought she'd had that night that Ian seemed like a dream walker.

"Is he all right?" she asked after a moment.

Lucien shrugged, his expression bleak. "He says he is, but to be honest, I think he's wretched. I wish I understood what's going on in that brilliant brain of his. He shares very little of himself. You can imagine how surprised his grandparents and I were when he suddenly declared he was leaving for Germany on a matter of business."

"Francesca is worried sick," Elise said.

His hooded glance gave her a sinking feeling. Oh no. Francesca had a right to be worried.

She studied every detail of his face. It seemed so amazing he was standing there when she'd just been longing for him with all her heart and soul that it was hard to think about anything else. For a moment, they just looked their fill of one another. She eventually swallowed thickly. "Lucien, if it's true that you didn't keep the truth from me because you didn't trust me, why didn't you tell me?"

Again, he glanced out at the lake, his eyes looking brilliant from the muted light.

"Don't you know?"

She shook her head. Elise sensed how uncomfortable he was . . . how much he was struggling.

"I didn't know until I stood there in Ian's office how much I've been avoiding telling him because I didn't want to share the pain. The burden. The shame," he added after a pause.

"Of what would you be ashamed? You never did anything," she said heatedly. "Neither did Ian. It was that man . . . that Gaines. He's the one at fault! Not you."

His eyes were bleak. "You don't know what it's like . . . to carry the knowledge of your father's sickness. His depravity. You can't escape it. It's in your very blood. You can't purge it." He gave a harsh laugh. "You can imagine how stupid I felt, trying to find a place where I belonged . . . a family where I fit in . . . wanting to escape the shame of Adrien's crimes and my mother's self-involvement . . . only to discover my biological father's sins were a thousand times more heinous than anything my adoptive parents could engineer."

"Lucien," she whispered feelingly. "You are your own man."

A small smile pulled at his lips. "I know. Thanks to you, I have coached myself in that concept for years now. I think it's been my saving grace. As terrible of a blow as it was for me to find out about Trevor Gaines, I think it might have been a thousand times worse for Ian, without the inoculation you and I had." He gave her a soulful glance. "You and I had struggled on that path before. We both had to do battle with the idea that we chose our own destiny, that our parents didn't determine who we are."

"There has never been another person I've ever met in my whole life who is as unique as you."

His jaw went tight. He stepped toward her at the same moment she stepped toward him, and then she was in his arms, her cheek pressed to his chest, inhaling his scent. It truly was a miracle, being in his embrace.

"It really is like holding on to sunlight, hugging you," he said gruffly near her ear. "You make the shadows fly."

"Why have you been so cold since you went away?" she asked in a muffled voice near his chest after she'd quieted the surge of emotion she experienced at his words.

"When I called once I'd reached London, I was cautious. Uncertain. And you sounded so distant. I wondered if I was correct to worry about telling you."

"You worried about telling me about Gaines?"

"Everything I said earlier about doubting myself in regard to telling Ian, I worried about a thousand times worse with you. I wanted to . . . but it seemed like such a toxic thing to spill. That secret along with my mission to find my mother has kept me from intimacy for years now. It never plagued me more than it did with you."

His naked pain flipped a switch in her. She hugged him tighter, like she thought her embrace truly could keep him safe from all the shadows in his life.

"I'm sorry for not telling you the truth," he said. "You must think I'm a hypocrite, for always encouraging you to be honest."

She shook her head against his chest. "No, I understand. You'd held on to that painful truth for so long. No . . . you'd *contained* it inside you. It's natural that you would worry about loosing it onto the world, onto people you care about. And as for the other, you were right to encourage me to speak the truth. We both know it. I'd lived a life of lies and provocations and manipulations for too long. You gave me the limit I needed. You knew very well I would have done just about anything—risked anything—for you, including learning a little self-restraint and loads of self-respect," she said in a strangled voice.

She inhaled, trying to breathe past the constricting band around her chest, and looked into his face.

"I love you. How's that for honesty? How's that for a risk?" she asked, laughing, a tear skittering down her cheek. "How's that for trusting in myself?"

His expression flattened; his nostrils flared. He abruptly seized her mouth with his own . . . and Elise was submerged in the truth, swimming in it, and she'd never felt less afraid of drowning.

"Do you mind?" he asked hoarsely a moment later when he bent and hooked the backs of her legs with his forearm, and he was carrying her toward the stairs, his gaze fiery.

"I'd mind if you didn't," she whispered next to this throat.

Minutes later, they lay naked on the bed together, Lucien on top, their bellies heaving together. He'd pinned her wrists above her head, his gaze never leaving her face as he slid his cock into her, and they fused. She shuddered. The sensation was poignant . . . powerful . . . as sharp as a knife blade. He remained motionless, poised on the sharp edge of desire, relishing it, wanting it to end in crashing, delicious pleasure and wanting it to last forever.

Wanting to stay one with her forever.

"I love you," he said, emotion and raw desire making his voice harsher than he intended. "I think I've always loved you. Not in the way I do now, but still . . . you have always been in my heart. You *are* the heart of me, Elise."

She stared up at him, rapt, and he was struck anew by her luminous spirit.

"Tell me what you need."

"I need you," she whispered.

His cock throbbed unbearably in her clasping sheath. He tightened his hold on her wrists and moved. They both gasped at the sharp pleasure. He stilled again, determined to make the moment last. He opened his eyes and met her stare. He palmed her jaw, wondering yet again at the softness of her skin. He would draw this out . . . stay perched on this exquisite cliff of pleasure for hours, keeping them tied together for as long as God would allow a mere mortal man.

She squeezed him with her vaginal muscles and he winced in pleasure, groaning and stroking her even though he hadn't meant to. She tempted him so sorely. . . .

"I will never teach you discipline," he rasped, fucking her with long, forceful strokes. "It was a losing battle from day one."

"I'm sorry."

"You are not. And neither am I. I wouldn't have you any other way," he managed before he took them higher, and all rational thought was forgotten.

Afterward, they lay as close as two people can get, their breath slowing together until it blended into a lazy, hypnotic synchrony, his penis still inside her. He felt her warm, soft body jump slightly beneath him and lifted his head to study her startled, perspiration-sheened features.

"What of your mother? Francesca told me that Helen was able to give you her name before she passed away. I thought you'd leave immediately for Morocco to find her!"

He leaned down and kissed the tip of her nose. "A day or two isn't going to make a difference after all this time. Besides, I had other family to attend to."

Her elegant throat convulsed. *"Me?"* she asked incredulously.

He smiled down at her. "If there's one thing that all of this has taught us, surely it's that *we* choose our families. Blood doesn't determine a family. Legal arrangement doesn't either, not necessarily. We were loners apart, but together . . . yes, we're a family, you and I. Or we can be."

"I had no idea you would ever feel that way," she said, wonder tingeing her tone. When she noticed his upraised brows, she said in a rush, "Of course I want to be your family. And of course you're mine. But . . . when did you realize?"

"It's been coming upon me slowly, but I think I even knew it, deep down, ever since that day you blazed into Fusion, insisting you were my new chef. I knew you were a risk to my mission here in Chicago, but I couldn't resist," he said, smiling wider at the memory. He shook his head. "What balls you have, for a tiny little woman."

"I'm not tiny," she refuted. Her frown melted away. "What do you mean, you felt that way ever since that day?"

He shrugged, his expression sobering as he looked down at her. "Just that I realized for the first time that I couldn't walk away from you again, especially when you'd strutted back into my life, practically grinding the red flag up my nose. If you could risk it so flagrantly, then surely so could I."

"You made our relationship sound like it was going to be purely sexual . . . for the mutual gratification of needs," she said, her scowl returning. But behind it, he sensed her dawning wonder.

"Well, it's certainly been that."

He laughed softly when he saw her wry expression. "It wasn't always as clear to me as it is now. I'm speaking in retrospect. But I suspect part of me knew, even back then, because I took on the challenge of you, even knowing it might sacrifice my chance of other family. Ian and my biological mother," he clarified when she gave him a puzzled look. "Besides, you didn't trust me. I had to say something that would keep you tied to me."

"So you settled for tying me up in the sexual sense," she said accusingly.

He lightly kissed her mouth, and despite her pique, her lips caressed his back.

"I really did need to teach you control, Elise. You would have burned me alive if I didn't. You may still," he admitted ruefully under his breath.

She reached up and ran her fingers through his hair. He closed his eyes in pleasure when she scraped his scalp with her nails, and his cock quickened in her warm channel.

"You were my own personal *sac de nœuds*," he said, growling softly as she caressed him and his body tightened and hardened. Her hands stilled on his head. He opened his eyes.

"You thought of me as a sack of knots?" she asked, sounding mildly offended.

He flexed his hips, thrusting. She gasped.

"Don't worry, *ma chère*," he rasped as he braced his upper body off her, withdrew, and stroked her again, deep and hard. He caught her soft moan with his skimming lips. "It's a challenge I'm more than up to, and unfurling the mysteries of you will keep me busy— not to mention amply rewarded—for a lifetime."

Now for the first time in print

CAPTURED BY YOU

A One Night of Passion Novella by Beth Kery

Chapter One

As one of the most successful landscape photographers in the world, Chance Hathoway was used to capturing the unexpected. A guy had to be ready when Mother Nature decided she'd show you the full extent of her power, because that fickle deity didn't approve of slackers. He was admittedly addicted to those rare, magical moments when he was granted a glimpse into the inner sanctums of pure beauty.

The evening he saw the woman walking out of Orchard Lake, water streaming down her smooth, naked skin, Chance figured Mother Nature had outdone herself.

He stood at the periphery of the forest photographing the setting sun over the wooded lake. The meadow grass and yellow daisies close to him provided ideal perspective and contrast texture to the calm water. Forty-five minutes ago the water had been peppered with falling rain, making it look like the lake was on a low boil. Presently, it was as smooth as glass. A hushed, soft silence prevailed in the aftermath of the storm. Sunlight clung in the humid air. The quality of the light could make a magnificent scene boring and a mediocre scene brilliant. The southern Illinois forest lake was pretty enough, but it was the saturated quality of the light that would make for some truly worthwhile images. *Hopefully, anyway,* Chance thought as he attached a wide-angle lens and began clicking off photographs.

He first saw her through the lens of his camera—a pair of lithesome arms breaking the liquid-mirror surface of the lake. He paused in his photo taking. The back of his neck tingled, and Chance knew instinctively that a special moment was about to unfold. He pressed with his finger repeatedly as she neared the shore. She drew close enough for him to make out the shape of her glistening calves and thighs as she kicked, propelling herself forward. He caught a glimpse of her buttocks, two round, pale globes skimming just beneath the surface of the water, breaking the surface every once in a while and teasing his senses. He felt his cock stir but continued to work with focus, capturing the essence of unexpected beauty.

When she got within thirty feet of the shore, he deftly changed his wide-angle lens to a telephoto and seamlessly resumed his photography. Something about her graceful, unhurried movements held him spellbound—a woman lost in the simple delight of a solitary summer swim, feeling the cool water licking her naked skin and the warm evening sun falling on her back.

She stood in the shallows, the water streaming down her dark hair, sloping shoulders and full breasts. Chance's intense focus fractured. He just stared through the camera lens, his forefinger held still, his breath stuck in his lungs. She walked slowly toward shore, taking her time, her skin gilded by golden sunlight and gleaming with moisture.

His finger moved as if of its own volition, attempting to capture her image . . . her essence.

Does nature actually make *women like this anymore?* he thought, stunned. She was like a 1950s film goddess—large, shapely breasts with luscious-looking, dark pink nipples; a small waist; taut, smooth belly and round hips. Was she mad, walking around naked in the forest with a body like that? Chance considered himself a modern man, but *blimey* . . . If anything could bring out the caveman in a male, it would be her. It was a little hard not to think of totally inappropriate things in that moment, like tossing her over his shoulder, laying her down in the grass and claiming her female glory in the most ancient, primal way a man could.

Something about her vulnerability admittedly excited him. As she rose from the lake, he saw that the dark pubic hair between her long, shapely thighs had been trimmed very short.

Without telling himself to do it, he zoomed in. Blood pounded into his cock, making him hard and ready in an instant, when he saw drops of water clinging to pubic hair and plump sex lips. What would it be like to see them dripping with juices of arousal?

As she came within feet of the shore, he clicked off more photos. Her full breasts struck an erotic contrast to her delicate, narrow rib cage. They trembled slightly as she moved through the water. He knew in a rational sense that he was invading her privacy, but the moment wasn't about logic or political correctness. Chance was a photographer. He could as easily have stopped himself from breathing as he could still his finger on his camera with such a miracle of unguarded feminine beauty standing before him.

His arousal mounted as the water level hit her knees and then her calves and more and more of her goddess-like form was revealed. He didn't normally photograph humans. They were so contrived in comparison to landscapes and wild animals. But this woman—this magnificent creature—was an exception. She epitomized natural grace. Sex was a primal, crucial part of nature, after all.

And she was sex walking.

She stood in the shallows, panting softly from her exercise, and brought a tail of long, dark hair around her right shoulder. She squeezed, releasing the excess moisture. He could hear the water dripping into the lake, see the droplets sprinkle on her heaving breasts. She slid her hand over the back of her head and released a restraining band. Wavy wet tendrils of hair fell around her shoulders and chest, coming within an inch of her voluptuous breasts.

He knew the precise moment when she realized she was being observed. Had she heard the click of his camera? She went still. He focused on her face. Her wet pink lips parted in dawning surprise. Her eyes were large and brandy-colored. They were trained directly on him.

He stood and looked at her with his naked eye. About thirty-five feet separated them. He'd photographed many a wild animal in locations across the globe. It was always an intoxicating, almost eerie moment when an animal first noticed him and, for a second or two, their awareness—human and beast, object and subject—melded.

Meeting this woman's stare sent a thrill through him unlike anything he'd ever known. What would she do? Rush over to him and yell at him for his presumption? Scream? As far as he knew, there wasn't anyone near the deserted location in the woods. The recent storm had chased most of the hikers and fishermen out of the forest. Perhaps she'd run. Something about her almost preternatural stillness reminded him of an animal before it took flight.

But then her arms fell docilely to her sides and her spine straightened, causing her breasts to thrust forward slightly. Otherwise, she remained immobile, her gaze never leaving him. He didn't know why, but her open, unmoving pose triggered something in him. He didn't know for *certain* if her posture was an invitation. It *felt* like it, though.

He bent to the camera and doggedly continued an impossible task—to capture the essence of a goddess.

Sherona Legion had grown up in southern Illinois, and she knew Orchard Lake like she intimately knew every inch of her diner and every inhabitant of the tiny town of Vulture's Canyon. Or at least she *thought* she knew her comfortable little corner of the universe. It was suddenly transformed into a mysterious, vast, exciting world when she walked out of Orchard Lake after her swim and saw the man at the edge of the forest photographing her.

For several seconds she stood stock-still, her muscles tensed and her heart starting to beat a throbbing alarm in her ears. She was easy prey. Thoughts of grabbing her clothing and making a dash for the forest raced past her consciousness, but then the man stood. He was a stranger to her. He was tall with shaggy, sandy blond hair. His skin was golden brown next to the white crewneck T-shirt he wore along with long army green canvas shorts and brown hiking boots. He apparently spent a lot of time outdoors, given that tan. His hips were narrow, but his chest and shoulders looked powerful. His athletic build, long legs and muscular calves told her loud and clear who would likely win if it came to a race.

A thrill of excitement went through her at the thought of him chasing her through the woods . . . catching her.

She blinked, shocked by her unexpected train of thought.

His hand remained on his camera, reminding her of the possessive, sure touch of a lover. Who was he? His clothing was outdoor casual, but along with his elaborate camera spoke of some degree of affluence.

All of these jumbled, anxious thoughts came to her in an instant as she stood there, naked and dripping with water, while he scored her with his stare. She should dress and demand he destroy the photos. Her gaze dropped over the front of his canvas shorts, and her breath burned in her lungs. Even from this distance, his arousal was obvious.

Heat rushed through her, the degree of it stunning her. She was vulnerable and naked. For some reason, his observation of her, the fact that he'd claimed her image both with his camera and naked eye, struck her as bold on his part. Dominant . . . exciting.

She recognized she was defenseless, but felt strangely powerful in the knowledge. She dropped her hands to her sides in an unfamiliar submissive gesture (Sherona was not known for being docile). Her naked body was nothing to be ashamed of. She knew from the thick ridge of the shaft of his cock riding along his left thigh that she was, in fact, beautiful to him.

It didn't surprise her in the slightest when he bent again to peer through the camera lens. She stood transfixed, a gentle breeze causing goose bumps to rise along her skin and her nipples to stiffen. The subtle movement of his fingers as he took her picture over and over struck her as highly erotic. She imagined what it would be like to feel those fingers on her skin, detailing her form using the sense of touch instead of sight. Liquid heat rushed through her, the strength of her response taking her off guard. Without really thinking, she pressed her fingers to the damp slit of her sex. Pleasure spiked through her, delicious and forbidden. Her nipples tightened painfully. She sensed him pause in his photo taking. He lifted his head slightly, spearing her with a narrow-eyed stare.

Good God. She was an exhibitionist, and she hadn't known it until that moment.

She blinked, disbelief and horror jolting through her at the realization. She lunged for the neatly folded sundress she'd placed at the edge of the meadow grass before she entered the water. Anxiety pressed down on her chest as she hurriedly donned it, covering her nakedness, and slid her feet into a pair of flip-flops. She glanced up as she tossed her panties into her canvas tote—she didn't want to make herself more vulnerable by pulling them over her legs in front of him—but the man still stood behind his tripod, unmoving. Sherona straightened, her heartbeat now pounding in her ears.

The forest preserve path that led to the parking lot was fifty feet to the right of her and perhaps seventy feet from the man. She had the advantage as far as distance. Besides, she somehow doubted he'd leave that expensive-looking camera behind to chase after her. Her heart was beating so fast, it felt as if it had swollen and was pressing against her breastbone.

She watched him warily as she walked quickly toward the path, her chin tilted defiantly, ready to break into a run at his slightest move. His mouth opened, and for a few tense seconds, she thought he was going to call out to her. He didn't, though, and Sherona gained entrance to the path. She plunged into the forest, the thick foliage blocking her view of him. She hadn't wanted him to see her run, but now she raced toward her car. By the time she reached the paved parking lot, she was breathing erratically and a fine sheen of sweat covered her skin.

She gave one backward glance toward the forest and opened her car door. Not until she sat in the driver's seat with the doors locked did she allow herself a moment to catch her breath. As her wild heartbeat slowed, she glanced to her left. The only other car in the parking lot was parked perpendicularly to her Ford Focus; a sleek, silver Jaguar coupe convertible. She noticed the rental plates.

It *had* to have been *his* car. Nobody in the vicinity of Vulture's Canyon, save Katie Pierce, drove such a luxurious, sporty vehicle.

Now that she was safe, she pressed her hand on her chest as if to calm her racing heart. Rationally, she knew she should have approached the man and demanded he destroy the photos he'd taken of her.

But something had *happened* out there in those woods. Something that Sherona couldn't see or touch, but could measure by its effect on her body and spirit. For some inexplicable reason, knowing that stranger had seen something in her that Sherona herself had never glimpsed caused the confining walls of her small, comfortable life to explode.

Her world suddenly seemed like a much bigger, breathtaking place.

Two days later, Chance strolled into the pleasantly cool, extremely clean interior of the Legion Diner. The good-looking, husky young man who stood behind the counter with a half apron tied around his blue jeans wasn't the person he'd been hoping to see. The only other people in the diner were a gray-haired man in his late fifties who gave him a suspicious, grouchy-looking once-over before he returned to his newspaper and a thin man wearing a cap, his jug ears sticking out from beneath it. The skinny man was eating his meatloaf single-mindedly, never glancing up once at Chance's entrance.

The kid behind the counter gave him a friendly nod.

"Sit anywhere you like."

"Thanks," Chance said, sliding into one of the booths that lined the front windows. He looked out onto the deserted Main Street of Vulture's Canyon. Better to call it *Only* Street. As far as Chance could make out, the desolate street lined with ancient, crumbling storefronts was the only paved thoroughfare in the back-hills town set in the midst of the Shawnee National Forest. The Legion Diner along with the Trading Company and the Last Stop Saloon appeared to be the only viable businesses in Vulture's Canyon.

He glanced around when the boy set a glass of ice water in front of him.

"I was looking for the owner? Sherona?" Chance said.

The young man's amiable countenance faded slightly.

"She's taking some bread and pies over to the Trading Company. She'll be right back. Are you English or something?" the kid asked.

"Australian. Ever visited the land down under?"

The young man threw him a dry glance. "The farthest south I've ever been is Nashville. What can I get you?"

"What's good?" Chance asked, peering at the blackboard menu behind the counter.

"Everything. My sister is the best cook in the county."

Chance did a double take. "You're Sherona's brother?"

"Derek Legion," the kid said unsmilingly.

Chance hid a grin. Derek had seemed perfectly friendly until he'd mentioned wanting to see his sister. Well, it didn't particularly surprise him that the little brother of a woman as beautiful as Sherona might be a little protective.

He stuck out his hand. "Chance Hathoway. I'm here at Rill Pierce's request to do some photographs for the Food for Body and Soul brochure," he explained as he shared a quick handshake with Derek. He'd known Rill since they'd met at UCLA during their undergraduate years, both of them students in the visual arts department, and both of them expats—Rill from Ireland and Chance from Australia. Rill had gone on to become a renowned movie director, and Chance had made his career in photography, but they'd remained friends over the years. When Rill had recently mentioned to him the charitable work he did for Food for Body and Soul, a cooperative farm that provided nutritious, healthy food for poverty-stricken and needy families in the Midwest and Appalachian region, Chance had been interested. It'd sounded like a worthy enough cause for him to take a quick vacation at Rill's house and help in any way he could. It'd been Rill who'd suggested how his expertise might best help out the organization.

"So that's why you want to talk to Sherona? Because of Body and Soul?" Derek asked.

Chance nodded. "I understand she's in charge of public relations for the organization. I wanted to get her ideas on where I should photograph and when."

"Well, she should be back any minute," Derek said, seeming partially mollified by his explanation. But Chance hadn't been entirely untruthful. Rill *had* told him Sherona was the person he should contact in regard to the brochure. He'd been chomping at the bit to meet her, however, ever since he'd learned the identity of the glistening goddess he'd blessedly glimpsed. The fact that his contact at Body and Soul and the woman at the lake were one and the same made Chance feel like Lady Luck herself had just dealt him a dream poker hand.

Chance had shared with Rill—in a highly edited form—his

experience of seeing a beautiful woman swimming in Orchard Lake two days ago. They'd been sitting together on the front porch of Rill and Katie Pierce's large house, enjoying the slow, cautious crawl of evening into the forest. Rill had asked him a few pointed questions about the female's appearance.

"*That* was Sherona Legion, the woman I told you to talk to about the photos," Rill had said in an unequivocal tone as he sat back in the Adirondack chair and took a sip of his iced tea.

"How can you be so sure it was Sherona Legion?" Chance had asked, amused.

Rill had given him a droll glance. "You think there are a lot of women who live in these parts who match the description you just gave me?"

Chance had taken a swig of his beer and stared thoughtfully at the lavender blue evening sky. "There aren't a handful of women on the *planet* that could match what I saw out at Orchard Lake yesterday."

Rill's eyebrows had gone up at that. "That's quite a compliment coming from a globe-trotting photographer who can expertly testify about the identities of the most beautiful women on the planet."

Chance had rolled his eyes at that and glanced toward the front door. They were expecting Katie to join them at any minute. "Don't say things like that in front of your wife. She'll think I'm a worthless root and never let me visit you again."

"Katie can make up her own mind as to your character without my input. She won't hold the fact that you're the heir to the Hathoway fortune or your popularity with the ladies against you unless you give her cause to," Rill had said with a smirk. He had grown a little more serious when he registered Chance's scowl. Chance liked Katie, considering her a brilliant light to Rill's dark, quirky brilliance. He didn't want her to hate him.

"Katie can see through a stereotype if anyone can. She's had her own struggle with being stereotyped as the blond Hollywood rich girl. Besides, she knows a few things about the truth behind the image from her brother," Rill had said, referring to Katie's celebrity sibling, Everett Hughes.

"And from being the wife of a famous director, I assume," Chance had said dryly.

Rill had just shrugged at that.

"I'll have the daily special and a glass of iced tea," Chance told Derek presently. Derek nodded and glanced sideways when the grouchy-seeming older man stood.

"You done eating, Errol?" the gray-haired man asked the thin man.

Errol nodded.

"Come on. I'll drive you home, then," the older man said with gentle gruffness, surprising Chance a little. The two men had sat at separate booths. Chance wouldn't have guessed they were acquaintances. The thin man wearing the cap set down his fork with an obedient gesture that reminded him of a child.

"That's for both of us," the older man said as he set some money on the counter.

"Thanks, Monty. Don't forget the bread Sherona set out for you, Errol," Derek said, waving at a paper bag sitting on the counter. Errol scooped it up as he passed, the gesture looking familiar.

"Have a good one," Monty said.

"See you later, Monty, Errol," Derek said as he checked his watch and opened the refrigerator door.

The man called Errol trailed after Monty through the front door. Chance realized belatedly that all three of the other occupants of the diner knew one another as intimately as extended family. Sherona Legion's diner appeared to be the tiny town's communal kitchen and dining room.

He looked around eagerly when he heard a sound behind the counter. Sherona walked through a swinging door tying a white half apron around her hips.

"Okay, I'm back. You can go. Mike is waiting for you in the front of the Trading Company," she said breathlessly to her brother. She gave her apron strings a final tug and glanced up, seeing Chance sitting there. She froze.

"Hello," Chance called.

If she wore any makeup, Chance couldn't see it. She didn't need it. Her lips, for instance, which had fallen open in shock upon seeing him, were a lovely, natural dark pink. She certainly didn't need any artifice to make them any fuller.

Or sexier.

Belatedly, Chance realized Derek was glancing uneasily between his sister and Chance as she gaped at him.

"I don't really have to go for a while," Derek said stiffly.

Sherona blinked and straightened, yanking her gaze off Chance.

"What do you mean? Mike is waiting for you, and you've been looking forward to this fishing trip since you got home from college."

This time, Sherona noticed the uneasy glance Derek gave Chance.

"I'll be totally fine," Chance thought he heard her say under her breath. She looked at Chance. "Has he taken your order yet?" she asked, her tone not necessarily cool, but definitely businesslike.

"I ordered the special and an iced tea," Chance replied.

She nodded once and began to move around briskly behind the counter. Derek hesitated, but seemed to take some reassurance from his sister's unconcerned attitude about Chance. He removed his apron and walked around the counter.

"I guess I'll be going then," Derek said.

Sherona set down a pan on the stove and walked over to him. They both leaned across the counter, and she gave him a quick hug and a kiss on the cheek.

"Call me if you need anything. And have a great time. You

deserve it, with grades like you got—and for your freshman year, no less," she said with quiet pride.

Derek gave a small smile and loped toward the front door. He gave Chance a guarded half wave and walked out.

He and Sherona were alone in the diner.

He thought it would be the right thing to do to approach her and say he was sorry for what had happened the other day by Orchard Lake. He walked to the counter and sat on a stool. She showed no sign of having any interest in an apology, or with having anything to do with him, for that matter.

He watched her with increasing fascination as she prepared his meal. Her outfit was kind of . . . well, *frumpy*, to be honest: a loose pair of jeans, black Converse tennis shoes and a shapeless white shirt. Not that Chance cared. She could be wearing Chanel and the only thing he'd see was her glorious naked form glistening with water. Did she dress like that to hide the fact that she possessed the body of a Venus? The disguise might have worked for some men, but it didn't for him. She could wear a tent and he'd find her sexy as hell.

She moved like she was doing a perfectly choreographed dance routine—open the refrigerator, grab a pan with one hand and a platter with the other, close the door with a small kick, set down the pan on the stove, flip on the gas, slide the platter into the oven, open the refrigerator again, grab the pitcher of tea, scoop some ice into a glass . . .

It went on. She moved with efficiency, but also extreme grace, the props of her pans and dishes and cutlery precisely where she wanted them to be when she reached out a hand. By the time she set a steaming plate of meatloaf, mashed potatoes, gravy, corn bread and fresh steamed green beans in front of him, sliding a napkin and silverware down next to it, Chance realized he hadn't spoken yet. Just like he had been down by the lake, he was completely mesmerized by her.

"Thanks," he said, appreciatively inhaling the divine aromas wafting off the plate.

She stood regarding him, her former methodical whirlwind of action coming to an abrupt halt. She wore her long hair in a low ponytail. Now that it was dry, he realized it was an auburn color that nearly matched the russet color of her eyes. Despite her calm, unreadable expression, he saw her pulse throbbing rapidly at her throat.

"What do you plan to do with those photos?"

He blinked. Her voice sounded low and smoky, but there was a definite trace of steely anger in it.

"I don't plan on doing anything with them."

Her nostrils flared slightly and her brown eyes sparked.

"Then why did you take them?" she demanded, crossing her arms beneath her breasts. His gaze flickered downward before he gave her a glance that was both apologetic and droll.

"Why do you think?" he quietly returned her challenge. He sighed when he saw her stiffen. "Sorry, I shouldn't have said that. It was wrong of me to take them. Truth is, I couldn't seem to stop myself. You're very beautiful."

They stared off in the silence.

He picked up his fork and sank it into the tender meat. He groaned in gustatory bliss a second later as he chewed. Did her lush lips tremble slightly in amusement? He set down his fork and stuck out his hand, hoping to take advantage of the temporary break in her irritation. She reluctantly put her soft, warm hand in his for a quick shake.

"I'm Chance Hathoway. I'm mates with Rill Pierce. I volunteered to do the photography for the Food for Body and Soul brochure. I understand I'm supposed to see you about the details."

"I think you've seen enough of me."

He laughed, his mashed potato and gravy–filled fork pausing halfway to his mouth. Her eyes flashed in annoyance, but he couldn't seem to help his mirth. Her response had caught him off guard. "I haven't seen near as much as I'd like," he replied honestly before he wolfed down his potatoes. His eyes went wide in appreciation. "Your little brother was right," he said after he'd swallowed. "You *are* an ace cook."

Her defensive posture told him loud and clear he wasn't going to charm her into forgetting his infraction.

"Look," he said, setting down his fork. He didn't *want* to make this offer, but he knew it was the right thing to do. "My computer is in my car. How about if I bring in the photos after I finish eating and you can be shot of 'em yourself?"

"You mean delete them?" she asked, obviously confused by his word usage.

"Yeah. If that'd be what makes you happy."

She lowered her arms and walked over to the sink, picking up a rag. "It would have made me happy to have my privacy respected in the first place," she said, starting to clean the counters briskly. "But since I wasn't granted that the other day, your offer will have to suffice. How do I know I can trust you not to have made a dozen copies of those photos?"

"I'm a professional photographer. I'd never release any photos including a person without their signed permission. If I ever did, said person would have the right to take me to court," he said, taking a bite of corn bread and butter that melted in his mouth. "*Blimey*, this is bloody good."

She rinsed off the rag and folded it neatly. "All right. I spoke to Katie Pierce about you yesterday, and she seems to find you fairly trustworthy. I guess I'll just have to take her word for it."

"*Fairly* trustworthy?" Chance frowned, pausing in the ravishment of his meal. He hadn't tasted food this good in a long time. Sherona's slow smile nearly made him forget his flash of disappointment at being judged only *fairly* trustworthy by Rill's wife, Katie. He'd been trying to make a good impression on his hostess in Vulture's Canyon.

"As trustworthy as a man with unlimited wealth, talent and cockiness can be," she said.

"Katie said that?" he asked incredulously.

"No. I listened to her describe you in much rosier terms and came to that conclusion on my own," Sherona said bluntly. She walked toward the swinging door behind the counter. "I have to unload some boxes in the storage room. Just yell when you finish eating and get your computer."

"You mean you *are* going to delete all the photos yourself?"

"You better believe I am," she told him with a cool sideways glance before she pushed through the swinging door.

Chance grinned and took another voracious bite of meatloaf. In the privacy of Rill and Katie's guesthouse he'd examined those photos more times than he'd ever admit to. He knew firsthand they packed a gargantuan punch. Sherona was going to have to look at each photograph before she deleted it, and he was going to be right there next to her while it happened.

He was looking forward to this.

Chapter Two

Sherona started when she heard Chance call her name and nearly dropped the can of tomatoes she was placing on the pantry shelf. Her nerves had been jumping ever since she'd glanced across the counter and seen him sitting in that booth, all long, lean, careless male virility. A man like Chance Hathoway didn't come through a town like Vulture's Canyon save once in a lifetime, and he was bound to cause havoc in at least one female heart during that ephemeral visit.

For some reason, fate had seen fit to make her heart the one at risk, Sherona thought wryly as she nervously smoothed her apron and rushed into her office, glancing at herself in the cracked mirror on her office wall. Or maybe not her heart, but certainly her body. She couldn't recall the last time she'd experienced her femininity and sexuality as acutely as she had the other day on the edge of that lake with Chance's camera trained directly on her. Knowing that he'd witnessed the sudden, sharp awareness of herself as a beautiful, desirable woman made her vulnerable to him.

Or maybe what made her vulnerable was that his *observance* of her was what had *caused* her potent arousal.

She knew who he was, of course. She hadn't out there at Orchard Lake, but she'd recognized his name when Katie mentioned their houseguest yesterday while she'd been visiting the diner, and Sherona had put two and two together. Her brother, Derek, had bought Sherona one of Chance Hathoway's books last Christmas when she'd taken up landscape photography as a hobby. Hathoway was one of the best-known nature photographers in the world. His photos had appeared in museums, art galleries, magazines, books and newspapers across the globe. He'd won multiple prizes for his work—actually, a surprising number for a man so young. The fact that he was also the heir to the Hathoway retail fortune and a gorgeous Aussie with a bad-boy, adventure-here-I-come smile only added to his mystique.

This was the man with whom Sherona Legion—diner owner, cook, waitress and lifetime resident of the skeleton of a forgotten town, Vulture's Canyon—was about to go and view naked photos with.

Nude photos of *herself.*

As she walked out of her office, her gaze flickered across the U.S. lotto jackpot ticket she'd bought the other day. She'd tacked it up on the bulletin board, along with the ten other ones she'd wasted her money on over the past decade. Stupid ritual, she knew, but it hadn't stopped her from buying one chance a year for the past ten years as an escape from Vulture's Canyon; one wispy, ephemeral shot at finally springing her life out of permanent stall-mode.

Sometimes you had to take a chance if you ever wanted to truly live.

She applied the no-nonsense, unflappable expression she'd acquired after years of being a cook and waitress in a quirky community of artists and nonconformists and pushed through the swinging doors.

He sat on his stool, his glass of ice water, his laptop and an opened package of mints sitting before him on the counter. She noticed his dinner plate was missing. Her gaze flicked to the sink, and she saw that he'd rinsed it off.

"Make yourself at home," she said with amused sarcasm.

"I was just trying to clean up after myself," he said, attempting an innocent look and completely failing. It was a little hard for a rugged, six-foot-and-so-many-inches, shaggy-haired, whiskered male who had seen it all in every location across the globe to come off as angelic. Her wry glance told him so.

"Don't open those photos out here!" she said, suddenly realizing that his fingers were tapping across the keyboard and his monitor faced the entrance to the diner. Just what she needed, for her customers to see her stark naked. Anger flickered through her once again at his infringement on her privacy.

"Come on," she said, waving for him to follow. She didn't look around until she'd reached her tiny, cramped office in the back room and sat at her desk.

"Shouldn't we lock up out front?" Chance asked as he maneuvered into the only other chair in the office. His knees pressed against the wood panel on the front of her desk when he sat. This room was much too small for him.

Or he was much too big for it. Chance Hathoway seemed much too large for her small, known world in general.

"No one will be in for probably an hour or two, but if someone does come, I'll hear the door chimes," she said, hoping she sounded calm and matter-of-fact. In truth, her heart was beating uncomfortably fast.

He placed his computer on her desk and started hitting a few buttons, his manner focused. The irises of his eyes were hazel flecked with gold, the warm tones perfectly suited to his sandy blond hair. While his skin, eyes and the hair on his head possessed tawny hues, his thick eyelashes, the hair on his muscular forearms and the light scruff on his jaw were a darker brown.

He turned the computer sideways so that they could both see the monitor. His expression had gone every bit as impassive as hers. Sherona felt like he'd just dealt her a hand in a high-stakes poker match.

She stared at the screen. Her mouth went dry.

The photograph had caught her in midstride as she walked toward the shore. The evening sun and the glistening moisture on her naked body made her skin glow . . . luminesce. It was the expression on her face that made her stare in wonder, however. She looked serene, but a small smile shaped her mouth.

It was as if Chance knew perfectly well he'd caught a part of her that she wasn't entirely sure existed until he'd captured it with his camera.

She knew now.

She felt odd . . . dizzy.

"The delete button is right there."

Her gaze flashed to his face at the sound of his gruff voice. He seemed somber . . . watchful. She remained unmoving.

"Would you like to see the rest of them?" he asked after a stretched, straining silence.

She nodded. It was all she could manage by way of a response.

His long fingers moved on the keyboard, reminding her of the lover-like way he touched his camera the other day—precise, knowing, masterful. She stared at the screen, overwhelmed by an emotion she couldn't quite identify. Here was an image of her squeezing the excess water out of her hair, crystalline droplets clinging to her right breast, a thin rivulet streaming down her ribs.

In this one, she stood at the water's edge. Chance had caught the expression of a woman who was entirely at peace with herself—who liked her own company. Tears burned behind her eyelids.

He clicked a key on the computer. Her breath stuck in her lungs at what she saw. She looked across the desk at Chance, her eyes going wide. He stared back at her unblinkingly, just like he had the moment after he'd taken this photograph, when he'd caught her startled wonder as she recognized his presence. Sherona had precisely the same feeling she'd had when he'd photographed her. A heavy, hot sensation of arousal pooled in her sex.

He tapped his finger. In the next photo, her gaze remained fixed on him, her hands by her sides, her shoulders back, her breasts thrust forward, a hint of defiance on her face.

"No, *don't*," she said sharply when he lifted his finger.

"Why not? These are the most beautiful shots of all . . . certainly the most honest," he said, his eyes looking very warm.

He hit a key. Her heart felt like it had lodged itself in her throat. She couldn't help but look. Stare. In the image, she faced the camera full-on, unafraid. Sherona wasn't sure if it was the setting sun causing the effect, but her skin looked flushed with a golden pink hue. A few droplets of water clung to her pubic hair and the two fingers she'd placed on her labia to staunch the sharp stab of arousal she'd felt.

Heat washed over her cheeks and chest. She reluctantly met Chance's gaze and felt that jab of lust all over again. Why did she find his observance of her so potently erotic?

"You can't possibly mean to delete them now that you've seen them," he said, his low, gravelly voice an audible caress in the tiny, still room. His accent perfectly suited him—lyrical and rough at once. His voice had nearly as palpable an effect on her as his eyes. "They're some of the best photographs I've ever taken."

She blinked in dazed surprise.

"I mean it," he said with quiet conviction. "I want to photograph you again."

"You mean . . . nude?"

He nodded. Their voices had gone hushed and intimate. Another wave of dizziness struck her, but the expanding ache at her sex seemed to ground her, keep her in the moment there with Chance. She couldn't escape him; she didn't want to.

"But not *just* nude," he said.

Confusion flickered through her, but so did another prickle of sexual awareness. It was as if his voice itself were touching her . . . seducing her. "What do you mean, not *just* nude?"

He nodded once toward the photograph on the screen. The captured Sherona stared back at both of them, her awakened sexuality a palpable thing.

"I want to see *more* of that," he said. "I want to liberate the hint of what I'm seeing there. I want to see it all, Sherona."

Her heartbeat drummed in her ears in the silent seconds that followed.

"What . . . what would you do with them? The photos?"

"Treasure them, I expect."

Her heart paused in her chest at his simple response.

"I'll never let another soul see them, save you. Please. I want the opportunity to show you what I see when I look at you. I want the chance to celebrate you. You're the most beautiful woman I've ever seen."

That pierced through the fog of mesmerized arousal he'd formed around her, striking her as patently ridiculous.

"Give me a break," she said, standing from her desk, feeling vulnerable. She lowered the screen on his computer, hiding the offending—compelling—image. "You probably say something similar to women in every city, village and hamlet you visit across the globe in order to get a woman to take off her clothes for you."

"No. I don't."

His quiet forcefulness caused her to pause. The door chimes tinkled in the distance.

"I don't photograph people. I'm a landscape photographer."

She swallowed thickly. She believed him for some reason. Maybe because he was so patently sexy, there'd be no reason for him to have to think of stupid scenarios to get a woman naked and into bed with him. Besides, she'd seen his magnificent nature photos. Something told her he'd never sully his camera by using it regularly for taking photos of naked women for lewd purposes.

But those photos of her naked were the exact opposite of lewd. They were sexual, yes, but powerful to the extreme. They didn't debase her sexuality; they celebrated it.

"I . . . I have to go. There's a customer," she said, coming around the desk.

He stood and took a step toward her, halting her exit.

"Sherona?"

"Yes," she muttered, staring at the buttons on his shirt, keeping her head lowered so that he couldn't see the throb of her pulse at her throat.

"Will you think about it?"

"I . . . I'm not sure."

Her eyes went wide when he touched her cheek. She looked up, startled. His face was suddenly very close, his features striking her as bold and chiseled, rugged and masculine, yet perfectly harmonious. She could smell his aftershave and something that reminded her of fresh air and the woods.

"You have every right not to believe me, but I'm completely captivated by you," he said gently, his warm, fragrant breath striking her lips. He brushed his mouth across hers in a questing kiss. Without thinking, she submitted to his heat . . . his touch. She moved her lips against his, sliding and shaping. She blinked when he made a low, gruff sound of arousal. He placed his hand along her neck in a possessive gesture and bent over her, sliding his tongue between her lips.

Liquid heat surged between her legs at the feeling of his tongue plunging into her mouth. His taste flooded her, blinding her to all else—peppermint and some subtle flavor she couldn't put a name to, but recognized with every cell of her female body. Her world narrowed to the sensation of his tongue dueling with her own, exploring her possessively, sucking on her sweetly until she moaned as if in answer to his call.

He shifted his hands to her waist and pulled her tight against him, his thumbs caressing the sides of her body in a lazy circular motion that caused pleasure to curl tight in her lower belly. She instinctively pressed closer to his body, seeking out the evidence of his arousal and gloriously finding it. He was warm and male and so hard, it sent a thrill of sexual anticipation through her unlike she'd ever experienced in her life.

He moaned roughly into her mouth. She whimpered in displeasure, shocking herself, when he broke their kiss. He nibbled at her upturned lips with a barely restrained hunger.

"I'll take such good care of you, Sherona," he murmured. "Let me capture you with my camera. I want to see pleasure blazing from your face. I want to see you wet like you were the other day when you came out of the lake, but this time with desire. I want to *show* you how you can look, how you can *feel*."

Sherona stared, overwhelmed, confused and blatantly aroused by his tensely uttered words. It was hard to think with his body pressed against hers, the taste of him still on her tongue, his large hands holding her so possessively, a hot promise in his eyes. She stepped back, breaking their embrace, her hand covering her lips as if she foolishly thought she could wipe away the memory of that kiss.

As if. She'd probably be able to perfectly describe that kiss on her dying day.

She gave him a wild, desperate glance and headed toward the diner. She was making some coffee for her customers a minute later when he came out of the back room.

"Is there a good time to come back tomorrow so that you can show me the cooperative farm and anything else you think should be featured in the brochure?" he asked her.

She glanced at him sideways. His voice had been decidedly neutral. She appreciated his backing off sufficiently so that she could think. Viewing those photographs with him, hearing him say those outlandishly sexy things, kissing him, had been a highly unsettling and intimate experience.

"The diner closes on Sundays at noon," she said.

"I'll pick you up at your house then. Where do you live?"

"No," she said, blushing when she realized how abrupt she sounded. Derek was gone for several days. She didn't entirely trust herself to meet with Chance in the confines of her empty house. Not after that kiss.

She glanced back cautiously at her three customers and lowered her voice. "Just meet me here. I have some work to do after the diner closes. Say around four o'clock? It ought to be cooling off a little by the time we get to the farm. I'll be able to show you the places we want featured in the photos for the brochure."

He nodded, his eyelids narrowing on her. "And you'll think about things between now and then?" he asked quietly.

"Yes," Sherona replied with a matter-of-fact manner she was far from feeling. She turned away from him and started to prepare her orders.

She doubted she'd do much else *but* think about his offer for the next twenty-four hours.

Chapter Three

Sherona stood back and watched as Chance Hathoway absorbed the interior of the Food for Body and Soul co-op store, where they sold a small portion of the food they grew and processed. He'd done the same thing when she'd escorted him around the farm. She couldn't think of another word besides *absorb* to describe his absolute focus as he took in his surroundings. She had the strangest feeling he saw things that were right in front of both of them to which Sherona was completely blind.

Thankfully, since picking her up earlier this evening, he hadn't mentioned the racy proposal he'd made at the diner. At least, she *thought* she was grateful for that. As she spent more time with him, however, growing to respect his solemn focus on his task, his pleasant conversation and effortless male sexuality, she was starting to wonder. His apparent ease at ignoring the fact that he'd photographed her nude and touching herself, not to mention his outrageous offer to photograph her doing even more sexy things, had started to grate on her in the past hour and a half. She'd never better comprehended the cliché about ignoring the white elephant in the room.

As he walked toward her with a sexy predator's stalk, his sandy blond hair falling onto his forehead and a small, intimate smile shaping his mouth, she wished he'd just pounce the topic on her once and for all and end her anxious anticipation about what the hell she was going to say.

It shocked her to the core that she was considering granting his request. She had girlfriends who would be scandalized by Chance's offer—not to mention her desire to take it—but they hadn't seen those photographs. Naysayers wouldn't have understood the incredible knowledge and power that had gone through her, catching a glimpse of her secret, sexual, *true* self portrayed in Chance's photos.

"I thought it'd also be nice to include a photograph of the river," she said, waving in the direction of the woods lining the Ohio River. "The view down by the water is really pretty, and it would give the feel of Body and Soul's natural habitat and roots. But you're the photographer," she added hastily when he didn't immediately respond. "I'll leave it up to you whether or not that would be a good addition to the brochure."

"I think it's a great idea," he said. He reached into the pocket of the simple crew neck T-shirt he wore and grabbed his sunglasses. "Besides, you don't have to convince me about including some natural photography. Why don't you show me the river?"

She nodded at Louis Vanhard, a long-haired, longtime Vulture's Canyon resident who was manning the cash register, and walked out of the store. They followed a forest path that led from the parking lot of the co-op to the river. The minute they entered the dark, still woods, Sherona felt an amplified awareness of Chance following her on the path. She turned to face him when they reached the clearing at the edge of the wide, flowing river.

"You're right," he said, glancing around. He removed his sunglasses and squinted at the opposite shore, then looked all around the area, as if gauging the light. "This will make a nice addition to the brochure. I should photograph in early morning, I think." He put his glasses back on and turned to her.

"May I ask . . . Why are you doing this?" she said.

"Why am I doing what?"

"Why are you taking time out of your schedule to come to a tiny, no-account town like Vulture's Canyon and take photos for free?"

"It's a good cause, isn't it? Healthy, nutritious food for needy families?"

Sherona just nodded, her gaze narrowed as she studied him. "You're a philanthropist, then?"

"I'm not a do-gooder, if that's what you mean. There are a few causes I feel strongly about, though. I'm a bit of a greenie, truth be told."

"A greenie?"

"You know . . . an environmentalist. I've photographed the most beautiful landscapes in the world. It's hard not to witness nature in all her glory and not want to preserve it in any feeble way I can," he said, putting his sunglasses back on. A prickle of awareness went through her. She couldn't see through his mirrored lenses, but she had the distinct impression his gaze had just slid down over her in appreciation.

"But you're the heir to a huge fortune. Don't your personal convictions conflict with the fact that you'll one day be the owner of a retail chain that epitomizes commercialization and the mighty dollar? What are you going to do when they come to you and tell you a portion of an Australian forest has to be mowed down to put up one of your stores?"

"I didn't ask to be born into the situation I was," he said levelly.

"So you plan to refuse your father's legacy?"

"I didn't say that. I just meant that my convictions are my own. I didn't just come up with them in an adolescent rebellion against my dad's lifestyle—or even if I did initially, my values have changed after my experiences traveling over the past fifteen years. I've seen things that have changed me on a permanent basis."

Sherona was impressed by his quiet conviction. There hadn't been an ounce of defensiveness to his tone.

"I admire you," she said honestly after a moment. "I'm envious of all the places you've seen . . . all the things you've done. I always wanted to see the world. Travel." She sighed and looked out at the glistening river. "Vulture's Canyon has been the limit of my world."

"That's not such a terrible thing," he said, joining her in admiring the sun-soaked, sylvan scene. "It's beautiful country, and the folks around here seem like they're good people."

She gave him a cautious glance of respect. "That's true. So . . . what will you do? About your father's fortune?" She couldn't stop herself from asking.

He shrugged. "My dad's got more bounce than a mob of kangaroos. He'll be around for a long time. When I do eventually gain control of his company and money, I'll make decisions about it based on who I am, not who he is."

Sherona couldn't help but smile incredulously. "And he *knows* this? Your dad?"

"Brandon C. Hathoway is no fool; he knows his own son. If he truly does leave me his fortune someday, he knows perfectly well his hard-earned money will end up in the hands of a tree-hugging no-hoper."

She smiled at his accented version of *no-hoper*.

"He must really love you if that's true."

Chance shrugged. "I'm his only son. I care about the old man enough to leave him to his corporate piracy, and he cares about me enough to confine his lectures about my wastrel life to once a year at Christmas."

"That sounds like a very mature relationship for two such different men."

"What about you? Where are your parents?"

"Gone. They died in a car accident when I was eighteen and Derek was eight."

His grin vanished. "I'm sorry."

"It's okay. It happened a long time ago. I miss them, though. Still. The diner was theirs. I've waitressed in it since I was twelve years old. I still feel them in there every time I walk through the door," she reflected quietly.

"Did you raise Derek?"

"Yes."

"No wonder you never left Vulture's Canyon," he said softly. "You never had much of a choice, I can imagine. Derek must be like a son to you as much as a brother. You became a parent at eighteen years old."

"He *is* like a son. Luckily, he's a wonderful person. I couldn't have gotten any more fortunate, as unprepared as I was to parent him. What if he'd been a rebellious basket case, and there I was, a teenage guardian with no clue what I was doing? I could have scarred him for life. It didn't turn out that way, thank God. Derek is thoughtful and smart and . . . just a great kid. He got straight A's during his freshman year at Washington University in St. Louis. He's in a very prestigious accounting program," she said proudly.

"He seemed like a good guy when I met him. He certainly is protective of you."

"What do you mean?" Sherona asked, turning toward him.

"I mean that he immediately put on his game face when I asked about you. He must be used to having guys come nosing around his gorgeous sister."

Heat flooded her cheeks. "Don't be silly," she muttered, studying her sandals pressing into the weeds beneath them. "There are only a handful of men around here, and I can assure you, they have better things to do than 'nosing around' me."

He whipped off his glasses. She sensed his head next to her neck. She glanced sideways in surprise and saw his face hovered a mere inch from hers. His gaze speared her. He inhaled as if to catch her scent off her neck.

"I honestly can't think of what activity would be more worthwhile than catching a nose-full of you, Sherona," his voice rumbled, making her ear tickle. She just swallowed, his stare making her temporarily unable to speak or look away. "Did you think about what I asked you yesterday?" he asked.

"Yes," Sherona murmured, her stare stuck on the amber dots in his eyes.

"I know you called Rill last night."

She started slightly. She considered Rill a friend worthy of a confidence. "Did he *tell* you that?"

"No. I just happened to be passing the kitchen when I heard him say your name. Were you doing a reference check on my character, Sherona?" he asked, his lips twitching.

"Does it surprise you that I was, considering what you're asking me to do?" For some reason, her words *what you're asking me to do* caused a heavy heat to flow down over her belly and sex. Or maybe that was because she was inhaling his male scent.

"No. Better for you to find out firsthand from someone who's known me for my entire adult life that I'm not a psycho," he said, his low voice mesmerizing her. His gaze ran over her face. He stepped closer, putting his hands on her shoulders. The front of his body brushed against hers, the zipper of his canvas shorts bumping softly against her lower stomach. The tips of her breasts hardened against his ribs. A twinge of excitement went through her clit.

"How would Rill know if you're a *psycho* in a sexual sense? I imagine you wouldn't advertise it to the world, would you?" she said, lifting her face to his so that their mouths were only inches apart.

"No, I'm pretty private about sex. Besides, I guess it all depends on what you consider to be abnormal, doesn't it?" he asked, surprising her.

She licked at her lower lip nervously. Here it was—the crux of the issue. "Yes, I suppose it does. So tell me what it is you plan to do besides take naked pictures of me."

A smile ghosted his lips. He had a very sexy mouth, Sherona observed.

"You must have felt it—out by the lake the other day," he said.

Her gaze skittered up to meet his stare. Had he sensed something similar to the electrical charge that had shot through her that evening by Orchard Lake? She saw the heat in his eyes and somehow thought he had.

"I thought it'd be exciting to take some fantasy photographs of you," he said, his warm, fragrant breath fanning her lips.

"Whose fantasy are you referring to?"

He stepped even closer, his hands grasping more tightly at her shoulders. She felt his erection against her belly and was reminded of seeing its fullness press against the fabric of his shorts the other day. Hot, forbidden excitement pulsed at her core.

"Mine. I think you share it, though."

"That's rather presumptuous of you to assume, isn't it?"

His brows went up at her challenge. "I'll tell you what I had in mind for the photos, and you can tell me."

Her breathing was suddenly shallow and erratic. Her nipples stiffened as they dragged against his torso. His thumbs circled on her shoulders in a massaging motion, distracting her even further.

"I was hoping you'd help me capture the essence of a fantasy," he murmured. "A really hot one that I never had until I saw you at the edge of that lake the other day."

She just looked at him in a silent challenge, trying to hide her soft panting and ignore the buzz of arousal at her clit.

"I'd like to photograph you somewhere private here in these woods. I want to make you look like a captive."

"Captive," Sherona repeated dryly, even though a surge of warmth had dampened her panties at the word.

He nodded, holding her stare. His hands moved as he began to languorously massage her back muscles. Distantly, she wondered if he was trying to relax her while he said such anxiety-provoking, exciting things.

"Yeah. An incredibly sexy one. I want to pretend that I've captured you and bound you and brought you to the woods for private ravishment," he said, his eyes glowing with both amusement and heat.

"That's how you want to photograph me? Nude and *bound*?"

"Yes," he said, his gaze running over her face as if searching for her reaction. His small smile faded when she licked at her lower lip nervously.

"And . . . and what about the actual ravishment part?" she asked.

"That would be up to you. All of this is up to you. I'm not going to do anything unless you agree to it. I'll stop whatever we're doing the second you tell me to." He dipped his head so that his mouth was a scant inch away from hers. She'd never known a man to appeal to her sense of smell more. She wanted to absorb his scent.

"Don't you think that's an awful lot to ask of me? I don't even know you," she whispered desperately. "What if . . . what if you do whatever you want when I'm bound and helpless?"

"I swear right here and now I'm not going to harm you. In fact, I want to give you more pleasure than you've ever known." He studied her soberly in the brief silence that followed. "You heard from Rill that I'm an upstanding citizen—for the most part," he added, giving her a small, concessionary smile. She couldn't help but return it in a shaky fashion. "But what's more, I think *you* trust me, Sherona. Instinctively. You trusted me not to attack you out there by the side of that lake. For a few seconds there, I think you *more* than trusted me. I think you *liked* having me see you in all your glory. And if you believe anything, believe this," he said, his manner suddenly almost grim, he was so serious. "You are the most *fuckingly* glorious woman I've ever seen in my life. You really can't blame me for wanting to capture you completely, can you?"

He dipped his head and seized her mouth with his own. A puff of suppressed air flew out of her lungs. Her arms snaked around his shoulders, and she participated in a kiss that struck her as both blisteringly hot and restrained.

Sherona wanted more—much more—but he lifted his head.

"What do you say, Sherona?"

She nodded once, her throat feeling tight.

His white teeth flashed in an unabashedly triumphant smile.

"Thank you. I have everything we need in the trunk of my car."

Alarm zinged through her. "What . . . You want to do it *now*?"

"Yeah. The evening light is perfect. Do you know someplace really private? In the woods?"

"I . . ." She glanced around nervously. Her heart started to do a drumroll against her sternum. "Yes, I think so," she said, anxiety edging her tone.

He grabbed her hand and squeezed it. She looked up at his face and saw his warm appraisal.

"I'll call Katie and Rill once we get to the car and tell them you and I plan to spend the evening together," he said.

Sherona blinked when she understood the message behind his words. He was reassuring her safety by telling dependable, mutual friends they were together that evening. Not only *she* would know she was putting herself in his hands for the night; Katie and Rill would know, as well.

It shocked her a little to realize she trusted him—a stranger—so much that she hadn't even considered such a precaution.

She nodded once, and they walked toward the path hand in hand.

Chapter Four

She directed him down a narrow, tree-lined country road.

"We'll have to leave the car and hike into the woods about a mile and a half," she said when he pulled into the empty forest preserve entrance. "This is one of the least known entrances to the forest, and hikers typically don't venture this far when they enter at other locations. If there's no one in the parking lot, then there's an almost one-hundred-percent certainty that there's no living person within a three-mile radius," she explained, pointing to the nearly invisible entrance to the parking lot. Chance turned.

She exhaled when she saw the empty lot, unsure if the leap of her heart came from nervousness or excitement.

"Perfect." Chance swung into a spot and gave her a swift smile.

She came around the opposite side of the vehicle from him when he popped the trunk. She glanced inside, seeing a large backpack that she suspected held his camera and equipment, although she also saw several bottles of water through a partially opened zipper, a soft-looking, folded ivory blanket and . . .

. . . rope.

He noticed her take a step back.

"It's okay. It's not harsh rope. It's nylon winch rope. I use it to haul equipment up steep elevations when I'm working in the mountains."

She just stared at him, suddenly reevaluating everything she'd agreed to.

Was she fucking *crazy*?

Was she so starved for some adventure, so desperate for hot, raw sex with a gorgeous man, that she'd put herself in danger?

One look at Chance's concerned expression and her anxiety eased.

"It's soft rope, Sherona, but it still looks like the heavy-duty variety. I thought it'd look . . . well, incredibly sexy, to be honest, for a made-up capture scenario—the texture of the black rope winding around your pale, soft skin." She blinked, heat washing through her at his quiet description. "But I also have some pieces of cloth in my pack. We could use those. Whatever you want."

Sherona strove to keep her expression impassive as she leaned into the small trunk of the sporty coupe and grabbed the two coils of rope. She gave him a sideways glance as she stood.

"Follow me," she said.

He didn't reply, but she heard him behind her, hastening to comply with her request.

Twenty-five minutes later, they broke the thick canopy of the woods and walked into a meadow filled with Queen Anne's lace, goldenrod and daisies edging a small lake cupped in the valley of the surrounding hills.

"Blimey," he breathed, staring at the meadow. "Look at that color."

Sherona turned to him for the first time since they'd undertaken their trek. He studied the scene through a narrow-eyed gaze. She'd been acutely aware of him behind her the entire time they'd been in the woods. It was the most amazing thing, but she kept having fantasies of running and having him chase her. The crotch of her jeans had actually grown quite damp, her scissoring thighs stimulating her sex even further as they hiked.

Did her body somehow *know* she could trust him, despite this risk?

"'Blimey,'" she repeated uncertainly. "That's good, right?"

His grin was sex distilled. "You better believe it, gorgeous."

She couldn't help but return his smile.

"Well . . . I'll let you decide where to set up. You know the best angles for light and everything," she said.

He nodded once and walked several feet ahead of her, casing the area with the tight focus she'd observed earlier at the co-op. Her heart did a little flip-flop when he paused, placed his backpack on the ground and spread the blanket on the meadow grass.

"Here?" she asked in a quavering voice.

He nodded and knelt to his pack. "The lake is great, but I like the evening light in the meadow more. Besides, the lake calls to mind a vacation getaway, while I want to convey—"

"A perv kidnapping an innocent woman so that he can have his way with her?"

His eyebrows rose at her droll comment. "You changing your mind, Sherona?" he asked, drawing his tripod out of his backpack. He also withdrew a bottle of water and handed it to her.

"Just tell me again that you're *not* that perv," she said, still clutching the black ropes with one hand as she grabbed the bottle.

"I don't think I'm a pervert," he said, standing up. "But if you think I am because I want to photograph you naked and tied up, then that's all that counts. We'll leave right now."

"Everybody is entitled to their thing when it comes to sex," she said quietly after taking a swig of water.

"I'm glad you think that. I happen to agree one hundred percent, as long as the participants are one hundred percent consenting and responsible adults."

She bit at her bottom lip and glanced down at the black rope.

"I'll pose for you for the photographs—do anything that you want. But . . . if you touch me at any time, I want the camera turned off. I'm not agreeing to having you take photos of me while I'm having sex."

"No worries. If that's the way you want it, that's the way it'll be," he said quickly, wanting to reassure her. He could tell it hadn't been easy for her to say that. On the other hand, her declaration had made his cock lengthen. Her comment had alluded to the fact that she expected to have sex with him, didn't it?

Was this a blessed day or what?

"So what do you want me to do?" she asked awkwardly.

"I suppose we could start by having you take off your clothes," he said, bending to straighten his tripod.

Sherona set down the black coils of rope and unbuttoned her blouse.

He saw her undressing from the corner of his vision, but forced himself to keep his gaze fixed on his task. Something told him that Sherona needed some evidence of his restraint, and drooling as she temptingly stripped down to her naked skin definitely wouldn't demonstrate that.

Still, he was only a man, and she was beyond sexy. He glanced up from his camera when she drew off her skirt and stood on the blanket, wearing only a tight camisole and matching panties. She looked up and saw him staring.

She held his gaze as she drew her panties down over her long legs.

Blood pounded into his cock, stiffening him to stone in an instant. Her image was arousing enough, but her *expression*; she *liked* showing herself to him, tempting him.

And was he ever tempted, he thought numbly as he stared at the juncture of her slender thighs. Her pubic hair was trimmed so short, he could clearly make out her fleshy sex lips, the slit between them beckoning him.

He couldn't wait to see her spread wide. His sexual hunger mounted until it felt as if it gripped at his throat. His nostrils flared in arousal when she reached for a strap of her camisole and started to lower it. She watched his reaction, seemingly as mesmerized as he was. The clinging material lowered slowly over the upper swells of her shapely breasts. The nipples popped out, pink and distended.

A sharp pang of lust caused his cock to lurch.

This was going to be more of a torture than he'd realized.

"Stop," he said suddenly.

Sherona paused with the camisole just beneath her breasts. The fabric was so tight, it pushed up the already firm, fulsome flesh slightly, exciting him.

"Leave it like that," he muttered, his gaze glued to her breasts. The woman was a walking wonder of femininity. His cock leapt again in the confines of his boxer briefs when she immediately lowered her arms, following his instruction. He gave her a sheepish smile and turned his attention to his camera with great effort.

"Is it hard for you?" he asked, trying to divert his attention momentarily from her goddess-like form. "To be so beautiful?"

When she didn't immediately respond, he looked up. Her cheeks were stained pink, but it was the incredulity and wonder he saw in her dark eyes that undid him.

"You *do* know you're beautiful, don't you?" he asked quietly, stepping toward her.

Again, she didn't respond, but he saw her delicate pulse leap at her throat. His gaze lowered over her, stunned anew by her ripe sexuality. He met her stare.

"The camera is turned off. Can I touch you—just for a moment—before we start?"

"Yes," she replied, the movement of her flushed lips sending prickles of excitement just beneath his skin.

He stepped closer and cradled her head in his palm, stroking her delicate jaw. She blinked. He had the distinct impression she'd assumed he wanted to touch her elsewhere and more intimately. Instead, he leaned down and placed a chaste kiss on her parted lips. His tongue dipped ever so briefly into her wet warmth. She was so sweet.

He lifted his head and held her stare as he slid the hair band at her neck off her ponytail. Neither of them spoke as he ran his fingers through the wavy, silken auburn tresses, spreading them around her shoulders.

"There. You're temptation itself. Are you ready to begin?"

She looked a little startled when he stepped away. He was a little surprised himself that he was able to walk away.

"I think so."

He picked up one of the coils of rope. "Why don't you lie down on your side while I restrain you? I want to make you as comfortable as possible."

Her breasts swayed alluringly as she knelt on the blanket. He noticed her glancing up at him, slightly puzzled, and realized he'd been staring down at her as she lay on her side, transfixed.

"Okay," he said with what he hoped was matter-of-fact briskness. He knelt near her feet. "Like I said, this rope is smooth, but be sure to tell me if it feels too tight. It should be snug, but I don't want it biting into your skin in any way," he said as he began to tie her ankles together. And what tender skin it was, he realized as his knuckles brushed against her calves. After a minute, he sat back and inspected his work.

"You're pretty good at that," Sherona said. She'd braced herself on her elbow and was looking at her bound ankles. He'd neatly wound the rope from ankle to lower calf. He'd been right. The contrast of the black, winding rope and her pale, smooth skin was electrifying.

His beautiful captive.

He scooted toward her waist, absorbing the image of her flawless skin and flagrant curves with his gaze.

"I told you, I have to use rope a lot when I travel in the wild," he said, grabbing the other coil of rope.

"And that's the only reason you're a rope master?" Sherona asked.

He glanced up to her face sharply and saw the small smile on her lips.

"Yeah, it is," he replied sincerely. He knew she was implying that he had a lot of experience restraining women, and he wouldn't deny it was a preference during sex. He'd never done it with anything as hardcore as ropes, however . . . nor did he typically bind a sexual partner at her ankles. The fact that Sherona was letting him amazed and humbled him.

She didn't respond, and he couldn't have said for sure if she believed him or not. All he knew for certain was that she held up her hands for him, her wrists together, ready to be bound.

"You really are something, you know that?" he said gruffly. "Don't think I don't appreciate how much courage this takes."

"Thank you for saying that," she said softly. He just nodded. He bound her wrists at the front of her body.

"Okay, you're all set," he said when he'd finished, realizing he was panting shallowly from excitement. Damn, this whole experience was scalding hot. He grimaced as he stood, trying to ignore his erection, which was increasingly feeling like a ponderous third limb throbbing next to his right thigh.

He approached his camera and got her framed up. He straightened.

"Okay, so let's get clear on our scenario," he said. He grinned when he saw her eyebrows go up in wry amusement. "You've been taken as my captive, but you end up being turned on by the whole capture scenario, too."

"Of course," she said drolly. "How convenient for you."

He chuckled. "I'm hoping you'll think it's just as convenient," he teased as he peered through the lens. His finger hovered over the button.

"Do you want me to look afraid?"

His mouth went dry at the sound of her low, smoky voice. He acutely felt his pulse throbbing along his cock. Damn, what had he gotten himself into with this woman?

"Sure. If you want to," he said, keeping his tone level with effort.

She didn't alter her expression drastically, but the whites of her dark eyes showed. *Holy shit.* He started clicking off photos. Despite the allure of her voluptuous body, it was her eyes on which he focused; they were large, velvety . . . like a doe's when it recognizes danger.

Sherona's eyes were damn near killing him.

"You're not really afraid, are you?" he asked as he photographed her.

"A little," she murmured.

"There's nothing to be afraid of. Just relax," he said as he took one final shot and removed his camera from the tripod.

"I'm going to take some from above you," he said, approaching her. He straddled her knees. The motion tightened his shorts over his rigid erection. He noticed those big brown eyes trained on his straining cock and hissed a curse.

"Excuse me?" she asked, looking disoriented. Her cheeks had grown bright pink now. Her lips had deepened in color as well.

"Nothing," he mumbled, lifting his camera and framing her up. "Do me a favor and lift your hands over your head. Arch your back. Now look at me with those gorgeous brown eyes. Ah, *too* right, Sherona. You've got it perfect."

"Is this when I'm supposed to start being turned on by the fact that I'm a captive?" she asked quietly, looking up at him with the whites of her eyes in full evidence, stretched before him like a delectable sexual feast ready for ravishment.

"I'll let you decide that."

He paused when she anxiously licked her lower lip with a quick pink tongue.

"You're a tease, Sherona Legion."

"I'm just playing the part."

"Be careful. You're playing it so perfectly, I'm starting to believe you," he said, clicking off photos.

"Maybe you should."

He paused and lowered his camera. For a few taut seconds, they just studied each other.

"Well, I suppose there's only one way we're going to find out if you're getting turned on or if this is an act. Come up on your knees and spread your thighs. Wide, beautiful."

He helped her adjust her position, although he only allowed himself the luxury of touching her smooth shoulders to steady her as she rose onto her haunches.

"Go on," he said in a tight voice as he inspected the bounty before him. Her bound wrists rested between her thighs, her arms next to her body plumping her breasts above the binding material of the camisole until they looked like some kind of ripe, succulent sex fruit.

"Spread your knees. Wider," he prompted when she did as he said, opening her knees while her ankles and calves remained restrained beneath her resting bottom. He took a decided step back because he suddenly wanted nothing more than to step forward and sink down on that blanket next to her. He lifted his camera.

"Now put your hands behind your head."

She hesitated, anxiety filtering across her beautiful, perspiration-glazed features. He moved his finger, capturing her reluctance and obvious arousal as she slowly lifted her arms, exposing her stretched naked torso and her spread, pink pussy. Her position forced her back into a slight arch, thrusting forward her large, firm breasts. The evening sunlight gilded her naked skin.

"Lord have mercy," he muttered as he clicked off photo after photo.

Chapter Five

She had the prettiest pussy he'd ever seen. It appeared vividly pink next to her white thighs, the delicate tissues flushed, the labia lips looking tender and slightly swollen from arousal. His nostrils flared as if he thought he could catch her scent from where he stood. And maybe he could; she was clearly very aroused, and he was nothing if not a primitive animal in those moments, every sense in his body sharp and honed. Moisture gleamed along the tempting slit of her outer sex.

"That's such a pretty sight, Sherona. Spread your thighs more."

When she complied without hesitation, he caught a glimpse of her tiny, slick opening with his camera. His cock lurched viciously, as if it had a mind all its own and knew precisely where it was supposed to be—buried fast in Sherona's tight, hot clasp.

"I think we have our answer," he murmured as he continued shooting. "The role has overcome you. You like the idea of being taken captive."

"I like the idea of you watching me. Seeing me."

He paused and lowered his camera. "I see you, all right. I see the sexiest woman I've ever witnessed in my life. I want *you* to see yourself that way, Sherona."

"Funny, how you're doing the looking, but I'm doing the seeing."

"What do you see?" he asked, raising his camera slowly.

"A sexy man who appears to be getting turned on seeing me naked and helpless," she said with a Mona Lisa smile that pierced straight through him.

"I'm the helpless one here," he assured her, clicking off photos in a desperate attempt to capture that punch-to-the-gut smile. "You have all the power in the world. *Show* me. Lower your arms and touch yourself."

He thought she'd hesitate, like she had when he'd asked her to come up on her haunches and spread her knees wide. But she didn't. She swung her bound hands down and let them rest between her thighs.

"You're blocking my view. Let me see the goodies," he teased, grinning as he snapped off photos.

She lifted her chin, her glance at him pure, proud hauteur.

"That's right, gorgeous. You know you hold all the cards," he muttered under his breath. He didn't think she could part her thighs much wider, given the rope restraints at her ankles, but she did. As she split her legs wider, she shifted her torso forward, displaying her magnificent breasts more prominently. He swore she knew precisely what she was doing, presenting herself so erotically. Her expression remained smooth, however, the only telltale sign of her arousal her flushed coloring and the glassiness of her doe-like eyes. He wondered if that potent combination of sensuality and innocence wasn't what had drawn him to her in the first place, what had driven him to this crazy scheme.

She lifted her hands as he'd demanded, showing him her sweet, pink pussy. Her taut belly heaved in and out in a subtle motion as she panted. She delved a finger between the fleshy sex lips that had been driving him near insanity for the past fifteen minutes. He knew for a fact how wet she was by the fluid movement.

Not to mention how glossy her finger looked when she pulled it out of the slick crevice.

He lost all sense of himself as he stood there and photographed her while she plunged her finger up and down between her labia, rubbing her clit strenuously. He went from a tight focus on her pussy to a wider shot of her entire body to narrowing down exclusively on her face as she abandoned herself to wanton lust.

There could be no doubt that she'd given herself wholly to the moment. Her pussy glistened with moisture in the soft evening sun, her breasts heaving delicately as she panted. Christ Almighty, if he couldn't hear the wet, clicking sounds from flesh rubbing together so briskly. When she subtly began to thrust her round hips against the pressure of her strumming finger and a shaky moan escaped those reddened lips, Chance lowered his camera.

He realized he was gasping for air like he was drowning. He turned away from the essence of beauty and sex, panting. If he kept looking at her, he'd go berserk.

"Chance?"

The uncertainty in her tremulous voice temporarily soothed his raging lust. He took a deep gulp of air and turned toward her.

"I'm sorry. You're so . . . incredible. This is harder than I thought it'd be."

She sat there spread before him, her pussy pink and wet, her cheeks flushed, her large nipples erect, her lips parted. She'd stopped touching herself, though. Knowing it was because of the way he'd reacted cut at him.

He returned his camera to his tripod. He was so excited, and he didn't want to ruin the photos with unsteady hands.

"Will you continue?" he asked her quietly after he'd framed her up.

She just stared at him for a moment while he existed on tenterhooks. Had he turned her off by turning away like that, overwhelmed? Had he frightened her? he wondered suddenly when he saw her gaze lower to the front of his shorts and his obvious erection. She opened her lips.

"Maybe in order to get into the spirit of things, you could tell me you were going to do something to me if I didn't touch myself," she said.

Chance froze. "Like what?"

He saw the elegant column of her throat convulse as she swallowed.

"Make me take you into my mouth," she replied softly.

Her own voice struck her as surreal in the hushed meadow. Had she really just suggested that Chance pretend-threaten to make her suck on his cock? She considered her position—bound naked with her thighs spread wide, masturbating before a near stranger—and realized her latest example of wanton behavior wasn't that far-fetched.

She studied Chance closely for his response to her suggestion, her heart racing, her exposed pussy tingling with excitement. She *so* needed to touch herself again. His handsome features had gone rigid and solemn.

"You want me to tell you that if you don't make yourself come for my camera, I'm going to force you to take my cock in your mouth?" he clarified.

She bit at her lower lip and nodded. His sheer incredulity mixing with his flagrantly obvious male arousal both assured her and fueled her unbridled lust.

"I'm not going to tell you that, Sherona."

"No?" she whispered, her pussy screaming out in protest.

He shook his head slowly, his nostrils flaring. "No, because this is how it's going to happen: You're going to keep touching that beautiful little pussy until you scream in pleasure. I'm going to turn off this camera. *Then* you're going to take my cock in your mouth."

Her heart slammed against her breastbone like a panicked bird in a cage.

"You know what to do," he said before he bent to his camera.

She lowered her bound hands, positioning them so that Chance had a clear view of her pussy. Her clit twanged with renewed pleasure when she slid her finger between the fleshy, creamy lips of her outer sex. She bounced her hips subtly against the pressure. Her moan intermingled with the sound of Chance's camera clicking away, capturing her image . . . her essence.

Either her unusual position or the sheer wantonness of her act was causing a singular excitement to mount in her. The nerves in her pussy were so inflamed, so needy of release, they seemed to be sending signals to all parts of her body. The soles of her bound feet burned in sympathetic excitement with her clit. Her nipples felt prickly, as if the still summer air kissed and licked at them. Her lips even felt overly sensitive, needing to be touched, abraded . . . abused a little. She stared hungrily at the thick ridge pressing against Chance's shorts.

Her arousal grew so pitched, she began to move her entire arm to stimulate her clit. Since she was bound, both arms moved up and down in a subtle jerking motion as she strained to ignite. She moaned as orgasm loomed, her gaze still glued to Chance's cock.

"Spread the lips wide," Chance demanded. "Bare all of that beautiful pussy to me."

She hardly heard him, she was so hot . . . so aroused . . . her nerves burning for release.

"Spread them, Sherona," he said in a harsher tone.

She parted her labia with several fingers, but had difficulty keeping the puffy flesh open, she was so wet with her sex juices. She stirred desperately in the crevice, agitating her clit and bucking her hips back and forth, back and forth against the intense friction. Her nipples pinched tight. A gasp rushed past her lips and her eyes widened.

"Aw . . . aw . . . ah . . ." Her cry left her throat like a quavering question. Distantly, she was stunned at the magnitude of pleasure that ripped through her, splitting her apart, cracking through her like a whip. Her body rippled and convulsed, helpless in the grip of the storm of desire that racked her.

A moment later, she blinked open her eyes, feeling like she saw the world anew—the golden meadow, the swaying grass . . . the beautiful, virile man who stood next to the camera, staring at her like she was as novel and miraculous to him as he appeared to her in those full seconds.

She panted softly, watching him as he hit a button on his camera. Her breath caught when she saw the shutter close. He walked toward her, his features rigid. When he came to a stop in front of her, her gaze was on level with his crotch. He touched her jaw and she looked up at him slowly.

"It doesn't matter how many times I tell you how beautiful you are. The words just don't suffice," he rasped.

She closed her eyes briefly. His stare burned her. Their gazes remained locked as he reached down to unfasten his shorts. A pang of renewed excitement shot through her clit. She wanted this. She wanted this so badly.

Her fingers moved in her slit, soothing the sensitive piece of flesh . . . exciting it all over again. Her gaze dropped over his torso.

How could she *not* get excited, watching Chance lower his shorts and step out of them? The boxer briefs he wore were snowy white against his smooth, tanned skin. His muscular legs were covered with brown hair. The contours of his aroused cock were obvious, pressed tightly against the clingy fabric of the underwear. Her pussy tingled as she watched him slide his fingers beneath the waistband and jerk the cloth forward over his testicles and the swollen root of his cock. Sherona waited with bated breath as he slid his hand beneath the shaft and lifted it from where it had grown trapped along his right thigh.

For a few lung-burning moments, he held his penis several inches from her face, stroking himself. He was beautiful to her; the shaft thick, straight and long, the head puffy and dark pink, the rim beneath it thick and defined. White semen oozed from the slit. She wasn't surprised; he looked near to bursting. Her mouth watered. The nerves in her lips prickled, needing friction.

"You're my captive. You're going to suck me off, Sherona," he said with a strange sort of rough tenderness that electrified her with excitement. Warm fluid gushed around her fingers. It amazed her that this sex-play scenario was turning her on, but how could she argue with all that abundant moisture anointing her? She looked up at him, her eyes wide. She parted her lips. He winced and cursed under his breath, his accent too thick for her to catch what he'd said.

He stepped forward and boldly pushed the thick head of his cock between her lips. She immediately clamped him tight enough to make her ache, needing the friction on her sensitized nerves. His shaft split her lips wide. He placed his hand at the side of her head, holding her stare, and flexed his hips forward, sliding his cock along her tongue, forcing her lips even wider to take his girth. She tasted his salty cum and hummed her approval.

He snarled in arousal and tightened his fingers, furrowing them into her hair. He fleetly unbuttoned his shirt and parted the folds, the better for him to watch her ministrations. "Suck, little captive," he uttered, not unkindly.

She gladly complied, sucking for all she was worth, making her lips such a tight clamp that pain mingled with her arousal. He began to move, thrusting in and out of her mouth to half-staff. "Ah, that's a sweet thing," he said from above her, his taut abdomen rippling in pleasure. "You've got a hot little mouth, haven't you? You're going to squeeze every bit of what I've got to give you out of me, aren't you?"

She began pulsing him faster, aroused by his language. Her fingers moved more avidly in her well-oiled slit, massaging her clit, making it burn all over again—more so, with Chance's big cock thrusting in and out of her mouth, faster and faster now. He filled her to capacity, and yet he refrained from pushing too far, harming her while she was in such a vulnerable position. He fisted the root of the shaft and began to stroke himself as he thrust into her mouth, using his hand to join in the lusty rhythm she set. As they both grew more excited, his fingers began to bump in an erotic tempo against her straining, overly sensitive lips, his action firing the nerves. She again hummed her approval into his throbbing flesh. Her hand moved more energetically at her pussy.

He suddenly stopped pumping. "Aw, holy mother of . . . *fuck* . . . Are you playing with yourself, woman?"

Her clenched eyelids opened slowly. His accent was so thick, and her arousal so great, it took her a minute to comprehend what he'd said. He stared down at her, his eyes looking a little wild. In the silence, the only sound that could be heard was that of her fingers moving in her well-lubricated, burning flesh. His already enormous member swelled further in her mouth, making her eyes go wide.

He swung his hips back, his mouth twisted into a snarl. She sucked like mad to keep him, but the bulbous head of his cock slipped out of the vise of her lips.

"I want your pussy," he said, his mouth set in such a grim line, it was a little intimidating. She panted and watched as he moved behind her.

"Lay down on your side again. I'm going to release your ankle restraints." His voice sounded tense, but his hands were gentle enough as he helped her down onto the blanket. She did what he asked, her awareness hazed by potent arousal. He knelt at her feet, releasing the knots he'd tied earlier. She lifted her head, admiring what she saw of his sun-gilded, lean torso through his open shirt. She spied a small scar along his ridged abdomen, white on his tanned skin. His cock hung at an angle from his body, the weight of the head pulling it downward, glistening with her saliva. His testicles looked full to bursting.

Instead of splitting her newly liberated legs wide and diving into her pussy—which was what she expected, given what he'd said—he laid down on the blanket and whipped his boxer briefs off his legs. His cock flopped heavily onto his flat belly. He touched her upper arm.

"Come here," he said with the strained sort of gentleness that drove her crazy. "Straddle me with your ass toward my head."

She struggled to do what he'd asked, encumbered slightly by her bound wrists. His large hands touching her naked body guided her into how he wanted her.

"Sit on my face, Sherona," he demanded, his hands grasping her buttocks, his fingers delving into the soft flesh.

Her heart charging like a locomotive, Sherona leaned forward in her kneeling position, bracing her forearms on his pelvis, and lowered her sex to his face. When his wet, hot mouth came into contact with her outer lips, she didn't just moan, she wailed. When his sleek tongue burrowed between her labia and gave her clit a brisk lashing, a high-pitched keen went through the silent forest.

He used his fingers to peel back her outer lips and torture the swollen berry of her clit. Sherona thrashed in his hold, the pleasure too acute, too overwhelming. He swatted her ass, the sound of skin slapping skin going off like a gunshot in the woods. He paused, kissing her swollen sex lips.

"You're dripping on my face," she heard him say thickly, making her hips move restlessly. He spanked her again, and she stilled with effort. She could feel his warm breath striking her tissues and screaming nerve endings. "I think you need something to occupy you while I make a meal of you." He moved his hand between them and found his cock. He lifted it, making it clear what he wanted.

What he expected.

Sherona shifted, her fingers encircling the rigid, pulsing member. She immediately stuffed him into her mouth, eager to resume her own consumption of his succulent cock. He gave a guttural grunt of satisfaction and returned his hands to her ass. He lifted her slightly off his face, spreading both her ass and pussy wide. She moaned as she slid his cock in and out of her mouth, her lips aching with her efforts.

She could feel his gaze scoring her.

"Prettiest pink pussy," she thought she heard him mutter before all consciousness splintered. He'd driven his tongue directly into her vagina, curling it, thrusting it in and out, ladling out her juices. He moaned roughly, the sound leaving her in little doubt that he highly approved of her taste. She drove down on his cock, gobbling him greedily, wanting to return the concentrated pleasure he gave her. Their heads both bobbed and strained. It was greedy consumption on both of their parts, lewd, raw . . . unbearably exciting. His fingers tightened on her ass in a painful grip. He maneuvered her skillfully up and down on his tongue, and she followed the demanding rhythm with her mouth on his cock.

He pushed her pussy down to his face tightly as he flexed his hips, filling her mouth. Her eyes sprang wide as climax loomed and his cock swelled to what seemed like twice its size. His tongue snaked up between her labia and whipped her clit ruthlessly. He opened his mouth over her outer sex and applied a precise suction. He thrust two fingers into her drenched pussy and continued to lash her clit with his tongue.

His cock stifled her scream.

She felt him spasm between her tightly clamped lips. A growl ripped out of his powerful chest and resonated from his throat, but he continued to eat her avidly. She convulsed in bliss. He held her to him tight, refusing her surcease from the almost overwhelming pleasure. Blinded by her own climax, she barely had the where-withal to jerk back slightly, preventing him from spurting semen into her throat. Instead, he came on her tongue: strong, abundant, musky emissions filled her mouth, more coming with each spasm of his thick member and grunt tearing from his throat.

Chapter Six

Her explosive climax left her feeling like a wrung-out dishrag. She sagged against Chance's body, highly aware of his heat and hardness, the sensation of his torso expanding and contracting as he recovered from his own orgasm. Her gasps for air blended with the tempo of his pants, both of them slowing together. An owl hooted soothingly in the woods. Sherona dazedly realized the sun had reached the tops of the trees as it set in the west.

She shivered in pleasure when Chance stroked her from hip to breast along the side of her body.

"Come here," he said, his voice sounding roughened and sexy.

She swung her knees over his head and rolled on her side, her abdomen muscles temporarily too relaxed in her satiation to lift her to a sitting position. He chuckled at her limp state and rose, beginning to untie the restraint of her wrists.

"Are we all finished taking pictures?" she murmured, feeling a little disappointment. A stab of incredulity followed at her sheer lasciviousness. Chance gave her a warm glance. His small smile really ought to be outlawed for the effect it had on her. He unwound the last bit of rope from her wrists and liberated her.

"The light is going to be bad in five minutes when the sun dips behind the tree line. We can come back tomorrow to finish the photos, if you like. In the meantime . . . " he said, reaching for her and reclining again on the blanket. Sherona went eagerly into his arms, sighing at the sublime feeling of her bare breasts and belly sliding against his smooth, warm skin. "I suggest you come with me to Rill and Katie's guesthouse so that we can finish the un-photographed portion of our project."

She laughed softly against his chest, brushing her lips against his skin. Fragrant male sweat coated her lips. Euphoria swelled in her breast. Risk-taking with a man like Chance Hathoway was an intoxicating experience.

"I'm not going to sleep with you at Katie and Rill's. They're my friends," she said, despite her thoughts.

"What's that got to do with anything?" he asked as he lazily stroked her hair. "The guesthouse is separate from their house."

"No. It'd be . . . disrespectful somehow," she said, feeling a little foolish. Still, it was true. She'd helped Katie pick out some items for the guesthouse and had seen it in various stages of completion. She'd feel ridiculous going in there, uninvited by the Pierces, to sleep with their houseguest. Chance touched her jaw, and she recognized it as a prompt. She looked up at him. His hair was mussed and his eyelids had the heavy look of a sexually satisfied male. He looked delicious. She slid an inch higher along his length, abrading her nipples against his solid body. His eyes darkened in appreciation.

"Are you serious? You're not going to spend the night with me because you're worried about imposing on Katie and Rill?"

"I didn't say I wouldn't spend the night with you. You can come to my house, if you like. Derek is gone for a few days."

Her softly spoken words seemed to cling overly long in the warm, golden light. His nostrils flared slightly as his gaze ran over her face. She couldn't help wonder what he saw there. "You've got yourself a deal, gorgeous," he muttered before he slid his hand to the back of her head, pushed her to him and kissed her so thoroughly, they almost didn't vacate the woods before nightfall.

By the time they reached her small, comfortable bungalow situated at the edge of Vulture's Canyon and the woods, some of her nervous excitement about spending time with Chance began to mount once again. It wasn't that she didn't believe she deserved a sexy fling with a gorgeous man. No, it wasn't that at all. Lord knows, living in Vulture's Canyon her entire life, she'd had rare enough opportunities for something so tempting. She wasn't foolish enough to run when the chance presented itself.

It was just that, sitting next to him in the car as he drove back into town, she'd started to realize just how attractive she found him—and not just sexually, either. He was warm and smart and had been to every corner of the earth and everywhere in between. In many ways, he lived the type of life she'd always fantasized about, knowing all along her dreams would never come true.

He put the car into park and peered curiously out the front windshield at her attractive little bungalow bathed in the evening light.

"It's a ripper. Pretty and neat as a pin," he said. "Just like you."

"Thanks," Sherona said, her cheeks warming.

She led him inside, glancing around anxiously as she tried to picture what her modest home looked like to his experienced eyes. He hardly seemed judgmental, mostly just interested. He walked around her living room, checking out her photos and studying her book collection..

"There's one you might find interesting," Sherona said when she came up behind him with two glasses of iced tea. She handed him a glass and pointed at his photography book. "Derek gave it to me last Christmas."

"What do you know?" Chance said, grinning. He flipped open

the coffee-table book and grimaced at his author photo on the back leaflet. "You've had my ugly mug in your house all along."

Sherona stepped closer and peered over his arm. "It's a good picture," she said fairly. She glanced up at him and took a swallow of her tea. "The real thing is nicer, though."

"Thanks," he murmured, leaning down to kiss her. When things started to get heated, Chance twisted toward her and spilled some of his tea on the book. "Sorry," he said, wiping up the drops of water with his hand. "How come Derek bought you this book, anyway?" he asked as he finished drying the page and replaced the photography book in her bookcase.

"Oh, I started doing some photography . . . just as a hobby, you know," she said, feeling the embarrassment most people feel when they admit to attempting an art form in the presence of a master. "Derek knew I was interested in nature photography, and we have so many pretty landscapes around here, he thought I'd like your book. He was right, by the way. Your talent amazes me."

"Thanks," he repeated with a warm, natural grace that appealed to her just as much as his careless male sexuality. "What kind of camera do you have?" he asked, sitting down on the sofa situated before her bookcase and fireplace. He nodded with interest when she told him. "Can I see some of the photos you've taken?"

Heat rushed into her cheeks. "Oh, no. I don't think so. I'm such an amateur, Chance."

"Did you take that one?" Chance asked, pointing at the framed photo of spring flowers in a meadow, in-focus bluebells and goldenrod and daisies in the foreground, the background a blur of wild, vibrant prairie.

"Yes," Sherona admitted, suddenly wishing she could melt into the sofa and disappear.

"It's really good. You're a natural," Chance said so matter-of-factly that she blinked.

"You're just saying that."

He gave her that devilish Aussie grin, his hazel eyes sparkling with amusement, and took a sip of his tea. "You mean to get you into bed?"

She snorted and rolled her eyes. "You already did that."

"Not really," he said, reaching out and touching her hand. She turned it over and watched, mesmerized as he stroked her palm with a long finger. "I've never been to bed with you, and I haven't spent anywhere near the time and attention I want to, making love to you. But that's not the point. Your photograph is good, Sherona. You have a natural understanding of light and perspective."

"Thanks," she said, genuinely flattered. She'd entered a sort of dazed trance, watching him stroke her palm, feeling it with every cell in her body. "I think I'll make you dinner for saying that."

"Just when I thought this day couldn't get any better."

She gave him a knowing glance, but grinned. He was an effortless charmer, to be sure. Still . . . it was nice to allow herself to be charmed for once. Chance was right. A day like today didn't come around but once in a lifetime.

Chance took a shower while she washed up and whipped together a chicken, wild rice and vegetable casserole. He came strolling out of the bathroom at the same time she was popping it into the oven. He looked more edible than her casserole, still buttoning up his shirt, his damp hair falling on his forehead.

"Something smells great," he said.

"Well, it's not me." Sherona smirked. "I'm going to jump in the shower, too."

"Okay. I'll set the table."

"Are you always this agreeable?" she asked, glancing at him sideways as she left the kitchen. He surprised her by reaching out and grabbing her hand. He pulled her back to him and suddenly she was in his arms, looking up into the amber, brown and green points of color in his eyes.

"I'm making it my mission to be agreeable to you."

Her eyebrows went up in a wry expression. "Well you're not doing a bad job, considering what happened in that meadow earlier. I've never done anything like that in my life," she said in an impulsive burst of honesty.

His eyelids narrowed as he studied her. Her pulse began to throb at her throat. "Then I really am the luckiest man around." She laughed and started to break free of his arms, but he pulled her back against him. His clean, male scent filled her nose. "How come you never think I'm serious?" he asked.

"I don't want you to be serious. I want you to be honest."

His expression sobered. She tried to ignore the disappointment that went through her when he dropped his arms, freeing her.

"What if they're one and the same, Sherona?"

She couldn't think of how to respond, especially when he seemed so genuine.

"Why did you?" he demanded suddenly.

"Why did I what?"

"Why did you agree to something so risky with a stranger?"

She licked at her lower lip nervously. "I don't know for sure," she prevaricated.

He stepped toward the counter and leaned his hip against it. "You said you wanted me to be honest. Don't I deserve the same consideration?"

She glanced away, embarrassed. A few strained, silent seconds passed.

"I've been stuck in this forgotten town for my whole life, Chance. I'm not complaining. It's like you said, it's beautiful country filled with good, honest people. But that doesn't mean I haven't longed for a chance to break away, for *something* to shake up my life a little bit. I don't want to grow old and die and know I've never stepped off the paved path."

"That's what I mean to you? A little rough country? A little risk?"

"A reminder that I'm alive," she said before she had a chance to censor herself. "That I'm still a vibrant woman, despite the fact that I've been stuck in the backwoods for my whole life, and been responsible for another human being since I was eighteen years old, but still haven't seen my thirtieth birthday. Yeah. Maybe that's what all this means," she said. When she realized how raw she'd sounded, she lifted her chin in a subtle, defiant gesture. "Given the life you've led, that must sound pretty naive and stupid."

He regarded her soberly. "The last thing it sounds is stupid."

Again, she looked away, ashamed by her burst of honesty. He stepped away from the counter.

"Plates?" he asked, obviously sensing her vulnerability.

She pointed at a cupboard, wavered on her feet, and turned away.

"You really are a fantastic cook," Chance said forty-five minutes later as he enthusiastically made his chicken casserole, salad and homemade seven-grain bread disappear. "You should be the one to publish a book. *Nutritious Country Cooking . . .* no . . . *Bohemian Country Cooking.* Get it? All the fresh produce you use from the co-op and hippy ideals blended with old-fashioned recipes," he said, pausing in his brainstorming to take a huge bite of apple walnut salad. "I'll do the photography for it, if you'd like."

"Oh, yes," Sherona teased fondly as she buttered her bread. "World-famous photographer working on a book that will sell ten copies; nine, if I can't get my brother to buy a copy."

"It'd be a great promotional tool for Food for Body and Soul," Chance told her pointedly.

She set down her knife and just stared at him. His eyes gleamed at her knowingly as he forked a large helping of casserole into his mouth.

"You're *right*. It would. Why haven't I ever thought of that? The proceeds could go to Body and Soul, but more important—"

"It would highlight everything the organization stands for—affordable, healthy food for needy families."

A thought occurred to her and her shoulders sagged. "We'd never be able to afford the costs to develop something like that, even if I could talk the other board members for Body and Soul into it."

"Tell you what. Give me a proposal for it—nothing fancy, just a page or so, something I can give to my accountant—and I'll back it. I'll pass it on to my publisher, too. Maybe they'll pick it up. With a wider distribution, it'd be a decent moneymaker for the organization." She gave him an incredulous glance. "What? I wanted to do some charitable work for Body and Soul. I told you I think it's a good cause."

"But you're already doing the photography for the brochure!"

He shrugged. "I'll be able to finish that tomorrow morning. I can do more," he stated matter-of-factly. "Besides, it'll give me a good reason to return to Vulture's Canyon soon."

All thoughts of a possible cookbook vanished. "When do you plan to leave town?"

"Day after tomorrow. I have a photo shoot in the United Arab Emirates scheduled at the beginning of the week."

Sherona took a sip of her tea, willing the sinking sadness and flash of disappointment she experienced to fade. Of course she'd known he'd be leaving Vulture's Canyon soon. Chance was a gypsy, given the nature of his job. It was just that in addition to the mind-blowing sex they'd had, she was starting to get used to his warm, natural male grace.

"It must be so exciting for you, going to countries like that . . . seeing those different cultures and ways of life," she said wistfully.

"I guess it's been hard for you to travel, bringing up Derek the way you did."

She nodded. "But not just because of Derek. He's in college now anyway, and gone for the majority of the year. The diner won't run itself, though." She realized she might have sounded maudlin as she nibbled on her bread thoughtfully and gave him a smile. "You know, it's never been closed once, except for Sunday afternoons, since my folks died."

"You're a hard worker."

"Or maybe I just haven't got anything better to do in this excuse of a town," she said, laughing.

After dinner, Chance insisted on cleaning up, claiming he had to earn his dinner. He shooed her into the living room with a cup of spearmint herb tea. Sherona leafed through a magazine, grinning every once in a while when she heard his boisterous efforts resounding from the kitchen—cupboards slamming closed, dishes rattling, and Chance singing a rousing, off-key tune as if to bolster his energetic cleanup.

He joined her ten minutes later carrying his own cup of tea and sank down next to her on the couch. Earlier, as they'd eaten dinner, it had occurred to her how easy it was to talk to him, perhaps because some of the sexual tension between them had broken after their first encounter. She'd even wondered if his down-to-earth insouciance wasn't the reason she'd felt intuitively comfortable enough with him to do something as risky as she had.

Now that they sat together sipping their tea and talking on her couch, however, Sherona realized that her intense sexual awareness and attraction to Chance Hathoway hadn't disappeared; it had just ebbed slightly following their charged encounter. As she sat there with her feet curled beneath her, admiring his profile and the shape of his long legs and his lean, muscular torso and just about everything else about his appearance, sexual anticipation mounted by the second, even surpassing her former attraction.

"So," he said once nightfall was complete and the lamp next to the couch glowed in the windowpane of her picture window, "will you be able to get away tomorrow evening to finish the photo shoot?"

"I probably shouldn't," she said quietly, studying her ceramic mug. Even at the mention of the photos and her wanton behavior, arousal curled in her lower belly and tightened her sex. "I'd have to find someone to watch the diner."

He set down his tea on the table and drew one knee onto the couch, turning to the side to more fully face her. "We can do it another time," he said so levelly that she glanced up in surprise. She'd thought he'd try to coax her. He smiled, as if he'd known what she expected.

"I'm not going to push you, Sherona," he said, his voice low and compelling. "You know I'd like to finish the photos, but it's not the most important thing to me at the moment."

"What is?"

"Getting to know you better. Making love to you in the way a man normally makes love to a woman for the first time."

She smiled. "What way is that?"

"Well, I don't want to give too much of a pat answer, but I'm pretty sure it usually doesn't involve having her strip down, tying her up and ordering her to pleasure me."

"I just thought maybe you Aussies didn't like to mess around with niceties on first dates," she murmured. He chuckled and reached out and stroked her elbow.

Their gazes held. His grin lingered on his lips. Her heart throbbed in her chest.

He was an incredibly sexy man.

"I want to take off all your clothes and touch you everywhere, Sherona," he said as he slid closer to her on the couch and his arm draped around her shoulders. She looked up at him, his face just inches from hers. "I know I'll remember the way you looked when you got out of that lake until my dying day. But I want to remember perfectly how you feel, too." His lips brushed against hers. "I don't ever want to forget how you smell and"—his tongue dipped into her mouth, a wet, elusive tease—"how you taste."

Chapter Seven

Excitement shot through her at his words and sexy caress. She put her free hand at the back of his head and pulled him down to her, pressing her mouth to his, shaping their lips together. He groaned in approval of her hunger and took command of the kiss, spearing her lips with his tongue and boldly exploring her mouth. He pulled her closer, his male hardness and heat tempting her beyond measure. She returned his kiss avidly, sliding her tongue against his, applying a focused suction that made his throat vibrate in a growl. He broke their kiss and set her mug on the coffee table.

"What are you— *Chance!*" she exclaimed loudly when he stood, bent down and lifted her into his arms like she weighed as much as a grocery sack. Heat flooded her cheeks. Sherona didn't consider herself to be overweight at all, but let's face it—she wasn't a delicate little thing. She was five feet nine inches with some fairly liberal curves.

"Chance, *please* put me down," she begged as he stalked through her living room toward the hallway. "You're going to hurt yourself."

He laughed, his white teeth flashing in the dim hallway. A sexual thrill went through her. He looked a little dangerous here in the shadows.

"Hurt myself carrying *you*? You don't weigh a thing." He paused outside the first door on the left. "This one?"

"No, the next," she said dazedly. He entered her bedroom and set her down at the edge of the bed. Before she could recover completely, he swooped down and planted a scorching kiss on her mouth that left her flustered all over again.

"I've carried packs up the Himalayas that weighed twice what you do," he said next to her lips a moment later, nipping at her in a completely distracting fashion.

"I'm not exactly Tinker Bell," she muttered as she nibbled him back.

"No, you're not," he said, standing. She caught the flash of his grin and saw him lunge toward her bedside lamp to turn it to a low setting. He turned back to her. "You're built just the way a woman should be." His hot, appreciative gaze left her feeling flushed. "Are you going to tell me you don't know you have the body of a bona fide goddess, Sherona Legion?"

She blinked at his teasing, challenging tone. The truth was, she *did* like her body just fine. Not enough to share with anyone lately, though. In fact, she only had two serious love affairs to her credit, and neither of those lovers had made her anywhere near as aware of her body as Chance had from the first.

"I watched you before you realized you were being observed when you were swimming," Chance said in a low voice, taking a step toward her. "You like yourself, Sherona. You're comfortable with yourself. It was the most compelling thing about those photos."

Sherona couldn't think of what to say. Her throat had gone dry. The sound of his voice mesmerized her.

"I also think you liked me seeing you. It gave you a jolt to know that I was staring at your beautiful face and your long legs and your sweet, round hips and your lovely, wet breasts. You liked knowing you had me at your mercy, didn't you?"

She swallowed with difficulty. She could tell by the tilt of his eyebrow that he expected an answer.

"Yes," she said throatily.

He smiled. "There's no shame in that. Why shouldn't a goddess glory in her beauty?" He sat on the edge of the bed next to her. "Would it please you to know you were pleasing me, Sherona?" he asked softly. She looked at him and nodded helplessly. "Then stand up and take off all your clothes. Show me all that glory."

She did as he asked, arousal flowing hot and fast now in her blood. She hadn't dressed in a particularly sexy outfit after she'd showered. It thrilled her for some reason to know that it didn't matter what she wore. Chance knew perfectly well what was under the loose, disguising clothing, and he seemed to find it appealing.

She removed her sandals first, highly aware of his focused, narrow-eyed gaze following her every move. Her fingers went to the zipper at the back of her floral skirt. It made a hissing metallic sound as she lowered it, the noise somehow illicit in the strained silence. The skirt fell around her ankles, and she stepped out of it. She glanced up as she began to unbutton her short-sleeved denim shirt. Chance's stare was trained at the apex of her thighs, his nostrils slightly flared. His gaze flickered upward as she peeled the fabric off her shoulders and the shirt dropped to the floor; it toured hungrily over her hips and belly. Her skin tingled beneath his perusal. For some reason, her fingers followed the path, stroking the skin that had been enlivened by his hot male gaze. Liquid warmth surged at her core when she saw his small, pleased smile.

"The panties next," he said. "And turn around while you lower them."

Another ripple of excitement went through her. She turned her back to him and lowered her white panties over her ass, looking over her shoulder for his reaction. Heat and triumph surged through her when she saw the feral gleam in his eyes as he stared at her bare ass. She bent slowly, alluringly, in order to remove the panties, and hid a small smile at his hissing curse.

"Now face me, Sherona," he said, his voice sounding harder . . . rougher. She turned toward him and saw that he'd parted his long legs. His erection pressed tightly against his crotch and the right leg of his canvas shorts. His eyes looked slightly glazed now, like a fever of lust was growing in him by the second. "Take off that bra and show me those gorgeous breasts."

She reached behind her and flicked open the hook. His strong throat convulsed as she peeled the cups off her breasts. His cock jumped visibly. He grimaced and stroked it through the shorts.

"You know what I want you to do," he said.

She wasn't sure, exactly, but she took a guess. She opened her hands on her smooth belly and caressed herself, enjoying the feeling of her warm, soft skin in a way she never had in her life. She cupped her breasts in her hands and squeezed.

"Ah, Jesus," Chance muttered. He was starting to look positively wild now. It excited her to know how much he was enjoying this. "Now pinch the nipples. Make them hard for my tongue."

That got her going. She did what he said, pleasure spiking through her as she teased and pinched lightly at her nipples, making them stiffen and distend. Chance looked so tense with lust, she wasn't really surprised when he stood suddenly and came toward her. She recalled that just recently she'd told him she was too big for him to carry, but he seemed to tower over her at that moment, all sinew and brawn and hard, aroused male. He put his hands on her waist and spun her toward the bed. She stumbled slightly and fell back on the soft mattress.

He fell on top of her almost immediately, his mouth fastening on the tip of one breast while he filled his hand with the flesh of the other. Her sex turned molten in an instant. She stared up at the ceiling as he finessed her breasts to perfection, drawing on the nipple with a hot suck, lashing tenderly to soothe the agitated crest, massaging the flesh with his big male hand in a way that struck her as thrillingly possessive and knowing at once. She dragged her fingers through his hair, holding him to her, gasping and whimpering in pleasure. He seemed both stretched tight as a wire and content at once as he feasted upon her breasts, moving his dark blond head occasionally between one nipple and the other, molding the flesh in a lascivious fashion that sent sharp spikes of arousal through her.

She whimpered in protest when he lifted his head.

"I'm going to eat your pussy now," he said, his voice rough, his face tight with desire. He put his hand on her waist and urged her to flip over. When she did, he unceremoniously grabbed a pillow and shoved it beneath her hips, making her bottom rise in the air. He parted her legs firmly and dove between her thighs.

Sherona shrieked at the sudden onslaught of pleasure of his mouth on her pussy. Chance certainly fit all the stereotypes of a daredevil, live-life-on-the-edge Aussie. He made love like he might attack a high mountain or a killer wave—with a gusto and thirst for life that left her stunned and breathless.

He groaned, deep, male and guttural, when he slid his tongue into her pussy, letting her know how much he approved of her taste. She moved her hips restlessly against his mouth, increasing the friction on her sex. Just like he had up in the woods, he swatted her ass, warning her to keep still as he made a meal out of her. He used his hands to part her buttocks and sex, splitting her wide for his consumption. When his wet, stiff tongue slid onto her clit, she let out a yelp and sank her fingers into the comforter. He pressed on that magic button with his tongue, lapped up the juices along her tender sex lips and sucked until she screamed and broke in orgasm.

The shudders of pleasure just wouldn't stop coming.

Through a thick haze of sensual overload and climax, she heard him chuckle. Vaguely, she was aware that he moved behind her and that his weight left the bed for a moment. He rolled her onto her back and scooted her farther onto the bed. She panted, still disoriented, as he crawled over her supine body. He wore a small smile on his mouth that struck her as slightly predatory and . . . a condom over his thick, long penis.

"I've waited for this for such a long time," he said, positioning himself over her and parting her thighs.

"Since two days ago, you mean?" she asked with breathless amusement, reaching for his shirt and unbuttoning it, starved for the feeling of his smooth skin and lean, hard muscles. She bit her bottom lip to still her gasp of anticipation when she felt his thick cock head press against her slit. He grabbed the back of her thigh and pushed it toward her chest, opening her to him.

"Bless it," he muttered in a blistering hiss when he thrust and drove his cock into her. Sherona's eyes sprang wide. God, he was huge and hard and . . . *bless it* was right. His cock was lodged so deep, it was kissing virgin flesh.

"Aw, Sherona. Screw two days. I've been waiting for this for my whole life," he muttered tensely before he began to fuck her, rocking her in a cradle of distilled lust, rocking the bed . . . her entire world.

Again she entered a timeless zone of sensual pleasure so rich, she nearly burst with it. He wasn't careful with her, fucking her with a kind of thorough, pounding, focused energy that she realized typified Chance. He thrust, slapping their pelvises together, then jerked up slightly, giving her an electric jab on her clit that made her squeak in helpless excitement with each stroke. A feral snarl twisted his mouth as he drove into her again and again, sparing her no mercy, forcing her to drown in the rich, carnal experience.

"God, you feel good. I'm finally fucking that pink, wet pussy. I was going starkers staring at it up there in those woods," he growled through a clenched jaw. "You're so tight, you're driving me mad, Sherona," he said in a heavily accented voice at the same time that he pounded into her so hard, she shifted away from him an inch on the mattress. "Come back here, gorgeous," he ordered, fixing her in place by grabbing onto the leg that was flexed into her chest with one hand and holding her shoulder with the other. He pumped with short, concentrated strokes, the intense friction making Sherona scream in pleasure. "That's right. There's no escaping that, is there?" he grunted before he drove into her one last time. She began to climax, her vaginal muscles rippling and pulling at his cock.

"Eeeowhhh," she wailed, her eyes going wide as his cock swelled hugely in her tight sheath, ramping up the strength of her orgasm.

He roared. She could perfectly feel his penis jerk and spasm as he fucked her shallowly and ejaculated into the condom.

His breath struck her face in jagged pants in the aftermath. Sherona was just as destabilized by the experience, struggling wildly to catch her breath.

"So," she panted after a moment, her heartbeat still throbbing in her ears. "That's how an Aussie usually makes love to a woman for the first time, is it? Nice and sweet and gentle?"

He shook with silent, breathless laughter. Her smile faded when he kissed her mouth and lifted his head to look at her.

"It's how I made love to you for the first time. That's all I know," he said.

She ran her fingers through his thick hair and drew him down for another kiss.

It was all she needed to know at that moment, too.

Chapter Eight

Sherona glanced eagerly toward the front door when she heard the chimes ring, but it wasn't the tall, rangy form she was hoping to see. Not that Chance was supposed to be here, of course. He wasn't due at the diner for another fifteen minutes.

Instead, short, round, friendly Olive Fanatoon entered the nearly empty diner, followed by Errol.

"Hey, you two," Sherona greeted them as Errol sidled over to his usual booth. This afternoon he was avidly studying a red race car. Sherona didn't know the model, but had no doubt Errol would fill her in on the make and record of the race car very soon.

"Hi," Olive said, smiling and coming over to the counter. "Not too busy, I see."

"No, the dinner crowd is due in a half hour or so. I have everything prepped for you. Hopefully it won't be too difficult."

Olive waved her hand casually. "It'll be fine. I've filled in enough times for you in the diner to know that if by chance I get behind or flustered, all I have to do is tell this crew to chill out. They'll get their food eventually—one way or another."

Sherona removed her apron. "I can't thank you enough for doing this."

"It's not a problem. Of course Errol is over the moon because he gets to eat dinner here tonight."

Sherona glanced over at the thin man studying the race car. The entire town of Vulture's Canyon helped look out for Errol, but Olive was his most devoted caretaker, spending several hours each afternoon at Errol's riverside house, cooking him meals and making sure he was doing the basics of self-care.

Sherona glanced toward the back of the diner and then at her watch. Olive must have noticed.

"We ran into that good-looking photographer out at the co-op store earlier this afternoon. He told me he'd be here to pick you up at five o'clock. Why don't you run into the back and do a little primping. Want to look your finest for a strapping man like that, I expect."

Sherona gave the older woman a dry glance. "I expect that's your subtle way of telling me I have flour in my hair or spinach on my face."

Olive laughed. "Nope. I may be old, but I'm still a woman. I know what a female wants to do before she goes out on a date with a guy who looks like Chance Hathoway."

"It's not a date," Sherona mumbled, turning away so that Olive wouldn't see her flaming cheeks. She'd known Olive for her entire life. Sure, Olive was an aged hippie, but even with her freethinking ways, she was bound to think Sherona was out of her mind for allowing Chance to do what he was going to be doing up in that meadow in a half hour.

She followed Olive's advice nonetheless, hurrying to the bathroom and combing her hair until it shone, then slicking on some lip gloss. She hadn't seen Chance since this morning when they both rose early, Sherona to race to the diner for the breakfast crowd and Chance to go back to the Pierce guesthouse and prepare for his day of photography at the farm and co-op. He'd asked her to call him on his cell phone if she was able to get someone to take her place at the diner that evening in order to finish their photography session.

And to spend his last night together before he leaves Vulture's Canyon, she reminded herself with a sinking feeling. Several times he'd alluded to the fact that he'd like to pursue the cookbook idea as they'd spent a long, idyllic, erotic night together, but Sherona was purposefully downplaying the likelihood of that happening in her mind. Chance was a man who likely had big dreams and made grand plans all the time. If only a small percentage of them came true for him, he still led a vastly more rich and full life than the majority of people on the planet. She couldn't put too much stock in his bedroom talk.

She'd just focus on the present. Tonight was all she'd likely ever have again with Chance Hathoway. She was going to appreciate every moment of it to its fullest while she could.

When she walked out into the main room of the diner several minutes later, he was just walking in. He looked windblown, tanned and very sexy after his photo shoot. Sherona paused at the back of the counter, staring at him, recalling hundreds of details from last night, some sweet, some funny, some so smoking hot she felt her body go into a steamy simmer. He did a double take when he saw her and let the door crash into his elbow. The chimes rattled.

"Hi, gorgeous," he said, wincing.

"Hi, graceful," she teased, walking around the counter. She approached him with what she hoped was calm aplomb, all of which went straight to hell when he cupped the side of her head and swooped down to kiss her. Hard.

"You two have a nice time!" Olive called, a sparkle in her eyes. "Don't worry about a thing here at the diner."

Sherona blinked as Chance took her hand and led her out the door. Chance's kiss had made her temporarily forget she was *at* the diner, let alone left room for her to worry about it.

She told herself that she should be less anxious than she'd been yesterday as they drove to the remote forest preserve entrance and hiked through the woods. By the time they finally broke through the canopy of the woods into the green, white and gold meadow, however, she admitted that she was *more* nervous.

This time, she knew precisely how powerful the experience could be.

The black nylon rope felt more erotic this evening as it wound around her naked limbs, binding her . . . freeing her. Today, he didn't fasten her wrists together at the front of her body, but at the small of her back. She lay with her belly on the blanket. The position made her feel even more vulnerable than she had yesterday. Chance's occasional caresses as he tied her up struck her as not only pleasurable, but entirely possessive. Yesterday she would have thought it was impossible, but his face looked even more rigid and focused as he bound her.

"How do you want me?" she asked when he'd finished and she lay on her stomach, her cheek on the blanket.

"Every way conceivable," she thought she heard him mutter grimly as he stood and walked over to his camera.

"I mean how do you want me positioned."

"I know," he said, framing her up. Just the simple action of him studying her through the camera lens sent a jolt of arousal through her sex. It sobered her a little—amazed her—to realize she had such a dirty, flagrantly sexy side to her character buried so deep for so long.

Chance started clicking off photo after photo. "Keep doing whatever you're doing. Keep looking right at me," he said, his tense order alerting her to the fact that he'd caught something he considered special.

It was like the camera was some kind of magical instrument, joining them somehow. She studied him through the lens, he chronicled her, and all the while their palpable connection caused things to grow wet and slippery between her thighs. The evening summer sun warmed her naked skin, but on the inside, Sherona heated to a low boil.

Chance straightened after a moment, wiping some sweat off his brow. He came over to her on the blanket. Sherona noticed his obvious erection.

"I want you up on your knees, your shoulders on the blanket," he said.

He helped her, as it was a little awkward with her hands tied behind her back. By the time he returned to his camera tripod, she was feeling very vulnerable indeed. Her bottom stuck up in the air, her shoulders and cheek pressed against the blanket. The sides of her breasts were fully exposed, the nipples stiffening as they brushed against the soft fabric.

Chance peered at her through the camera, jerked slightly and then fleetingly grabbed his swollen cock. A small moan flew past her lips at the erotic sight. The air seemed to tease the wet tissues of her sex, but her thighs were clamped tight from the restraints. She longed to spread her thighs and feel the air licking at her pussy . . .

. . . to feel Chance licking at it. Heat flooded her at the memory of his exceptional talent doing just that.

"You doing okay?" he asked her as he continued to photograph her.

"Yes."

"You were looking a little uncomfortable there for a second."

"I was just thinking about something," she murmured, watching him. She'd been thinking about something that made her uncomfortable, all right: the fact that Chance's tongue wasn't laving her tingling, burning clit.

He stood after a moment and came toward her again. She realized she panted shallowly from arousal, her nipples feeling chafed and sensitive as they moved subtly against the blanket.

"I'm going to turn you so that your bottom is facing the camera."

A sharp pain of desire stabbed at her clit. She turned her face, her forehead against the blanket and bit her lower lip to stifle a groan. He was going to use his camera to stare directly at her most private places. It shamed her a little that the idea aroused her so greatly.

After he'd positioned her, she was on her knees with her bottom raised several inches above her bound ankles, her shoulders and head on the blanket. She was highly aware of Chance kneeling next to her right hip, hating when he slid his hands off her shoulders, wishing he'd touch her again. Her entire body screamed for the friction of his caress.

Her heart squeezed when he didn't immediately move away. It leapt when he suddenly opened his big hand between her thighs, his finger sliding between her labia.

"You're so turned on, your clit is swelling between the lips," he said gruffly.

His finger twitched, flicking her clit for emphasis.

"Chance," she said in a choked voice.

He didn't reply, just stood. She couldn't see him in her position, but she could hear his camera clicking, knew he was zeroing in on her bound body, her ass, her obvious arousal, capturing the evidence of a captive who *clearly* enjoyed her captivity.

Her breath caught in her lungs when the clicking sound ceased. A second later, she felt his weight on the blanket. She turned her chin as far as she could and saw him kneeling next to her. He touched her ass, stroking the sensitive skin, letting his fingertips trail into the crack in a teasing caress.

"Would it be all right if I spanked you? Not hard. Just enough to make your ass pink."

She strained to see his face with her right eye. It was glazed with a light perspiration and tight with arousal, but his eyes on her were warm.

"Yes," she replied.

He gave her a small smile and the hand on her ass lifted. Her eyes sprang wide when he brought it back again, this time landing a brisk smack on her buttocks. Again and again he slapped her ass, making it tingle. He didn't strike her hard, but he did spank her frequently.

"Do you like being spanked, little captive?" he murmured.

"No," she spat, lying through her teeth in order to play the part. He paused, his hand caressing her buttocks, and she hissed under her breath, *"Yes."*

"That's what I thought," he said smugly.

In order to redeem her pride just a little, however, she tried to avoid the blows, shifting her hips and nearly causing herself to spill over on her side. Chance reached across her ass and held her in place to receive the spanks he administered with his other hand.

Sherona realized tears wet her cheeks and the blanket, but they weren't from pain. They were from pure sexual frustration. She wanted to come so badly, she was about to scream.

By the time he stood, her bottom burned. Her pussy felt as if it were aflame.

She heard the camera clicking and bit her lip to stifle a whimper. She was so hot, she was about to spontaneously combust. When would Chance end this torture?

This time when the camera stopped and he came to the blanket, she begged softly, her arousal surmounting her pride.

"Chance, please," she moaned.

"I know," he said, sounding grim. "Do you think I'm not suffering, too? Just one more position, one more round of photos, and we'll be finished."

She felt him unbinding the ankle restraints and moaned into the blanket. Her cheeks were hot and damp from her tears and perspiration. She knew what he was going to do, and she was right.

He made her split her legs wide, still in the bent-over position, her tail in the air, her sex fully exposed.

"Jesus, Sherona," she heard him hiss.

She clamped her eyelids shut in a mixture of shame, excitement and arousal. She could only guess what she looked like, her pussy soaked and swollen and red from uncontrollable lust, her bountiful sexuality displayed for Chance's eyes and his camera.

Her eyes remained clenched shut the entire time he photographed her in that bent-over position, her enflamed, dripping pussy and spanked ass on display. She'd thought it would be better to have the air lick at her exposed sex, but it wasn't. It tortured her all the more. But it was Chance's observance of her raw desire that tormented her the most.

This is what he'd turned her into—an alive, sexy, liberated woman who would likely be forever captive to one thing and one thing only.

Him.

She let out a sharp, tremulous cry when she made the poignant realization. It was heaven to fall into the dizzying depths of desire, but it was a pain unlike anything she'd ever known to know that it would never, *could* never last.

"Shhhh," she heard him soothe, and she realized in her dazed lust and need that he'd stopped photographing her and knelt next to her on the blanket. He stroked her sun-warmed back with his hand. "I've turned off the camera, Sherona."

"Then *hurry*," she whispered hoarsely, her lips feeling swollen and sensitive.

She thought that given their frantic state that he'd take her with the force of a locomotive, but he didn't at first. She keened softly when he entered her slowly, his girth stretching her tissues, making her grind her teeth at the pleasure spiked with just a touch of pain. He caressed her bottom and her back with one hand as if he wanted to quiet her clamoring nerves at the same time he excited them into a frenzy.

The moment his engorged cock filled her, throbbing deep inside her, and his balls pressed against her hypersensitive sex, Sherona exploded in climax. She quaked as pleasure tore at her, freeing her from the captivity of her need and enslaving her to it, as well.

She distantly became aware of him murmuring to her tensely as she came.

"That's right. Come on my cock. I've captured you, beautiful. Now we're in each other's blood, and I'll fuck you like you're mine. All mine," he grated out.

Then he began to move, proving the truth of his words. She was his, and he was proving that to her, fucking her with the sort of barely restrained energy and abandon that typified Chance, branding her very spirit with his mark.

Chapter Nine

After their scalding first joining, they made love again, this time with Sherona free of her bonds, loving Chance in the golden evening sun just as fully as he loved her. In the aftermath, he held her against his naked chest and stroked her hair.

"Come with me tomorrow," he said.

Sherona blinked open her eyes from her satiated doze. He touched the side of her face, prompting her to look up at him. The sunlight was turning his hair into a burnished gold.

"To the airport in St. Louis?"

"No," he said, a smile twitching at his mouth. "To the Middle East. Not just there, though," he added, his grin fading. "I want to show you the world. I want to see your face when you look at the pyramids for the first time and the Simonas Petras Monastery on the Athos peninsula and the Italian coast and Ha Long Bay . . . all of it. It'll be like discovering the world all over again. I want to see it all again through your eyes."

For an unguarded second, she pictured it—the two of them standing side by side, staring enraptured at the miracles of man and nature, making love in exotic lands, the smell of spice and adventure in the air. She'd dreamed of traveling her entire life. To do so in the company of Chance would be a fantasy she'd never even begun to conjure in her imagination until now.

But of course, it was just a dream.

"That's lovely of you to ask," she said, moved by his invitation.

"Then say yes."

"Chance, I can't," she exclaimed, wincing when she saw his handsome face darken with disappointment.

"Why not?"

"I couldn't afford a trip like that in a million years, and even if I could, I couldn't leave Derek alone."

"Why not? Isn't he on his own when he's at college?"

"Well, yes, but that's different. At a university, there's some kind of supervision built in." Chance gave her an incredulous glance. "There *is*. At least if he gets into trouble, he has places where he can go."

"Sherona," he said, giving her a give-me-a-break glance as he stroked her hair, "everyone in Vulture's Canyon would rally to help Derek if he should need it. But if you can't come this summer, maybe you can travel with me in the fall when Derek is at school. I'll come back to do the cookbook photography, and then we'll leave after that," he said, staring off into the distance as if he were working out all the logistics in his mind.

"Chance, I can't do something like that."

"I don't see why not," he said, his manner completely practical.

She rolled her eyes at him in fond exasperation. As a wealthy heir to a fortune and a famous photographer, Chance didn't even consider finances a major issue in making decisions. Of course, it was different for Sherona.

Quite different.

"I don't have unlimited financial resources like you do," she said slowly, as if she were explaining things to a child.

"I told you, it doesn't matter. I *do*."

She shook her head and gave a mirthless bark of laughter. "Do you really think I'd just drop everything and leave my entire life here?"

"I thought you said you'd always wanted to see the world," he said, suddenly looking grim.

"I do, but—"

"Is it me, then? You don't want to go with me?"

"No!" she exclaimed before she could censor herself. She paused, her breasts heaving against his chest, willing him to understand with her eyes. "I'd love to travel around the world with you. It'd be . . . incredible."

His expression softened. He stroked her cheek. "I'm glad we agree on that, at least. So there's no problem."

She closed her eyes briefly in frustration and rolled away from him, hating the absence of his smooth, warm skin.

"There *is* a problem, Chance. I refuse to live off you financially. I'm not going to even consider a crazy proposition like that when I know I don't have the money to do it."

He sat up abruptly as she began to dress.

"I told you that I have plenty of money—"

"I'm not living off you, Chance. I'm not going to be some kind of kept woman," she said abruptly, cutting him off. She regretted her harshness immediately when she looked into his eyes. Longing flooded her, so potent it stole her breath for a moment. She fastened her bra and pulled her blouse around her as she tried to recover her voice. He still hadn't moved when she turned to face him.

"You're the adventurer, Chance. I'm just a small-town girl with a small-town life. This is where I belong," she said, blinking back tears.

"Your life is as large as you want it to be," he said somberly.

She gave him a tremulous smile. "I didn't set the boundaries of my life. They were just given to me. You're the one who was born into a world without any limits. And it *should* be that way," she said, her gaze on him warm . . . loving. "You're the last person on the face of this earth who belongs in a tiny world, Chance Hathoway."

"So that's it?" he asked after a tense moment. "You're refusing to come with me?"

"I *can't*," she repeated, her longing making her sound desperate.

"I'm falling for you," he said starkly. "I think I might have fallen good and hard from the first second I saw you walk out of that lake. Don't bring this to a halt before it's really had a chance to get started, Sherona."

"I'm not purposefully halting anything. It's just that I belong here, and you . . . *don't*. We both know that."

His face looked set and grim as he stood up and grabbed his clothing.

Chapter Ten

He left town the next morning. To say that Sherona was miserable was a blatant understatement. They'd spent the night together, touching and making love almost constantly, as if they wanted to store up a deposit of caresses and murmured words and ecstasy to last them a lifetime.

Which is perhaps precisely what they were doing, Sherona thought presently as she opened up the diner.

She let the door close behind her. For a few seconds, she just stood in the dim diner and stared. She could maneuver around the thirty-by-fifty-foot space blindfolded. This place was where she'd seen her parents working side by side with congenial familiarity, where she'd first learned the value of hard work, and prepared meals for thousands of people.

These walls held her entire world, and she'd always been comforted by that knowledge.

She wasn't sure whether to thank Chance or curse him for making her feel suddenly imprisoned by the confines of Vulture's Canyon.

Later that night, after she'd exhausted herself at the diner and returned home, she checked her e-mail. Her attention was immediately caught by Chance's address. They'd exchanged e-mail addresses, but she hadn't expected him to be in contact so soon.

She opened the message and read:

I'm not going to make it easy for you to forget. Look for one of these every day. I miss you like hell already.

She opened the attachment with a trembling hand. She stared at the image of herself lying on her side, naked and bound. Her eyes looked enormous. How had he managed to catch the nuances of expression on her face, those unlikely combinations of wariness and curiosity, anxiety and blatant arousal?

She shut her eyes and felt the burn. Damn him. He knew she'd longed to participate in the fantasy, to leave with him . . . to see the world. Did he think that tempting her in this fashion would alter the limits of her world?

The captured image of her eyes in that photograph haunted her that night, making sleep elusive.

Fortunately, Derek returned home the next afternoon, giving her something to focus on other than herself and her morbid thoughts. Her brother was in good spirits after his fishing trip and gladly agreed to help her unload a new shipment of supplies that had been delivered.

"You know how Mike's dad is an accountant over in Carbondale?" he asked her as he helped her carry some packages of paper into her office for the printer. Sherona nodded. "Well, he's offered to let me intern with him next summer. It won't be paid or anything, but he says I can stay rent-free at their house, and I think it'd be a great experience, don't you?" he asked, dropping the armload of paper onto the copier table with a loud *thump*.

"Yeah, I do," Sherona agreed, her eyes going wide. "Wow, I didn't expect you to be working at an accounting internship until your senior year."

"I know, that's why this is so great," Derek enthused. "What?" he asked when he noticed her staring at him, a small smile on her face.

"Oh, nothing. You're just growing up so fast."

He rolled his eyes. "I'm in college, Sherona, not the third grade."

"I know. Oh, never mind," she said, waving her hand as if she were making her emotional moment vanish. "Let's go finish before the dinner crowd gets here."

"Okay," Derek agreed, pausing next to her bulletin board. "Hey, they drew the numbers today for the lotto jackpot. Mike and I heard about it in the car on the way home from Prairie Lake."

"Did they?" she asked distractedly, her mind already on what she needed to prep for dinner. "I'll have to check them."

"You don't have to. I memorized them."

She glanced back, something about the flat quality of Derek's voice grabbing her attention. She wasn't surprised that he'd memorized the numbers. Derek had an exceptional talent for numbers and math, thus choosing accounting as a major. Was it her imagination, or did Derek's face go pale as he stared at her ticket?

"Ha. Don't tell me," she joked uneasily. "I picked all the winning numbers."

"No, you didn't," he said.

"Of course. Story of my life," she said, grinning and turning toward the storeroom.

"You picked five of them, though."

Sherona came to a dead halt on the threshold at the sound of Derek's quiet voice.

"I did not."

The color had definitely washed out of his face, she realized. He turned to look at her, his dark eyes wide with shock. His nod of affirmation went through her like a lightning bolt.

"You paid for a multiplier for the five numbers. I think they said the five-number winners got two hundred and fifty thousand each. With the four-times multiplier, you just won a million dollars, Sherona."

Two weeks later, Chance sped down the familiar country road, his mind ablaze with anxious anticipation. Sherona had called him four days ago, but he'd been on a shoot in the dune fields of the Empty Quarter in the United Arab Emirates, where cell phone coverage was nonexistent. He'd only received her message when he'd checked into his hotel in Najran.

He'd been on a plane within six hours of hearing her message.

She'd said she'd received some important news and hoped she could speak with him as soon as possible. He'd been sending her e-mails and a single photo a day, as promised, but she'd never once acknowledged his messages. Her phone call had sent a shock through him. He'd tried to call her, but the reception was spotty. He hadn't been able to get through to her until he was at Heathrow, waiting for his flight to the states.

"Is everything all right?" he'd demanded immediately when he'd finally heard her voice coming clearly through the phone connection. He'd begun to suspect that the difficulty in contacting her wasn't on his end, but with the remote location and surrounding hills of Vulture's Canyon.

"I'm fine."

He'd breathed out a sigh of relief.

"I'm sorry, I hope I didn't alarm you," she'd said worriedly. "I just . . . I have some good news."

"Can you tell it to me in person?"

"What? I mean . . . I'd love to," she'd said earnestly.

"Good. Because I'm about to get on a plane to St. Louis."

He'd called her once he'd landed and was in a rental car, driving to Vulture's Canyon.

"Can you meet me at the forest preserve?" she'd asked when he'd called her.

"*The* forest preserve?" His body had perked into alertness.

"Yes. I'll meet you in the parking lot in . . . forty-five minutes?"

"I'll be there," Chance had said.

And now he was.

He pulled into the forest preserve entrance, wildly curious about the news and brimming over with excitement at the thought of seeing her again. He couldn't help but be optimistic given the hopeful tremor in her voice when she spoke to him.

He immediately saw her standing next to her car when he reached the lot. He swung his vehicle next to hers and bounded out to her.

She leaned against the trunk of her car, watching him with huge eyes. He immediately wanted to hug her so tight she couldn't breathe. He'd missed her like he'd left a vital organ behind when he'd left two weeks ago. All he wanted to do was touch her again, meld with her, but something about her sober expression stilled his desire to wrap her in his arms. He came to a halt a few feet away from her, suddenly wary.

A small smile tilted her lips. Her auburn hair was loose, fluttering around her cheeks. She looked so pretty, wearing a pair of jean shorts that showed off her long, shapely legs and an old T-shirt that had been washed so many times, it looked touchably soft. It hugged her full breasts, teasing his senses. She didn't usually wear such obviously sexy clothes, did she?

"Hi," she said.

"Hi."

"Thank you for coming."

"Of course I came. I would anytime you asked."

She smiled full-out then. It hit him like a punch to the gut. He started toward her, caution be damned, his arms outstretched. She moved so quickly, slipping away from his arms, that he blinked in shock.

"Sherona?" he asked, staring over his shoulder to where she'd come to a stop after eluding him.

"That was cruel of you, to send me those photos every day."

"I wasn't being cruel," he said. "I wanted to remind you of what we have between us."

"Do you think I need reminders, Chance?"

His gaze narrowed as he studied her. He couldn't quite interpret her expression.

"You know I would have come with you if I could, don't you?" she asked.

He swallowed thickly. "I do know that. I was just trying to make the point that you *could* if you wanted to."

"I couldn't, though. Not then."

His nostrils flared slightly. "What do you mean, 'not *then*'?"

"I have a secret, Chance."

He stared at her in openmouthed amazement that segued to arousal in a second. There had been a playful, slightly singsong quality to her voice. It struck him with a jolt that the expression he hadn't been able to identify was pure excitement. She practically *vibrated* with it. Her little avoidance of his arms had been a goading tease, he realized when he saw the gleam in her dark eyes and the small, electrical smile on her pink lips.

"Tell it to me, then," he demanded, turning toward her and taking several steps in her direction. She backed away from him, her grin widening.

She was a witch, he swore.

"You're going to have to *make* me tell you. But you'll have to catch me first," she said quietly.

Then she was running toward the woods, long legs pumping, her gorgeous ass daring him with every lunge.

"Son of a—"

He tore after her.

At first, Sherona suppressed giggles with effort as she ran into the shadowed forest. She hadn't planned to say or do anything so outrageous when she went to meet Chance today. But after sitting there for a few minutes and recalling all their erotic interludes in the forest, including the first time they'd seen each other, her excitement at seeing him had mounted to unbearable levels. Seeing his much-longed-for face and long, lean body had sent her passion to unprecedented heights.

Her mirth faded after only a moment of being on the path, however.

She could hear him behind her, his rapid footfalls informing her he was closing in fast. Her heart felt as if it would burst straight out of her chest. Her breathing came ragged and harsh. She ran faster, trying to elude him and yet wildly excited to be caught at once.

"I'm playing with you, gorgeous, just like you're playing with me. I'm going to *catch* you."

She whimpered and put on another burst of speed. The evenness of his voice when he spoke both alarmed and thrilled her. She understood. He didn't even sound winded. He was toying with her, knowing perfectly well he could capture her anytime he wanted.

His footfalls pounded closer now. She imagined she could feel the male heat resonating off him, although she knew that couldn't be true. If he were that close, he could grab her . . .

. . . *take* her.

A shiver tore through her. Her scissoring thighs stimulated her sex, making her hot and aroused. She tried desperately to increase her speed, but it was difficult on the uneven forest path, her feet having trouble getting traction. Chance's tread sounded much more steady and rapid than her own. She glanced over her shoulder, her eyes wide in trepidation, and she tripped when she saw how close he was to her.

He immediately caught her, the abrupt halt of her movement rattling her brain. He spun her and jerked her back against him, his mouth covering hers.

It was a conqueror's kiss, no doubt of it, forceful and ravenous. She whined when she registered his familiar taste. His hands moved over her body in a bold claim, cupping the sides of her breasts, squeezing her waist, molding her ass to his palms before he gave her a sharp spank.

"You're caught now, aren't you?" he breathed out as he ravished her throat with his hot mouth.

She twisted against him, wiggling, her softness against his hardness. He captured her wrists and pinned them behind her, leaning over her until she arched her back, pressing her breasts against his chest. It thrilled her that he held her for his consumption so easily. She cried out in excitement when he bent his tawny head and nipped at her breast. Then he enclosed a tip in his mouth, laving at her nipple with a stiffened tongue through the cloth of her bra and shirt. Sherona's mewl of pleasure was like a wild animal's cry in the forest.

He lifted his head but continued to kiss and take tender bites of her breasts as he pushed her to the side of the path. The world suddenly spun, and Sherona found herself facing the trunk of a wide oak tree. Chance's hands were at her waist, unfastening her shorts with deft haste. He pressed his groin against her ass, making his arousal flagrantly known to her.

"What am I going to do?" he asked, his gruff voice sending a thrill through her.

She bit her lower lip. "Fuck me?" she asked shakily.

"You'd better believe it," he said, shoving her shorts down to her knees. Her underwear followed. "Put your hands on the trunk," he ordered. He sounded angry, but Sherona knew he was really just tense with arousal. She did as he said while he held her with one arm looped around her waist, making sure she didn't elude him this time. She felt his breath coming in pants against the skin of her back and his hand moving around her bare ass as he unbuttoned his jeans.

A moment later, he shoved his hand between her thighs, but his touch on her pussy was gentle enough. Sherona shrieked as he rubbed her clit, quick and ruthless.

"You're soaking wet," he mumbled. "My little captive likes to be chased."

Sherona leaned against the tree, her mouth going wide when she felt the thick, swollen head of his penis press against her slit.

"You're never going to run from me again, are you?" he rasped, his fingers delving into the flesh of her ass.

"I can't promise that," she managed between clenched teeth. She pushed back against him, longing to feel his big cock lodged deep inside her. He spanked her briskly and she stopped.

"If I don't run, you couldn't catch me," she rasped.

"Good answer, because I'll always catch you, Sherona. Always," he muttered thickly before he thrust. She screamed. One second she'd been empty, and the next she was filled with Chance's cock. Overfilled. He began to thrust immediately, not giving her time to recover from his abrupt penetration. Nerves that registered the sting of his forceful, total possession began to burn with pleasure. His pelvis slapped against her ass repeatedly as he pounded into her, the arousing sound mixing with the wild heartbeat in her ears and his grunts of pleasure.

They became two animals in that moment, a male claiming his mate, two creatures straining and pumping and pushing, feeding an atavistic flame until they'd explode with it. He slammed into her, his hands holding her captive to his pistoning cock, until Sherona gave a plaintive, desperate scream.

She knew she'd be sore tomorrow, but right now her pussy burned unbearably, craving more. She pumped against him with the little leeway his tight hold gave her, wild with excitement. He responded by slapping her ass with each driving downstroke, riding and prodding her to the finish line. She gave a disbelieving cry when she crossed it and orgasm shattered her awareness.

After a moment of blissful ecstasy, she came back to herself, climax still shuddering through her.

"Ahhhh!" she shrieked when she felt Chance's cock lurch viciously inside her. His fingers sank into her hips and ass in a desperate hold. He roared as he came, emptying himself into her farthest reaches.

She'd never heard him breathing so hard following their lovemaking. His pants sounded like they tore at his throat as he struggled to collect himself in the aftermath of their lightning strike of need. His cock still throbbed inside of her, his climax ebbing. She felt him shift his hand, caressing her ass and then spanking her softly as his cock twitched and she felt another thrill go through him.

"What's the secret?" he demanded through ragged pants.

Sherona grinned, hiding her face. She was breathing heavily as well, her body still recovering.

"Let me look at you," she said.

He caressed her ass with both hands. His cock jerked slightly inside her. Sherona opened her mouth, wishing she hadn't spoken when she felt him withdraw. She straightened, feeling a little disoriented. He steadied her and turned her into his embrace.

When she looked into his face, she saw that he wore a small, sheepish smile. She immediately went up onto her toes and kissed his grin, her heart swelling at the sight.

"Did I tell you how glad I am to see you?" she whispered next to his lips.

"I figured your telling me to chase you was the equivalent," he said wryly. He leaned down and kissed her again. When his kiss grew hungrier and she felt him stir next to her lower belly, she broke apart with reluctance.

"I told you I'd tell you the secret when you caught me," she breathed.

He blinked as if he were trying to bring his eyes back into focus. "Oh. Yeah. What is it?"

She smiled widely and touched his scruffy jaw. He looked gorgeous, every inch bad-boy Aussie, as usual.

"I've won a million dollars."

"What?"

She nodded, laughter bursting out of her throat. Saying it to him was like hearing the news for the first time herself. She rapidly explained the circumstances—her traditional one-time-a-year shot at her dreams, and how inexplicably, miraculously, fate had dealt her a winning hand.

Chance appeared speechless.

"It's true," she said, tears leaking out of her eyes. "I want to travel with you, Chance. I want to see the world. That is . . . if the offer still stands," she said hesitantly, not quite able to interpret his frozen expression.

"Are you teasing me, Sherona?" he asked tensely. "Because if you're joking about something like this, I might have to turn you over my knee."

Her eyebrows went up. "Sounds interesting. Unfortunately, I'm one hundred percent serious."

A disbelieving bark of laughter erupted from his throat. His expression grew rapt as he studied her face, as though searching for signs of a trick. She just looked back at him steadily, her pure joy at looking upon his face shining unguarded from her eyes.

"You're going to come with me? You'll be with me, Sherona?"

"Yes. I've already got my passport. And I've made arrangements for the diner, for the short-term, anyway. I'll have to come back sometime soon, though, Chance. I can't break all ties with Vulture's Canyon."

"I know that. I wouldn't want you to never come home. We still have to finish the cookbook, too, remember?"

She shook her head, tears overfilling her eyes. "You really were serious about that, weren't you?" she asked, amazed.

"Course I was. It's a great idea, don't you think?"

She nodded, and a tear spilled down her cheek. He dried it with his fingertips.

"You're going to love it, seeing the world," he breathed out, his mouth just inches from hers. "I'm going to *love* seeing it with you, Sherona."

She nodded, staring at his soul shining from his hazel eyes.

"You made my little world a bigger, more beautiful place, Chance."

"I feel the same way about you."

She smiled, warmed by his admission, even though it struck her as a little silly. "Your world? *Small?* You've been to every corner of the globe," she teased, nipping at his lower lip.

He shook his head, suddenly sober.

"It's seemed like the tiniest, most hateful trap ever created for the past two weeks, seeing the world without you," he said.

Her lips parted in surprise. He seemed to take her amazement as an invitation and swooped down to give her another blistering, heartfelt kiss.

Keep reading for an excerpt from
Beth Kery's next Ian and Francesca novel

BECAUSE WE BELONG

Available November 2013 from Berkley Books

Francesca walked out of the dressing room carrying a blouse, jeans, and underwear, pausing when she saw Ian enter the suite. Her fiancé met her gaze, somber as a judge, and locked the door. A smile pulled at her lips.

"I was about to shower," she said.

His eyebrows went up, his bland expression conveying dry disbelief. *You're doing no such thing,* she could just imagine him thinking. Francesca chuckled. She knew what he intended every time he locked that door. His actions would have made her smile—not to mention her heart begin to pound faster—at any time, but today, it made her uncommonly happy. He'd been so preoccupied and worried about his mother's health, tortured that he'd made a wrong decision in regard to her medication and care, convinced there was something else he *should* be doing, but wasn't. The care and protection of his mother had been ground deeply into his very bones since he was a child too young to be forced to consider such matters. He couldn't escape the heavy responsibility as a man. Sadly, Helen Noble was making little to no improvement. Ian had been making frequent trips to London, crowding his already packed work schedule.

"Lucien and Elise are coming for dinner. We don't have time," Francesca reminded him.

He walked toward her. She wondered how long it would last, that shiver of anticipation she experienced every time she saw that hungry gleam in his blue eyes and that predatory stalk. They'd been together now for over half a year, and her excitement had only grown. His recent preoccupation and worry only made that need to join with him sharper and more imperative.

"I called Lucien and asked them to come an hour later," he said calmly as he removed the garments from her hands and set them on an upholstered chair.

"And Mrs. Hanson? She's busy making roast beef and Yorkshire pudding."

"She's turning down the temperature in the oven. I told her I needed a nap."

She studied him as he came toward her again. His lie to Mrs. Hanson, the housekeeper, was a true one. He looked as arrestingly handsome as usual, wearing a white and blue striped dress shirt open at the collar and dark blue trousers—casual wear, for Ian—but the months of worry over Helen Noble had taken their toll. His facial muscles were drawn tight from tension and there were shadows beneath his eyes. He swore he hadn't lost weight, and his clothes hung on his tall, fit frame as appealingly as ever, but she and Mrs. Hanson agreed that he looked thinner. He'd been trying to diminish his anguish through his already rigorous exercise routines, the result being a leaner, harder . . . impossibly more intense man. She reached up and touched his jaw as his arms encircled her waist.

"Maybe you really should rest. It would do you good," she said as he pulled her against him. A jolt of arousal awakened her body at the sensation of his masculine contours fitting against her so perfectly.

"It would do me much, much more good to watch your beautiful face while you're tied up and helpless," he said quietly before he leaned down and kissed her.

She opened her heavy eyelids a moment later, drugged by his potent kiss and the sensation of his body hardening against her.

"Helpless against what?" she murmured next to his plucking lips.

"Helpless to resist me."

"But I . . . don't . . . want to . . . resist you. You know . . . that," she managed between kisses, her body melting against him as he leaned over her, demanding every existing modicum of her attention. He lifted his head and his hand slid down her arm. He grasped her hand and led her toward the bed.

"The ropes will just reassure me," he replied.

"Ropes?" Francesca asked, dazed. He'd used cuffs to bind her during foreplay and sex, and padded restraints and whatever else he might improvise with on the spur of the moment, including his own hands. But *ropes*?

"Don't worry," he said once he'd led her to the edge of the bed and encouraged her to sit. He leaned down and nibbled at her lips fleetingly . . . but convincingly, Francesca decided. "The ropes are made of silk. Do you think I'd ever put anything next to your beautiful skin that would mar it?" he asked near her ear a moment later, his low, rough voice causing goose bumps to rise along her nape.

She just stared up at him, enraptured by his small Ian-smile.

Less than ten minutes later, she lay completely nude horizontally at the foot of the large, luxurious four-poster bed, her hips and body near the perpendicular angle of the edge. She'd watched in amazement and growing arousal as Ian had meticulously—and knowingly—bound her wrists to her calves in an elaborate, precise design of black silk rope twists and knots. She lay on her back, her knees bent toward her chest, her thighs spread wide. He'd instructed her initially to hold her calves, the pressure of her gripping hands pressing her folded legs into her body. Then he'd begun to bind her, forearms to calves and then calves to thighs.

She was trussed up good and tight, although she was not uncomfortable. Unless the erratic pounding of her heart and the mounting need for friction on her exposed, naked sex counted as discomfort.

She watched Ian anxiously as he returned from the room at the right side of the suite, their private sanctuary—the room that was typically kept locked and contained all manner of instruments for bondage, punishment, and pleasure.

"What have you gotten from your room to torture me with?" she asked teasingly, her head twisted to see what he held in his hands. She saw little, however, his body blocking what he set on the top of a bureau. He turned toward her, still completely dressed. Her nipples prickled beneath his hot stare as he examined her, his gaze striking her as cool and assessing and blazingly possessive all at once.

"*My* room?" he repeated as he came toward her. Her clit twanged in conditioned excitement when she saw the small pot of cream he held in his hand. It was the clitoral stimulant that he always rubbed on her when he was doing something new to her . . . something challenging. Francesca had dubbed it a "wicked cream" because it was known to make her want in ways she'd never before imagined. It was known to make her beg.

"Yes. To whom else does the room belong?" she asked distractedly.

"You, of course," he said, holding her stare and untwisting the lid of the pot. She watched his every move with tight concentration as he dipped a thick finger into the little pot, a dull ache mounting in her by the second.

"You are the only one who has a key," she said as he withdrew his finger and a dollop of white cream. He placed a knee on the trunk at the foot of the bed and leaned over her supine, bound form. "Therefore it is yours."

"I control the room, yes," he said, reaching. She lifted her head off the mattress, holding her breath as he neared her spread pussy, her mouth watering uncontrollably, her nipples tightening into almost painful hard points. He'd conditioned her body so exquisitely. "But the room exists for your pleasure," he continued. She gasped as her head fell back and he knowingly massaged the cool cream between her labia and onto her clit. "Therefore, it is fair to say it is both of our domain, wouldn't you say?" he growled softly as he rubbed.

"Oh . . . *yes*," she moaned. Already the cream warmed beneath the hard, agitating ridge of his forefinger. Soon, very soon, it would make the nerves tingle and burn. It would make it so that she did just about anything to climax. Despite her growing arousal, what Ian meant was not lost on her.

Before they'd met, that room had been for Ian alone, the ecstasy he gave other women a mere by-product of his personal pleasurable aims. He was still the master of that room, but for him to say the room was *theirs* was special, and she was touched.

He straightened and stood, screwing the lid on the pot as he looked down at her with a hooded gaze, his expression hot but also vaguely frustrated.

"Why do you look at me like that?" Francesca whispered.

His nostrils flared slightly and he turned away. "I was thinking there is nothing more beautiful than you on the face of the earth," he replied, his back still turned to her. "And that . . ."

"What?" she prompted when he faded off as he picked up some items on the bureau.

He turned and walked toward her, and for once she was so preoccupied by his intensity and what he was telling her, she didn't immediately try to ascertain what was in his hand or determine what he planned to do to her, like she normally would do.

"Ian?"

"I wish I could . . ." He paused, his gaze once again trailing over her from face to bound legs and arms. "Keep you with me always," he said after a moment. He came toward her.

"I am with you always," she said. Sensing his dark mood, however, she strained to lighten the moment. "Just try to get rid of me, and you'll discover how hard it is to escape."

He gave her a swift smile. "It would be an utter impossibility for me to escape you." She opened her mouth to continue the conversation—she sensed it was important—but he sidetracked her by setting the items he carried on the bed and reaching between her thighs. He rubbed her clit with a quick, expert touch. She gasped. She'd always wondered at the fact that he touched her even more knowingly than she touched herself, as if he were inside her head and could feel what she did.

"Is the cream starting to work?" he murmured.

"You know it is," she accused between gritted teeth. He met her eyes and she felt his smile all the way to the pit of her stomach. God, she loved him so much. Sometimes she worried he didn't realize how much . . .

"I'm going to put something into your ass," he said quietly, still rubbing her clitoris.

"Okay," she said, sensing the pointedness of his comment, but not the significance. He didn't use plugs on her all the time, but it was certainly one aspect of their sex play with which she was familiar. He must have noticed her slight confusion, because he pulled his hand away—making her whimper in protest at his absence—and reached for something on the bed.

"This," he said, holding up a four-inch plug with a base. It wasn't that different from ones he'd used on her before, with one exception. The base and the plug itself were completely transparent.

"Is it all right?" he prompted.

"Yes," she replied without hesitation, even though she blushed.

Something leapt into his blue eyes . . . something she cherished. He quickly lubricated the clear plug. He watched her face as he carefully inserted it. She moaned softly and bit her lip. The stimulation of her anus seemed to make the clit cream go into full action. She tingled and burned. He pressed until the base came into contact with her skin. She felt beads of sweat pop onto her upper lip.

She jumped when Ian abruptly shoved the heavy wooden trunk away from the foot of the bed and leaned down over. The tip of his tongue flicked over the top of her lip, gathering her sweat, before he kissed her with barely restrained passion.

"I have never loved anything or anyone the way I do you," he said gruffly when he sealed their kiss.

"I love you, too," she whispered feelingly. A shudder of pleasure went through her as his fingertips found their way beneath her bent knee and he began to finesse a nipple. He put his hand on her shin, gently pushing her knee toward the other one, exposing her breast. His dark head lowered. She blindly stared up at the elaborate crystal chandelier over the bed as he kissed the nipple with warm, firm lips before he took it into his mouth and sucked, sometimes gently . . . sometimes not. Her ass muscles tightened reflexively around the plug and her clit pinched in achy pleasure. By the time he lifted his head, both of her nipples stood at attention, reddened and hard. He gave the left nipple one last gentle pinch. She whimpered in mounting pleasure and he released her.

"Have I ever told you that you have the most beautiful breasts in existence?"

"Once or ten thousand times," she replied.

"They deserve even greater praise."

The air between her spread thighs seemed to lick at the moisture gathering there. She watched, her breath coming erratically, as he straightened. Her heart lurched in excitement when he began to unbuckle his belt. When he'd lowered the zipper, he reached into his white boxer briefs and removed his cock, releasing the long, thick veined shaft so that the base fell against the waistband of the briefs. His penis bobbed before settling, the heavy, swollen head causing it to fall at a slightly downward angle as it protruded from his body. Her mouth watered instinctively. Her pussy became even damper. The sight of his cock had once both intimidated and aroused her. After months of making love with Ian, however, only excitement remained.

As if he knew precisely the reaction he was giving her, he stepped closer to her face and pressed his thighs against the bed. She turned her cheek against the edge of the mattress and opened her lips. He leaned closer and delved his fingers into her hair. She no longer needed him to direct her to meet his need. Not in this, she didn't.

She strained her head, bathing his warm, rigid length with her tongue. He tightened his hold in her hair and she took the fleshy, firm crown into her mouth, her lips stretching around it, squeezing him. She gave the slit a firm polish with her tongue, making his fingers tighten in her hair, before she slid the shaft into her mouth and sucked.

"Jesus, that's good," she heard him say roughly from above her as he pulsed his cock in and out of her mouth. "You always seem so hungry for it . . . as hungry for me as I am you."

Her increased fervor was an assurance that what he said was true. After a moment, she closed her eyes and let him have control, trusting in him completely. Her attention narrowed to a concentrated channel, every sense pinpointed on him—his familiar, delicious taste and scent, the arousing texture of his cock, how his flesh became even more rigid and swollen with every thrust and draw of her clamping mouth. She loved the way his fist tightened in her hair, his unspoken demands not harsh, necessarily, but as always, unapologetically firm. Ian relished in pleasure, and she'd come to adore giving it to him without reservation.

The cream had gone into full action on her clit, making nerves sizzle and burn. The pressure of the plug in her ass added a primal, dark edge to her arousal. She was bound and couldn't relieve the swelling ache in her, and that made her pleasuring of Ian more desperate and wild. He'd become a part of her in the past months, his pleasure her own.

Her excitement mounted as his thrusts into her mouth came faster and his cock swelled. She strove to take him deeper and succeeded, her reward his rough, slightly stunned groan of pleasure.

"No," she protested, her voice roughened from his cock when he swung back his hips and his cock slid out of her mouth with a wet suction sound. His cock was like a drug, his pleasure addictive to her. He loosened his grip on her hair, his fingertips lightly massaging her scalp before he backed away.

"Yes," he said simply, and she didn't argue. She wasn't surprised. He occasionally spent himself quickly, taking her in a greedy rush that she loved because it betrayed the depths of the desire of a man whose self-control was legend. Typically, however, he drew things out, drowning her in pleasure and excitement, making their need mount to unbearable levels, building the fire so that when climax came, it was explosive. This evening, she sensed his need to hold on to her for as long as he could, to mingle their essences and prolong the sharp intimacy.

She swallowed thickly when she saw him pick up a red rubber vibrator from the bed. It was new, one he'd never used on her before. It had an unusual ring at the tip. She saw his thumb move and the tool began to vibrate almost silently. He held her stare as he pressed the rigid, pulsing ring against her mouth, both soothing and exciting the sensitive flesh. Her lips felt feverish and swollen from his earlier strident thrusting between them. She willingly opened them as he moved the vibrator, his actions striking her as more intimate and arousing than she would have expected. She moaned softly as he pressed the vibrator deeper, sliding it against the moist flesh just inside her mouth. Her vagina tightened as she stared up at him in helpless arousal and granted him full, undeniable right over her body.

"So beautiful," he murmured, and she knew he'd seen her submission as clearly as he'd seen her face. "I could look at you forever when you're giving yourself to me."

He removed the vibrator from her damp lips and caressed her cheek tenderly. She turned her face into his palm and kissed the center of it. He made a rough sound in his throat and removed his hand. He once again pushed one of her knees toward the other one, exposing her naked breast, using the wand of the vibrator to stimulate the curving flesh. She bit her lip, trapping her soft cry when he inserted a taut nipple into the vibrating loop and pressed softly.

"Feel good?" he murmured, his gaze returning to her face.

"Yes," she whispered.

And it did. Her nipple was surrounded by the pulsing loop. The mysterious pathway of nerves connecting her nipples to her clit flared to life. She twisted her head on the mattress and moaned, her need growing sharp and untenable.

"Shhh," Ian soothed gently.

She cried out when he parted her labia matter-of-factly and encircled her clit with the vibrating loop. Her cry segued to a groan of ecstatic misery when he turned up the power on the vibrator. She closed her eyes and shuddered at the intense, concise stimulation, her hips twisting on the bed. He placed his hands on the coil of rope at her calf and kept her in place. She had no choice but to accept the distilled pleasure full on.

"Come," Ian said a moment later.

She followed his command to the letter, her bound body shaking in the onslaught of release. After the first, most powerful waves of climax had passed, he removed the vibrator. Her head came off the bed and she bit off a scream when he pressed his cock to her pussy, grabbed her thighs and impaled her with one stroke.

"Oh God . . . *Ian*," she gasped as she continued to climax around his penis. The sudden intrusion overwhelmed her. It primarily felt wonderful, but it also hurt a little, overfilled as she suddenly was with Ian's large cock in her pussy and the plug in her ass.

"That's right," he rasped as he began to thrust, his handsome face rigid with restrained pleasure. "That's what I wanted to feel. So hot. So wet," he grated out as he fucked her and her vagina clamped around him as she continued to come.

"No," she muttered desperately a minute later when he again withdrew from her. She lifted her head, staring at the erotic sight of his heavy, glistening cock poking out from his open fly and lowered briefs. He often didn't remove his pants completely as he played with her while she was bound. It drove her wild with thwarted longing. It drove her a step away from madness to watch while bound and helpless as he ran his large hand over his moist, rigid shaft. Her vagina and ass muscles clenched tight. He gave a harsh moan.

She realized he stared fixedly between her parted thighs at her spread pussy and the inserted plug. Her cheeks heated. She experienced an overwhelming desire to cover herself. She'd never felt so exposed to him as she was at that moment. Was she foolish for opening herself to another human being so wholly . . . for allowing herself to become so vulnerable?

His facial muscles convulsed slightly as he stared, the expression somehow speaking of longing so intense, it bordered on pain for him. All of her doubts about her vulnerability faded to mist. In many ways, Ian laid himself as bare during their lovemaking as she did for him.

"Ian," she murmured. He looked up, meeting her stare, and she knew her heart was in her eyes.

"You shouldn't look at me like that. You know what it does to me."

"I'm sorry," she replied.

"No, you're not," he said grimly, moving toward her head and unbuttoning his shirt fleetly as he did so. He whipped the shirt over his shoulders. Her stare lowered covetously over bulging, lean muscle. She'd learned over the past several months that when she was bound, her eyes had to take the place of her greedy fingers, making her a more keen observer. Since Ian also blindfolded her at times, her nerves, too, had become exquisitely sensitive to his every move and touch. "And I'm not either, to be honest," he continued. "If I could bottle that look in your eyes, I would."

She was in such a powerful, strangely combined state of both satiation and sustained arousal, it took her a moment to notice his rigid and yet somehow hesitant expression as he stroked her neck, the sides of her breasts and ribs, making her quiver with pleasure.

"What is it?" she asked quietly, puzzled by his mood.

He didn't speak for a moment, just continued to caress her with his large, warm hand.

"I would like to video you while we continue. Just your face," he added quickly when she didn't immediately speak.

"Why?" she asked, even though she thought she knew the answer.

His expression grew unreadable, but she sensed his turmoil nonetheless. "Like I said, I would bottle your sweetness if I could," he admitted. "Carry you with me everywhere."

Her heart seemed to swell two sizes in her chest. He'd known so much pain in his life . . . been so fearful of abrupt rejection, been primed for unexpected fearful and even violent reactions from a schizophrenic mother.

"All that I am is always here for you, Ian," she said softly. "But of course you can video me, if you think it will help . . . somehow."

His averted gaze zoomed to her face. "You're sure? Of course you know it will only be for me. I will guard it assiduously."

She smiled. "I know that. Do you think I'd allow it otherwise?"

His nostrils flared slightly as he studied her. "You think it's an odd request, don't you?"

"No. I don't share your need, but I understand it, Ian. I do," she added pointedly.

He leaned down and kissed the diamonds on her bound hand—the engagement ring he'd given her weeks ago.

"Thank you," he said.

His solemn manner made her eyes moisten. She was glad when he moved away. When he returned to her field of vision, he carried a small video camera. He set it on the bureau and quickly focused it, the lens aimed toward her head.

"It's trained on your face," he said as he approached her again a moment later. She noticed that far from diminishing during the brief absence from her, his erection appeared every bit as firm, heavy, and flagrant. Her love and trust in him made her glory in the evidence that it aroused him to tape her during sex. It was merely another level of intimacy for them to explore. She wasn't put off by his request.

"You know I love seeing you give yourself to me," he said, stroking her hips and then her lower belly, his long fingers inching toward her mons and spread pussy. "This way, I will have the vision always available to me."

"Wouldn't you rather have me in person?" she asked, her cheeks flushing as he teased her, his long, talented fingers tickling skin just inches away from where she burned. She whimpered when he caressed her humid inner thighs.

"I would prefer to have you in person a million times over," he assured, his mouth twitching into a small smile. "What sane man wouldn't want this . . . ?" He paused, plunging a thick, long finger into her slit, making her inhale sharply. "This exquisite flesh?" he finished.

She was so aroused, she could hear him as he moved in her wet pussy, finger-fucking her. He withdrew and immediately transferred his lubricated finger to her clit, rubbing her so accurately her eyes rolled back in her head and she clamped her lids shut. His innate talent in combination with the clitoral stimulant was almost unbearably potent and precise.

"No, lovely. Open your eyes. Look at me."

She strove to do what he demanded, focusing on his much-loved face. He continued to stimulate her clit bull's-eye fashion. Her lips trembled. He was going to bring her off again very, very soon.

"What do you enjoy more?" he asked unsmilingly. "A vibrator or my hand?"

"Your hand," she said without hesitation, pressing her hips against the divine pressure. "Always your hand. Your touch," she added shakily.

"The video will be the same for me. I allow you to use a vibrator in my absence, don't I?"

"Yes," she mouthed, too overwhelmed with growing arousal to speak audibly.

"But you would rather have me?" he asked, and despite his typical palpable confidence, she heard the thread of uncertainty in his voice . . . of naked need.

"A *million* times over." She repeated his words brokenly, looking into his scoring blue eyes. Emotion overcame her. She clamped her eyes shut, a tear shooting down her cheek, and came against his hand.

She returned from the realms of bliss at the sensation of the plug sliding out of her ass. He was almost immediately there—a fuller, throbbing replacement. He held her stare as he slowly entered her, his eyes a brilliant contrast to his rigid features. The raw intensity of the moment overwhelmed her. There wasn't a spot in her body or soul she wouldn't willingly give him.

"Don't look away," he said harshly when he pressed his testicles against her buttocks and she gasped for air that didn't seem to adequately expand her lungs. He must have sensed how powerful the moment was for her. He spread his hands on her hips and began to fuck her, his pelvis slapping rhythmically against her ass. "Don't ever look away, Francesca."

He sounded almost angry, but she knew he wasn't. It was the intensity of the moment that strained his voice. She merely shook her head, too inundated by the sensation of his cock plunging in and out of such an intimate place, too saturated with love and desire to do anything but surrender. The clitoral cream in combination with Ian's primal possession made her burn yet again. Even the soles of her feet heated and prickled. He spread his hand over her lower belly, continuing to thrust his cock in and out of her. She cried out sharply, her back arching slightly off the bed, when he slid his thumb between her labia and rubbed her clit.

"Oh no," she gasped, hardly aware of what she was saying.

"Yes," he corrected between clenched teeth. "Open your eyes."

She did as he demanded, not realizing she'd closed them as ecstasy mounted. The sounds of their bodies smacking together faster and faster seemed to match the pounding of her heart in her ears. His thumb moved, creating a delicious friction. She was about to ignite like the tip of a struck match. She focused on him with effort, biting off a moan. Sweat sheened his face, chest, and ridged abdomen.

"Tell me you love me," he rasped.

"I love you so much."

"Always."

"*Yes*. Always," she said, her lips trembling as she crested. She felt him swell inside her, the slight pain of discomfort only fueling her desire, providing the edge she needed to come. Her sharp cry was silenced by Ian's roar of release.

A moment later, he fell between her bound legs, holding himself off her with his arms braced on the mattress, both of them still quaking and panting in the aftermath of the storm of climax. A drop of sweat fell in her eyes. It burned, but she didn't blink; the image of him was too beautiful.

"I'll call Lucien and Elise and cancel for tonight," Ian said, his gaze running over her face.

"It'll be too late. They'll already be on their way. Besides, you could use an evening with friends. You always seem to relax and enjoy yourself around Lucien. He has a good effect on you."

His mouth twitched. "I enjoy myself much more around you. And you wouldn't believe how relaxed I am at the moment."

"You know what I mean. You've been under so much stress lately, with your mother being ill." Her grin faded. After a moment of studying him, she reconsidered. "Do you really want to cancel?"

He straightened and slowly withdrew from her, grimacing as he did so. "Yes," he answered honestly as he began to unbind her arms and legs. "I'd rather spend the night with you right here," he said after a moment. He shot her a darkly amused glance as he whipped the rope around her limbs, releasing her restraints with as much methodical precision as he'd made them. "But I suppose I shouldn't be so selfish. A couple hours spent with friends isn't going to make a big difference in the scheme of things. I'll be back in bed with you soon enough, right?"

"Absolutely."

An inexplicable chill passed over her heated flesh like an invisible shadow, and was gone in an instant. She sighed with relief as she straightened her freed legs and stretched like a content cat.

She hardly thought about her automatic, certain reply until later. Naturally she and Ian would be here together later.

They would be in one another's arms, where they belonged.

About the Author

Beth Kery lives in Chicago, where she juggles the demands of her career, her love of the city and the arts, and a busy family life. Her writing today reflects her passion for all of the above. She is the *New York Times* and *USA Today* bestselling author of *Because You Are Mine*. Find out more about Beth and her books at BethKery.com or Facebook.com/Beth.Kery.